*He's always been driven by the need to succeed,
so can he surrender to love?*

Tycoon's Choice

Three sizzling, sparkling romances from three
beloved Mills & Boon authors!

In July 2010 Mills & Boon bring you four
classic collections, each featuring three favourite
romances by our bestselling authors

THE PRINCES' BRIDES
by Sandra Marton
The Italian Prince's Pregnant Bride
The Greek Prince's Chosen Wife
The Spanish Prince's Virgin Bride

TYCOON'S CHOICE
Kept by the Tycoon by Lee Wilkinson
Taken by the Tycoon by Kathryn Ross
The Tycoon's Proposal by Leigh Michaels

THE MILLIONAIRE'S CLUB:
JACOB, LOGAN & MARC
Black-Tie Seduction by Cindy Gerard
Less-Than-Innocent Invitation by Shirley Rogers
Strictly Confidential Attraction by Brenda Jackson

SAYING 'YES!' TO THE BOSS
Having Her Boss's Baby by Susan Mallery
Business or Pleasure? by Julie Hogan
Business Affairs by Shirley Rogers

Tycoon's Choice

LEE WILKINSON
KATHRYN ROSS
LEIGH MICHAELS

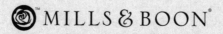

All the characters in this book have no existence outside the imagination of
the author, and have no relation whatsoever to anyone bearing the same name
or names. They are not even distantly inspired by any individual known or
unknown to the author, and all the incidents are pure invention.

First published in Great Britain 2010
Harlequin Mills & Boon Limited,
Eton House, 18-24 Paradise Road, Richmond, Surrey TW9 1SR

TYCOON'S CHOICE © by Harlequin Enterprises II B.V./S.à.r.l 2010

Kept by the Tycoon, Taken by the Tycoon and *The Tycoon's Proposal* were
first published in Great Britain by Harlequin Mills & Boon Limited in
separate, single volumes.

Kept by the Tycoon © Lee Wilkinson 2006
Taken by the Tycoon © Kathryn Ross 2006
The Tycoon's Proposal © Leigh Michaels 2006

ISBN: 978 0 263 88107 3

05-0710

Printed and bound in Spain
by Litografia Rosés S.A., Barcelona

KEPT BY THE TYCOON

BY
LEE WILKINSON

Lee Wilkinson lives with her husband in a three-hundred-year old stone cottage in a Derbyshire village, which most winters gets cut off by snow. They both enjoy travelling and recently, joining forces with their daughter and son-in-law, spent a year going round the world 'on a shoestring' while their son looked after Kelly, their much loved German shepherd dog. Her hobbies are reading and gardening, and holding impromptu barbecues for her long-suffering family and friends.

CHAPTER ONE

THE physiotherapy room at Mayfair's exclusive Grizedale Clinic was quiet and peaceful, the only sound the muted background roar of London's traffic. A deep-pile carpet covered the floor, a vase of crimson roses scented the air and a black leather couch was spread with a spotless sheet ready for its next occupant.

At the open window muslin curtains lifted in the slight breeze, allowing light to enter but keeping the lingering summer-in-the-city heat at bay.

Wearing a silky, charcoal-grey suit and an ivory blouse, her long, naturally blonde hair taken up in a coil, Madeleine was sitting at the desk, updating her previous patient's file, when there was a tap, and the door opened.

Neat in her blue uniform, dark curls secured in the nape of her neck by a gilt clip, Eve came in with some notes.

Eve Collins, along with her brother Noel, had been Madeleine's friend since their nursery-school days.

It had been Eve who had mentioned this post at the clinic. 'If you're interested, Maddy, the woman who usually fills it has taken maternity leave, which means it will only be temporary.

'But I promise you the surroundings are pleasant, and the money's good, so this might be just what you need to tide you over until you've built up a clientele of patients...

'That is, if you don't mind working four evenings a week throughout the summer months…'

'I don't mind at all,' Madeleine had said gratefully, 'and I'd be glad of both the money and the experience.'

'I'll mention your name to Mrs Bond, who deals with personnel.'

On being offered the post, Madeleine had started work immediately. It meant she could no longer see her mother in the evenings, but she had reorganised her daytime routine to fit in visits to the nursing home between her private patients.

Smiling at her friend, Eve put the notes she was carrying on the desk and, her blue eyes gleaming with excitement, hurried into speech. 'Your last patient for tonight is a new one, a Rafe Lombard…'

Then dropping her voice to a whisper, 'And boy, is he *gorgeous*! A real hunk, with all the charm of a young Sasha Distel! Tall, dark and handsome may be an overworked phrase, but there's no other way to describe him.'

Madeleine sighed and raised her eyes to heaven. 'The last time you told me someone was gorgeous he turned out to have pimples and dandruff.'

'Scoff if you must, but this time you'll have to admit I'm not exaggerating. All the female staff are in a tizzy, married and single alike.

'When he smiled at Thelma, who you must admit is a bit of a man-hater, she went weak at the knees and dropped all the papers she was carrying.'

'Well, you'd better send this gorgeous hunk in,' Madeleine said drily. 'Otherwise I won't have time to take a look at him.'

A moment or so later the latch clicked, and, pushing aside the notes she had just scanned through, Madeleine glanced up.

The man who entered the room carried with him an air of power, of self-reliance and quiet authority.

As she looked at this ruggedly handsome, perfect stranger, everything stopped—her breathing, her heart, the blood in her veins…even the world ceased to spin on its axis.

It was as if she'd always known him. As if she had just been marking time, waiting for him to appear. Waiting for him to fill the void she had been only too aware of, even while she was married to Colin.

Rather than rushing into speech, as many of her patients did, he stood quite still, his forest-green eyes fixed on her face.

Dragging air into her lungs, she struggled to pull herself together. Though it seemed an eternity, it could only have been a few seconds before she succeeded in regaining at least some outward semblance of composure.

His effect on her had been pure and immediate and total, and she knew instinctively that she must stay cool and aloof, or be lost.

For perhaps the first time she understood fully why every tutor on the physiotherapy courses—apart from Colin—had found it necessary to warn their pupils not to allow themselves to get emotionally involved with any of their patients.

And, when it came to the crunch, how useless that warning was.

Drawing another deep, steadying breath, she rose to her feet and, daring her knees to tremble, advanced to meet him, holding out her hand. 'Mr Lombard, I'm Madeleine Knight…'

He took her hand in a firm grip and smiled, he looked deep into her eyes and nearly stopped her heart for a second time.

Her breathing impeded, her throat desert dry, she began, 'I understand you've suffered a possible whiplash injury. When did it happen?'

'Earlier this evening.'

His voice, low-pitched and slightly husky, shivered along her nerve ends.

Those clear green eyes lingering on her face, he added, 'Since then I've had some discomfort. I don't think it's anything to worry about, but I was advised to see a physiotherapist just in case there was any muscle damage.'

In spite of all her efforts her voice wasn't quite steady as she asked, 'How did it happen?'

'I was taking my racing car round a private circuit when the steering went.' Drily, he added, 'Straw bales can seem remarkably solid at speed.'

He was still watching her and that steady appraisal threw her far more than any of her previous male patients' attempts at flirtation.

'If you could strip to the waist and get up on the couch so I can check it out, please?' She tried to sound cool and professional, in control.

While Madeleine kept her eyes fixed firmly on his notes he took off his jacket and shirt and draped them over a chair, before hitching himself up to sit on the couch.

Only when he was settled did she look up.

His back was straight and muscular, the line of his spine elegant, as the broad shoulders tapered to a lean waist and narrow hips. His clear, tanned skin carried the glow of health and gleamed like oiled silk, making her want to touch it.

Even the back of his well-shaped head was attractive and sexy, the short dark hair curling a little into the nape of his neck.

Taking a deep breath, she went over to him and, concentrating fiercely on her professional task, with firm but gentle hands began her examination.

Though he must have been well aware of his effect on women, he made no suggestive remarks, nor did he try to chat her up. Instead he sat quietly, obediently raising his arms and flexing his muscles when asked to.

As soon as she had finished the examination, she said briskly, 'Right, Mr Lombard...' and moved away to a safer distance.

As he swung his feet to the floor she confirmed, 'Though there's some obvious stiffness in the neck and shoulder muscles, luckily there's no evidence of any real damage. In a few days, if all goes well, you should be back to normal.'

'That's great.' He smiled at her, his smile a white slash across his tanned face.

She watched as his lean cheeks creased, and a fan of fine laughter lines appeared at the corners of those fascinating almond-shaped eyes. Eyes that tilted up at the outer corners. Eyes that would have made even the most ordinary face appear extraordinary. And his face was far from ordinary…

Dragging her gaze away with an effort, and trying to ignore the way his smile had sent her pulses racing madly, she went on, 'Rest is all it needs until after the weekend. Then I suggest you have a further check just to be on the safe side.'

Looking directly into the clear aquamarine eyes of this cool, fascinating woman, who seemed totally unaware of her own beauty, he asked, 'So when shall I see you again?'

His intent gaze and the question, phrased as it was, shook her rigid.

But seeing him again, even in a professional capacity, would be far too dangerous. It would be courting disaster.

The clinic's policy was that a strict protocol should be observed between staff and clients, and, faced with soaring costs at the nursing home, she couldn't afford to lose this job.

'Perhaps you'd like to come in again on Monday or Tuesday morning?'

He shook his head. 'Evening would suit me better.'

Biting her bottom lip, she made a pretence of studying her appointments before she suggested evenly, 'In that case, suppose you make it Monday evening at the same time?'

Mrs Deering, the plump, middle-aged and happily married part-timer who worked weekends and Monday evenings, could hopefully help him without any threat to her peace of mind or her position.

'That suits me fine.'

'Then I'll say goodnight, Mr Lombard.'

'*Au revoir*, Miss Knight. Many thanks.' He strode to the door and made his way out.

Some element of vitality went with him, and she was left feeling, *life goes that way*.

With a hollow emptiness in the pit of her stomach she sank down at her desk and, with the image of his dark, attractive face filling her mind, started to update his notes.

The notes finished, she was sitting there gazing into space when the door opened and Eve came back in. 'I wondered if you were still here… Almost everyone else has gone.'

With nothing to look forward to but a solitary supper, there had been no incentive for Madeleine to hurry home.

'So what did you think of Rafe Lombard?'

'He was every bit as gorgeous as you said,' Madeleine answered as lightly as possible.

Eve looked gratified. 'And there's more…'

'More?'

'According to Joanne, who always seems to know these things, he inherited Charn Industries from Christopher Charn, his godfather… Which must make him a multimillionaire, and a prime catch.

'Though so far apparently he's managed to elude the hook and stay a bachelor. Which is a challenge in itself. A challenge I wouldn't mind taking up if I got half a chance. After all, a multimillionaire must be worth the risk of getting fired.

'Ah, well,' Eve sighed as she continued, 'I suppose I mustn't let myself dream. He's hardly likely to be interested in the likes of me. With those kinds of looks and that amount of charisma, Rafe Lombard must have women queuing up to throw themselves at his feet.'

No doubt Eve was right, Madeleine sighed, and pushed all thoughts of Rafe Lombard firmly to the back of her mind.

'Finished with these?' At the other girl's nod, Eve gathered up the notes and headed for the door. 'Well, I'm off. I've a date with Dave. See you Tuesday. Don't spend all weekend at the nursing home. Try to get out a bit.'

'I'll try.'

Since her mother had suffered severe head injuries in the gas explosion that had wrecked their rented house, she had spent most of her free time by the sick woman's bedside.

Sitting hour after hour with the corpse-like figure, talking or reading to her, not knowing how much, if anything, her mother understood, had taken a heavy toll on Madeleine.

As had the death of Madeleine's husband, Colin, in the same tragic accident. An accident she could only blame herself for.

As the weeks turned into months, finding she was no longer any fun, most of her friends had drifted away, and only Eve and Noel had stuck by her wholeheartedly.

Eve, in her usual cheerful, down-to-earth way, had provided an emotional crutch, while Noel had been there for her in a practical capacity.

First he had helped her find somewhere to live, then he had taken her out, chivvied her to eat and done his utmost to raise her spirits while she tried to pick up the pieces of her shattered life.

As a shoulder to cry on, Noel was the first to admit that he was useless. But when she had needed someone to make her laugh, to forget for a short time at least that she needed a shoulder to cry on, he had been ideal.

When he'd gone to work abroad, troubleshooting for an oil company, she had missed him. Missed his unstinting support, his irreverent tongue, his spiky sense of humour and laid-back attitude.

Missed having a man in her life.

Since she had been on her own several men had tried to get on more than friendly terms with her. But, well aware that, in the circumstances, the odds were stacked against any new relationship succeeding, she had steered clear.

After being alone so long it was time to move on, she knew, yet no one had attracted her enough to act as the catalyst to make her *want* to take the chance.

Until today. And that attraction, fierce though it was, was futile.

Becoming aware that time was slipping past, she closed the window and collected her shoulder-bag before letting herself out through a side-door and heading for the main gates.

On rainy days she caught the bus back to her Knightsbridge flat, but during the dry, settled spell of weather that had lasted for almost a week now, she had enjoyed walking home.

Tonight, however, having reached the imposing gates and turned west along Grizedale Street, she felt oddly weary and dispirited, in no mood for the thirty-minute walk.

She had just drawn level with a midnight-blue limousine that was parked by the kerb, when its rear door opened and a tall, dark-haired figure climbed out.

Dazzled by the low evening sun, she took a moment to realise that the man blocking her way was Rafe Lombard.

Surprise stopped her in her tracks, and as she shielded her eyes to look up at him he said easily, 'I thought if I hung around a while I might catch you. Have dinner with me?'

He was tall, dwarfing her with his height. If they were standing closer her head would rest on his broad chest.

Confused by the thought, she found herself stammering, 'N-no, thank you.'

'Perhaps it was stupid to spring it on you like this, but now I've admitted I'm an idiot,' he laughed, 'won't you reconsider and go out with me?'

With a flash of humour, she said, 'What? Go out with a self-confessed idiot?'

He gave her an appreciative grin. 'Think of the entertainment value.'

She shook her head. 'I can bear to give it up.'

'Surely not!' he mocked gently.

'Afraid so.'

'Go on. I promise I don't bite.'

Madeleine lowered her eyes. 'I'm sorry, but I can't.'

Putting his head on one side, he asked, 'Why not?'

His face was so full of charm that it took her breath away and turned her very bones to water.

Her voice sounding impeded, she said, 'It's against the clinic's policy for staff and clients to get familiar or meet on a social basis.'

He grimaced at the prim phrasing. 'If we do get familiar I promise not to breathe a word to a soul.'

'I'm not dressed for eating out.'

'You look absolutely fine to me.' He grinned.

Before she could make any further protest, she found herself drawn towards the car and urged into the back seat.

He slid in beside her, and she went hot all over when his muscular thigh pressed against hers as he reached to fasten first her seat belt and then his own.

Sensing that heated confusion, and warning himself not to rush things, he moved away to leave a little space between them.

With a silent sigh of relief, she glanced at him.

He met her gaze directly. The sun slanting in showed that her long-lashed aquamarine eyes had in their depths a sprinkle of gold dust, and her flawless skin a peach-like down.

His fingers itched to stroke it.

Controlling the urge, he asked lightly, 'Anywhere in particular you'd like to go?'

Wits scattered, knowing she shouldn't be here at all, she shook her head. 'No, I—'

Touching a button, he instructed the chauffeur, 'Just drive around for a while, Michael.'

As the limousine pulled smoothly away from the kerb, feeling rather as though she'd been hijacked, Madeleine began weakly, 'What made you...?'

'Chance my arm?' Rafe suggested when she hesitated. 'Sheer determination. If I'd been sure of seeing you again, I might not have rushed things. But when I made a few tactful enquiries I discovered that you wouldn't be here Monday evening...

'Which could have meant one of two things: either I was just another patient you didn't mind if you never saw again...or else someone you *could* be interested in and felt, because of the clinic's policy, you should steer clear of. I rather hoped it was the latter...'

Trying to control the surge of excitement that ran through her, she bit her lip.

Though his phrasing had been reasonably cautious, there was an air of confidence about him that suggested he felt fairly sure it *was* the latter.

And the way she had allowed herself to be shepherded into the car without protest must have reinforced that assumption.

'It opens up such possibilities...' He smiled at her. 'And I'm only too pleased you're free to explore those possibilities...'

The sexual chemistry between them was like an electrical force she could sense through every pore in her skin.

But recalling what Eve had said about women throwing themselves at his feet, and disinclined to let him believe that she might be one of them, she tried to appear cool and unmoved.

Judging by his face, her strategy hadn't worked.

In an effort to take the wind out of his sails she looked him in the eye and asked, 'What makes you so sure I'm free?'

Apparently unruffled, he answered, 'Well, for one thing, you're not wearing a ring—'

'That's nothing to go by these days.'

'True. That's why I waylaid your colleague.'

'Which colleague?'

'The pretty, dark-haired girl who first took my details. I happened to see her leaving the clinic and spoke to her. Eve, isn't it? I gather she's a good friend of yours.'

Without a blush, he added, 'I managed to coax quite a bit of information out of her.'

An edge to her voice, Madeleine asked, 'What kind of information?'

'I needed to know if you were married or in a steady relationship. When I asked her, she told me you'd lost your husband and been alone for quite a while now. I couldn't imagine a beautiful woman like you being on your own, but she seemed fairly sure there was no man in your life at the moment.'

When Madeleine merely looked at him, he added, 'Which means you have no commitments, no one waiting at home for you?'

'No.' As though he was willing her, she found herself unable to lie.

'Then I'd like to think that having dinner with me is *marginally* more appealing than eating alone?' he said quizzically.

When she made no immediate response, he urged, 'Please say it is, for the sake of my fragile ego.'

She smiled in spite of herself, a smile that brought her beauty to life and set those tiny gold flecks in her eyes dancing.

As he stared, entranced, she said a shade tartly, 'I have the distinct feeling that your ego is robust enough,' then, throwing caution to the winds, added, 'But yes, it is. *Marginally*.'

He laughed. 'A woman with spirit, I see… So where would you like to go?'

His mouth was beautiful, she thought, at once controlled and sensitive, the lower lip a little fuller than the upper. It was a mouth that tied knots in her stomach.

Somehow she managed, 'I really don't mind. Anywhere you choose.'

That was the first hurdle cleared, Rafe thought triumphantly as he instructed the chauffeur, 'The Xanadu, please, Michael.'

Knowing he shouldn't touch her—yet—but desperate to do so, he took her hand and, his thumb stroking across her palm, went on softly, 'I think you'll agree that it's the perfect setting for a romantic evening.'

She shivered.

Things were moving fast. Too fast.

Knowing she needed to apply the brakes, she withdrew her hand and, gathering herself, stared resolutely out of the car window.

But she was still breathing unevenly when they drove through tall ornamental gates and drew up outside the celebrated Mayfair restaurant.

Once a private house, the Xanadu was built in the style of a Spanish hacienda, and stood in its own discreetly floodlit gardens. Mature trees and shrubs provided a pleasant backdrop to smooth green lawns, and flowering shrubs climbed the stuccoed walls.

When the middle-aged chauffeur got out to open the door, Rafe told him, 'Don't bother hanging around, Michael. Get off home to the wife.'

His look grateful, the man said, 'Thank you, sir. Goodnight sir, madam…'

Rafe opened the thick smoked-glass door with an easy courtesy that she soon came to know was part of his nature.

Inside the foyer, his jacket was whisked away and they were greeted by the proprietor. 'Good evening, Mr Lombard…madam… How nice to see you. Your usual table?'

His *usual* table… Did he make a habit of bringing his women here? Madeleine wondered.

'Please, Henri.'

The *maître d'* appeared to show them through a series of archways to a secluded corner table in the stylish, white-walled restaurant.

Long windows looking onto the gardens were open wide, letting in warm evening air fragrant with the scent of roses and honeysuckle. A few bright stars were appearing, and a thin, silvery disc of moon floated in the blue sky.

As he'd said, it was the perfect setting for a romantic evening.

Watching her glance round, and instantly on her wavelength, he queried, 'Yes?'

'Yes,' she agreed with a smile.

While they sipped an aperitif she tried to concentrate on the menu, but, try as she might, she couldn't prevent herself looking at him, and whenever he wasn't watching her her eyes were drawn to his face.

He wasn't merely good-looking. With a cleft chin, a mouth that was at once ascetic and sensual, a strong nose, high cheekbones, brilliant, thickly lashed green eyes and dark, curved brows, he was intriguing, riveting.

But it was more than his looks. Much more. There was something about the man himself. Something she couldn't quite put a name to, but something that fulfilled a need in her. It felt right to be with him, as if she had always known him, as if they belonged together.

While they ate an excellent meal he kept the conversation light and general, moving from topic to topic, finding out what interested her, seeking her opinion on the subjects that did.

In spite of her *awareness* of him, the heated attraction that lay just beneath the surface, she found herself responding with an ease that, when she thought about it later, surprised her.

It wasn't until they reached the coffee stage that he deliberately moved into more dangerous territory.

Needing to know, and recalling the levelness of her gaze even when she was flustered, he went for the direct approach. 'Tell me about your husband.'

Every nerve in her body tightening, she said, 'There's not much to tell.'

'What was his name?'

'Colin. Colin Formby.'

'You kept your maiden name?' he queried.

'Yes. It was what my family wanted,' she said quietly, taking a sip of her drink.

He raised an eyebrow quizzically. 'You were an only child?'

'Yes,' Madeleine answered.

Rafe paused, leaning back in his chair. 'What field was your husband in?'

'Physiotherapy.'

'When did the pair of you meet?'

'At university.' Madeleine lowered her gaze, focusing on anything but Rafe's probing gaze.

'You were students together?'

'No. I was in my final year. Colin was a tutor.'

Rafe was intrigued. 'So he was older than you?'

'Eighteen years.'

'A big gap.'

'Yes,' she said shortly. Madeleine had always thought that the age gap, big as it was, wouldn't have mattered if she had truly loved him.

Rafe could sense her growing discomfort, but having got this far, he decided to press on. 'How long were the two of you married?'

'Six months.'

'Not long.'

'No,' Madeleine almost whispered.

Rafe paused, knowing his questions were difficult for her. 'How did he die?'

'He was killed in an explosion.'

Quelling the urge to ask any further questions, Rafe commented, 'Tough.'

Madeleine raised her eyes to his. 'Yes, it was.'

There was sadness there and some other emotion Rafe couldn't put a name to. But it wasn't the utter desolation, the inconsolable grief, of someone who had lost all they held dear. Of that he was sure.

He breathed an inward sigh of relief. The absence of a man in her life had made him fear that she was still in love with her dead husband, but the vibes he was picking up convinced him he was wrong.

Which must make his chances of succeeding, a great deal easier, he thought.

Refilling her coffee-cup, he changed the subject smoothly. 'What does Madeleine Knight do in her spare time? Are you a secret television addict?'

Relaxing again, she laughed and shook her head. 'No, I much prefer a book.'

'Ah, a woman after my own heart! Have you read Matthew Colt's *Funny Business*…?'

'Oh, yes… I loved the part where Joe tries to steal his ex-wife's poodle…'

For a little while they talked about the book, laughing over the bits that had amused them the most, before Madeleine remarked, 'I read somewhere that it's going to be turned into a play.'

'So I understand. Should be worth seeing… Do you like the theatre?'

'Love it.'

'Have you had a chance to see the new West End play everyone's talking about?'

'*Beloved Impresario*?' She shook her head and, unwilling to admit she couldn't really afford to go to the theatre these days, said, 'I imagine tickets are like gold dust.'

'I'm sure I could get hold of a couple, if you'd like to see it?' he asked casually.

Her heart starting to hammer against her ribs, she bit back the urge to accept. She was being foolish in the extreme just having dinner with him. No doubt all he wanted was a brief fling.

But while many women might have jumped at the chance, that kind of thing wasn't her style.

Plus, it could cost her her job.

Her expression tight, controlled, she refused with formal politeness. 'I don't think so, thank you.'

He was having none of it. Green eyes looked into aquamarine. 'You mean you don't want to see it? Or you don't want to see it with me?'

Feeling as though she'd been set down in the middle of a minefield, she found herself wishing the evening were over. Wishing she could escape.

And he knew it.

Lifting her chin, she answered as steadily as possible, 'I don't have much spare time, so I don't want to commit myself.'

He had known from the start that getting anywhere with this woman wouldn't be easy. Now he realized that it was going to be a great deal harder than he had anticipated.

But he had wanted her on sight, wanted her with a passionate hunger that had surprised and shaken him. And no matter what it took, he vowed, he intended to have her.

But it would be a mistake to come on too strong.

With a graceful movement of his hand he conceded defeat and, his expression bland, steered the conversation into less perilous channels.

Feeling relieved, she followed his lead.

Watching her, he noted that relief and wondered why she was so wary, so reluctant to get involved.

Still, the night was young. There was time to change her mood.

His charming nature soon set her at her ease once more, and by the time they finally rose to leave she could have stayed there all night.

And he knew that too.

Watching her face, soft and dreamy now, he felt a strange tenderness mingling with satisfaction as he escorted her outside.

Moonlit air caressed her skin like velvet, and the stars were so close she felt she only had to stretch out a hand to pluck one from the sky.

The taxi Rafe had ordered was waiting for them, and his hand a warm weight in the middle of her spine, he ushered her towards it.

When they were settled in the back, he said, 'I understand from Miss Collins that you live in Knightsbridge. Where exactly?'

She gave him the address of her flat and, sliding open the glass panel, he relayed it to the driver.

As they reached the gates and joined the late-night stream of traffic, he looked deep into her eyes. His look was so intent and searching it made her heart beat faster and her breath grow short.

While she stared back at him as though mesmerised, he took her heart-shaped face between his palms and, bending his dark head, touched his mouth to hers.

His kiss, light and fleeting though it was, seemed to melt every bone in her body and filled her with an almost uncontrollable longing.

Drawing back, he said quizzically, 'There now, that's what you've been fearing all night, but it didn't hurt a bit, did it?'

When she just looked at him with big, dazed eyes, he said, 'So shall I do it again?'

Somehow she found her voice and lied jerkily, 'I'd rather you didn't.'

'OK,' he said, and kissed her again. This time there was nothing light or fleeting about it.

When, without conscious volition, her lips parted beneath the light pressure of his, he deepened the kiss until her head was reeling and her very soul had lost its way.

He could feel her trembling and, sensing that she was his for the taking, he suggested softly, 'My apartment is quite close to here. Will you come up for a nightcap?'

Somehow she found her voice and objected huskily, 'It's late. I should get to bed.'

'Exactly what I had in mind...' he murmured.

She didn't dare look at him.

'With so much chemistry between us...' He let the sentence tail off.

But then he didn't need to say any more. Sex with him would be good, she knew that instinctively. Better than good. Mind-blowing.

Heat running through her, she said, 'I've never gone in for one-night stands,' and was uncomfortably aware that she sounded stuffy and old-fashioned.

Raising a dark brow, he asked, 'Who said anything about a one-night stand? I have the distinct feeling that having you in my arms for a million and one nights wouldn't be enough.'

Struggling to close her mind to the seduction in his voice and words, she looked down at her lap. For once in her life she was sorely tempted to do what Eve was always telling her to do, and live a little.

But the guilt that had been her albatross now became her saviour, reminding her that she couldn't afford—either financially or emotionally—to get involved with this man.

Taking a deep, steadying breath, she said, 'I don't want to go to bed with you. I'd like to go home, please.'

CHAPTER TWO

MADELINE braced herself, expecting him to be angry, to try and persuade her to change her mind, but, showing no signs of temper or disappointment, Rafe said evenly, 'Very well. If that's what you want.'

Relieved that he'd accepted her decision, that she'd won so easily, she made an effort to relax her taut muscles.

The relief turned out to be premature, as he returned to the attack.

'Have lunch with me tomorrow?' Before she could answer, he swept on, 'According to the forecast, it's going to be another lovely day. We could go for a drive, and picnic in an idyllic spot I know.'

'I'm afraid I can't.'

'You're not working tomorrow, are you?' he questioned.

'No. But I've a lot to do.' In a rush, she added, 'Saturday mornings I clean the flat, and then I do some shopping.'

She always bought a selection of small gifts for her mother, before catching the two-thirty bus to the nursing home.

He raised dark brows. 'Surely housework and shopping can wait? While this good weather holds, having a drive in the country and a picnic would be a lot more fun.'

Thinking of what had happened to her mother and Colin,

and feeling the black taste of guilt in her mouth, she said sharply, 'There's a lot more to life than just having fun.'

Then, seeing the shadow that had fallen across his face, and regretting lashing out, she touched his sleeve. 'I'm sorry. That wasn't very gracious of me.'

'No.' He covered her hand with his. 'But you don't have to be gracious with me. I'd much prefer honesty…'

She was surprised. None of the men she'd known had particularly valued honesty.

'Tell me why the idea of having a little fun upset you so much,' he pursued.

It wasn't something she could tell him.

It wasn't something she could bring herself to tell anyone. Not even Eve and Noel.

Pulling her hand free, she said jerkily, 'It isn't the idea of having fun… It's just that…' The words tailed off.

'You really can't stand the sight of me?'

She should have said yes, and be done with it. Instead, she said, 'No, it's nothing like that.'

'So what is it?'

'I—I don't have time for commitments…'

'I wasn't asking you to sign your life over to me,' he said mildly, 'merely to spend a few fleeting hours in my company. If you're busy Saturday morning, let's make it the afternoon.'

'I'm not free Saturday afternoon. I have to be out by two-thirty.'

'What time will you be home?'

Naturally truthful, she admitted, 'About six.'

'Then have dinner with me.'

Before she could think of an excuse, they were turning into Danetree Court, an old-fashioned block in a tree-lined square.

As they drew up outside her ground-floor flat, fumbling in her bag for her key, she said quickly, 'Don't bother to get out.'

Ignoring her injunction, Rafe asked the driver to wait and

accompanied her across the pavement. In the amber glow from the street lamp he unlocked the door and handed her back the key.

'Thank you.' Dropping it into her bag, she slipped inside and turned to face him.

He was standing so close that she could feel the warmth of his body and his breath stirring her hair.

She glanced up.

His mouth was only inches away. Just the thought of it touching hers again sent shivers down her spine and brought her out in goose-pimples.

She backed a step. 'And thank you for a very nice evening. I've had a lovely time.'

'I'm pleased you've enjoyed it.' Then, as though it was all settled, 'I thought we'd go to Annabel's tomorrow evening…'

She hesitated, knowing full well she should stop this thing in its tracks but wanting desperately to see him again.

Looking into her face, seeing her waver, he added firmly, 'I'll pick you up at seven-thirty.'

Though common sense told her she was being a fool, she agreed, 'All right.'

When he lifted a quizzical brow at her lack of enthusiasm, her voice unsteady, she added, 'I'll look forward to it… Well, goodnight.'

He tilted his head to one side, a gesture she was coming to know. 'Rafe?'

'Rafe,' she echoed obediently. It was the first time she had used his name.

'Goodnight, Madeleine. Sleep well.'

'Goodnight,' she said again.

He didn't turn away as she had expected. Instead he stood quite motionless, watching her.

She knew she should step back and close the door, but, fascinated by the unnerving stillness that generated so much sexual tension, she was still rooted to the spot when he bent and kissed her.

This time his mouth was not only sweet, but also *familiar*. His arms went around her, and he drew her close. His kiss was firm and masterful and when he sought to deepen it her lips parted as though there was no help for it.

The last obstacle removed, his mouth began to move against hers in a sizzling kiss that melted her last defences as easily as a blowtorch melted butter.

He tasted like ambrosia. Her stomach clenched and her heart began to race wildly, while desire dried her throat and ran like red-hot lava through her bloodstream.

She was no longer capable of thinking straight when, a few seconds later, he freed her mouth and, his voice husky, murmured, 'You're the most beautiful thing I've ever seen. I can't wait to feel your naked body against mine, to make love to you…'

Looking up into his shadowy face, she knew she ought to send him away. But she couldn't.

'Is that what you want?' he murmured.

She nodded silently and, her breathing shallow and ragged, waited impatiently while he went to pay off the taxi.

He came back and, taking her chin in his hand, lifted her face and began to kiss her again, kisses sweeter than wine, as he eased them inside and closed the door.

In the gloom, he continued to kiss her while he removed the clasp that held her hair. She heard his little murmur of satisfaction as the silky mass tumbled around her shoulders and he ran his fingers through it.

Then his hands slipped to the warmth of her nape and began to travel over her, tracing her shoulders, her ribcage, her slender waist, the flare of her hips and the curve of her firm buttocks.

'I've never met a women I wanted so much,' he murmured against her lips.

His touch was all she had ever hoped for or needed, and above his softly spoken words she could hear his heart beating. Or was it her own?

Caught up in a whirl of sensual delight, on a flight to the stars, she was hearing things, tasting things, feeling things that she had never heard or tasted or felt before.

While he continued to kiss her he unbuttoned her blouse and, unhooking the fastening of her bra, slipped one hand inside. Her breast fitted neatly into his palm. Enjoying the warm weight of it, he brushed his thumb over the velvety nipple and felt it firm beneath his touch. Shudders of pleasure running through her, she gasped deep in her throat. Hearing that muffled sound and interpreting it correctly, he bent his head to take the other nipple in his mouth and suckle until her whole body was on fire with longing.

When she could stand no more she pushed him away and, taking his hand, urged him towards the bedroom.

As the door closed behind them, the small voice of reason warned her that she was acting completely out of character. Acting like a fool.

But, having jumped into the deep end, she was in over her head and unwilling to be saved. Brushing reason aside, she moved to close the slatted window blind and shut out the night.

Turning to him, she saw the gleam of his eyes in the semi-darkness before he switched on the bedside lamp, flooding that part of the room in amber light.

On the dressing table close by was a framed snapshot of a smiling, fair-haired man.

Reaching out, Rafe picked it up and, his voice a little wary, asked, 'Is this your husband?'

She answered distractedly, 'Oh, no, that's Noel. He's out in the Middle East. In the oil fields.'

'An ex-lover?'

'A friend.'

Rafe replaced the photograph with care, and turned to gaze at her.

She had expected him to skip over the preliminaries and hurry her into bed, but with no suggestion of haste he said softly, 'I want to look at you. Take off your clothes for me.'

As though under a spell, she began to take off her suit and blouse. But modesty once ingrained was hard to dislodge, and, aware as she was of his appreciative gaze, the lick of flame in his eyes, her cheeks were hot as she stripped off her panties.

When she straightened and stood before him naked, he made a half-smothered sound deep in his throat, a very male sound, and without taking his eyes off her for an instant began to divest himself of his own shoes and clothing.

As she watched him discard his dark silk boxer shorts, it was her turn to smother the gasp that rose in her throat. Too turned on to move, she swallowed hard, her stomach tightening with anticipation.

'Come here,' he said.

When she obeyed, he lifted her onto the bed and stretched out beside her. Then, propping himself on one elbow, he leaned over her and, his hand fondling her breast, he said softly, 'You're exquisite. The loveliest thing I've ever seen.'

Colin had been an unexciting lover, with a low sex drive and little skill. Not only had he preferred to make love in the dark, but also he had never told her she was beautiful, nor had he caressed her in that way.

Rather, he had avoided touching her, as though he found the idea of enjoying sex something to be slightly ashamed of.

Rafe obviously had no such inhibitions.

Inhaling the fragrance of her skin, he murmured, 'You smell as fresh and delightful as apple blossom,' before his mouth began to roam over her.

She shivered deliciously as his unshaven jaw rasped against the smooth skin of her flat stomach.

When he had kissed and tasted every inch of her golden flesh, his mouth returned to pleasure her breasts while his fingers found the nest of pale, silky curls and began to explore further. Shivering, she gave herself up to the sensations those skilful fingers were engendering.

It wasn't long, however, before the exquisite torment grew too much to bear and she writhed under the lash of pleasure while desire rode her, digging in its spurs so that she began to make little whimpering sounds deep in her throat.

He paused, then, drawing her back against him, spoon-fashion, he eased her hips towards him before returning his hands to her breasts.

Just at first he was careful, as though gauging her reaction. Then he began to thrust more strongly, building a tension that spiralled and grew until the sensations, almost too great to be borne, peaked, and stars exploded inside her head.

Hearing her little gasping cries with pleasure, he held her there, drawing out the moment, until he too was caught up in the surging excitement.

For a while they lay together quietly while their heart rates and breathing returned to normal. Then he drew away, and, turning her to face him, gathered her close and kissed her tenderly.

Knowing she'd been married, he had been somewhat thrown, partly by her obvious shyness, and partly by her instinctive reaction to their lovemaking. Her obvious pleasure had been followed by what he could have sworn was *gratitude*. Frowning, he wondered if her husband had been clumsy and lacking skill, or simply uncaring.

Seeing that frown, she asked a shade anxiously, 'I hope you weren't disappointed?'

'Anything but,' he assured her.

Then, picking up her very real concern, he kissed her and, leaning his forehead against hers, told her with soft emphasis, 'You're very special, and I'm immensely flattered that you let me into your bed.'

Feeling her relax, with a little sigh of relief he settled her head on his shoulder. She felt limp as a rag doll. The power and intensity of his lovemaking had left her exhausted, totally drained, yet at the same time full of bliss, brimming with rapture.

Never for a moment had she imagined love could be like this—and yes, it *was* love—never imagined that this strength of feeling could take root and blossom so quickly. It wasn't just the result of sexual deprivation, nor was it simply the chemistry between them. This was different. This was more. Much more.

They seemed to meet on every level, physical, mental and emotional. And as she slid into sleep she found herself thinking that if she searched the world over she would never find a man who was more right for her.

The same thought was in her mind when she stirred and surfaced slowly, her body relaxed and satisfied, a quiet happiness singing through her.

She was in love, truly in love, for the very first time. It was a big risk, letting herself fall so hard and so fast for a man she had only just met.

But she couldn't say she hadn't known what she was doing. Well aware that she was vulnerable, well aware that she was teetering on the brink of falling for him, well aware that making love with him could easily push her over, she had walked into it with her eyes wide open.

And it had been wonderful beyond words. She had never felt so utterly content. Not even her guilt over Colin could spoil things, or alter the way she felt about Rafe.

Sighing, she stretched out a hand to touch him, but she was alone. Jolted wide awake, she opened her eyes to find he was standing by the bed fully dressed, a cup of tea in his hand.

'I'm sorry to wake you, but I thought it best if I left early.'

He set the cup on the bedside cabinet and smiled down at her. The blind was still closed, but even in the half-light his thickly lashed green eyes were brilliant, and with his hair a little rumpled, a dark stubble adorning his jaw, he looked irresistibly virile and attractive.

Her heart doing strange things, she pushed herself into a sitting position.

'What I'd really like to do,' he went on, 'is stay and make love to you until such a time as the sight of a strange man leaving your flat wouldn't raise a single eyebrow...'

Just his words made her go hot all over and sent a surge of desire running through her.

'But bearing in mind what you said about having a lot to do, I'm restraining the urge...'

Disappointment pricked sharp as a thorn.

'I'll pick you up at seven-thirty.'

He stooped and kissed her, a lingering kiss, as if he couldn't bear to leave her. She was on the verge of begging him to stay when he straightened and strode to the door.

An instant later he was gone.

For a moment or two she felt empty and lost—*bereft*—as if the whole thing had been nothing but a wonderful dream. But the cup of tea sitting by her elbow was tangible proof, not only that he was no dream, but also that he'd cared enough to think about her. Gladness returning, she reached for the cup and took a sip. Only the day to get through and she would be seeing him again.

Excitement and anticipation buoying her up, the morning passed quite quickly, and even her afternoon visit to the nursing home didn't seem quite so fraught as usual. For the first time in what seemed an age, happiness was crowding out guilt. Or at least masking it.

By a quarter past seven that evening, showered, dressed and lightly made-up, Madeleine was ready and waiting. Standing by the window, she watched as a silver Porsche drew up by the kerb promptly at seven-thirty, and Rafe jumped out. He looked breathtakingly handsome in well-cut evening clothes, and she wondered if she was underdressed for Annabel's.

Taking deep breaths to calm herself, she let him ring the bell before picking up her evening purse and going to open the door.

He smiled at her. 'Ready?'

Madeleine nodded. 'Will I do?' she asked a shade anxiously.

His glance swept over her from head to toe.

She was wearing a simple black dress that clung lovingly to her slender curves and set off her flawless, pale gold skin. Her blonde hair was taken up in a gleaming coil that served to emphasise her pure bone structure, and in her neat lobes were small gold hoops.

A light in his eyes, he said, 'You look stunning,' and bent his dark head to kiss her.

Her heart leapt in her breast, and she knew he held everything she was, everything she hoped for, in the palm of his hand.

It was a beautiful evening, warm and still, and she could smell roses in the heart of town as she was escorted to the car.

When she was settled, he slid in beside her and started the engine. As they left the square behind them and joined the evening queue of traffic, he queried lightly, 'Missed me?'

The true answer was yes, but she said primly, 'I haven't had time.'

'So what have you been doing all day?'

'Nothing very exciting. I spent most of the morning cleaning and shopping.'

'But you went out in the afternoon? Anywhere nice?'

Flustered by the question, she said, 'No, not particularly.' She had meant to sound casual, but it came out as defensive, and she bit her lip.

Intrigued by her tone, he wondered what she was hiding. Deciding not to push it—he'd find out when he knew her better—he changed tack.

'What made you decide to become a physiotherapist?'

She relaxed, glad to chat about her work. 'You might call it following in my father's footsteps. Physiotherapy was his chosen profession, and it was widely acknowledged that he had healing hands. When I was a child he became prominent in his field, and so much in demand that he turned into a work-aholic.'

'So you didn't see much of him?' Rafe questioned.

'No.' There was a remembered hint of sadness. 'When he wasn't at his consulting rooms in Baker Street, he was often in the States giving lecture tours.'

'Why the States? Any particular reason?'

'My father's American by birth. He was brought up and had done his early training in Boston.'

'So you're half American? Any relatives over there?' he asked.

'Just an aunt and uncle we used to visit. They were always delighted to see us.' Madeleine smiled as she reminisced.

Rafe asked no further questions, and they lapsed into silence until the Porsche drew up outside the famous basement entrance in Berkeley Square.

When he had helped her out, he handed the keys to the doorman and they made their way down the steps and in through a door at the bottom.

'Good evening, Mr Lombard. Nice to see you.' Clearly well-known, Rafe was welcomed inside.

As he signed in he was greeted by a couple who looked

inclined to attach themselves, until he said with smooth politeness, 'Well, if you'll excuse us?' and led Madeleine away.

When they were out of earshot, he added, 'Jo and Tom are very nice, but I wanted you all to myself tonight.'

She flushed with pleasure.

There was a mere handful of people in the bar, even fewer in the restaurant, and the dance floor was empty, its dark mirrors reflecting nothing.

'It doesn't get busy until later, so we'll have plenty of time to dine in comfort and then we can dance later.'

Just the thought of being held in his arms made her temperature rise even more.

When they were settled at a table and had been given menus, he asked, 'Is there anything in particular you fancy?'

Wanting only to watch his face in the candlelight, she shook her head. 'You order for me.'

The order given, they were sipping an aperitif when he reached across the table and, taking her slim but strong hand, examined it.

'You said your father had healing hands. Have you?'

'I'm afraid not,' she said honestly. 'Nor have I my father's sheer dedication.'

'So you're not a committed career woman?' He glanced up and met her gaze.

'Not really. I could be just as happy being a wife and mother.'

'At the risk of sounding chauvinistic, I find that highly commendable in this materialistic age. Most of the women I've met have been career-orientated. Being 'just' a wife and mother comes a very poor second to their independence. No wonder so many men feel threatened...'

His white smile flashed suddenly. 'Don't get me wrong, I wouldn't want a brainless, compliant woman, no matter how beautiful she was, nor would I want a clinging vine...'

'What *would* you want?' She laughed.

'An intelligent, independently minded woman who was capable of standing beside me as my equal. Yet a woman who would be willing to put her home and family before her career.'

Had he stayed single because he couldn't find the right kind of woman? she wondered. Or was that just an excuse so he could go on playing the field?

As though he knew exactly what she was thinking, he added, 'Someone with all those qualities isn't easy to find. That's one of the reasons I haven't been in a hurry to marry.'

'Then you intend to?' The instant the words were out she wished them unsaid, and the warm colour rose in her cheeks.

A hint of amusement in his voice, he said, 'Oh yes, I fully intend to…'

To Madeleine's relief the arrival of the first course provided a welcome diversion, and during the rest of what proved to be a very enjoyable meal Rafe kept the conversation light and general.

They had reached the coffee stage before he returned to more personal matters, by asking, 'Do you enjoy your work at the clinic?'

'Yes. Though of course it's just a temporary post, and part-time.'

'You have private patients as well?'

'Some. But by the time this job ends I'm hoping to have more,' Madeleine said, taking a sip of her coffee.

'Do you treat children?' Rafe asked.

'Oh, yes. At the moment I'm visiting a young boy who injured his knee playing football. Why do you ask?'

'My sister, Diane, and her husband, Stuart, have a problem. A couple of months ago their ten-year-old daughter, Katie, was quite badly injured when she fell from her horse. Since leaving hospital Katie has been treated at home, but it seems she's grown to dislike her present physiotherapist and has refused to have any further treatment. Would you be willing to take a look at her?'

A little flustered, Madeleine agreed, 'Of course. If you think I'll be able to help.'

'If Katie takes to you, and I can't imagine she won't, you could be the answer to all our prayers… More coffee?'

'I don't think so, thank you.'

Rafe smiled a dazzling smile and asked. 'Then would you like to dance?'

The club had started to fill up, and there were several couples already on the floor.

Madeleine's eyes lit up. 'Yes, I'd love to.'

Even in her own ears her words sounded eager and breathless, and as he took her hand and led her onto the floor she wondered where the old cool and composed Madeleine had gone.

Though it was a long time since she had been on a dance floor, she had always enjoyed dancing. But this was something special.

He was a good dancer, light on his feet and with a purely masculine grace. As he held her to his heart, his cheek against her hair, they moved round the floor as though made for each other.

For Madeleine the rest of the evening passed in a kind of dream as, without speaking, just enjoying the music and the closeness, they danced every dance.

When the floor started to get crowded, Rafe murmured in her ear, 'About ready to go?'

She nodded, a little shiver of excitement running down her spine. She hadn't allowed herself to think any further than dining and dancing at Annabel's, but now the evening was over and the night lay ahead.

When she was settled in the Porsche, he turned to look directly into her eyes. 'I shared your bed last night. Will you come to Denver Court tonight and share mine?'

A betraying catch in her voice, she agreed lightly, 'That seems only fair.'

As they drew up outside the imposing tower-block complex and he helped her out, one of the night security staff came hurrying over.

'Evening, Mr Lombard… Anything I can do for you?'

'Could you put the car away, please, Jim?' A folded note changed hands.

His arm around her waist, Rafe escorted Madeleine into the building and across the pale marble-floored foyer to the lift.

On the top floor they stepped out into a wide, luxuriously carpeted area with a white and gold decor and extravagant arrangements of fresh flowers.

When he let them into his apartment and flicked on the lights, she saw that he occupied one of the corner penthouse suites. From the spacious and attractive L-shaped living room, French windows led onto a walled patio and garden.

She gasped as she looked around her, taking in the luxurious surroundings. Rafe smiled and bent to touch his lips to the warmth of her nape, before asking, 'Would you like a nightcap?'

Shivering a little at the caress, and impatient for the pleasures to come, she shook her head.

Taking her hand in his, he led her through to a large *en suite* bedroom with pale walls and a thundercloud-blue carpet and curtains.

Opening a connecting door into a similar room decorated in ivory tones, he suggested, 'If you'd like to use the guest-room facilities you'll find everything there you need.'

In the well-appointed bathroom there was indeed everything a guest could want, including slippers and a white towelling robe.

She found herself wondering how often he brought his women back here.

It was an uncomfortable thought, and she pushed it hastily

away. This might only be another brief and casual affair as far as *he* was concerned, but for her it was special, a once-in-a-lifetime love affair, no matter how short a time it lasted.

When she had cleaned her teeth and showered, she brushed out her long, silky hair and, a little shy, put on the towelling robe before making her way back to Rafe's room.

He was just emerging from his bathroom, stark naked apart from a towel slung round his neck that he was using one-handed to rub his dark hair.

As she hesitated in the doorway, tossing aside the towel, he held out both hands. 'Come here.'

Loving that touch of arrogance, she went to him, and was rewarded with a lingering kiss.

He had shaved, and she could smell the fresh, spicy scent of his cologne. Eyes still closed, she put up a hand and stroked his smooth cheek.

'Mmm...' she murmured.

Nuzzling his face against her throat, he said, 'I intend to kiss every inch of you, and bristles can play havoc with delicate skin.'

Untying the belt of her robe, he slid his hands inside and, like a blind man reading Braille, ran his fingers over her slender body, savouring the purely tactile pleasure.

It was strangely erotic, and by the time his hands returned to her breasts she was quivering all over. When his thumbs brushed lightly across the sensitive nipples, she gasped.

As he continued to tease, soon aroused to fever-pitch, she pressed her hips against his.

But, refusing to be hurried, he said, 'We've got all night. Plenty of time to take things slow and easy, to ravish you, in the best sense of the word.'

She wondered how he could be so patient, so willing to wait for his own pleasure.

As though reading her mind, he said softly, 'Your body

responds so delightfully to my every touch, it makes the pleasure mutual.'

He put his mouth to her breast and laved the nipple with his tongue. 'You like that, don't you?'

She shuddered, and, holding his dark head between her hands, breathed, 'Yes, but I don't think I can stand much more...'

'Oh, I think you can.'

When he finally lifted her onto the bed and stretched out beside her, she was almost mindless, poised on the brink.

He stoked a caressing hand down her slender figure and, finding the warm, silky skin of her inner thighs, used a single long finger to tip her over. Her whole body bucked convulsively, and she lay quivering and helpless until the exquisite sensations began to die away.

She felt a little *triste*. She had wanted to make love *with* him, to share the experience, to know he was feeling the same delight and joy she was feeling.

When she opened dazed eyes, he was watching her.

Smiling at her, as though he understood perfectly, he said, 'It's all right,' and with those skilful hands he proceeded to reawaken the desire she had thought sated.

Then slowly, very slowly, as though to draw every last ounce of pleasure out of it, he made love to her, building up a molten core of heat, a spiralling tension, until the tension snapped and sent them both rocketing into space.

She drifted back to earth to find his dark head was lying on her breast and his hand holding hers. It was one of the sweetest sensations she had ever felt.

Her heart overflowing with love and gratitude she lay quietly enjoying their closeness until he moved away and, turning onto his back, gathered her against him and settled her head on his shoulder.

CHAPTER THREE

AFTER a night OF love-making, it was almost ten o'clock when Madeleine woke. She was alone in the big bed, but just as that fact registered the door opened and Rafe came in carrying a tray.

His dark hair was still damp from the shower, and he was wearing a short, navy-blue silk robe. 'Good morning.' He smiled lazily as she pushed herself upright. 'I thought we'd be decadent and have breakfast in bed.'

He put the tray on the bedside table and, leaning over to kiss her, remarked wickedly, 'After the night we've just spent, I don't know how you can look so beautiful and fresh.'

'I'm happy,' she said simply. She had never thought she would say those words again.

He smiled at her. 'Happiness suits you.'

As he sat on the bed and fed her toast and scrambled eggs and coffee, his voice casual, Rafe suggested, 'Tell me some more about yourself.'

Instantly uneasy, she said, 'There's not a great deal to tell.'

Sensing that unease, and wondering what was causing it, he decided to go slowly. 'Do your parents still live in London?'

'They got divorced when I was twelve.'

'Presumably it was your father's dedication to work that caused the break-up.'

'Yes. Though my mother loved him passionately, eventually she got fed up with him never being there for us.' Madeleine turned her head away from him.

'Was it an amicable parting?'

'As amicable as these things ever can be.'

Rafe probed further, 'But you must have missed him?'

'Yes, I did, and I don't think my mother ever really got over it.' She felt her eyes begin to water, but she smiled as she looked up at Rafe.

'She didn't marry again?'

'No. I believe she still loves him. Certainly there was never anyone else.'

'Do you still see him?'

Madeleine shook her head. 'Some time after the divorce he remarried and went to live in Los Angeles. We haven't had any contact for years.'

Then, wanting to escape from the spotlight, she said quickly, 'Now it's your turn to tell me something about yourself.'

His face straight, he replied, 'There's not a great deal to tell.' He laughed and kissed her, before beginning, 'I lost my father when I was twelve. A year after he died, my mother married again. Her new husband was an ex-army officer.'

'Did you all get on as a family?'

'Diane, who's seven years older than me, was away at university, so that left just the three of us, and unfortunately my stepfather and I *didn't* get along. I resented him taking my father's place and showed it, which, with hindsight, must have made life extremely difficult for my mother. My stepfather was a strict disciplinarian and after he'd whacked me a couple of times for what he termed insolence, I began to seriously hate his guts.' Rafe paused for a moment before continuing.

'Things went from bad to worse, and the whacks changed to beatings. On the final occasion, when he began to lay into me with his belt, my mother tried to intervene. He pushed her out of the way so roughly that she stumbled and fell. I saw red and went for him. I wasn't quite fourteen at the time.'

Her aquamarine eyes full of concern, Madeleine asked, 'What happened?'

Matter-of-factly, he said, 'I managed to split his lip before ending up in Casualty.'

As she winced he added, 'I think he may have been genuinely sorry afterwards. But it was patently obvious that things couldn't go on like that, so I was hastily packed off to live with my godparents.'

Madeleine reached out to touch his arm. 'Were you very upset?'

'For a time I was very bitter,' he admitted. 'Though my godparents were amazing.'

'Had they any children of their own?'

'One daughter, Fiona. But they had always hoped for a son, and were only too delighted to have me.'

'Fiona wasn't jealous at all?'

His face softened. 'Oh, no. We got to be very close. In fact for a while she hero-worshipped me. She was nearly three years younger than me, and I always called her my kid sister.'

'So it was a good move?'

'Oh, yes. The whole family treated me exactly like their own, and I was very happy with them until I went up to Oxford. My godfather died eighteen months ago and it was like losing a father...

'But that's enough doom and gloom—let's talk about something else. What shall we do for the rest of the day? Would you like to—'

'I can't,' she broke in desperately. On Sundays she always had lunch at the nursing home, and spent the rest of the afternoon and evening there. 'I mean, I'm already going out.'

When she made no effort to elaborate, he asked, 'What time do you need to start?'

'In about an hour.'

'Then as soon as you've showered and dressed, I'll take you home.' Though his voice was even, she knew he was vexed by her reticence, but she couldn't bring herself to tell him about her mother. He was sure to ask questions that, burdened with guilt, she didn't want to answer.

His profile cool and aloof, he drove through the Sunday streets in silence. She longed to break that silence, but could think of nothing to say.

When he drew up outside her flat and, still without speaking, helped her out, she felt a sudden panic in case this was the end.

What would she do if he simply drove away?

As though to keep her guessing, he unlocked her door and handed her back the key, before asking, 'Are you free tomorrow evening?'

'Yes,' she said eagerly.

'Then if you like, I'll take you to see Katie and her parents. I've already mentioned your name to them.'

'There's just one thing…' Madeleine began a shade awkwardly.

Reading her hesitation, he said, 'You prefer to keep your private and professional lives separate?'

'Yes, I do.'

'That's fine by me. All they know up to now is that you're the physiotherapist who checked me out, and we can keep it that way. I'll pick you up at six-thirty, and afterwards we can have dinner.'

Madeleine liked Rafe's sister and brother-in-law on sight. Over drinks on the sunny terrace of their Surrey home she learnt that Diane, with her brother's seal-dark hair and green eyes, was a lawyer, and Stuart, a pleasant, easy-going man, worked as an architect.

They both doted on their only daughter and were over the moon when Katie took an immediate liking to Madeleine, and agreed to have further treatment.

The liking was mutual. Madeleine instantly lost her heart to the quiet, sensitive child, with her long dark hair, her big brown eyes and shy smile.

Over the next few weeks, with regular treatments, Katie's condition improved enormously, and a strong bond developed between her and Madeleine.

Rafe was delighted for everyone's sake, but he stayed well out of things and, though his and Madeleine's relationship grew and blossomed, it was never mentioned.

They spent as much time with one another as possible, dancing, dining, talking, simply being together.

Several times, while the good weather held, he barbecued for them on his patio. Afterwards, safe from prying eyes, they made sweet, delectable love in the sun.

As the days and weeks passed and Madeleine got to know him better, her happiness increased. Apart from his physical attributes and his prowess as a lover, he proved to be even-tempered and generous, an intelligent, stimulating companion, always sensitive to her needs.

She knew that never in her lifetime would she find another man who suited her so well, and, eternally grateful, she said many a prayer of thanks to the goddess of destiny for the miracle that had brought him into her life.

Only her visits to the nursing home cast a shadow. Rafe said nothing openly, but she knew he was ruffled by her un-explained absences. Even a little jealous of whom she might be meeting.

Each time she tried to tell him the truth guilt made the

words stick in her throat, and she chickened out. But one of these days, she promised herself, she *would* find the courage to tell him everything.

In the meantime, though she still spent most of Sunday at the nursing home, she had changed her Saturday visit to the morning—struggling with the shopping and housework when she could—to leave the afternoon free.

That Saturday afternoon they had something very special planned. Jonathan Cass was one of her favourite artists, and Rafe had accepted an invitation to a one-day private showing of Cass's new, and so far unseen, works.

He had arranged to pick her up at twelve-thirty so they could have lunch together before going on to the Piccadilly gallery, and she left the nursing home earlier than usual to make certain she was home in good time.

She was only just back when the phone rang.

Sounding tense, unlike himself, Rafe said, 'Some urgent business has cropped up. Would you mind very much if I picked you up after lunch?'

'Of course not.'

Sounding relieved, he said, 'Then I'll see you about two.'

It had been a damp, grey morning, and by two o'clock it was pelting down with rain.

Rafe was always on time—she had never known him to be late—and as the hands of the clock moved with maddening slowness—two-fifteen, two-thirty, a quarter to three—and he failed to arrive, she began to get anxious and jumpy.

As she stood staring blindly out into the wet, windswept square, watching the raindrops run down the windowpane like tears, she saw the ghost of his face blurry in the glass and felt a queer foreboding.

Oh, dear God, suppose something had happened to him? The panicky thought made her heart begin to race uncomfortably fast.

Don't be a fool, she chided herself. Of course nothing had happened to him. No doubt he'd just been held up. But if that was the case, why hadn't he phoned? It would have only taken a moment to reassure her.

After waiting until three-thirty without hearing from him she called his mobile, only to find it was switched off. In desperation she tried his flat at Denver Court, but it rang hollow and empty, until the answering machine picked up her call.

By the time five o'clock arrived, convinced that her worst fears had been realised, she was a mass of jangling nerves. She was wondering agitatedly whom she could contact, when she saw his car pull up outside. The rush of relief was so great that it made her feel giddy and light-headed.

He had his own key by now, and she stood, her knees trembling so much they would hardly support her, while he crossed the streaming pavement and let himself in. She wanted to run to him, but she could neither move nor speak.

'I'm sorry I couldn't get here any sooner.' As he spoke he took off his coat and hung it up.

When he turned she noticed some angry-looking marks on his face, as though a cat had raked its claws down his cheek.

'What have you done to your face?'

'It's just a scratch,' he said dismissively.

Taking a deep, steadying breath, she remarked, 'I wondered what had happened to you.'

'I was unavoidably detained.'

She waited for some kind of explanation, but he said nothing further.

After so much anxiety, his casual dismissal of the subject caught her on the raw.

Seeing her mouth tighten, he said, 'We can still go to the gallery this evening.'

'It's not that,' she assured him stiffly. 'I was worried to death about you. I just wish you'd given me a ring.'

'I'm afraid my mobile went on the blink.'

The obvious excuse did nothing to help matters.

'Forgive me?' Seeing her set face, he smiled. 'Oh, dear, obviously not.'

His eyes fixed on her mouth, he bent his head to kiss her. She moved back a step.

He sighed. 'And here I've been, waiting all day to kiss you. Waiting all day just to touch you, to take you to bed and make love to you.'

Angry with him for his cavalier attitude, she looked at him stonily.

'In that case, I'll have to resort to a spot of friendly persuasion.'

Catching the lapels of her jacket, he pulled her towards him. Then, one hand beneath her chin, he lifted her face to meet his kiss.

It wasn't until his lips touched hers that she realised just how urgent was her need to have him kiss her. Just how much she needed to be reassured that he was really here, to be with her.

But, unwilling to let him know it, she tried her utmost to hide how she felt. Though she badly wanted to, she refused to put her arms round his neck, refused to melt against him as she normally did.

Even so, they were standing so close she could feel the warmth of his body, the ripple of his muscles, the firmness of his flesh.

His hand slid up and down her spine in a restless movement that told her he didn't like restraining himself, but was doing it anyway while he waited for some sign that he was forgiven.

After a time, when none was forthcoming, he lifted his mouth enough to murmur huskily, 'Are you persuaded yet?'

Her anger having drained away, she answered, 'Not yet; keep trying.'

His lips curved into a smile before his arms closed around her and he kissed her again.

Unable to resist him any longer, she reached up slowly, her fingertips tenderly tracing the scratches, before her palm cupped the hard planes of his cheek.

She heard his indrawn breath before he covered her hand with his own and, carrying it to his lips, kissed the palm.

Her whole being melted with love for him, and she wondered, how on earth had she managed to live before she met him?

When she tugged her hand free he frowned, a frown that changed to a glint of satisfaction as her fingers began to undo his shirt buttons.

It was only later that she realised she ought to have pressed him for an explanation first, but how could she, when so many times she had failed to give *him* one?

His need urgent, he swept her up in his arms and carried her through to the bedroom. When he had swiftly undressed her and lifted her onto the bed, he stripped off his own clothes.

Though she had seen him naked many times, she caught her breath yet again. He was a magnificent male animal, and she was his chosen mate. It was as wonderfully simple, as down to earth, as that.

Mostly he was a slow, skilful lover who took his time and enjoyed pleasuring her, building up the intensity until often she was gasping and writhing, hardly able to bear all the exquisite sensations he was engendering.

But now he wasted no time on foreplay, and trembling enough to rouse him even more, she accepted his weight eagerly.

She could hear his quickened breathing, feel the thump of his heart, and knowing she had caused it gave her pleasure.

Briefly she was pliant beneath him, waiting. Then she was taut as a drawn bow string as he drove hard and fast, carrying them both to a shattering climax.

She experienced a complete losing of self, then a gradual

gathering back as they lay in an erotic tangle of limbs, both breathing as if they'd just run a race.

After a while he lifted himself away and, leaning over her, brushed a loose tendril of silky blonde hair away from her flushed cheek.

'All right?' His expression held a mixture of concern and tenderness.

'Of course,' she assured him. 'Why shouldn't I be?'

'Well, I wasn't very gentle.'

His words made her think, made her suddenly appreciate that normally he was *careful* with her. But something—that brief touch of discord perhaps?—had thrown him off balance.

'You don't have to treat me like porcelain,' she told him a shade tartly. 'I won't break.'

Suddenly he was laughing. 'Are you trying to tell me you prefer it hard and fast to slow and easy? Well, well, well…'

'I'm not trying to tell you anything of the kind. I like…' She broke off and, feeling her colour rise, tried to wriggle free.

Putting an arm either side of her, he said silkily, 'Do go on. It's about time you opened up and told me. What *do* you like? I'm always willing to oblige.'

He was in a strange mood, she thought, and accused, 'You're trying to embarrass me.'

'Succeeding too, if the way you're blushing is anything to go by,' he said arrogantly.

Pushing herself up, she made another, more determined, attempt to escape.

He foiled her by the simple expedient of pulling her elbows from beneath her.

'Don't be shy. Tell me.'

'Rafe, *please*…'

'That's my intention as soon as I know what pleases you the most…'

When she remained silent, he sighed. 'Oh, well, if you're

determined not to tell me, I'll just have to experiment and make my own judgement…'

'Not now.' She tried once more to sit up.

Pushing her gently back, he said, 'Now.'

Secure in the knowledge that all hunger was sated, she said, 'You'll be wasting your time.'

'I don't think so.'

She quivered like a plucked string under his hands as he effortlessly re-aroused her desire. Soon she was spinning in some crazy world of sublime sensations while his every touch, his seeking mouth and tongue added more…

When finally she lay limp and emotionally drained, he gathered her close and kissed her. 'Sleep now.'

After a short time she awoke refreshed to find he was up and dressed.

'If we have a quick meal at the Xanadu we've still got time to go to the gallery.'

'We don't *have* to go.'

'I know you want to.' Bending down to kiss her, he added, 'And I don't want you to miss out on anything that gives you pleasure.'

As she showered and dressed, she thought—as she'd thought before and was to think many times in the coming weeks—how lucky she was to have Rafe. With a quiet but radiant happiness, she found herself daring to anticipate the day when he would tell her he loved her and ask her to be his wife.

Then, one golden evening in late September, a woman arrived at the clinic asking to speak to Madeleine on a matter of some urgency.

Presuming it was business, she agreed, and when a tall, good-looking brunette was shown in, she held out her hand with a friendly smile. 'Hello… I'm Madeleine Knight.'

The expression in her dark eyes unmistakably hostile, the newcomer, beautifully dressed and thin to the point of gauntness, ignored the proffered hand. 'And I'm Fiona Charn, Rafe's fiancée…'

Sitting down in the visitor's chair, she crossed slim, silk-clad legs. 'To put it bluntly, I gather that while I've been away this last time, he's been bedding you…'

Watching the hot colour pour into Madeleine's cheeks, Fiona added, 'But I'm wearing his ring.' She flashed a large, square-cut emerald.

Somehow Madeleine gathered herself enough to say jerkily, 'I had no idea he had a fiancée.'

'Oh, I don't blame *you* in particular. Rafe's always been a red-blooded man, and if it hadn't been you it would have been some other woman. He's extremely attractive to the opposite sex. Women throw themselves at him, so in a way one can't wonder that he takes advantage…

'But now I'm home it has to stop. Rafe's mine.'

Her voice sounding thin and tight, Madeleine said, 'If he's that kind of man I'm surprised you still want him.'

'Oh, I want him all right, so if you were thinking of suggesting that I set him free, forget it… For one thing he doesn't want out, and for another, we have a bargain…'

'A bargain?' Madeleine echoed.

'When it became clear that I was to be an only child, Daddy was bitterly disappointed. He held the old-fashioned belief that no mere woman could be expected to run a business empire successfully. Then Rafe came to live with us, and it was like a dream come true. The son he'd always wanted.

'Daddy was a wealthy man, but most of his money was tied up in the business and, to give him his due, he was concerned about my future.' Fiona paused, tossing her silken hair over her shoulder.

'After his first heart attack, he talked things over with Rafe and agreed to leave Charn Industries to him lock, stock and barrel if he would marry me and take care of me…'

Yes, Madeleine remembered being told that Rafe had inherited the Charn empire from his godfather.

'Rafe and I had been lovers for some time, so he was quite happy to make it legal. We'd have been married by now and there wouldn't have been a problem if I hadn't been diagnosed with a rare blood disorder. I've had to spend long periods in a private clinic undergoing treatment, which meant Rafe was left alone, and, as I say, he's a red-blooded man who needs a woman. Any woman.'

Her voice brittle, Fiona went on, 'Then I discovered I was pregnant, which made this last treatment more prolonged and complicated, and in the end I lost the baby…'

Shocked and horrified to think that she and Rafe had been lovers while his fiancée went through such an ordeal, Madeleine stood rooted to the spot, staring at her.

'But now I'm back home for good, and we'll be getting married fairly soon. I don't intend to let him stray, so I suggest you find yourself another man, preferably one that doesn't belong to some other woman.'

Getting to her feet, Fiona stalked out without a backward glance, leaving Madeleine devastated, shattered, her insides fractured into tiny pieces like a car's windscreen smashed with a hammer.

She was still standing staring blindly into space when Eve came in carrying the next patient's notes. 'Dear God!' she exclaimed, after a glance at her friend's face. 'You're as white as a sheet. What on earth's wrong?'

Madeleine focused with difficulty, and her voice impeded, said, 'Fiona Charn, the woman who just went out, is Rafe's fiancée.'

'What?'

'She's Rafe's fiancée,' Madeleine repeated.

Seeing her sway, and afraid she was going to faint, Eve pushed her into a chair.

'You're sure? You haven't got the wrong end of the stick or anything?'

'She was wearing his ring.'

'No! It can't be right; he loves you… I felt sure he did.' Eve was angry and indignant on her behalf. 'But if he's that kind of man, perhaps you're better off without him…'

She gave her friend a quick hug and, seeing the blankness of shock still on Madeleine's face, said, 'Look, why don't you go home? I'll tell Mrs Bond you're ill and get someone to fill in for you.'

'No… I'll be all right. I'd rather keep working. Just give me a few minutes.'

When Madeleine went home that evening, Eve insisted on going with her. 'Noel might well be out, and I don't think you should be alone,' she said soberly.

But Noel, who was just back from the Middle East and currently sleeping on Madeleine's bed-settee, *was* at home.

When he heard the news he was sympathetic, even angrier than his sister, and a great deal more vocal. 'I'd like to break the bastard's neck,' was one of his more restrained comments.

But as Madeleine pointed out bleakly, though Rafe had treated the woman who was to be his future wife with a callous disregard that was unforgivable, he had told *her* no lies. Promised *her* nothing.

He had never said he was free, never said he loved her or asked for her love. She had given it freely, and foolishly perhaps, *presumed* he was free, *presumed* he cared about her.

She couldn't have been more wrong. But perhaps, after what had happened to Colin and her mother, she didn't deserve to be happy. Perhaps it was poetic justice that Rafe hadn't loved her, any more than she had loved Colin... Perhaps this was what she deserved...

'Don't make excuses for him,' Noel broke into her thoughts. 'He's just been using you... I take it you won't be joining him in Paris?'

'No!' she said determinedly.

Rafe was in the French capital on business, and he had made all the arrangements for Madeleine to join him for a long weekend. It was a romantic trip she had been greatly looking forward to—staying on the Champs-Elysées, dining on the Bateaux Mouches, walking hand in hand down the Rue de Rivoli...

But now everything had changed.

'When he gets back,' Noel went on, 'face up to the swine and tell him what you think of him.'

'I can't,' she whispered.

How could she let Rafe see how heartbroken she was, how utterly devastated? It would be humiliating, mortifying. Somehow she had to walk away with at least her self-respect intact.

Guessing what was in her mind, Eve approved her decision. 'It might be best to let him think you don't care, that it doesn't mean a thing to you. At least that way you won't be just another scalp dangling from his belt...'

'So how are you going to get out of this Paris trip without letting him suspect the truth?' Noel asked.

'I don't know,' Madeleine said helplessly.

After the three of them had talked it over for a while, Eve exclaimed, 'I've got it! Send the brute a 'Dear John' email. Tell him you've met someone new and you're finishing with him.'

'I don't think that would work,' Madeleine demurred. 'He's only been in Paris two days—there hasn't been time for me to have met anyone else.'

'In that case make it someone you already know,' Eve said thoughtfully.

Madeleine shrugged. 'But I don't know anyone I could begin to pretend was a new lover…'

'What about me?' Noel asked. When Madeleine stared at him blankly, he said, 'Don't look at me like that, or you'll seriously damage my ego. Aren't I tanned and handsome, personable enough to play the part of your lover?'

'Of course, but—'

'Then all you have to do is tell the lowdown skunk that I'm the man you really care about. Go on to say that I've been away working, and now I'm back he's redundant, so to speak. That would do the trick, don't you think?'

'It might,' Madeleine admitted. 'He once saw a snapshot of you and wanted to know who it was. When I told him, he asked if you were an ex-lover. I said no, a friend.'

'That's fine, then. You wouldn't have been likely to admit to your current lover that I was more than just a friend, would you?

'Right…' He produced his laptop. 'Get cracking, and make it offhand enough to trample his masculine pride in the dust. That way you'll never have to set eyes on him again.'

After some input from both Eve and Noel, the short email read:

Noel has returned from the Middle East sooner than
I'd expected, so I'm afraid I won't be able to join you
in Paris after all.
Sorry it's a bit last-minute, but I'm sure you'll
be able to find someone else to take my place.
Thanks for all the good times.
Madeleine.

'That should do the trick,' Noel approved.

Eve agreed, and the email was duly sent.

It wasn't until after supper, when Eve had gone home and

Noel was settled on the bed-settee, that the full realisation of what she'd done struck her, and she gave way to the bitter unhappiness that crowded in.

Climbing into bed, she buried her face in the pillow and cried until she had no more tears left, before falling into an exhausted sleep.

Next morning when she awoke, Noel was already up, and as she tidied the bedding away and folded the settee she could hear the shower running.

Still in her night things, she was making coffee when he strolled into the kitchen with a towel knotted around his lean hips.

'Mmm…smells good.'

Madeleine had just turned to hand him a mug when she saw a car pull up outside and a familiar figure jump out.

Filled as she was with a sudden panic, her hand trembled so much that a lot of the coffee slopped over.

'Steady there.' Noel took the mug from her.

White to the lips, she whispered, 'Oh, dear God, it's Rafe. I don't want to see him. I can't bear it.'

'So don't answer the door.' Noel shrugged.

'He has a key,' she admitted miserably. Then in desperation, 'What am I going to do?'

'I'll soon send him packing… No, better still… Come on, kiddo, let's give the cheating swine an Oscar-winning performance.'

Grabbing her hand, Noel hurried her into the bedroom, coming to a halt in line with the open door.

'Put your arms round my neck and close your eyes,' he instructed. Dropping the towel, he pulled her close and began to kiss her just as the front door opened and Rafe walked in.

Noel broke the kiss, and they both looked towards the man standing there as though the sky had fallen in on him.

Shock, and a kind of raw disbelief, showed in his face,

closely followed by anger. Then the shock and anger iced over and with a razor-sharp edge to his voice he said, 'So this is Noel… I can quite see why you didn't want to come to Paris…'

Tossing the key he was holding onto the coffee-table, he added, 'We'll meet again, Madeleine, one day. Mark my words…' and, turning on his heel, walked out.

'That's put paid to the swine,' Noel remarked with satisfaction, and, using one hand to cover Madeleine's eyes, stooped to grab the towel.

'Now, then, if you promise to keep your eyes shut while I make myself decent, I'll allow you to pour me another mug of coffee…'

Though she kept them shut, there was no real need to—they were blinded by tears…

CHAPTER FOUR

As THOUGH the fates had conspired against her, the bitter end to the affair coincided with a further blow. After slipping into a deep coma, her mother died three days later at the age of just forty-four.

At the funeral Madeleine was dry-eyed, too frozen for tears. Blaming herself for her mother's death, as she had blamed herself for her husband's, she felt leaden, desolate, weighed down by grief and guilt.

Eve and Noel were the only other mourners. Madeleine's aunt and uncle wrote to offer their condolences, and to apologise for not being there.

The letter ended, 'If you feel like getting right away come and visit with us, do, and stay for as long as you want to.'

The suggestion seemed like a lifeline.

Her job at the clinic was almost over, and Noel, on summer leave, and with nowhere to live, professed himself happy to flat-sit for her.

With Eve's encouragement, Madeleine notified her private patients, and accepted her aunt and uncle's invitation to visit them in Boston.

Her only regret was leaving Katie, who, on hearing the news, threw her thin arms around Madeleine's waist and, her big brown eyes overflowing with tears, cried, 'I don't want you to go.'

'But you're almost better now. If you keep on doing your exercises you don't really need me any longer.'

'I do, I do,' the child wailed.

'I promise I'll come and visit you as soon as I get back, and then you'll be able to show me how well you're managing.'

Tears still running down her cheeks, Katie sniffed dolefully. 'How long will you be gone?'

'I'm not sure,' Madeleine told her. 'A few weeks… A month maybe.'

'I'll miss you, the little girl said, brushing away her tears.'

'Tell you what—suppose I write to you?'

'Can I write back?'

'I'll expect you to. Now, give me a smile, and don't forget to do those exercises.' Madeleine smiled, an ache in her heart as she said goodbye to the little girl who reminded her so much of Rafe.

'I won't.'

When Madeleine arrived in Boston, her aunt and uncle, who had a big house on the edge of the Common, welcomed her with open arms and, seeing how shattered she looked, did their utmost to cheer her up.

For their sakes she tried to appear cheerful, but her mother's death had left her desolate, and she missed Rafe with a raw, ragged, savage pain that made her feel as if she'd been mauled and left for dead.

She had intended to stay in Boston for a month at the most, but, unable to regain her grip, and giving in to her aunt and uncle's urging, the visit lengthened to five weeks.

After six weeks had gone by, feeling unable to accept their generous hospitality any longer, she declared her intention of returning to England.

'Do you *want* to go home?' her aunt asked.

'No,' Madeleine admitted—suppose she ran into Rafe, or saw the announcement of his wedding in the papers?—'but I must get back to work.'

'You're not just worrying about money, are you? We're not exactly poor, and I'm sure—'

'You're very kind, and I appreciate it. But I do want to start work again as soon as possible.'

Agreeing that that might be for the best, her uncle offered her a position in the physical-therapy unit of the Wansdon Heights Fitness Center, which he owned.

After some thought, she accepted. If she stayed safely in Boston, surely sooner or later she would forget about Rafe?

Either that or she was afraid she would grieve for the rest of her life.

Her aunt and uncle were delighted that she was staying and, when she announced her intention of finding a small apartment to rent, urged her to live with them.

'We love having you here, and we've five spare bedrooms. We can turn the biggest into what you Brits call a bedsit.'

She thanked them sincerely but, needing to be independent, insisted on paying a fair rent and keeping herself.

Unable to change her mind, they agreed.

A phone call to London settled that when Noel went back to the Middle East he would hand in the keys to her flat, and Eve would store her relatively few possessions.

That part was easy. The letter to Katie, who was looking forward to having her back, was much harder to write.

The answer came by return. Her parents, apparently to soften the blow, were buying the child a computer for her birthday, and after extracting a promise that Madeleine would keep in touch by email Katie seemed reasonably cheerful.

The fitness centre was extremely busy, and in an effort to put the past behind her and give herself less time to brood

Madeleine chose to work long hours, finding it rewarding and, after a time, therapeutic.

The bleakness of disillusionment, mingled with the longing for what might have been had Rafe proved to be the man of principle she had thought him, began to fade but still never truly left her thoughts. By the time Alan Bannerman joined the staff, she was over the worst. Or so she told herself.

Somehow—perhaps it was his mild manner, his charming diffidence—he got through to her, and when they had been colleagues for some six weeks she accepted a date. A pleasant, undemanding companion, he proved to be an antidote to loneliness.

When they had known each other for three months he asked her to marry him. Thinking him placid and unemotional, she was surprised by how ardently he pressed her. Unable to give him an immediate answer, she asked for time to think it over. She was relieved when he agreed to wait a week, and they arranged to have dinner the following Saturday evening.

When Saturday morning came and Madeleine still hadn't been able to make up her mind, she decided to phone Eve and ask her opinion.

Listening to the familiar voice answer laconically, 'Hello?' she felt a surge of homesickness.

'Hi, it's me.'

'Maddy! It's great to hear from you!' Eve exclaimed. 'How are things?'

'I've got something of a problem.'

'Hang on a minute while I switch off the telly... Right, fire away.'

When Madeleine had told her, Eve exclaimed, 'A man who's not only nice-looking but also decent and dependable wants to marry you and you call *that* a problem?

'Even though the love of my life finally moved in with me six weeks ago, I can't get him to make any sort of commitment, let alone offer to marry me...' Eve moaned. Then quickly added, 'Don't worry, I'm sympathetic really. It must be tough when it's something as important as marriage and you can't make up your mind!'

Madeleine laughed. 'Be serious for a second, Eve; this is important.'

'What's he like in bed?'

'I don't know,' Madeleine admitted.

'So you've been keeping him at arm's length? I can't say I blame you. Once bitten, twice shy... Though if you *do* decide to marry him, it might not be a bad idea to find out what kind of lover he is before you actually say "I will"...'

'That's the problem, Eve,' Madeleine sighed, 'I'm fond of him, but there's no passion.' Then, striving to be fair, 'At least on my side.'

'I thought not. Otherwise you wouldn't still be hesitating. It's Rafe, isn't it? You're still in love with him.'

'No!' Realising her denial had been too vehement, Madeleine added more moderately, 'No, I'm not still in love with him.'

'But you've never really got over him,' Eve concluded.

'It has nothing to do with Rafe.'

Eve grunted her disbelief. 'I think it has everything to do with Rafe.'

'As far as he's concerned it's over and done with. All in the past. Truly.' Madeleine tried to make her voice sound as persuasive as possible.

'Well, I'll believe you, thousands wouldn't. So what do you want me to say?'

'I just want a truthful opinion. Whether or not you think I should go ahead and marry Alan.'

'If you need to ask my opinion, you don't love him enough and you shouldn't be marrying him.'

Put like that it was blindingly simple.

'Thank you,' Madeleine said gratefully.

'Don't thank me until you've made up your mind.'

'It's made up.' Madeleine smiled, relief flooding her voice.

'Atta girl! Is it yes or no?'

'It's no. You're quite right. If I needed to ask your opinion, then I don't love him enough. It wouldn't be fair to marry him. We're having dinner together tonight; I'll tell him then.'

'What will you do when you've told him? I mean, if you work together it could make things difficult.'

Madeleine paused, trying to decide what to do. 'I think, for his sake, I'll have to give in my notice and find another post.'

'I agree. Leave him alone so he can gather up the pieces and get on with his life.'

Madeleine gasped at Eve's bluntness.

'Look on it as being cruel to be kind,' Eve said briskly. 'You'll be doing him no favours by hanging around. Now, how do you feel?'

'I'm not sure. Relieved…a bit sad…restless…unsettled…and just hearing your voice has made me feel dreadfully homesick.'

'You've been there for over a year, Maddy. Why don't you come home?'

All at once, Madeleine very much wanted to. But if she did she would be in the same city as Rafe and run a risk, however small, of seeing him.

And that she couldn't bear.

Just the thought made her skin chill with panic and the fine hairs on the back of her neck rise.

Picking up Madeleine's unspoken fear, Eve brought it into the open. 'Unless you're afraid of running into Rafe?'

'Well, I…'

'London's a big place, Maddy, and it's not as if you normally move in the same social circles.'

'That's true.' Then, saying aloud something she had only thought about, 'He'll no doubt be married to Fiona by now.'

'I guess so. I haven't noticed any mention of it in the papers, but then I don't often get to read the society columns. So how about it? Are you coming home?'

'I'd like to, but…' Madeleine hesitated as the practicalities of the situation struck her. She hadn't managed to save a great deal, and by the time she had paid her airfare she would have very little money left.

'If I come home I won't have a job.' She voiced one of the most serious considerations.

'Presumably you won't have one there when you've left Wansdon Heights, and there are plenty of openings in England for a good physiotherapist.'

'I'd have nowhere to live.' Madeleine sighed.

'Come to me until you find somewhere.'

'You've only got one bedroom.'

'Well, I've a fold-away put-you-up, and I've recently bought a bed-settee, like you used to have, for the lounge.'

Momentarily tempted, then suddenly remembering, Madeleine said hastily, 'I couldn't possibly. What about Dave? He wouldn't want another woman cluttering up the place, even for a short time.'

'He wouldn't dare raise any objections. I'd kick him out if he did.' Eve laughed.

'Please, Eve,' Madeleine cried anxiously, 'don't fall out with him on my account.'

'Hey there, I'm only joking. Where's your sense of humour gone?'

'I'm sorry. I guess I'm just depressed.'

'Then it's high time you pulled yourself together and came back home. You've only been marking time in the States. Why don't you *really* put the past behind you and start living again?'

After a moment, Madeleine said slowly, 'I might just do that,' and started to mean it.

'Honest?' Eve queried.

'Honest.'

'With regard to a job, you could always treat patients privately. Visit them in their own homes, or even take a live-in position, until you find the right kind of opening and accommodation.

'Tell you what, I'm working tomorrow morning, filling in for Tracy. I can check the list of clients who want home-visits and see what new enquiries are coming in. I'll let you know if there's anything that seems suitable… Now, before you go, there's someone here who would like a word with you. Just at the moment he's sleeping on my bed-settee while he looks for a flat.'

'Hi, beautiful!' said a familiar voice.

'Noel!' Madeleine cried, her gladness evident.

'What's my favourite girl been doing?'

'Behaving like an idiot.'

'I don't believe a word of it,' he joked.

'It's great to hear your voice.'

'I thought you'd be pleased. Hurry back, sugar. Seeing me in the flesh is bound to give you an even bigger thrill.'

Laughing, she said, 'I didn't know you were home.'

'I'm back for good, ready to settle down to a nine-to-five job behind a desk.'

Madeleine didn't believe him for a second. 'You're joking, of course.'

'Yes and no. I'm going to give it a try, anyway.'

'Any special reason?' she pried.

'You mean, is there a woman involved? Yes. Her name's Zoe. She's five feet three, with a figure like a dream, short dark hair, and eyes the colour of chocolate. Added to that, she's clever, good-natured and loyal, and she thinks I'm the bee's knees,' he added smugly.

'Well, she would, wouldn't she? You always did have a good sales pitch. Just take care she doesn't discover too many faults,' Madeleine giggled.

'Faults?' He sounded affronted. 'I don't have any faults—like most men, I'm perfect.'

'Of course you are. Sorry.'

'I should think so. However, just in case she hasn't realised all my finer qualities, it wouldn't do any harm to have you on hand to sing my praises…'

'Such as?'

'Well, if you can't think of anything better, you could always tell her how shy and sweet and utterly wonderful I am. If necessary I'll pay you.'

'You want me to lie to her for money?'

He groaned. 'Where are your friends when you need them? Still, I'll forgive you if you come back as soon as possible.'

'I intend to.' Whether or not Eve found anything suitable, Madeleine now knew for certain that she was going home.

'Any chance of making it back for Christmas?'

'I seriously doubt it.'

'There's a cold snap on the way and good odds on it being a white one this year. Remember how, as kids, we used to wish for a white Christmas?'

'I remember,' Madeleine answered wistfully.

'Well, the long-range weather forecast has been for snow nationwide, the mistletoe is up and my lips are pursed ready.'

Madeleine laughed. 'Even with such an incentive, I'm afraid I can't see myself making it until the New Year. But I'll get things moving as fast as possible.'

'You do that. Bye, now. See you soon.'

With a sigh, Madeleine replaced the receiver.

The fact that she was going home would be a blow to her aunt and uncle, and she hated the thought of telling them almost as much as she hated the thought of telling Alan. But it had to be done.

* * *

In the event, telling Alan proved to be an even worse ordeal than she had anticipated. Displaying an unexpected streak of tenacity, he hung on like a terrier, refusing to accept her decision, trying to change her mind.

By the time the uncomfortable meal was over, Madeleine felt totally shattered.

Pleading a headache, which was the truth, she opted for an early night and, fearing a continuation of the pressure, refused his offer to take her home and waved for a cab.

It was obvious that he wasn't going to take no for an answer and, knowing that for both their sakes it would be best to make a quick, clean break, she decided to leave Boston as soon as she could. But as it was only a few days to Christmas, she realized it might prove impossible to get a flight until after the holiday.

As soon as she got back to her bedsit, she called Logan Airport.

Her luck was in.

Due to a last-minute cancellation, there was a seat available on a flight leaving the following evening. Though it was in first class, and she couldn't really afford the extra, she booked it on her credit card.

That done, she breathed a sigh of relief.

When she reached London, she would have just about enough money to enable her to stay in one of the cheaper hotels for a few nights.

How well she managed after that would depend on how soon she could get back to work. If Eve came up with anything suitable…

Thinking of her friend, she reached for the phone. It would be the early hours of the morning in England, so she couldn't tell Eve what she'd done, but she could leave a message.

Having tapped in the familiar number, she waited for the answering machine to cut in, then said, 'Eve, it's Maddy. I've managed to get a seat on a flight leaving Boston tomorrow night. I'll ring tomorrow afternoon, when you're home from work, and give you the details. Bye for now.'

Then, her head throbbing dully, she emailed Katie to tell her the news, before putting on her nightdress and going through to the bathroom to brush her teeth.

She had been sleeping badly lately, but, now she had come to a decision and taken the first positive step towards going home, she should be able to sleep better, she told herself bracingly as she climbed into bed.

For months she had tried not to think about Rafe, but, as though the decision to go back to London had opened the floodgates of memory, she found herself doing just that.

She could see in her mind's eye how his thick, sooty lashes brushed his hard cheeks when he looked down…how his clear green eyes could go silvery with laughter, or dark and smoky with desire…how the creases in his lean cheeks—too male to be called dimples—deepened when he smiled.

She remembered how generous and caring he had been. How willing to give and take, to compromise. Remembered too how masterful and resourceful he could be when he thought it necessary. She had been at the Mayfair clinic one Friday evening when, returning early from what she knew had been a tiring business trip, he'd phoned to suggest that they had dinner together.

Having agreed to work later than usual, and unwilling to keep him hanging about, she had said no, and arranged to meet him the next day for lunch. She had then spent the rest of the evening regretting her decision, and wishing she'd said yes.

When she had left for home, he was waiting for her.

Leaning nonchalantly against his Porsche, wearing casual clothes and, though the sun had gone down, sunglasses, he had straightened at her approach and moved purposefully to bar her way.

Her heart had leapt and gladness fizzed through her like champagne.

'What are you doing here?' As he took her arm and drew her towards the car, she added lightly, 'And why the shades?'

'This is an abduction, doll,' he said in the accent of an American film gangster.

'Good gracious! Didn't I ought to scream?'

'If I was following the script, I should say menacingly, "Not if you know what's good for you".'

'Oh.'

'On the other hand, it would give me an excuse to kiss you,' he drawled laconically.

Lifting her face, she asked demurely, 'Do you need an excuse?'

'An invitation's better. Not that I really need either.' Bending his dark head, he kissed her with a hungry passion that showed how much he'd missed her.

Then, as though his lips couldn't bring themselves to part from hers, he murmured between soft, baby kisses, 'I can't wait to make love to you. I've thought about nothing else while I've been away.

'This afternoon, in Paris, I brought an important board-meeting to an early close because I couldn't concentrate. I kept imagining I was undressing you, touching you, feeling your response... I couldn't wait to get back, to make it all happen...'

A little breathlessly, she asked, 'So what are we doing standing here?'

'That's a good question.'

He hurried her into the car and, sliding in beside her, started the engine.

When they turned down an unfamiliar road, she queried, 'Where are we going?'

Sounding happy and carefree, he told her, 'To a little inn

called the Woolpack. It's right off the beaten track and no one will care if we stay in bed for the entire weekend.'

'Oh, but I…'

He glanced at her sharply. 'I hope you're not going to tell me you have other commitments?'

Judging from his tone, if she said yes it would precipitate a showdown, and she wasn't prepared.

Brushing guilt aside, she decided that just for once she could miss her usual weekend visits to the nursing home.

Never easy at telling lies, she swallowed and said, 'I was going to say I haven't got a toothbrush or any clean undies.'

She felt him relax.

'That's all been taken care of,' he told her. 'I paid a visit to your flat and picked up what I thought you might need.'

Giving her a wicked sidelong glance, he added, 'I didn't bother to pack a nightie.'

The carefree mood was back, and with a little sigh, she rested her head lightly against his arm for a moment. 'I've missed you.'

He gave her knee a brief squeeze. 'Next time I have to go to Paris I'd like you with me.'

By the time they arrived at the Woolpack, a blue dusk was spreading gauzy veils over the countryside and bats were flittering about.

The lamplit inn, a lopsided, half-timbered black and white building with overhanging eaves and tall, crooked chimneys, looked as if it belonged in some Charles Dickens novel.

They were greeted by a plump and smiling landlady who showed them up to a small room under the eaves with a tiny *en suite* bathroom and black oak floorboards that creaked at every step.

The ceiling sloped steeply, and the low casement windows were thrown open to the balmy night air. A high, old-fashioned double bed, with a goose-feather mattress and sheets that smelled of lavender, took up most of the space.

A tray with a bottle of champagne and a plate of hors d'oeuvres was waiting by the bedside.

When they had thanked the landlady she wished them a cheerful, 'Goodnight,' and bustled away.

Rafe dropped their bags on a low chest and helped Madeleine out of her light jacket, before shedding his own. Then, glancing at the tray, he queried, 'Hungry?'

'Yes. But not for food.'

He gave a low growl and, sweeping her into his arms, carried her over to the bed.

Even though his need was every bit as urgent as hers, he didn't hurry as he stripped off first her clothes and then his own and joined her.

Her arms went round his neck while his hands shaped and moulded her, clasping her hips to pull her firmly against his lower body, before making love to her with an unleashed passion that sent her up in flames.

When the heated rapture settled into a contented glow they lay in bed, kissing occasionally and feeding each other delicacies between sips of champagne.

It was lovely and romantic, and Madeleine had never been happier.

Afterwards, as though they couldn't get enough of one another, they had made love again, and again, and, reliving that night, all the pleasure and warmth, she found herself trapped in a sensual haze.

Only when the haze cleared and she realised she was alone was the warmth replaced by such bleak desolation that she felt like crying.

Though what good would crying do? It was over. All in the past. She must forget Rafe. Forget the way he had made

her feel. Forget the happiness he had brought her. Dismiss him
from her thoughts and not look back.

But that was easier said than done.

After a restless night spent tossing and turning, she woke
next morning heavy-eyed and unrefreshed, still feeling cold
inside.

Jumping out of bed, she headed for the bathroom. But,
while a hot shower heated her skin, it failed to cure that inner
chill of loss.

When her aunt and uncle returned from church and asked
her to join them for lunch, she broke the news that she had
refused Alan's proposal and was returning to England.

Though they were sorry to lose her, they accepted her
decision without attempting to change her mind… Grateful
to them both, she kissed them and thanked them sincerely for
all they'd done.

Then, after writing and posting a short, difficult letter to
Alan, she tidied her room and packed her few belongings.

Her cases zipped and ready, she made herself a pot of tea
and was just reaching for the phone to call Eve, when it rang,
making her jump.

Wondering if it might be Alan, she answered cautiously,
'Hello?'

'Maddy?'

'Eve! I was just going to ring you. I presume you got the
message I left?'

'Yes, I did. Now, that's what I call getting a move-on. How
did Alan react when you told him you couldn't marry him?
You have told him, I presume?'

'Yes, I told him last night. He refused to take no for an
answer.' Madeleine sighed.

'In that case you're doing the right thing. You need to get

out of there as quickly as possible for both your sakes. How did your aunt and uncle take it?'

'Better than I'd expected. They're disappointed, of course, but they didn't try to put pressure on me.'

'Thank the lord for small mercies. Now for my news. As soon as I got to the clinic I checked through the requests for physiotherapy. There was nothing that seemed up your street. Quite disappointing really.

'Then just before I was due to go home I had a phone call from a Mrs Rampling, who desperately needs help. Her husband had a stroke some three months ago, and at the same time fractured his hip. She's worried that he's making very little progress. It seems he's a difficult man who hates hospitals and clinics, but he's agreed to have a physiotherapist treat him at home.

'She told me that what she really needs is someone who would be willing to live in for as long as it takes to give him a better quality of life.'

'Where do the Ramplings live?'

'I gather that at the moment they're living in Kent, in a big house near the village of Hethersage.

'Apart from the fact that Mr Rampling can be 'uncooperative', I must say that it sounds like a good bet. The salary she mentioned is generous in the extreme, and you'd have your own self-contained accommodation. Interested?'

Without hesitation, Madeleine said, 'Very.'

'Then perhaps you should give her a ring? If you can find a pen and paper, here's the number…'

When Madeleine rang the number Eve had given her, a woman's pleasant voice repeated the number, then added, 'Harriet Rampling speaking.'

'Mrs Rampling, it's Madeleine Knight.'

'Oh, Miss Knight… How good of you to ring me so promptly. I gather from Miss Collins that you're still in the States?'

'That's right.'

'If the salary I suggested is acceptable, would you be willing to come to us on your return? For a trial period at least?'

'Yes, certainly,' Madeleine answered eagerly.

'Oh, that is good news!'

'I understand you live in Kent, near Hethersage?'

'Yes, we've been living there since my husband came out of hospital. Normally we live in London, but we're having our house at Regent's Park extensively altered, to make life easier for George. Until it's finished, which looks like being several more weeks, our son suggested we stay with him at Hethersage Hall.

'It is a good-sized place and we have our own ground-floor accommodation. There's also a comfortable self-contained flat we hoped might be suitable for you. It's not huge, but it does have a reasonable living room, a bedroom, a kitchen and an outside stairway which gives some degree of privacy.'

Then a shade anxiously, 'I think you'll like it.'

'I'm sure I will,' Madeleine concluded.

She heard a distinct sigh of relief before Mrs Rampling went on, 'You can either eat with us or do your own thing, whichever suits you. I gather you're returning to England quite soon?'

'I'm leaving Boston tonight. I should be arriving in London tomorrow morning.'

'Do you have any immediate plans? Anyone you want to spend Christmas with before you come to us?'

While Madeleine knew that Eve would make her welcome, she also knew there was very little room in the small flat. And now Dave had moved in, and Noel was sleeping there, it would be quite impossible.

Added to that, Eve and Dave and Noel and Zoe made a foursome. *She* would be the odd one out. It wasn't a situation she fancied. 'No, not really.'

'You have no family?'

'No. My mother died just over a year ago, and my father's in California. I shall probably book into a hotel until after the holiday.'

'Perhaps you *want* to stay in London…?'

'Not particularly,' Madeleine added.

'Then wouldn't it make more sense to come straight to the hall?'

Tempted, Madeleine hesitated. The thought of spending the holiday alone in a hotel wasn't particularly appealing, and, now that she'd splurged on a first-class ticket, money was even tighter than she had anticipated.

'Well, I…I wouldn't want to intrude on your family over Christmas.'

'My dear, of course you wouldn't be intruding… Though, as a matter of fact, George and I are flying up to Scotland first thing tomorrow morning. We're staying with our son and daughter over Christmas and the New Year.' Her excitement evident, she added, 'They have a brand-new baby boy, and both George and I are looking forward immensely to seeing our latest grandson.'

Then, getting back to practicalities, 'Our being away from the hall will give you breathing space, and also a good chance to settle into your flat. What do you say?'

It would be ideal in some ways, Madeleine thought, though it would leave her with Mrs Rampling's other son and his family. Unless they too were going away?

But even if they weren't, she needn't feel she was intruding. The flat was self-contained, so she could keep herself to herself.

'In that case I'll be happy to, if you're sure that arrangement suits you, and your son won't mind?'

'Quite sure. That's all settled, then.

'Mary Boyce, the housekeeper, will have everything ready for you, and if you can tell me your flight number and what time you're due to land, we'll send Jack, Mary's husband, to pick you up.'

'Thank you.' Madeleine gave her the information.

Sounding warm and friendly, Mrs Rampling added, 'Do make yourself at home. Though it will be January before we actually meet, I'm looking forward to it. Have a good flight.'

'Goodbye, and thank you again.'

Relieved and excited, Madeleine quickly called Eve to give her the good news and thank her.

'What are friends for?' she asked. Then, with more than a hint of uncertainty, 'But are you sure you want to give this a shot? After all, you don't really know what you'll be letting yourself in for.'

'Hey, everything's arranged. Don't try and talk me out of it now. It's much too late.'

Then curiously, 'You seemed to be all in favour earlier. Why have you changed your mind?'

'At the time I was quite convinced it was in your best interests, but now I…I can't help having second thoughts.'

'Don't worry, I'm sure everything will be fine.'

Still sounding anxious, unlike herself, Eve said, 'I just hope everything turns out all right. But if it doesn't work, you can always come to us, you know. We'll manage somehow.'

'Thanks,' Madeleine said gratefully.

'Now, don't forget, if you're not happy with the situation, let me know straight away.'

CHAPTER FIVE

AFTER a technical fault that made the big jet almost two hours late getting airborne, the flight was smooth and uneventful.

Madeleine could never sleep on planes, and after so many disturbed nights she was feeling shattered by the time they landed.

The formalities over, she changed her dollars into pounds and, bearing in mind the warnings she had received, slipped half the money into her handbag and the other half into her flight bag.

Both bags on her shoulder, she was heading for the exit when a uniformed chauffeur approached her and queried, 'Miss Knight?'

Wondering how he had managed to pick her out of such a crowd, she answered, 'Yes, that's right.'

'Mrs Rampling asked me to meet you.'

'I'm sorry you've had to wait so long.'

'That's all right, miss,' he said politely. 'When I discovered the flight was running late I used the time to get some breakfast. Now, if you'll come with me, miss, the car's waiting outside.'

She willingly surrendered the unwieldy baggage trolley and followed his short, thick-set figure out to a sleek grey limousine.

It was a bitterly cold, curiously still day, with a sky that gleamed grey and pearly, as iridescent as the inside of a mussel shell.

After the warmth of the terminal, Madeleine found herself starting to shiver in the bleak air. But with a speed and efficiency she could only admire she was installed in the luxurious car, and her luggage stowed away.

The comfortable seats were covered in soft fawn leather and it was pleasantly warm. Almost before they were clear of the airport, lack of sleep catching up on her, her eyelids began to droop and she slipped into a doze.

When she surfaced they were travelling along a quiet country road with skeletal trees on one side and an old lichen-covered wall on the other.

Stifling a yawn, she sat up straighter and looked around her just as they reached a stone-built gatehouse with tall, barley-sugar chimneys and mullioned windows.

As they turned towards the entrance, a pair of black ornamental gates slid aside at their approach and closed behind them.

Rolling parkland stretched away on either side as they followed a serpentine drive that ran between high, mossy banks.

Hethersage Hall, hidden from sight until they had rounded the final bend, was wrapped snugly in a fold in the hills. It was a homely, rambling place, not at all stiff and starchy as its name suggested.

The walls were mellow stone, the roofs a natural slate. Half a dozen gables peaked and sloped at various odd angles, yet the whole thing had a charming symmetry. There were diamond-leaded windows and an oak front door that was metal-studded and silvery with age.

When the car drew to a halt on the cobbled apron and the chauffeur helped Madeleine out, the door was opened wide and a small, plump woman with curly grey hair appeared, smiling a greeting.

'Miss Knight… I'm Mary Boyce, the housekeeper… Do come in out of the cold…'

Returning her smile, Madeleine followed her into a large

wood-panelled hall with polished oak floorboards and dark antique furniture that glowed with the patina of age.

The huge fireplace was full of pine logs, and above the stone mantel there were green spruce boughs and spectacular swags of ivy and scarlet-berried holly. A bunch of mistletoe hung from a fine old chandelier, and a tall, beautifully decorated Christmas tree filled one corner.

Cheerful and garrulous, Mrs Boyce went on, 'You must be weary. Goodness knows jet lag's bad enough, but when there's a long delay on top of that…!'

'Mr and Mrs Rampling send their sincere apologies that they weren't able to greet you in person. They've gone to Scotland to spend the holiday with their son and daughter and their family.'

'Yes, Mrs Rampling did explain.'

'Well, now, if you'd like to come through to the living room…'

The living room was white-walled and spacious, with oak beams and casement windows that looked over a pleasant garden.

It was furnished with an eclectic mix of old and new—some beautiful antiques, a modern suite upholstered in soft natural leather, an Oriental carpet that made Madeleine catch her breath, and several paintings by Jonathan Cass. The sight of which gave her a pang. Rafe had owned several of Cass's snow scenes.

When she was ensconced in a deep armchair in front of a blazing log fire, Mrs Boyce said, 'I'll get you something to eat while Jack takes your luggage up.'

Feeling too tired to eat, Madeleine said, 'Thanks, but I'm not at all hungry. Though a cup of tea would be lovely.'

'Then a cup of tea it is.'

By the time she came back with a tray of tea and homemade cake, made even more soporific by the warmth of the fire, Madeleine was having a serious struggle to stay awake.

Watching her stifle a yawn, Mrs Boyce put the tray down on a small oval table and, proceeding to pour the tea, said sympathetically, 'You must be more than ready to get some sleep.'

'I am tired,' Madeleine admitted.

'Well, as soon as you've finished your tea you can get your head down.' Adding, 'I'll be back in a few minutes to show you round the flat,' the housekeeper bustled away.

Madeleine was just finishing her second cup of tea when Mrs Boyce returned and queried, 'If you're ready?' Then, in concern, 'I'm not rushing you, am I?'

'No, not at all, I'm quite ready.'

As she followed the housekeeper across the hall and up a graceful curving staircase with a griffin head as its newel post, she looked around her.

It was a beautiful old house, she thought, utterly charming and unpretentious, with its simple white walls and black beams, its polished oak floorboards and linenfold panelling.

At the top of the stairs Mrs Boyce turned left down a short, wide corridor, and opened a door at the end.

'Here we are.'

The living room was warm and cosy with an old, gently faded rose-pink carpet, matching curtains and a comfortable-looking suite. On the mantel was a small chiming clock.

Though there was discreet central heating, a log fire burnt in a delightful little fireplace with a tiled surround and an elaborately carved fender. To one side, a basket was filled with pine logs and cones that gave off an aromatic scent.

'What a lovely room!' Madeleine exclaimed.

Mrs Boyce looked worried. 'There's just one thing; I discovered earlier that the phone up here isn't working. I really don't know what's wrong with it.

'Of course, you could always use one of the downstairs phones.'

'That won't be necessary,' Madeleine assured her. 'I have a mobile.'

Looking pleased that the problem had been solved so easily, the housekeeper led the way into a pretty, feminine bedroom with an *en suite* bathroom.

Having turned back the duvet on the double bed, she indicated the cases which had been placed on an oak linen chest next to a cheval-glass. 'If you want any help with your unpacking, I'm sure Annie will give you a hand…

'And this is the kitchen…'

Madeleine glanced around the well-equipped kitchen, which was bright and airy, with a natural pine table and chairs, primrose tiles and muslin curtains at the casement windows.

'I hope it meets with your approval?'

'It certainly does,' Madeleine assured her. 'The whole flat is really lovely.'

The housekeeper beamed. 'Mrs Rampling will be pleased. She was anxious that you should like it.

'Now, you'll find plenty of food in the fridge and cupboards,' she opened the relevant doors to prove it, 'but if there's anything else you want, Annie will no doubt be shopping in the morning. She's taking over the household duties until after the Christmas holiday.

'There, now,' she said as, the short tour over, they went back to the living room, 'I'll leave you to get some sleep.'

At the door she turned. 'Oh, I almost forgot; as it's your first night here, the master is hoping you'll join him for an evening meal…'

There had been no mention made of either a wife or a family, Madeleine realised, though presumably there was a Mrs Rampling junior.

She was just about to ask, when the housekeeper added,

'Pre-dinner drinks are served at seven in the study, which is directly across the hall from the bottom of the stairs.'

A second later she had closed the door behind her and departed.

Though the invitation to dinner had been carefully phrased, it held an underlying hint of command that for some reason Madeleine found vaguely disturbing.

She was a free agent, Mrs Rampling had made that clear, and if 'the master' had any ideas to the contrary… Well, he wasn't employing her, she reminded herself, and, if the worst came to the worst, she could always leave.

Irritated with herself, she sighed. She'd only just got here. Why was she thinking of leaving before she'd even met the man?

It wasn't like her.

Deciding that it was simply because she was so tired, she pushed her irritability aside and glanced around the living room once more.

On the far wall, a door with irregular panels of old glass gave access to an outside stone stairway guarded by a wrought-iron rail.

The doors to the bedroom and kitchen were plain oak, while the door to the main part of the house was handsomely carved. As she admired it she noticed there was no key in the ornate lock, and felt a faint stirring of unease.

Be sensible, she scolded herself; as the flat was part of the house, there should be no need to lock the door. Yet still that slight feeling of unease persisted, refusing to be banished.

A closer inspection showed that, though the door leading to the stone stairway was securely locked and bolted, neither it, nor any of the internal doors, boasted a key. Not even the bathroom.

But if the lack of keys became a problem she could always talk to Mrs Boyce about it, she decided as she went through to the bedroom.

Much too weary to do all her unpacking, she dug out a change of clothing for the evening, her night things, her sponge bag, her cosmetic purse and her alarm clock.

As she stripped off her clothes and donned her nightdress she saw with delight that it had started to snow, big flakes that drifted down like feathers from an angel's wing.

From being a child, she had always loved snow, and for a short time she watched the magical sight before closing the curtains.

To make certain she didn't sleep too long, she set the alarm for six-thirty, then climbed thankfully into bed.

Madeleine had been asleep for some time when she began to dream. She heard a noise in the outer room, the faint click of a latch as a door was opened and closed quietly. That was followed by the stealthy brush of footsteps crossing a carpet, and in the way that dreamers did she knew that something menacing was standing just outside her bedroom door.

She got out of bed, but couldn't bring herself to open the door and confront whoever or whatever stood there. Instead, she went through a door on the far wall and found herself in a dark, narrow corridor. Almost immediately she heard the footsteps behind her and fear clutched at her heart…

She began to run blindly, down endless pitch-black corridors, the thing at her heels getting closer…gaining on her… She could hear whatever it was breathing now…

Abruptly the corridor came to a dead end. She was feeling frantically for a door, or some other way out, when a cold hand reached out of the darkness to touch her…

With a half-stifled scream she woke up, shuddering and panting, her heart thudding against her ribcage.

As consciousness kicked in the nightmare faded, and just briefly she was disorientated until she remembered where she was.

Reaching for the light switch, she flooded the room with light, blinking a little as her eyes adjusted to the brightness.

A glance at the clock showed it was just turned six. Thankfully she realised that there was ample time to shower and change before she had to go down to dinner.

She would have much preferred to stay in the flat and have a snack in front of the living-room fire rather than dining with the family, but as she would be living in their house it would make sense to start off on the right foot.

In spite of the abrupt awakening she felt rested and refreshed, and, turning off the alarm, she stretched luxuriously before climbing out of bed and heading for the bathroom.

Through the frosted glass she could make out that everywhere was covered with a white blanket and it was still snowing heavily. It looked as though Noel had been right when he'd forecast a white Christmas.

By half-past six she was showered and dressed in a simple dinner dress in a silky grey material, her make-up in place and her blonde hair taken up into a gleaming coil.

Intending to make a quick phone call to Eve, she went through to the living room, which was still comfortably warm though the fire had burnt out, and looked around for her handbag.

Her flight bag was there but not her handbag. Where on earth had she put it?

A brief search revealed no sign of it. Neither did a more thorough one.

She could almost have sworn that she'd brought both bags up, but she'd been so dazed with tiredness, she couldn't be absolutely sure.

Had she left it in the car?

No, she thought with certainty, she could definitely remember having the two bags with her in the living room. She had put them down between the side of the chair and the coffee-table, so she must have only picked up her flight bag and left her handbag behind.

But there was plenty of time to fetch it and still have a word with Eve before dinner.

Everywhere was still and silent, not a soul in sight, as she descended the stairs. Through the diamond-leaded panes of the landing window she could see that the snow was coming down even faster and a rising wind was whipping it along.

As she crossed the hall she paused for a moment to admire the Christmas tree with its gleaming star on top and all its candlelights glowing. For anyone to have gone to so much trouble, there must be children in the house.

Unwilling to burst in on the family unexpectedly, when she reached the living room she knocked.

There was no answer, and she opened the door to find that the room was deserted. Crossing to the chair she'd sat in earlier that day, she bent to pick up her bag.

It was no longer there.

For a moment she was nonplussed.

But of course the housekeeper must have found it and, unwilling to disturb her, taken charge of it.

Oh, well, she thought philosophically, she could always ring Eve after dinner.

When she reached the study she found that too was deserted. It was a comfortable, homely room. Built-in bookcases flanked the fireplace, and in the corner a grandfather clock ticked sonorously. Next to it, an octagonal table held a phone and a silver-framed photograph of a gentle-faced woman with greying hair.

Several standard lamps cast pools of golden light, and a log fire blazed and crackled on the wide stone hearth. Below the mantel were bright garlands of holly and mistletoe and ivy.

On the far left, through a partly open door, Madeleine

glimpsed an adjoining office with an imposing desk that held a computer and an array of state-of-the-art equipment.

She glanced at the clock and, finding it was still only ten minutes to seven, sat down in one of the deep leather armchairs drawn up to the fire.

As she gazed into the flames, her thoughts went back to an old pub near Rye that Rafe had taken her to more than a year ago. It had been a chilly September day and they had lunched in front of a blazing fire.

She could see his face with the firelight flickering on it. Visualise the tiny crescent-shaped scar at the corner of his mouth, the way he tilted his head, the quick, sidelong smile, the tough male beauty that never failed to make her heart beat faster…

Though she hadn't heard anyone come in, some instinct made her lift her head and look up.

A tall, dark-haired man stood only a couple of feet away, his eyes fixed on her face.

Shock hit her in the chest like a clenched fist.

But it couldn't be Rafe. It *couldn't*.

Convinced she was seeing things, she squeezed her eyes shut.

When she opened them again he was still standing there, his green eyes cool, his face shuttered, silently watching her.

Her heart began to pound like a trip-hammer, her head went dizzy and the blood roared in her ears, while darkness swooped, threatening to engulf her and drag her down into the depths.

Somehow she fought against it and won.

But still she could neither move nor speak, and for what seemed an age she simply sat and gaped at him.

Wearing charcoal-grey trousers and a fine black sweater that pulled taut across his wide shoulders, he looked both disturbing and dangerous.

He was the first to break the silence. 'You're even lovelier than I remember.' His tone was as cool and biting as his gaze, so that the remark sounded more like condemnation than a compliment.

'Why are you here?' Her voice shook so badly that the words were barely intelligible.

He smiled thinly. 'This is my house.'

She made a movement of denial. 'Mrs Rampling said her son owned Hethersage Hall.'

'I'm Harriet's son. Or, rather, her godson.'

'I don't understand,' Madeleine said jerkily. 'I thought your godparents were called Charn…'

'Yes, they were. However, when Harriet had been a widow for almost two years, she met and married George Rampling, a middle-aged widower with three grown-up children and a couple of grandchildren…'

But Madeleine was no longer listening. Her thoughts skittering about like mad things, she realised that, as Rafe and Fiona must be married by now, *this* was Fiona's house.

Oh, dear God. She might walk in at any minute! Panic-stricken at the thought, Madeleine jumped to her feet. She must get away.

She had only taken a couple of steps when Rafe's fingers closed around her wrist like a steel manacle.

'Don't rush off.'

'Please let me go…' For a moment or two she tried to pull free.

When, finding it was useless, she stopped he loosened his grip a little and, leading her back to the chair, pressed her into it.

'I want to leave,' she whispered.

He shook his head. 'Harriet was so pleased you were coming, so you really must stay. Otherwise I'll get the blame for driving you away.'

'What about your wife?' Madeleine blurted out.

He raised dark brows.

'*She* won't want me here.'

'What makes you think that?' he asked interestedly.

For a moment she almost admitted the truth, then better sense prevailed and she began carefully, 'As Mrs Rampling isn't here and your wife *is*—'

Once again he shook his head. 'She isn't.'

For a moment all Madeleine could feel was relief that Fiona wouldn't walk in and find her there.

'But I'm neglecting my duties as a host,' Rafe went on smoothly. 'What can I get you to drink?'

'I don't want anything to drink, thank you.' Then, more firmly, 'I've no intention of staying. I'm going back to London. Now.'

'I'm afraid I can't ask Jack to turn out again on a night like this.'

'I'll phone for a taxi.'

'And do you think you'll get one?'

'Surely the conditions can't be that bad?' she protested hoarsely.

'When I came home some time ago it was all I could do to get up the drive, and it's been blowing a blizzard ever since.'

She lifted her chin. 'If necessary I'll walk down to the main road and wait for it there.'

'Do you know how long the drive is?'

'No,' she admitted.

He smiled mirthlessly. 'I thought not. It's the best part of a mile, and because it's in a dip the snow is collecting there. And even if you *could* struggle to the end of the drive, in weather like this I doubt if they've managed to keep even the main road open. In any event, you haven't a hope in hell of getting a taxi, so you may as well sit down and relax.'

'I'd prefer to go back up to the flat.' She got to her feet and started for the door on trembling legs.

Rafe easily reached it first and stood with his back to the panels, barring her way. 'And I'd much prefer you to stay here.'

She wanted desperately to push past him, but he looked so tall and dark and menacing that she hadn't the nerve to try.

When she hesitated, he added silkily, 'I've been looking forward to having a talk with you.'

'Then you already knew it was me your godmother had engaged?'

'Oh, yes. When Harriet mentioned your name I was able to tell her I knew you, that you'd been Katie's physiotherapist. She could hardly believe her luck.

'I would have been at the airport to meet you, but I didn't want you to change your mind about coming to Hethersage.'

Firmly, she said, 'Well, I've no intention of staying. If I can't go tonight, I'll leave first thing in the morning.'

He smiled a little. 'We'll see, shall we? In the meanwhile, suppose we sit down and talk?'

'We've nothing to talk about.'

'That's just where you're wrong.' Cupping her elbow, he led her back to the chair and waited for her to sit before moving to the drinks trolley.

Just briefly, Madeleine debated making a run for it, but common sense told her she would be wasting her time. He would catch her before she even reached the flat, and if she *did* manage to get there first she wouldn't be able to lock him out.

Turning to look at her, he queried, 'So what's it to be?'

'I've already told you I don't want a drink.'

Ignoring her churlishness, he filled a glass with a pale Amontillado and offered it to her, his green eyes daring her to refuse.

Weakly, she took it.

Pouring himself a whisky, he sat down opposite and regarded her. He looked eminently satisfied, she decided resentfully, well-aware that he was the master of the situation. Well-aware that she knew it.

From being a life-saver, she thought bleakly, this offer of a job had turned into a nightmare. Sipping the unwanted sherry, she stared into the flames, trying to sort out the confusion in her mind. Surely being offered a post in Rafe's house was too much of a coincidence?

Yet it couldn't have been planned... Or could it?

But if it *had* been planned, why? What could Rafe possibly hope to gain?

The answer was, he had nothing to gain and everything to lose if Fiona found out.

But still the suspicion was there, and Madeleine wondered, had Rafe, for whatever reason, put his godmother up to it? Had George Rampling really any need for a physiotherapist, or had the whole thing been an elaborate hoax?

Though how could they possibly have known she was coming back to England? It had been such a last-minute decision that no one other than Eve and Noel had known.

Except Katie.

She had emailed the child late on Saturday night, so it would have been the following morning before she read it, and later on that same day Mrs Rampling had contacted Grizedale Clinic...

But how had she known to do that? How *could* she have known...?

'Penny for your thoughts.' Rafe's voice sounded amused, a little mocking.

Madeleine looked up slowly and met those gleaming eyes. 'Does Mr Rampling really need physiotherapy, or was the whole thing just a pack of lies?'

'No, everything that Harriet told you was true. She's been on the lookout for a live-in physiotherapist for weeks now.'

'So are you saying that my being here is nothing but a coincidence?'

Rafe raised an eyebrow mockingly. 'Would you believe that?'

'No,' she replied sternly.

He smiled briefly. 'I wouldn't have expected you to. As a matter of fact it was carefully planned.'

Fear sidled up to her and took her hand. With a sickening feeling that she'd walked into some kind of a trap, she felt her mouth go dry and the blood in her veins turn to ice.

Putting the sherry glass on the table with shaking fingers, she crossed her arms and rubbed her palms up and down her bare arms as though she was cold.

The last time they had met, he'd said, '*One day we'll meet again…*' That was all. He hadn't said what he would do when they did meet, but there had been an underlying threat in the quietly spoken words, a hint of menace, that even now made her shiver at the memory.

Making an effort to fight off the panic, she told herself stoutly that she was just being silly. What could he possibly do to her?

But there was a hardness about him, a barely leashed anger, that made her afraid.

Unsteadily, she demanded, 'How did you know I was coming home?'

'How do you think?'

'Katie?'

'Got it in one. Knowing I was—shall we say?—*interested*, Diane has been keeping me up-to-date on what was happening in Boston. When she got your email, Katie was so excited she couldn't wait to tell her mother.' The ice clinked in his whisky glass as he took a sip.

'That still doesn't explain how you found out enough to be able to trick me into coming here. How you knew I was looking for a live-in post. Only Eve…' She stopped speaking abruptly.

Remembering their last conversation, her friend's strange volte-face, her obvious uneasiness, the way she had admitted to having second thoughts, Madeleine asked sharply, 'When did you talk to Eve?'

'When Diane told me you were coming home I wanted to know exactly what your plans were, and I felt sure Eve would know. I finally managed to contact her at the clinic, and after some initial resistance on her part we had quite a long talk. She told me what she was trying to do for you, and I mentioned I might be able to help.

'All I had to do was suggest to Harriet that she rang the clinic's physiotherapy department and talked to a Miss Collins—which she was only too pleased to do.'

So as well as using his godmother, he had used Eve… But what had he said to her to get her to talk to him? And why hadn't Eve told *her*?

As if she'd spoken the thought aloud, he said, 'In the end it was easier than I'd anticipated. I didn't even need to ask Eve not to say anything. It was she who suggested that it would be better if you didn't know I was involved until we'd had a chance to talk. I think she was afraid you might change your mind about coming back…'

There was a tap at the door, and the housekeeper put her head round to say, 'Dinner's all ready when you are.'

'Thank you, Mary, we'll serve ourselves. You can leave anything else that needs to be done until Annie gets here.'

'Thanks… I'll say goodnight, then.'

'Goodnight.'

As the latch clicked, realising belatedly that she should have used the opportunity to escape, Madeleine jumped to her feet and started for the door, crying, 'Mrs Boyce—'

An arm snaked round her waist and a cool hand covered her mouth.

Pulling her back against him, Rafe put his lips to the side of her neck and murmured softly, 'That's not on, my sweet. I don't want Mary involved.'

Trembling, shaken to the core by the caress that was no caress, she stood quite still.

As soon as he released her, she rounded on him. 'And I don't want to be kept here against my will.'

Then, helplessly, 'I can't understand what you're hoping to gain, why you went to so much trouble to get me here.'

He took a stray tendril of blonde hair that had escaped and tugged it gently, making her flinch away. 'It was no trouble. In fact the whole thing worked incredibly smoothly.'

She gritted her teeth. 'Why—?'

'We'll talk about it after dinner.'

'I don't want any dinner.'

His green, lazy-river eyes heavy-lidded and sensual, he said, 'Well, if you really don't want to eat, I can think of something a great deal more exciting to do…'

Wondering frantically if he meant what she thought he meant, she stared up at him.

Softly, he went on, 'So it will suit me fine if you decide against eating.'

He held out both hands. 'Shall we go upstairs?'

CHAPTER SIX

HER normally low, well-modulated voice shrill, she cried, 'No, I don't want you to touch me. I couldn't bear it.'

'The choice is yours.' He smiled. Seeing her expression change, he sighed. 'I gather eating's preferable.'

'*Anything* would be preferable,' she said primly.

'Sassy, eh?' Taking her chin, he tilted her face up to his.

Every nerve ending in her body jerked, and it was all she could do to keep from crying out.

Watching what little colour she had drain away, he remarked silkily, 'I'm beginning to think you're scared of me.'

'Well, you're wrong,' she retorted.

'You mean you're not?'

'No, I'm not,' she lied. 'I just can't bear you to touch me.'

'So you said. But I'm afraid you're going to have to get used to it…'

The faint hum and beep of a fax machine cut through his words.

'If you'll excuse me for just a moment, I'll make sure that's nothing important.' He disappeared into the office.

Her legs feeling too weak to support her, she sank down in the nearest chair. As she did so her eyes lit on the phone on the nearby table. Eve had said, 'Now, don't forget, if you're not happy with the situation, let me know straight away.'

If she could put Eve in the picture, it would seem like a lifeline. With a nervous glance towards the office, she hurried across and picked up the receiver.

She was just tapping in the number when a lean, tanned hand reached over her shoulder and depressed the receiver rest. As she caught her breath, he took the receiver from her hand and replaced it.

'Dear me,' he said mildly. 'It seems I can't take my eyes off you.'

Turning to face him in the confined space, she said as steadily as possible, 'I promised to ring Eve…'

He studied her face, and she tingled under the scrutiny of those green eyes. 'There'll be time for that later.'

'I'd prefer to do it now,' she insisted.

'Our meal will be spoiling…' He reached out a lazy hand and stroked a fingertip down her cheek. Her body trapped between his and the table, she stood perfectly still, afraid to move.

'Unless you've changed your mind about eating?' he queried.

'No, I haven't changed my mind,' she said thickly.

He sighed. 'A pity, but still…'

One hand cupping her bare elbow, he led her to the white-walled, black-beamed dining room, where a candlelit refectory table was set for two.

Several huge logs blazed cheerfully in a Crusader grate, and over the mantel were more garlands of holly and ivy and mistletoe threaded through with gleaming scarlet ribbon.

A thick sheepskin rug lay in front of the stone hearth, and a couch was drawn up before the blaze. Waiting on the coffee-table was a tray with cups and saucers, cream and sugar.

When Madeleine was seated at the table Rafe turned to a massive sideboard, where on a hotplate a glass jug of coffee was bubbling away next to an array of silver dishes.

Removing the covers, he began to fill two plates with roast chicken and vegetables. Then, setting one of them in front of her, he sat down opposite, poured the Chablis and waited pointedly until she picked up her fork and began to eat.

His remark about her having to get used to his touch had sounded very much like a threat and, afraid to ask, she wondered nervously just what he'd meant by it.

'Worried that you'll end up in my bed?' His voice was laced with intent.

Glancing up, she answered with spirit, 'Not when you have a wife.'

'I don't have a wife.'

Wits scattered, she stammered, 'Y-you said your wife wasn't here.'

'Well, as I haven't got one, she wouldn't be, would she?' he countered reasonably.

'You're not married?' She could hardly believe it.

'No, I'm not married,' he said patiently.

'But I thought…'

'What did you think?'

For a second or two she floundered, then, gathering herself, said, 'That with a house like this you'd be married and starting a family.'

'It isn't mandatory,' he responded drily.

'Neither is ending up in your bed.'

He saluted her spirit. 'But you will.'

'Is that misplaced confidence, or merely conceit?'

'Try fate.' He laughed.

Teeth clenched on her bottom lip, she returned her attention to her plate.

Rafe said nothing further, and for a while only the sound of the wind roaring in the chimney and the mellow tick-tock of the casement clock in the corner broke the silence.

While she made a pretence of eating, Madeleine's thoughts

tumbled about like ringside clowns. Why wasn't he married after more than a year? Fiona had made it sound as if the wedding was practically a *fait accompli*.

Was he still hedging? Trying to wriggle out of the bargain? Meanwhile taking what amusement he could get on the side?

Her lip curled. Well, he wasn't going to use *her* again. She was wiser now. Not so vulnerable.

Or was she?

Though she took care not to look up, she was aware that his eyes seldom left her face. That steady regard was nerve-racking; it made her feel like some specimen on the end of a cruel pin.

The main course over, he removed the plates and helped her to a generous portion of apple pie and a piece of white Stilton.

So he'd remembered that she preferred cheese to cream with her apple pie, she thought as she glanced up unwarily, and met those brilliant, heavily lashed eyes. Twin candle flames were reflected in the black pupils, and, fascinated, mesmerised, she found herself unable to look away.

After what seemed an age, he broke the spell by saying conversationally, 'So tell me what's been happening since I last saw you.'

'I thought you were being kept informed,' she responded tartly.

Unruffled, he said, 'There are some important things I still don't know for sure. For example, why you ran away to Boston in the first place…'

Well, if he didn't know, she had no intention of telling him.

'I presumed it was because of Noel, that the pair of you had split when he discovered how you'd been two-timing him…'

He was a fine one to talk about two-timing, she thought bitterly.

When she said nothing, Rafe pursued, 'You certainly fooled me with that pretend shyness, that butter-wouldn't-melt routine.

'Though I should have realised by the way you disappeared at regular intervals with no explanation that you weren't the sweet innocent you pretended to be, nevertheless it came as quite a shock to discover just what kind of woman you were…'

Yes, she could still visualise his expression. He wasn't used to having the tables turned on him.

'So how many other men have you managed to fascinate and delude since then?' Rafe's question brought her back to the present with a bump.

When she looked at him mutely, he said, 'I know of at least one who wanted to marry you. Alan, I believe his name was.'

It must have been Eve who had told him, she realised. When she had mentioned Alan in her emails to Katie, it had been simply as a colleague.

'Did he get angry when he realised you'd been stringing him along? Is that why you came home?' His voice was full of resentment.

'I'm not in the habit of stringing men along,' she said stiffly.

'If you weren't stringing him along, why didn't you marry him?' he asked.

Madeleine's eyes dropped from his gaze. 'I didn't love him enough.'

'Not counting your husband, have you ever truly loved any man?'

A bitter, cold, gritty feeling in the centre of her chest brought such pain that Madeleine felt tears sting her eyes, and was forced to bend her head while she blinked them away.

He laughed mirthlessly. 'No, I thought not.'

'Well, you're wrong,' she flared, then, terrified he might have guessed, added with perfect truth, 'I've always loved Noel.'

'Clearly not enough, or you wouldn't have been happy to cheat on him… No, I'm afraid I don't *seriously* believe you've ever cared a jot about any man. Though there must have been plenty of men who loved you. Different men, but they were all drawn into the same old game, danced to the same old tune.' He moved to stand closer to her. 'But now those games are over, and, for the foreseeable future at least, I'll be the one calling the tune.'

'I—I don't know what you mean,' she stammered.

His little smile was like a breath of cold air on the back of her neck. 'I mean that everything has gone according to plan and you're here with me. Now all I have to do is *keep* you with me.'

'I might be stuck here for tonight because of the snow— which incidentally I don't believe even *you* could have arranged—'

With a wry grin, he said, 'I have to admit that the snow was fortuitous.'

'But I shall certainly be leaving first thing in the morning.' She tried to sound confident.

'I shouldn't bet on it.'

Going to the window, he drew aside the heavy red velvet curtains. Through the diamond-leaded panes she could see that thick snow, whipped along by a fierce wind, was swirling past.

'The previous owner admitted that during a bad winter this area, and the hall, can be snowed up for days at a time,' he added.

While her skin crawled with apprehension, she made a determined effort to put the situation on a more prosaic footing. 'Wouldn't you find being snowed up very inconvenient?'

'Just at the moment I find it the exact opposite,' he answered smoothly.

She ignored that, and, taking a deep breath, ploughed on determinedly. 'What made you decide to move to the country?'

'I was tired of living in town. I'd always intended to move to a rural area when the right house came on the market…'

Madeleine was surprised; she had always thought of Rafe

as a sophisticated city man. But then she had been wrong about so many things.

'As soon as I saw this place I knew it was what I'd been waiting for.'

'So you gave up your flat at Denver Court?'

'No, I still have it. It comes in handy for the odd night or weekend I want to spend in town.'

Relaxing a little, and determined to lighten the mood, she asked, 'Don't you find commuting a pain?'

'Not really. These days I work from home a good deal of the time. When I need to go into London I use a small chopper I pilot myself.'

'I didn't know you had a pilot's licence.'

He swished the curtain to, then suddenly he was by her side, looming over her. 'There are a lot of things you don't know about me. A lot you still have to learn.' A brittleness to his voice, he went on, 'For instance, I don't like being made a fool of by any woman, especially one I imagined loved me…'

The tension suddenly tightening like a hempen noose around her throat, she gazed up at him with wide, greeny-blue eyes. 'That's why I inveigled you here.'

That answered the first of her questions, but not the second. 'I can't imagine what you hope to gain,' she burst out agitatedly.

'Can't you?'

Watching her bite her lip, he glanced in the direction of the thick sheepskin rug. 'Shall we move in front of the fire and—?'

Flinching away, she cried hoarsely, 'No!'

He raised a dark, mocking brow. 'Anyone would think I was about to strip you naked and have my wicked way with you.'

When, her heart pounding against her ribs, she said nothing, he added softly, 'But that comes later…'

'If you lay a finger on me, I'll scream.'

He clicked his tongue. 'How melodramatic. Unfortunately, there's no one to hear you.'

'There's Mrs Boyce and her husband.'

'They've retired for the night... And, as their accommodation is several hundred yards away, above the old stable block, you'd have to scream very loudly indeed.'

She swallowed, her throat tight and dry. 'There must be other servants...'

'What staff I have live in modern bungalows on the estate. I'm afraid we're quite alone, so screaming would be useless.

'In any case, it's unnecessary at the moment. I was only going to suggest that we had our coffee in front of the fire.'

Feeling a little foolish, and realising vexedly that that was what he'd intended, she crossed to the hearth and sat down on the big leather couch while he collected the glass coffee jug from the hotplate.

Surely this was just some cat-and-mouse game he was playing in order to frighten her? she thought distractedly. And if it was, all she needed to do was keep calm and refuse to be frightened.

Which was easier said than done.

And if it wasn't?

No, she couldn't let herself think that way. There was only tonight to get through.

Only?

Then tomorrow morning she would find *some* way of leaving, she promised herself, even if she had to abandon her cases and walk...

'Planning your escape?'

She jumped, and as her colour started to rise he laughed. 'I've hit the nail on the head if that blush is anything to go by.'

How could he walk in and out of her mind like that? she wondered agitatedly as she accepted the cup of coffee he handed her.

He sat down beside her and, as though answering her question, went on, 'You have a very expressive face. Just then you looked fiercely determined...

'But I remember when you used to look eager and expectant, full of anticipation, hungry with desire and passion. Then afterwards, soft and dreamy, sated with love...'

'Stop it!' she cried.

He raised an eyebrow. 'Does the remembrance make you uncomfortable? As you profess to have loved Noel, do you regret two-timing him?'

'I regret ever meeting you,' she cried.

'Life's full of regrets. When we were in bed together, did you ever think of him? Regret that he wasn't the one holding you, making love to you?'

'Many times,' she flashed and, seeing the way his mouth tightened, realised with a feeling of triumph that she'd scored a hit, even if it was only his pride that was hurt.

'Was Alan a good lover?'

Rattled by the unexpected question, she answered sharply, 'That's nothing to do with you.'

'How many other men have you had apart from him?'

'How many other women have you had apart from—?' About to say 'Fiona', she brought herself up short.

'Apart from...?' He raised an eyebrow at her.

When she said nothing, he suggested, 'You? Well, I—'

She shook her head violently. 'I don't want to know. I really don't care.'

In truth, the idea of him making love to another woman still had the power to hurt. But his question had smacked far too much of the pot calling the kettle black.

Slowly, he said, 'I can't say I've lived like a monk, Madeleine, but neither am I any Casanova. One woman in my life is enough...'

You could have fooled me, she thought bleakly.

'But not just any woman will do. In fact my bed's been empty for quite a while…'

If that was the truth, where was Fiona? Unless she was once again in some clinic?

'The only thing I've had to warm it has been the dream of having you there…'

Though she knew now how faithless he was, her heart seemed to turn over in her breast.

Unable to stand any more, she put her coffee-cup down so that it rattled in the saucer and jumped to her feet. 'I'm going up to the flat.'

'Not just yet.' He caught her wrist and, before she could brace herself, pulled her onto his lap and held her there, both hands encircling her waist.

After a moment's useless struggle she sat stiff and straight, her head turned away.

'Relax,' he said, looking at the pure curve of her cheek. 'At one time you used to enjoy sitting on my lap in front of the fire… Especially if I—'

'Well, now I'd hate it!' she flashed.

'If I weren't a perfect gentleman I might move my hands a few inches higher and see whether or not that's the truth.'

Alarm made her heart race with suffocating speed. Her voice hoarse, she said, 'You'd be wasting your time. As far as you're concerned, I'm immune.'

'I'm not sure I believe you. Your heart's already beating faster, which, as you swore you weren't afraid of me, suggests that you want me.'

'I don't want you. I don't love you.'

'You didn't love me then, but you're a very passionate woman and your body always responded to mine without reservations.'

As she made to shake her head, he said, 'Don't bother to deny it. There are certain signs that couldn't be faked. It's something I'm sure of, and I don't believe that's altered. I could easily make you want me…give you a lot of pleasure…'

Boldly, she rejoined, 'My body *possibly*…but not my mind…and you once told me that a lot of sexual pleasure is generated in the mind…

'Now I'd like to go to bed.'

'Exactly where I want you.' Taking the pins from her hair, so that it tumbled round her shoulders in a pale cloud, he added softly, 'It's high time you made some reparation.'

Jolted, she asked through stiff lips, 'What is there to make reparation for?'

'No man likes to be made a fool of, to be taken for a ride then shrugged off—'

'I didn't—' she began.

'Oh, come! When your long-term lover returned to England you couldn't get rid of me fast enough. I have to say it rankled… Now I expect you to make up for it…'

So he was out for revenge, out to satisfy his wounded pride.

Her voice choked, she said, 'I don't want to go to bed with you. I *won't* go to bed with you.' Then in desperation, 'You can't force me to do anything I don't want to do.'

'I've no intention of using force. It won't be necessary.' He sounded so sure of himself.

Shudders running through her, she begged, 'Oh, please, Rafe, don't do this to me. I want to sleep in my own bed…alone…'

When he released her, hardly daring to believe she'd won, Madeleine struggled to her feet.

Rising at the same time, he put a light hand at her waist. 'I'll see you up.'

Very conscious of his hand in the small of her back, she was partway across the hall when he stopped her, and said quizzically, 'I'm afraid I can't bring myself to kiss Mary, and it's a shame to waste it.'

As he turned her into his arms and tilted her chin, she caught sight of the mistletoe hanging over them. A second later everything was wiped from her mind as his mouth covered hers.

Though his kiss was light to begin with, it had a devastating effect on her, and, shaken to the very core, she parted her lips beneath his the way a flower opened to the sun.

He made a sound almost like a groan and, running his fingers into her hair, deepened the kiss, taking his own sweet time, until her head was spinning.

There was nothing in the world but this man, his lips, his arms, the warmth and strength of his body, the memories of how it had been, and what he'd once meant to her.

When he finally freed her mouth, blind and dizzy, she swayed and clung to him.

He steadied her, then, lifting her high in his arms, carried her up the stairs. It was like something that was happening in a dream, something she was experiencing, yet not quite real.

When he set her down and flicked on the light she saw that she was in a strange room, a masculine room with a dark blue and white decor, a central chandelier and a king-sized four-poster bed with a blue and silver canopy.

'You told me you wanted to sleep alone in your own bed. If you still want that, you're free to go.'

Her whole body crying out for him, she could feel the heat running through her, the passionate hunger, the overwhelming need.

She knew with blinding clarity that she was still in love with him, and no matter that he didn't love her, no matter that he just wanted to use her, he was the only man she would ever love. She was forever tied to him.

'Do you still want that?' he repeated.

No!

She wasn't sure whether she'd spoken the word aloud, or

whether he'd read her surrender, but, his eyes never leaving her face, he began to strip off his clothes.

Her throat dry, her heart beating fast, she stood wide-eyed and defenceless, as if bewitched, and watched him.

He discarded his shoes and socks before taking off and tossing aside the black sweater. Then slowly he unfastened the belt of his trousers, dealt with the clip and zip, slid them down over lean hips and stepped out of them. A moment later his dark silk boxer shorts followed.

Naked, he sat on the edge of the bed and said, as he'd once said before, but this time it was a command, 'Take off your clothes for me.'

With trembling fingers, she began to strip off her things—shoes, stockings, dress and slip. When she reached behind her to unfasten her bra he got to his feet and, gripping her hands, trapped them there. Then he smiled into her eyes, and bent his head to put his mouth to her breast.

Through the delicate lace of the low-cut cups she could feel the heat and dampness, and her nipples firmed, needing more, aching for the exquisite sensations his mouth and tongue could bestow.

She tried to free her hands, but he wouldn't allow it. Instead he traced the upper curve of her breast with his tongue, coming tantalisingly close, but carrying on to the valley between and the other breast without giving her what she craved.

Then, holding both her wrists with one hand, he used the thumb of his free hand to stimulate without satisfying, while his mouth worked its way up to the warm hollow at the base of her throat and lingered there sensually.

Then suddenly she was free and he was back on the bed, watching her with green eyes that had gone dark and smoky.

She tossed aside the bra and slid the matching panties down over slender hips.

'Come here,' he ordered softly.

When she went to him he turned her round and pulled her down between his spread knees. Then, sliding his hands beneath her arms, he began to fondle her small, well-shaped breasts.

She could feel the roughness of his legs against her thighs and his firm flesh pressing urgently against the base of her spine. Even so, he seemed to be in no hurry, but to enjoy pleasuring her.

In the cheval-glass opposite she could see the pair of them reflected, the blonde head and the almost black, his tanned, muscular body in sharp male contrast to her pale, very womanly curves.

See what he was doing to her. How, his lean fingers dark against the creamy skin of her breasts, he was alternately stroking and teasing the dusky-pink nipples, pinching and tugging slightly, rolling each of them between a thumb and forefinger.

In some indefinable way the erotic sight added to the sensations, making them more intense.

Just when she thought she couldn't stand it a moment longer he slid one hand between her thighs, and with long, probing fingers drew all the exquisite sensations into a glorious whole.

When she jerked and began to shudder helplessly he put an arm around her and, drawing her back, held her more firmly against him. It was like holding a lit sparkler, all fire and light.

She was still quivering, still breathing fast when, his hands at her waist, he lifted her to her feet. 'Now let's see what you've learnt.'

Startled, she turned to look at him.

His green eyes mocking, he said, 'The days when women were expected to lie down and think of England are well and truly over. In these modern times women are men's sexual equals, so now it's your turn to make love to me.'

Stretching out indolently on his back, his hands clasped behind his head, he waited.

While her heart hammered against her breastbone, she dragged air into her lungs and, her hands unsteady, pushed back the long strands of blonde hair that were clinging damply to her cheeks.

'In the past you've always made a pretence of being a little shy and innocent,' he added caustically. 'Now you don't have to pretend any longer, so let's see what you know or what you've learnt since then.'

Her eyes filled with unspoken anguish and she bent her head and looked down, the overhead light casting the shadow of her long lashes onto her cheeks.

That look punched a hole in his heart.

He reached out and, taking her hand, squeezed it gently. A consoling gesture she remembered from the past. A gesture that now seemed to be merely mocking.

Snatching her hand away, she said raggedly, 'Very well, if that's what you want.'

When she awoke it was almost ten-thirty, and she was alone in the bed. While her body felt sleek and satisfied, her mind was a jumble of thoughts and mixed feelings.

After her somewhat clumsy attempt to make love to him, mortified by her own inexperience, she had been turning away when he stopped her.

'Let me go.' She tried to break free. 'I'm going back to the flat to spend the night.'

'I don't think so. It's too late.'

Suddenly he rolled and, reversing their positions, trapped her body beneath his. His weight sparked off a heated rush of desire that made her quiver.

Feeling that betraying movement, he put his mouth to her breast and felt her hips jerk in response.

As he recognised that her need was almost as great as his own, his lovemaking was hard and fast and intense, focused simply on the twin goals of pleasure and release.

Caught up in the dark glory of it, her breath ragged, she let go of the hurt and anger and abandoned herself.

This was real. This was enough.

Only it wasn't.

Despite the explosion of ecstasy, despite the bodily bliss, there was so much missing—the caring, the warmth, the commitment.

She started to cry, and the tears simply wouldn't stop.

He gathered her up and cradled her to him.

When she was all cried out, he kissed her wet cheeks and, holding her in the crook of his arm, settled her head on his shoulder.

Totally drained, emotionally exhausted, she slept almost at once.

In the early hours of the morning, still tangled in the gossamer threads of a lovely dream of a summer picnic she and Rafe had once shared, she reached out and touched him.

He stirred and turned his head, so that his face pressed into the curve of her neck.

Warm and sleepy, she snuggled against him and felt his immediate response, the hard hammer-blows of his heart as his arms closed round her. Then in the darkness his lips had found hers, and he was kissing her with a passion that once more set her alight.

They had kissed and caressed and made love a second time with an undiminished hunger, before falling asleep again in each other's arms.

Recalling the piercing beauty of their lovemaking, she felt her eyes fill with tears. She wept then for a lot of things. For past mistakes that couldn't be altered, for still loving him in spite of everything, but most of all for giving in and going to bed with him.

If she had been strong enough to hold out against him he wouldn't have forced her, she was sure of that. It was her own need for him that had been her downfall, that had wiped out this last year as if it had never been and left her once more in his thrall.

Despairingly she asked herself, how was it possible to go on loving a man who, once he'd had his revenge, for that was what it amounted to, wouldn't give her a second thought?

Even so, and though she despised herself, she knew that she might be tempted to stay and give him what he wanted from her, if only Fiona didn't exist…

But the other woman *did* exist and presumably *she* still loved Rafe in spite of everything. Still hoped to marry him.

Poor Fiona.

How was it possible for two women to go on loving a man who was basically rotten?

Three women, if she counted Harriet Rampling.

Out of the blue and for the first time, Madeleine found herself wondering about the relationship between Rafe and his godmother.

How was it that, after he had treated her daughter so shabbily, and apparently reneged on the bargain he had made with her husband, Harriet Rampling and her godson were still so close that she would choose to live in his house?

It didn't seem to make any sense.

CHAPTER SEVEN

MADELINE was drying her cheeks with the back of her hand when the bedroom door opened and Rafe came in carrying a tray of coffee.

He was wearing stone-coloured trousers and a fine olive-green sweater with a loose, sleeveless jerkin. His thick dark hair, a shade longer than was fashionable and trying to curl, was brushed back from a high forehead.

Needing to be in control, she sat upright and, pulling the duvet up to cover her nakedness, trapped it under her arms.

His eyes on her tear-stained face, he put the tray on the cabinet and, sitting down on the edge of the bed, reached out a hand to tilt her chin. 'Regrets?'

'It's too late for regrets.' In spite of all her efforts her voice shook betrayingly.

He freed a strand of hair caught in her earring, curled it round his finger and tucked it behind her ear, before cupping her cheek.

There was tenderness in his eyes, in his touch, and, feeling an uncontrollable wave of love, she turned her face into his palm.

The breath hissed through his teeth and then he was holding her close, his mouth muffled in her hair. 'I think it's about time we were—'

The trill of a phone cut through his words.

He drew back and, taking the mobile from his jerkin pocket, walked across to the window, saying over his shoulder, 'Don't let your coffee get cold.'

There were two cups on the tray, and, as she turned to pick up the coffee-pot and fill them, she heard him say a business-like, 'Lombard.'

A second later his voice changed to a softer, more caring tone. 'Hello, sweetheart, how are you…?'

Fiona, Madeleine realised, and something inside her shrivelled up.

'That's good… Yes…yes, that's right. No, I'm afraid we're snowed up, you wouldn't get here by road today. Probably not tomorrow, either…'

Her heart starting to race, Madeleine wondered if perhaps the other woman was in some clinic, and wanting to come home for Christmas?

'Yes, that would be fine,' Rafe agreed. 'I'll make the arrangements. As a matter of fact it will fit in very nicely with my other plans…'

If Fiona *was* intent on coming here, somehow *she* had to get away. The panicky thought was going through her mind when he added, 'I'll ring you back in a little while… Yes, yes, I will… Bye.'

He dropped the phone back into his pocket and returned to sit on the bed, making the mattress depress beneath his weight.

She was taken completely by surprise when he asked casually, 'How do you feel about a trip to London?'

'A trip to London?' she echoed blankly.

'I thought we might have lunch at the Denaught.'

'Lunch at the Denaught… But I—I thought…' She stammered to a halt.

'That I meant to keep you a virtual prisoner?'

Annoyed by his amusement, she demanded, 'Wasn't that what you intended me to think?'

Taking a sip of his coffee, which he liked black and sugarless, he admitted blandly, 'I did mention keeping you with me. But I was hoping to rely on persuasion rather than actual physical confinement.'

Wondering what kind of game he was playing, why he'd suggested having lunch out, she said, 'Didn't you just say we were snowed up?'

'To all intents and purposes we are. But we have a small snowblower that Jack can use to keep the helicopter pad clear. Ever been in a chopper?'

'No.'

'Fancy the idea?'

The true answer was no. She was afraid of heights and didn't much care for flying in any form. But it would be a chance to leave the house. A chance, once they were at the Denaught, to escape. If she excused herself to go to the powder room, hopefully she could get a taxi and be away before he missed her.

Trying to keep the excitement out of her voice, she readjusted the duvet and said, 'Yes, that would be very nice.'

'Of course, I'll want your word that you won't try to run. That you'll stick with the role of the physiotherapist Harriet hired.'

Try as she might she was unable to meet his eyes and, with a hark back to childhood, the hand hidden beneath the duvet had the first and middle fingers crossed as, after the briefest hesitation, she agreed, 'Very well.'

'Good. Then while you shower and dress I'll have a word with Jack and get everything organised.'

The second the door had closed behind him, she jumped out of bed, pulled on her clothes and hurried along the corridor to her flat.

As soon as she had dried herself and dressed she put on her make-up and coiled her hair, leaving the same small gold hoops in her ears that she'd worn the previous night.

She couldn't wait to get away. It would mean leaving her cases, but once she was safely in London she could arrange to have them picked up. In the meantime, Eve would lend her whatever she needed.

Dressed in a cream blouse and a fine wool suit the colour of molasses, she pulled on a pair of matching suede boots and crept downstairs.

As soon as she'd found Mrs Boyce and retrieved her handbag, she would go back to the flat and phone Eve.

There was no sign of the housekeeper, and, having peered into several rooms, including the kitchen, she was returning to the hall when Rafe appeared wearing a hip-length leather jacket.

'Lost?' he queried.

'I was looking for Mrs Boyce.' Instinctively she spoke the truth.

'Mary's off until after Christmas. Annie will be filling in for her, when she gets here.'

'Oh…' Madeleine said. But, thinking back, she could vaguely remember Mrs Boyce mentioning it.

'Were you wanting the housekeeper for any particular reason?' he asked.

Doing her best to sound casual, she explained, 'Last night I couldn't find my handbag. I thought I must have left it in the living room, but when I went to look it wasn't there. I presume Mrs Boyce must have found it and put it somewhere safe.'

'Well, if that's all it is, there's no problem.'

'But I need my purse and—'

He smiled lazily. 'Don't worry, I promise I'll buy lunch. Now, about ready to start?'

There was money in her flight bag, and she would need money for a taxi. Her mind working overtime, she said, 'Not quite… I'd better fetch a coat,' and fled back upstairs.

It was a moment's work to unpack her cream coat, and her

flight bag was where she'd left it. Knowing how useful its contents would be, she hesitated, sorely tempted to take it.

But the last thing she wanted to do was alert Rafe. Giving up the idea, she unzipped it and felt for the money she'd slipped into the inner pocket alongside her passport and other papers.

The pocket was empty.

It must be the one on the other side.

That too was empty.

Feeling as though she'd been kicked in the solar plexus, she made a more thorough search.

Everything else was there, but her money, her passport and other travel documents were gone.

Suddenly it all added up.

There were money and papers missing, a phone that wasn't working, no keys in the doors, a handbag that had mysteriously disappeared…

Realising that the whole thing had been carefully planned, she clenched her teeth.

'Got a problem?'

Looking up, she found Rafe was standing in the doorway, watching her.

Her voice tight with barely controlled anger, she began with the least important. 'The phone up here isn't working…'

'So Mary said,' he agreed blandly.

'There are no keys to the doors, and, before you try to fob me off with excuses, I know they've been purposely removed…'

Those lazy green eyes regarded her calmly. 'Then presumably you know why?'

'Oh, yes, I know why. To prevent me locking myself in, and to enable you to come in and out whenever it suits you— which you've no right to do…!'

'It *is* my house,' he pointed out when she paused to draw breath.

'It might be your house, but that doesn't give you the right to walk in and take my belongings…' she said breathlessly.

When he simply stood there and watched her, her voice shaking, she accused, 'You came in while I was asleep—' recalling the dream that the slight noise he must have made had triggered off, she shuddered, before going on '—and you stole my handbag and the money and papers from my flight bag. Don't bother to deny it.'

'I wasn't going to deny it,' he said mildly. 'Though *stole* is hardly the correct word. I'm merely keeping them safe until I'm satisfied you don't intend to do anything silly.'

'How dare you?' she cried hoarsely. 'You've no right to treat me like this—'

'Perhaps we could leave the recriminations until later? The chopper's warming up ready and Jack will be standing around waiting for us.'

Then, with a glance at her mutinous face, 'Unless you've changed your mind about going? If you have, we could always stay at home.'

She had opened her mouth to say that she had no intention of going anywhere with him, when she hesitated. There would be no chance of escaping if they stayed here. Better to put on a reasonably amicable front and go with him. Then at the first opportunity she would slip away. Either Eve or Noel would pay her taxi fare…

'Well?'

'I haven't changed my mind.'

Picking up her coat, he helped her into it. 'Then let's go.'

Outside it was a perfect winter's day, with a cloudless sky as blue as lapis lazuli. Though the sun shone brightly, the air was glacial, and frost sparkled like glitter on a Christmas card.

Snow covered everything in a thick white counterpane, filling in hollows, redefining the landscape, piling on sills and ledges, burying shrubs and plants, clothing bare branches and weighing down the green arms of the pine.

The apron outside the front door had been partially cleared and, harnessed to what appeared to be a child's sleigh, a small, sturdy pony waited placidly.

'Courtesy of the previous owner, who was going to live in Australia,' Rafe explained as he helped Madeleine into the sleigh and fitted himself in beside her.

Pressed as they were, hip to hip and thigh to thigh, there was just enough room for the two of them.

'It belonged to his children... Cosy, wouldn't you say?'

Robbed of breath by such close contact, Madeleine said nothing.

'We do have a snowmobile,' he went on, 'but there's something wrong with the engine and Jack is having to work on it.'

Finding her voice, she asked, 'How far is it to the helicopter pad?'

'Only a few hundred yards. But considering the conditions, I thought this mode of transport might be preferable to walking, and Jack says Hercules can do with some exercise.'

He made a clicking noise with his tongue, and apparently eager to live up to his name, Hercules set off with a will.

Though the sleigh ran easily enough, the pony's short legs sank into the snow alarmingly until they got under the lee of a wall bordering the path to the flat, raised ground where the helicopter pad and hangar were situated.

Looking for all the world like a plastic bubble, the helicopter was waiting, its door open, its rotor blades turning gently.

Jack came to meet them and take charge of the sleigh while Rafe, a hand at her waist, escorted her across to the small silver machine.

After a momentary hesitation, she ducked her head and climbed in.

Rafe closed the door and, a moment later, swung in beside her. Then, having fastened both their seat belts, he put on the headset and turned his attention to the controls.

The engine note rose to a whine and a second or so later, the downdraught from the rotor blades whipping up the surrounding powdery snow, they lifted off into the blue, blue sky.

As they levelled out Rafe glanced sideways at her, noting her absolute stillness, the slim hands clasped into fists, the way her eyes were fixed blindly on the control panel.

'OK?' he asked above the engine noise.

She nodded without moving her gaze.

Reaching out, he took the nearest hand and squeezed it reassuringly.

She gave him a small, wavering smile.

'That's my girl.'

After a minute or so she took a deep breath and forced herself to look down. She was rewarded by a truly fantastic view. A winter wonderland of glistening snow, a montage of fields and hedgerows and silver filigree trees.

Fascinated, she began to pick out small dwellings and isolated farms, streams and roads, and clearly, on the smooth white snow, the tracks of animals.

Then in no time at all, it seemed, the countryside gave way to town and they were coming in to land on the Denaught's clearly marked helicopter pad.

With its high grey stone walls, its towers and turrets and battlements, the place looked more like a castle than a hotel, Madeleine thought.

On the same wavelength, as he so often was, Rafe raised his voice to tell her, 'Long before it became one of London's top hotels, the Denaught was a fortified country house belonging to Sir Ian Bolton.

'After the Bolton family died out, the place stood empty for a time until some property developer realised its potential.'

When they touched down and the rotor blades slowed, he removed his headset and, unfastening their seat belts, queried, 'So how do you feel about your first helicopter flight?'

She surprised herself by saying, 'I enjoyed it. I hadn't expected to, as I'm terrified of heights.'

'It's somewhat different from standing on the edge of a precipice.'

'I pictured it as being just as terrifying.' She laughed.

'But still you came.' His voice was dry.

She hoped he hadn't guessed what she had in mind. It would make getting away all the more difficult, if he had.

But if the worst came to the worst, she would refuse point blank to go back with him. And if he tried to force her she would kick up a fuss, she decided as he came round to help her out.

The Denaught appeared to be very busy, and she was greatly cheered to see a red-coated doorman dealing with a steady trickle of taxis arriving at, and leaving, the main entrance.

There was much less snow here, a mere carpet compared to the thick covering they'd left behind them, which made walking easy even in fashion boots.

'Better make the most of it,' Rafe said, when she remarked on the fact. 'If the forecast is right, we've more heavy snow coming overnight, with blizzards in our neck of the woods…'

'Good afternoon, Mr Lombard…madam…' A youngish, round-faced man in a smart navy-blue uniform appeared from nowhere. 'Lovely day.'

'It is indeed,' Rafe answered.

'If you and the lady want to go straight in, I'll take care of things.'

'Thanks, Steve.'

'You seem to be well-known here,' she remarked, as they made their way across the concreted area and through a side-entrance.

'Yes, it's a place I often use. Apart from the fact that they have an excellent chef, the helicopter pad is extremely useful, and I keep a car here,' he added nonchalantly.

As they reached the foyer, with its crackling log fire and seasonal decorations, a grey-haired, distinguished-looking man wearing a cream carnation in his buttonhole, bore down on them.

'Good afternoon, Mr Lombard…'

'Afternoon, Charles. This is Miss Knight.'

'Miss Knight…' Obviously one of the old school, the manager made her a courteous little bow.

'I must apologise for giving you so little notice, at a peak time,' Rafe said.

Charles waved away the apology. 'It's always a pleasure to have you here, Mr Lombard.'

As their coats were borne away by one of his minions, he added, 'Your usual table's ready, and your guest has arrived.'

Rafe nodded. 'Thanks.'

'The young lady's waiting for you in the private lounge.' He indicated a door to the right.

Madeleine's thoughts began to race as, a hand beneath her elbow, Rafe escorted her across the foyer towards the lounge.

Remembering his previous phone conversation, she felt hollow inside.

As Fiona couldn't get to the hall, had he suggested that they meet here?

But if he had, why had he included *her*? Unless he'd decided that she was safer under his eye than left to her own devices.

After all, he had no idea that she and Fiona had ever met, no idea that she knew about the bargain he had made with his godfather.

And she was hardly likely to tell the other woman how he'd tricked her into going to the hall. So perhaps he was hoping to present her simply in the role of physiotherapist?

The role he had asked her to play.

Another thought struck her. Did he mean to take Fiona back in the helicopter? Though how did he intend to extract 'reparation' from *her* with his fiancée on the scene…?

Well, whatever his intentions, if it was Fiona waiting in there, he had a nasty shock coming.

But if it was Fiona, she'd rather tell him the truth now than have to face the other woman.

At the door to the lounge, her insides churning, she dug her toes in and asked jerkily, 'Who is it that's waiting?'

'You'll see.'

'I'd like to know.'

Shaking his head, he said decidedly, 'That would spoil the surprise,' and, opening the door, propelled her inside.

She was aware of a log fire burning in what seemed to be a deserted room, before a small figure came hurtling towards her. Almost knocked off balance, she found herself being hugged with a warmth and enthusiasm that went straight to her heart.

'Katie!' she exclaimed, half laughing, half crying. 'How you've grown. You're getting really tall. You almost come up to my chin.'

'*You* haven't changed at all,' Katie declared. 'You're just as beautiful as ever.' She turned to Rafe and gave him a hug. 'Thank you for bringing her, Uncle Rafe.'

Then, taking Madeleine's hand, she went on happily, 'I'm so glad you're back. I've missed you. Aren't you pleased to be home?'

Glancing up, Madeleine met Rafe's ironic gaze. Dragging her eyes away, she said, 'Of course I am.'

'School's broken up for Christmas, so when Mum told me you were staying at the hall so you could treat Uncle George, I asked if I could come and see you. But Uncle Rafe said you were all snowed up…'

So it had been Katie Rafe had been talking to when he used the endearment *sweetheart*, not Fiona.

'Did you enjoy flying in the helicopter?' Katie asked eagerly.

'Yes, I quite liked it.'

'I thought you would,' the child said proudly. 'That's why I asked Uncle Rafe if he could bring you to see me.'

So though he must have known he was running a risk, known that she might refuse to go back with him, he'd brought her to please Katie.

'He didn't tell me,' Madeleine said.

'I asked him not to say anything because I wanted to surprise you.'

'Well, you certainly did that.' She squeezed the child's hand. Then, puzzled, asked, 'But surely you didn't come alone?'

'No, Helga, the au pair, brought me. She'll be coming back for me at two o'clock…'

Which meant she would have to delay her escape, Madeleine realised. There was no way she could disappear while Katie was still here.

'Mum is at work,' the child went on. 'She's going to join us as soon as she can get away. But she said to start eating without her, just in case she can't make it for lunch.

'I'm hungry already. I was too excited to eat much breakfast. Are *you* hungry, Maddy?'

Still feeling churned up, Madeleine lied, 'Yes, I am.'

'Well, if my two favourite girls are hungry—' Rafe put an arm around each of them '—let's go and eat.'

Katie fairly danced along, her dark, glossy plait swinging. 'While we have lunch I can tell you all about Bertrand…'

When, seated by one of the long windows in the pleasant dining room, they had finished ordering, Madeleine asked, 'Who's Bertrand?'

'He's the Labrador that Uncle Rafe is giving me for Christmas. Though I'm fine again now, Mum and Dad don't want me to ride any more until I'm grown up, so they agreed I could have a dog. Bertrand's about six months old and I'm getting him tomorrow, because the sanctuary doesn't open on Christmas Day.

'I decided to call him Bertrand because that's Uncle Rafe's middle name…'

'Is it really?' Madeleine laughed. 'I didn't know that.'

Rafe grimaced. 'Not a lot of people do.'

Then to Katie, 'Do you *have* to tell all my most shameful secrets? And come to that, how do you know?'

The little girl giggled. 'Mum told me. But she thinks Bertrand is rather grand for a puppy, so I'll probably call him Bertie for short.' She turned her attention back to Madeleine. 'He was rescued when his previous owner left him shut in the basement of a derelict house,' she explained. 'He'd almost starved to death before he was found. But he's very friendly and he still likes people.

'He's from the Mill House Animal Sanctuary. Uncle Rafe gives them lots of money to help the animals…'

While they waited for the meal to be served, and between courses, Katie chatted away non-stop.

Madeleine smiled and listened and marvelled that a child she had regarded as quiet and a little shy could be so talkative.

Catching her eye, Rafe said with a wry smile, 'As a rule Katie doesn't say much, but when she gets excited she could talk for England.'

They had almost finished their coffee before Diane herself came hurrying in, wearing a businesslike grey suit and carrying a black shoulder-bag-cum-briefcase. Her cheeks were flushed and she sounded more than a shade breathless as she said, 'Hi there.'

'You're very late, Mum,' Katie pointed out.

'Yes, I know, darling, and I'm sorry. I began to think I wasn't going to make it at all. I was trapped into having lunch with a client.'

She gave her brother, who had risen at her approach, a peck

on the cheek and, stooping to hug Madeleine, said with obvious sincerity, 'It's good to have you back.'

'I expect you can do with some coffee?' Rafe asked.

'You're a mind-reader.' Dropping into the chair he'd pulled out for her, Diane smoothed a hand over the dark hair that fell straight and gleaming to her shoulders, and grumbled, 'Sometimes I wonder why I keep on working.'

He smiled. 'You know perfectly well that you love your work. If you didn't have it, you'd be lost.'

'That's true. I just don't want to be a mirror image of Mother.'

He raised an eyebrow. 'I don't think you need to worry on that score.'

'But you wouldn't want *your* wife to have a career,' Diane noted.

'I'd prefer her not to. Unless it would make her seriously unhappy to give it up. If that was the case, I'd have to withdraw my opposition…' He sat back confidently.

They chatted for a minute or so until the fresh coffee had arrived and been poured, before Katie reminded him, 'Uncle Rafe, you promised you'd show me the inside of your helicopter some time and let me sit in the pilot's seat…'

'Well, I will, sweetheart.'

'Can't you do it now?' She glanced at her watch. 'It's only a quarter to two.'

As Rafe hesitated, Diane said, 'Go if you want to. Maddy and I can catch up on some gossip.'

'Oh, *please*, Uncle Rafe.' Katie was already on her feet and tugging at his arm.

He cast his eyes heavenwards. 'I should have more sense than promise these things.'

'Go on,' Diane urged, 'you know you want to.' Then to Madeleine, 'Men always enjoy showing off their toys.'

'Femaled into it,' he said with mock-resignation. 'Come on, then, Poppet. We'll pick up your coat on the way out.'

'It's Helga's yoga class this afternoon,' Diane reminded her daughter, 'so if you see her come while you're out there, you'd better go straight home with her. Daddy should be there by the time you get back.'

'All right… Bye, then, Mum.'

'Bye, darling. I won't be late tonight.'

'That's good. Bye, Maddy. Come and see us soon—then you'll be able to meet Bertie. I think you'll like him.' Katie ran back and put her arms round Maddy.

'I'm sure I will,' Madeleine agreed, and hugged the slight figure.

'Come on, then, Uncle Rafe…' She took his hand.

Over the child's head his eyes met Madeleine's, an unmistakable warning in their cool green depths, as he said lightly, 'I'll be back in ten minutes or so. Don't go anywhere.'

As the tall, broad-shouldered man and the slender dark-haired child turned away, they heard Katie coax, 'If I'm very careful, will you let me try on the earphones, Uncle Rafe?'

He smiled down at her. 'I dare say.'

'Oh, goodie!'

While the pair made their way to the door, Diane sipped her coffee and looked after them fondly. 'I'll be pleased when Rafe settles down and has a family of his own…'

Madeleine felt her heart constrict as if an iron band had tightened round it as Diane added, 'He'll make a really good father. He's great with Katie, and she fairly dotes on him.' Then a shade diffidently, 'I hadn't realised how things were— between you and Rafe, I mean—until he told me…'

Madeleine found herself wondering exactly how much he'd told his sister, and where Fiona fitted into all this. It didn't sound as if Diane knew about the bargain Rafe had struck with his godfather… Or if she did, she certainly didn't seem to be blaming him for not keeping it.

'He hasn't been happy while you've been away,' Diane

went on. 'But now you're back, thank the lord, and I'm only too delighted that things finally look like they're working out…'

Not knowing what to say, Madeleine stayed silent.

'Poor Rafe… In some ways he's had a raw deal…'

Seeing the sceptical look on Madeleine's face, she hurried to defend her brother. 'Oh, yes, I know he *appears* to be the man who has everything, but so far, through no fault of his own, he's lost out in ways that have really mattered to him.

'Though he was never deprived of material possessions, he didn't have a very happy childhood. In fact it's a miracle he didn't grow up warped…'

Recalling the story he'd told her about his stepfather, Madeleine began, 'You mean…?'

'I mean he could so easily have ended up weak, psychologically damaged. But thank the lord he's turned out to be one of the strongest, most stable people I know.

'The only thing I've ever known to really throw him off balance was when you went to the States…' She glanced up at Madeleine and then went on, 'But to get back to the point. Our mother wasn't a home-maker. She never wanted children. She was a career woman through and through, and well over thirty when she married Dad. Even then she only agreed to a wedding because I was on the way.

'Children bored her, and she couldn't wait to get me off her hands so she could be free. Unfortunately for her, there was still Rafe to come.

'She believed she was in the menopause, and by the time she found she was pregnant again, it was too late to do anything about it. No child asks to be born, yet, as though he was to blame, she always resented him.

'Dad and I did our best, but he needed a mother's love, and the more he tried to get close to her, the more she pushed him away. He was much too young to understand why…'

Madeleine's heart bled for the poor, bewildered child who'd been so cruelly rejected. But after the way he'd treated Fiona he didn't deserve her pity, she reminded herself.

'Then when he was twelve and I was nineteen our father died, and six months later, to our surprise, Mother remarried. Unlike Dad, who was a kind man and wouldn't have hurt a fly, her new husband was a brute and a bully. It's not surprising that Rafe came to hate him…

'To cut a long story short, when Rafe was barely fourteen, for his own safety, he was sent to live with his godparents.'

Her face clouded.

'It's true that they welcomed him with open arms, but even there he had his share of problems…'

Madeleine was taken aback. When Rafe had talked about his godparents, he'd made no mention of any problems. Rather he'd emphasised how well they'd treated him.

As if pushing aside unpleasant memories, Diane made a dismissive gesture and went on, 'Though at that time the Charns could well afford it, he was anxious not to be a financial burden. He wanted to be independent, to be able to fund his own schooling.

'As though in answer to a prayer, when our paternal aunt died she left us a small legacy in her will. I used my half to further my career, while Rafe, with his godfather's help and approval, put his into stocks and shares.

'When it comes to finance, my brother has the Midas touch. Everything he invested in turned to gold, and by the time he went to university he had the independence he craved.

'He could have cut free then from the Charn household, but he didn't,' Diane said proudly. 'He continued to call their house home, continued to treat them as if they were his own parents. And when Christopher ran into trouble, Rafe stood by him through thick and thin…'

Well, he would do if he was expecting to inherit Charn Industries, Madeleine thought cynically. But once again there had been no mention of Fiona.

She was about to jump in with both feet and ask where the other woman was, when Diane exclaimed, 'Oh, lord, aren't I rabbiting on? But I wanted you to know, to understand, that Rafe isn't—'

'Isn't what?' Rafe asked.

Both women jumped.

'Oh, you're back,' Diane said. And, obviously flustered to be caught talking about him, hurried on, 'Did Katie enjoy the helicopter?'

He grinned. 'Enormously. She's quite determined to get a pilot's licence as soon as she's old enough.'

'I take it she's gone?'

'Yes. Helga was running a few minutes late, otherwise she would have stopped for a word.'

Diane picked up her shoulder-bag. 'Speaking of being late, I'll have to get a move-on myself. Thanks for the coffee.' She turned back to her brother. 'We'll be at home all over Christmas. Stuart's mum and dad are coming to stay with us, so you must bring Madeleine for a meal as soon as you can make it.'

'Will do.'

'Keep in touch, and let me know how things are.' Glancing at her watch, she added, 'I've got an appointment at three-fifteen, so I'll have to dash. But first I must pop into the ladies' room and check my make-up.'

'I'll come with you.' Madeleine seized her chance as Diane gave Rafe a sisterly kiss.

Then, leaving him to signal a waiter and pay the bill, the two women walked back to the main lobby. Though her heart was thudding, Madeleine tried hard to appear casual, in case he was watching them.

As soon as Diane was safely out of the way, she'd slip outside and ask the doorman to get her a taxi. It would mean leaving without her coat, but that was a small price to pay, and no doubt Eve would be able to lend her one.

CHAPTER EIGHT

THE blue and gold powder room was momentarily deserted. Meeting Diane's green eyes in the mirror and watching her run a comb through her hair, Madeleine took a deep breath and broached the subject that had been weighing so heavily on her mind.

'I was wondering about Fiona...'

As the other woman began to apply a fresh coat of lip gloss, Madeleine hurried on, 'Is she all right now? I understand that she had a lot of problems in the past...'

'Lord, did she have problems! The whole family were worried sick about her, but because she'd always clung to Rafe he bore the brunt of it. Now she's doing fine, I'm pleased to say. When she was finally given a clean bill of health it must have taken a great weight off his mind as well as Harriet's. I know it did off mine... Well, I really must fly or I'm going to be dreadfully late. Take care. See you soon...' Diane waved goodbye.

Madeleine sighed. After all that, she was little wiser. The only thing she knew for certain was that Fiona was well, and not languishing in some clinic.

The most important questions remained unanswered. Was she still hoping to marry Rafe? Still hoping that he would keep his part of the bargain? But if that was the case, why wasn't she with him?

As Diane hurried out, a small group of women came in, laughing and talking.

It occurred to Madeleine that if she waited until they went out and mingled with them she would be a lot less conspicuous if Rafe was keeping an eye on the lobby.

They seemed to take an age, and she made a pretence of re-coiling her hair and checking her make-up while she waited on tenterhooks.

When the group finally headed for the door she joined their ranks and slipped out with them.

She had half feared Rafe would be waiting, but a hasty glance around the lobby showed no sign of him.

With a sigh of relief she hurried to the main entrance, where a door with panels of thick stained glass was opened for her by the red-coated doorman.

There were vehicles coming and going, and a silver Mercedes was drawn up a few paces away, its engine idling. But there seemed to be no cabs.

'Can you call me a taxi, please?' she asked, aware that she sounded breathless.

'Certainly, madam.'

As he moved to do her bidding, Rafe appeared by her side, her coat over his arm. 'That won't be necessary, James. The lady's with me.'

'Right, Mr Lombard.'

While shock kept her rigid, motionless, he slipped a note into the doorman's hand and put her coat around her shoulders.

She had drawn breath to tell him she had no intention of going back with him, when he tipped her face up and, letting his thumb graze along her jawline, said softly, 'I'm very well-aware that you had your fingers crossed.'

Though his voice was cool, careless, it held a bite that made her feel small. As the heat rose in her cheeks he smiled into her eyes and, bending his head, kissed her.

That sorcerer's mouth worked its black magic, scattering her wits and making her head reel. As if under a spell she allowed herself to be steered to the nearby car and installed in the front passenger seat.

He slid in beside her, clicked their seat belts into place, and they were away before she could catch her breath.

It was a good thirty seconds before she was able to think straight. Then she began to berate herself. Why had she weakly let him take charge of her again? Why had her fighting spirit, her determination to resist at all costs, died so easily? Why had she allowed her common sense to be submerged, her basic instinct of self-preservation to be swamped by the magic of his kiss?

Because she couldn't help it. She was held in thrall by her love for him.

It wasn't a comfortable thought. It stripped her of her freedom, her independence, even her pride, and put her at the mercy of a man who had treated his sick fiancée without any consideration.

Well, she wouldn't be put in that position. Somehow, she resolved, she would find the strength to fight, the strength to leave him…

They were pulling out of the hotel forecourt to join the main traffic stream before it occurred to her to wonder about their mode of transport.

Earlier, Rafe had talked as if the roads around Hethersage would be impassable for the next couple of days, so why were they going back by car rather than in the helicopter?

When she voiced the question, he answered calmly, 'We're not going back to Hethersage, at least not straight away. I'd like to go back tomorrow and have Christmas there, but right now I've plans which necessitate spending the night in town.'

'Spending the night in town?' She was surprised.

'Have you any objections?'

'No.' Being in London suited her just fine. It would give her a much better chance of carrying out her resolve than being snowbound at the hall.

But she couldn't help but wonder *why* he wanted to spend the night in town. Rafe wasn't a man to do anything without a good reason.

Perhaps it was something to do with Fiona. Thinking back to his phone conversation with Katie, she recalled him saying, 'As a matter of fact it will fit in very nicely with my other plans.'

Taking a deep, calming breath, she asked, 'What *are* your plans exactly?'

'As parking will be a nightmare, I intend to leave the car at Denver Court and take a taxi into the centre of town to do some shopping.'

'Shopping?' It was the last thing she had expected. He gave her a glinting sideways glance. 'For your birthday present, amongst other things…'

Her birthday… Even Eve and Noel hadn't remembered, and so much had happened in the past two days she hadn't given it a thought.

'How did you know it was my birthday?'

'You once mentioned that if you'd been born a few minutes *after* midnight instead of a few minutes *before*, your birthday would have fallen on Christmas Eve.'

And he'd remembered. Just for a moment she struggled against tears.

As though he sensed her emotion, he went on briskly, 'So what would you like for a present? It's up to you to choose.'

'I don't want a present from you.'

There was a telling silence, then she rushed into speech, 'I'm sorry if I sounded rude and ungrateful. I'm not ungrateful…'

'Just rude?'

Knowing she had been brought a flush to her face. Still she persevered, 'I really don't want you to buy me anything.'

As though she hadn't spoken, he said, 'It might be a good idea to start our shopping trip at Harrod's.

'As you haven't got either a handbag or an overnight bag with you, you'll need a number of things. A dress for this evening, accessories, underwear, night wear, toiletries, make-up…'

'But I—'

'Don't argue.'

'I don't want to be forced into having anything I can't pay for,' she informed him stiltedly. 'I hate to feel beholden.'

She saw by the way his beautiful mouth tightened that her words had angered him.

But as though striving to be reasonable, he said equably, 'Look on it as your Christmas present.'

'I don't want a Christmas present.' Flatly, she added, 'I can't afford to buy you one.'

'So indulge me, and call it your Christmas present to me.'

Little shivers started to run up and down her spine, as he added, 'Strictly speaking you won't *need* a nightdress… But we'll get one anyway, so I can have the pleasure of taking it off…'

London's busy streets and most of its pavements were clear of snow, but with frost laying icy fingers on everything, its parks and gardens and squares clad in bridal white, it looked an enchanted city as they headed towards Denver Court.

As well as apartments the complex had a small, select shopping mall, a comprehensive fitness centre, an indoor and an outdoor swimming pool, and two of the most exclusive and expensive restaurants in town, the Starlight Room and the Jacobean Room.

When they stopped at the main entrance to the court one of the security staff came over. 'Good afternoon, Mr Lombard. Nice to see you back.'

'Afternoon, John. Can you call a taxi, preferably one I can hire for the rest of the afternoon, and then take care of the car for me?'

'Consider it done.' A mobile phone appeared in his hand. After a brief conversation, he reported, 'Danny, who has his own cab, is just dropping a passenger. He'll be with you any minute.'

As Rafe helped Madeleine out and handed over the car keys a well-kept taxi appeared, and in a moment they were installed in it and heading for Knightsbridge and Harrod's.

Everywhere was crowded with last-minute shoppers, but miraculously both the human traffic and the vehicular managed to keep moving.

It was starting to get dusky, and in the centre of town the Christmas lights were just coming on.

Teddy bears wearing festive hats tumbled and clowned, Santas and sleighs, reindeer and elves, stars and angels blinked on and off, vying with glittering shop windows full of seasonal displays of wines and foodstuffs, furs and jewellery, toys and luxury goods.

On the street corner a Salvation Army band, the brass instruments gleaming under the lights, was playing carols, while one of its female members wielded a collecting box.

While their taxi was held up by a red traffic light, Rafe rolled down his window and passed her a wad of notes.

'Thanks,' she called. 'Happy Christmas.'

'You're very generous,' Madeleine remarked.

'I can afford to be, and I have great respect for the Salvation Army; they do a good job.'

When their taxi drew up outside Harrod's, whose window displays were a delight as always at this time of the year, having thanked the driver, Rafe asked, 'Can you find somewhere to park, then come back for us in…say…an hour?'

'Can do,' the man agreed laconically. 'But it'll cost a packet.'

'That's not a problem,' Rafe said smoothly, and more notes changed hands.

He turned to Madeleine and, shrugging out of his leather jacket, said, 'I suggest you leave your coat in the car; you won't need it.'

When, still unhappy about him spending money on her, she had reluctantly slipped out of her coat he hurried her into the huge store.

'We'll start in the dress department.'

Despite the crush of shoppers, focused and positive, Rafe got attention with no apparent effort.

Unlike most men he had very clear ideas about what would suit her and how he wanted her to look, and when, her mouth stubborn, she refused to choose, he chose for her.

In a remarkably short space of time she had everything he had previously listed, including an evening bag and a shoulder-bag. Amazingly, it was still a few minutes short of an hour when, loaded with boxes and packages, he shepherded her towards the main doors.

Just as they reached the pavement their taxi drew up, the lights gleaming on its polished bonnet.

When the packages were stored in the boot and she was settled in her seat, Rafe gave the driver an instruction she didn't catch and got in beside her.

As they pulled away from the kerb, he asked quizzically, 'There, that wasn't too painful, was it?'

Hating to be railroaded like that, she stayed mutinously silent.

He picked up her hand, which was clenched into a fist, and, straightening the fingers one by one, said, 'Tell me something; if you were my wife, or we were about to marry, would you still object to me buying you things?'

Her heart did a little flip before she answered, 'No, of course not. But that's different.'

Instead of just wanting to use her to satisfy his lust and

soothe his wounded pride, it would mean that he loved and respected her. It would change everything.

'As it is, I feel like a…a paid mistress.'

'That denigrates us both.' Though he spoke softly, she heard the edge of anger in his voice.

Responding to that anger, she said, 'I suppose you've never had to pay for sexual favours.'

'No, I haven't,' he replied curtly. 'And I wasn't thinking of starting now.'

Suddenly ashamed of herself, of her behaviour, she admitted, 'I shouldn't have said that. I'm sorry…'

With a little sigh, he lifted her hand to his lips and kissed the palm. 'And I'm sorry we didn't do the more important shopping first.

'Had we done things the other way round, it might have made all the difference to how you feel.'

She shook her head. 'I don't see how it could have made any difference.'

'Wouldn't that rather depend on what I was thinking of buying?'

Confused, she said, 'I don't know.' Then, curiously, 'What were you thinking of buying?'

'I'll tell you when we get there.'

Uneasy, she insisted, 'Tell me now.'

'Apart from your birthday present? A ring.'

'A r—ring?' she stammered.

'An engagement ring,' he said deliberately.

Once, when she had fondly imagined he might love her, that would have been like a dream come true. Now it was bewildering and unsettling.

'Why would you want to buy me a ring when you said all you wanted was reparation?'

'Shall we say for the look of the thing? So that other people—'

'I don't want a ring,' she broke in, her voice thick. 'It would just be a sham.'

'You've made it clear that you don't want to feel like a paid mistress. As my fiancée you would have no cause to feel that way, and while we're together you'd have a certain status.'

'You can keep your money. I don't need a ring. I've no intention of staying with you. Apart from the fact that you want revenge, I mean nothing to you—'

'I'm afraid you've become something of an obsession, and I've no intention of letting you go until I'm good and ready.'

'You can't *force* me to stay.'

'No,' he agreed, 'but you will. There's a part of you that *wants* to. A part of you that—at the risk of sounding melodramatic—is still in thrall. Otherwise you would never have slept with me last night, never have left the Denaught with me today.'

When, thrown by such an accurate assessment, she stayed silent, he went on, 'Maybe you need to get me out of your system, the same as I need to get you out of mine…'

Chilled by his words, she shivered.

'And the best way to do that, and set both of us free, would be to stay together until the torment, the fixation, the obsession, call it what you will, dies a natural death…'

If only it were that simple.

'Ah, here we are.' The taxi had drawn up outside Marshall Brand, one of the best known and most exclusive jewellers in town, whose windows invariably displayed the minimum of rare and beautiful objects.

'Can you give us half an hour or so?' Rafe asked the driver.

The man nodded. 'We're in luck. I've just spotted a free meter a few yards further on.'

Opening the door, Rafe jumped out, and before Madeleine could argue she found herself urged out of the taxi and across the pavement.

A uniformed security guard opened the heavy glass door and, after an assessing glance at Rafe, ushered them into the palatial shop.

With mirrored walls, crystal chandeliers and vases of fresh flowers, the sales area was set out like a salon. Velvet-covered couches and easy chairs, interspersed with elegant display cabinets and small glass-topped tables, were widely spaced on a thick, plum-coloured carpet.

As Madeleine glanced around her, a delicate gold bracelet in one of the cabinets caught her eye, and for a moment or two she was lost in admiration of its beauty and simplicity.

'Mr Lombard?' A well-dressed man with silver hair and rimless glasses appeared from nowhere.

Turning from watching Madeleine, Rafe said easily, 'That's right.'

'Good afternoon. I'm Carl Brand.'

The two men shook hands.

An arm at her waist, Rafe made the introduction. 'This is Miss Knight, my fiancée.'

'Miss Knight…' Carl Brand inclined his head.

'I'm sorry that we're somewhat later than I'd first antici-pated,' Rafe said.

'Please don't apologise.' Brand waved them to the nearest couch. 'If you would care to take a seat, I have a selection of rings the size you indicated, ready to show you.'

As he proceeded to unlock the nearest display cabinet they heard a pop, and a young woman appeared with a still-smoking bottle of vintage champagne and two glasses on a silver tray.

When the flutes had been filled, feeling as though she was an actress in some play, Madeleine accepted one and took a sip. The wine was cool and sparkling, like quicksilver on her tongue.

While they sipped the champagne, half a dozen rings on

individual stands were placed on the table. There was a ruby, an emerald, a beautiful aquamarine on a chased gold band, a sapphire, a cluster of small, perfect opals and a huge diamond solitaire.

All were superb of their kind.

'I'll give you a moment,' Brand murmured, and moved discreetly into the background.

'What do you think, darling?' Rafe asked.

Caught on the raw by the *darling*, she wondered how he'd deal with it if she announced that she hated them all, and walked out.

But she very much doubted if she could drum up sufficient nerve.

As though he'd read her mind, he glanced at her, his green eyes holding an unmistakable warning, as he suggested, 'Suppose you try one on?'

'Do I have any other option?' she asked pleasantly.

He deliberately chose to misunderstand her. 'If you don't care for any of these, we can always ask to see some more.'

She shook her head. 'I don't want to see any more.'

'Does that mean there's one here you like?'

In the circumstances it didn't matter, though for her one particular ring stood out.

Unwilling to say so, she cooed with saccharine-sweetness, 'As you're buying it, *darling*, I'd much prefer you to choose.'

'Sure?'

'Sure.'

Though he smiled, she knew he was annoyed, both by her mockery and her refusal to co-operate.

'Very well.'

She felt a fleeting regret. He would probably insist on buying the diamond, her least favourite. Though she couldn't deny it was a magnificent ring, and many women would have preferred it, it was too large and showy for her taste.

Reaching out, he selected a ring and slipped it onto her finger. 'This would be my choice.'

Madeleine found herself staring down at the aquamarine as he added, 'It matches your beautiful eyes.'

It fitted to perfection, and looked wonderful on her slim, but strong, hand.

Had this been a real engagement it was the ring she would have chosen, and suddenly she found herself gazing at it through a mist of tears.

He tilted her chin, and she looked into his eyes, her own open wide, afraid to blink. Seeing the shimmer of tears, he said, 'Of course, if you have any other preference…'

She shook her head, mutely.

He kissed her lightly on the lips. 'In that case we'll take it.'

Soft-footed, Carl Brand returned to ask, 'Is there anything here that takes your fancy?'

'We've decided on the aquamarine.'

'An excellent choice, if I may say so. It's a particularly fine stone. The colour and clarity are superb, and it was cut by Jean Pierre Falgayras, a master craftsman. Would you like to have it wrapped?'

'I don't think so.' As Madeleine made to take it off, Rafe stopped her. 'Keep it on, darling. I'd like you to wear it.'

'At the moment it's still fully insured,' Brand told him. 'But if you want to check the details…'

'I don't think that's necessary.'

Rafe got to his feet and, taking the older man on one side, engaged him in a low-toned conversation.

'We can certainly do that, Mr Lombard,' Madeleine heard Brand agree. Then, 'We do indeed, and they come from the same house. If you'll give me a moment…'

He raised a hand and, when a young woman hastened over, issued a quiet instruction that had her hurrying away again.

She returned after a minute or so carrying a midnight-blue leather case, with Marshall Brand stamped in gold on the lid.

At a signal from Brand, she handed the case to Rafe and unobtrusively refilled the champagne glasses before moving away.

He opened it and, after scrutinising the contents, snapped it shut again, nodding his approval.

'Would you like that gift-wrapped?' Brand queried.

'Please.'

While Rafe and Carl Brand dealt with the financial side, Madeleine stared down at the aquamarine and sipped her champagne.

She felt strange and light-headed, a confusion of thoughts whirling through her brain like autumn leaves in a wind-storm.

Why had he insisted on her having a ring? Had he really been considering her status? How she would feel about being his unwilling mistress?

Oh, surely not. It just didn't add up. If all he wanted was reparation, why should he take *her* feelings into account?

Recalling what Diane had said about him being knocked off balance when she'd gone to Boston, she wondered if he might once have cared a little for her.

Obviously he no longer did, but he certainly *wanted* her. He'd admitted to being obsessed, admitted that he needed to be free of her...

Perhaps his idea was to try and get her out of his system before he married Fiona.

But if it was, it still didn't explain why he'd insisted on a ring.

And surely Fiona wouldn't be a party to another woman wearing his ring, even if it meant nothing...

Or would she?

If she wanted Rafe badly enough, and agreeing to do things on his terms was the only way she could get him, she might.

Madeleine sighed and, her mind shifting focus, began to consider things from another angle.

All this time she had blamed Rafe for treating Fiona so badly, for reneging on the bargain he had made. But perhaps if he hadn't met *her* when he did, if they hadn't become lovers, he would have gone ahead and married Fiona.

She wouldn't have deliberately taken another woman's man, but she had never asked if there was anyone else, merely presumed that there wasn't. So could part of the blame be laid at her door? It was a most unsettling thought. She had more than enough to feel guilty about.

Making a tremendous effort, she tried to clear away the confusion in her mind and decide what her course of action should be. Was she going to run at the first real opportunity? Or was she going to go down the bitter-sweet path of staying with Rafe whenever he wanted her?

No, she thought violently, with the shadow of Fiona still in the background, she couldn't do that.

But loving him as she did, could she find enough strength to walk away from him?

She still hadn't reached a decision when, carrying two gift-wrapped packages, Rafe returned to ask, 'All set to go?'

Wondering if one of them was for Fiona, she rose to her feet to accompany him.

They were escorted by Brand, who, at the door, wished her, 'A very happy birthday,' and put a small box wrapped in silver paper into her hand. She thanked him with a smile that made him her slave for life.

Outside a few flakes of snow were drifting down, adding a touch of magic to the Christmassy scene, as Rafe steered her through a busy throng of shoppers to where the taxi was waiting.

'Shall I take that?' He relieved her of Brand's gift and put it, along with the two small packages he was carrying, into the capacious pockets of his leather jacket.

As soon as they were settled in and underway, she found herself having to stifle a yawn. Wondering muzzily whether

her tiredness was due to champagne or jet lag, she fought against the urge to sleep.

But it was a slow journey back to Denver Court and when Rafe, seeing her eyelids start to droop, gathered her close, all she could feel was relief.

Comfortable, safe, at home, she let go and drifted into oblivion, her head on his shoulder.

When they reached their destination and drove into the forecourt she awakened naturally and, sitting up, looked around her.

There was a light covering of snow and it was still falling, whirling past like handfuls of thrown confetti, obliterating the tyre tracks of vehicles almost as soon as they were made.

She felt refreshed by the sleep. All the previous muzziness had vanished, and her head was clear.

'Feeling better now?' Rafe asked.

'Yes, I'm fine.'

'That's good. Later we're having dinner at the Starlight Room.'

When they had put on their coats and the bags and boxes had been retrieved, Rafe paid the driver, gave him a handsome tip and watched him sketch a salute as he drove away.

They crossed the foyer, with its Christmas tree and festive trimmings, and took the lift up to the penthouse. As it always had in the past, it made her nerves tighten and left her stomach behind.

When the doors slid open, juggling with the various packages, Rafe let them into his service flat and flicked on the lights.

With a little ache in her heart she realised that nothing had changed. It was the same as it had been when Rafe had brought her here more than a year ago, except that the patio and garden area now had a white coverlet.

Watching the snow falling softly, Madeleine found herself

thinking back to how pleasant it had been the summer she had known it, how they had drunk red wine and made love in the sun. How happy they had been.

Knowing that was a dangerous path to go down, she tried to push away the memory, but it crowded in, swamping her, overwhelming her.

Once again she could feel his beloved weight and the warmth of the sun on her face, smell his aftershave and the patio roses, taste the smooth dry wine on her tongue and the sweetness of his kisses…

'Penny for your thoughts.'

'What?'

As she turned away from the window, he said, 'You were miles away. Your face was soft and absorbed, and *waiting*, as though in your mind you were being made love to.'

Watching the hot colour pour into her cheeks, he said, 'It looks as though I hit the nail on the head. So who was it? Me?'

When she bit her lip and stayed silent, he shrugged. 'So long as it's turned you on, it doesn't really matter who it was.'

He carried the Harrod's packages through to the guest bedroom and dropped them onto a chaise longue covered in peach-coloured velvet, before helping her off with her coat.

At that moment the phone in the living room rang.

'If you'll excuse me, this might be the call I've been waiting for.' He went out, closing the door behind him.

Fiona? Madeleine wondered.

She was glad there wasn't a bedside phone. Had there been, she might have felt tempted to eavesdrop. But Rafe refused to have phones in the bedrooms on the grounds that, whether he was sleeping or making love, he didn't want to be disturbed.

Recalling what he'd said about having dinner at the Starlight Room, and realising she would need to get organised, she began to unpack the Harrod's parcels.

First of all the various toiletries, which she put into a toilet bag patterned with silvery-blue dolphins. Then, with a little quiver of excitement, she took out the evening dress Rafe had selected, and draped it over one of the button-backed chairs.

A simple ankle-length sheath with a modest neckline it was—on the surface—the kind of thing she might have chosen for herself. What made it totally different, apart from the designer label, was the superb cut, the colour and the material.

It was a clear, light gold—a colour she wouldn't normally have dreamt of buying—and it was made of silk chiffon.

As she had started to shake her head, the saleslady had said, 'It would look beautiful on, and madam certainly has the figure for it.'

'Try it,' Rafe had urged.

Soft and insubstantial as gossamer, it had slipped over her head and settled into place, a silken caress that clung lovingly to every curve.

The sight of herself in the full-length mirror had kept her momentarily rooted to the spot. She had never imagined she could look like this.

When, her knees feeling weak, she emerged from the fitting room, after one long look Rafe had said simply, 'Yes, we'll take it.'

As soon as a matching wrap and evening bag, strappy sandals and silk stockings had been purchased, he nodded his satisfaction. 'That's the most important part done. Now the lingerie department…'

The ivory silk undies, delicate as a spider's web, would have been any woman's dream, as would the dainty satin and lace nightdress and negligee he had picked out.

She had always bought pretty, feminine lingerie because it boosted her morale, but she had never aspired to anything in that class, and the thought of *wearing* such beautiful things had caused a shivery sensation to run up and down her spine.

Now looking down at them, she felt that same shiver of anticipation.

But she mustn't feel like this, she warned herself sharply. She mustn't allow herself to be lulled into meekly accepting what he wanted to give. She mustn't let herself enjoy the things he was almost forcing on her, perhaps just to salve his conscience.

If he had a conscience.

But after the way he had treated Fiona she couldn't believe he had.

Looking down at the ring on her finger, she wondered, not for the first time, how she could keep on loving a man like Rafe. A man who could treat one woman so badly, and coerce another into wearing his ring for 'the look of the thing' and for just as long as it suited him.

If he'd loved her it would have been different. Even if he hadn't intended to marry her it wouldn't have mattered. If he'd loved her, she could somehow have lived with that.

But he didn't love her. He might *want* her, but he didn't love her.

She must remember that and not weaken.

And if she stayed, she *would* weaken. So somehow she must find the will to leave him, and soon.

If she went back to Hethersage she would be trapped there, so it had to be tonight.

Judging by what he'd said in the taxi, he was confident that she would stay. So his guard would be down. With a bit of luck she could be in a cab and away before he missed her. Surely either Eve or Noel would be there to pay the fare. But if the worst came to the worst and they were both out, she would find some way of coping.

Feeling the need for action now she had made up her mind,

she decided to shower and start to get ready. Removing the ring and the small gold hoops from her ears, she put them on the bedside cabinet and took the pins from her hair. There was still no sign of Rafe as she gathered up the toilet bag and the negligee and headed for the *en suite* bathroom.

CHAPTER NINE

WHEN she emerged some fifteen minutes later, fresh and perfumed, the negligee whispering around her, her long hair a gleaming cloud around her shoulders, he was lounging on the chaise longue.

Stretching out a lazy hand, he pulled her down beside him in a proprietary manner, and nuzzled his face against the side of her neck. 'You smell delightful.'

Her heart starting to beat faster, she sat stiff and still, telling herself she mustn't weaken. If he was at all ruffled by her lack of response, he didn't show it.

Indicating the four small packages assembled by his side, he said, 'There's plenty of time to open your birthday presents before we need to get ready.'

Selecting the nearest, he handed it to her.

The gift was the one Carl Brand had given her and, stripping off the paper, she found a silver filigree case that opened to disclose a pale, padded lining with a dozen slots to hold rings. It was obviously an expensive item, and she realised that to give her something so valuable he must regard Rafe as an extremely good customer.

The second gift was a handmade card and a bottle of perfume from Katie. Absurdly touched that, as well as going to so much trouble over the card, the little girl had remem-

bered that *Janvier* was her favourite perfume, Madeleine had
to bite her lip.

Diane's gift was matching soap and bath oil.

'How did they know it was my birthday?'

'Apparently Katie once asked you when it was, and she'd
remembered. That was one of the reasons she wanted to see
you.' Rafe smiled at her. 'But when I told her I was planning
to take you into town to buy your present, and that I had
wanted it to be a surprise, she and Diane agreed not to say
anything over lunch.'

He picked up the final package and, handing it to her, said,
'Happy birthday.'

The wrapping off, she saw it was the midnight-blue case
with Marshall Brand in gold on the lid.

As, a tightness in her chest, she sat staring down at it, he
asked, 'Aren't you going to open it?'

When her fingers, so sure at most times, fumbled ineffec-
tually, he took it from her and used his thumbnail to flick
open the lid.

Madeleine caught her breath involuntarily.

Lying on the velvet lining was a beautiful gold necklace
set with six sparkling aquamarines. Alongside it were
matching drop earrings that were equally lovely.

Watching her as she sat staring at the exquisite set in stunned
silence, Rafe suggested crisply, 'Suppose you try them on?'

Her fingers far from steady, she fastened the earrings to her
delicate lobes.

Head tilted a little to one side, he studied her. 'Perfect. Now
for the necklace…'

As she made to pick it up, he said, 'No, let me.' Taking it
from the case, he moved behind her and, having fastened it
around her slender neck, bent to touch his lips to her nape.

She was still quivering from that caress when he turned her
so that he could look at her.

'Yes… Though for the best effect they should be displayed against the skin.'

He brushed aside the ivory satin of the negligee.

The necklace felt smooth and cool against the warmth of her flesh, and through the dressing-table mirror she could see that the aquamarines were exactly the same colour as her eyes.

Remembering Rafe's comment, just for an instant she was overcome by emotion.

He saw that emotion and, misinterpreting it, said coldly, 'I suppose you're going to tell me that in spite of the ring, you feel like a kept woman.'

Angry that she'd weakened, she retorted, 'How else would you expect me to feel?'

He got up, his jaw tight. 'Well, if that's the case, I may as well have my money's worth.'

His hands beneath her elbows, he lifted her to her feet and, unfastening the belt of her negligee, slipped it from her shoulders. As it fell in a satin puddle at her feet he swept her up in his arms, carried her to the king-sized bed and laid her down.

Then quickly, but with no appearance of haste, he discarded his clothes and, like some sultan, stood looking down at her.

She was beautiful, with a slender body, long, balletic limbs and subtle curves.

But she was more than merely beautiful.

A great deal more.

That warm, generous mouth and those thickly lashed almond eyes made her a fascinating combination of wholesome girl-next-door and the exotic.

Her long blonde hair spreading over the pillow, and the blue-green aquamarines sparkling and glittering like a sunlit tropical sea against her creamy, flawless skin, added to that exoticism.

Slowly he ran a single finger from her throat to her navel, and back again.

Her heart thudding against her ribs, she stared up at him, her wide eyes fixed on his face.

Holding her gaze, he traced the curve of her breast and heard her breathing quicken as he circled the velvety nipple.

Knowing it would be useless, she made no attempt to fight him, but neither would she yield, she thought fiercely.

As though he could read her mood, he smiled a little grimly. When he moved to join her on the bed, she stiffened involuntarily. He might be aroused enough to just take her.

Perhaps, for one angry moment, he had intended to simply take, to impose his will, but it wasn't in his nature to force any woman.

Stretching out beside her, he touched his lips to hers in a slow, unhurried kiss, as though he was quite happy to spend the rest of the evening doing nothing else.

When her lips quivered and parted beneath his, he let his hands move over her, touching her as though she was some priceless treasure, more precious than the aquamarines she was wearing.

The caring, the tenderness, wrapped streamers of warmth around her heart and melted her resistance as easily as the heat from a candle flame melted wax.

His mouth followed his hands, leisurely, caressingly, finding the most sensitive areas. When he reached the soft skin of her inner thigh and began to flick with his tongue, she shuddered and made a little sound in her throat.

Softly, he murmured, 'Just lie there and enjoy what I'm going to do to you.'

Already on fire with need, she couldn't have done any other. He could feel her surrender to the sensations, surrender to him, as he teased and probed, building up the heat until pleasure exploded inside her and, her back arching, she clutched at the sheet she was lying on.

Still he didn't stop. Making the need build again and again.

Satisfying it again and again. Every time she knew there could be no more, there was more. When she finally felt his weight, she thought dazedly that she had nothing left to give, nothing left to gain.

But he proved her wrong.

Then common sense kicked in. Once again she had given in to him, allowed herself to be seduced, manipulated, when she should have been strong.

He might have *seemed* tender, caring, but it had merely been a show, and, while she couldn't deny how much pleasure he had given her, it had solved nothing. Altered nothing.

As though her thoughts had disturbed him, he stirred and lifted himself away. Then, sitting on the edge of the bed, he leaned over to kiss her lightly.

'It's about time we were moving.'

As she raised her hands, intending to take off the earrings and necklace, he stopped her. 'I want you to wear them…' Though he spoke softly, there was a steely edge to his tone.

He reached for the ring and, his expression precluding any argument, slipped it back on her finger. 'And your ring.'

Realising it was useless to argue, she agreed, 'Very well.'

She could get either Eve or Noel to return the jewellery and her unwanted finery to Rafe, and pick up her own things.

Watching him pad barefoot to the other bathroom, she thought, not for the first time, what a magnificent male animal he was. The lean hips and waist, the broad shoulders and elegant line of his spine, could have belonged to a Michelangelo statue. While his carriage, the way he held his head, spoke of a natural self-confidence, an innate authority.

Yet, if Diane was correct, he could so well have ended up weak and psychologically damaged. But while he appeared to be neither, he had no scruples about the way he treated women, Madeleine thought as she set about getting ready for the evening. But was that because, having been rejected by his mother, he was getting his own back on females in general?

That might explain his cruelty to Fiona.

But it didn't necessarily excuse it.

She had just finished putting the finishing touches to her make-up when Rafe reappeared wearing an immaculate dinner jacket, his seal-dark hair neatly brushed, his jaw freshly shaven.

Feeling, as always, the pull of his magnetism, she thought how devastatingly handsome he looked in evening clothes, and just how much she loved him.

Her breathing constricted, she wished she didn't have to leave him, wished that things could have been different, even while she knew how hopeless such a wish was.

Standing stock still, his head tilted a little to one side, he looked her over from head to toe, taking in the clinging dress with its matching gold sandals, the greeny-blue gems glittering at her ears and throat, the elegant knot of hair and the discreet touch of make-up.

Unnerved by the sheer intensity of his gaze, she asked awkwardly, 'Do I look all right?'

He smiled, the lopsided smile that never failed to touch her heart, and, lifting her hand to his lips, said huskily, 'My love, you look enchanting.'

Shaken to the core by the endearment, she was still standing motionless when he picked up her wrap and put it around her shoulders. 'As we won't be leaving the building, that's all you'll need.'

For what lay in store she could have done with a coat, but, unable to argue, she collected her small, gold evening bag and, on legs that felt unsteady, accompanied him out of the apartment.

As they went through an archway at the far end of the hallway and made their way along a series of marble galleries, she forced herself to think, to try and form a plan of escape.

Would it make sense to come back the same way? Or

would it be quicker to find another exit on the other side of the building?

As she was unsure where the exits were, or how easy it would be to get a taxi at any of them, it might be safer to stick with what she knew.

But it could take longer. Which would give Rafe a better chance of catching her up. For she was sure that when he missed her, he would come after her.

Though as soon as she was in a taxi and underway, she would be relatively safe. Of course, he would know only too well where she was heading, but once she got to Eve's she would be home and dry.

Then, somehow, she would put the last few days out of her mind and start to live the rest of her life. A life in which Rafe played no part.

She took a quick, ragged breath as the thought of never seeing him again cut into her heart like a knife. But it was the best way.

The only way.

Lifting her chin, she glanced up and found with a shock that his eyes were fixed on her face.

'Looking forward to the evening?' he asked, his voice casual.

'Oh, yes, enormously.' Wondering if she'd made the mistake of sounding too enthusiastic, she added, 'I've always dreamt of dancing and dining at the Starlight Room.'

'Then I'm delighted to have chosen the right venue,' he said smoothly.

The Starlight Room was, as its name suggested, a rooftop restaurant. It lay at the far end of the complex beyond a large skating rink, which in the summer became an open-air swimming pool.

Two storeys up and circular, an exotic mushroom on a thick stalk, the Starlight Room's projecting windows provided magnificent views over London.

Madeleine had seen it from a distance, but never yet been

inside, and as they stepped into the lift at the base she felt a little flutter of excitement.

As soon as they entered the luxurious foyer, a young man wearing immaculate evening dress wished them, 'Good evening, sir, madam,' and took Madeleine's wrap.

A moment later a larger-than-life *maître d'* appeared, who greeted Rafe by name, and with some ceremony led them through to the restaurant proper.

It was every bit as Arabian Nights and glamorous as she could have wished, with a table to each window and a central dance floor.

The majority of the tables were already occupied by a top-notch clientele wearing dinner jackets and evening gowns. The scent of French perfume hung on the air, and there were enough jewels on display to restock the Rue de la Paix.

It was the kind of gathering where ordinarily Madeleine might have felt out of her depth, even slightly intimidated by such a display of wealth. But with a little thrill of pride, she knew herself to be one of the best dressed women there. And on the arm of one of the most strikingly handsome, imposing men.

On a raised dais, like the hub of a wheel, a small orchestra was playing a Latin-American dance number, a soft, romantic tune, with a shiver of maracas.

Above them, the ceiling was a dome of indigo studded with lighted stars, and through the windows she could see snow was still falling gently, adding its own touch of magic to the scene.

Instead of a table for two, as she had imagined, they were shown to a table set for six. She glanced at Rafe, expecting him to point out the mistake, but he said nothing.

As soon as they had been seated, a waiter appeared with a magnum of champagne in an ice bucket and queried deferentially, 'Shall I open it, sir?'

'No, not yet, thanks.'

As the man moved away, Rafe turned to Madeleine, and asked, 'Shall we make the first part of your dream come true?'

Leaving her bag on the table, she went into his arms. He held her lightly but firmly, his spread hand at her waist steady, his chin just brushing the top of her head.

It was more than a year since they had danced together, and as they moved as one to the haunting rhythm she thought how happy she had been then.

Even now he'd contrived to make it lovely and romantic, and had things been different she could have danced the night away in his arms and been utterly content.

When the Latin-American medley came to an end with a scattering of applause, they started to make their way back to the table.

All at once, catching sight of who was sitting there, Madeleine's jaw dropped and she stopped dead in her tracks.

'Your mouth's open,' Rafe murmured in her ear, 'and it's giving me ideas I can't follow through in a public place.' He used a finger to lift her chin.

Then, an arm at her waist, he urged her towards the table, where, looking in their direction and smiling, were four people—Eve and Dave, Noel and, presumably, Zoe, all dressed up to the nines.

The four rose at their approach, and there was a smiling chorus of, 'Happy birthday,' before, gladness in her voice, Eve exclaimed, 'Just look at you!' and leaned forward to kiss Madeleine's cheek.

When Noel had followed suit, the three men shook hands with great cordiality.

How had Rafe and Noel come to be on such good terms? Madeleine wondered dazedly as, his glance moving from her to Rafe, Noel said with formal politeness, 'May I introduce Zoe Denholm…?

'Zoe, this is our lifelong friend, Madeleine Knight, and—' taking note of the aquamarine on Madeleine's finger '—her fiancé, Rafe Lombard.'

As they exchanged handshakes, Zoe said pleasantly, 'It's nice to meet you both.'

Looking at Madeleine's thunderstruck face, Eve turned to Rafe and remarked with satisfaction, 'It's quite obvious that you managed to keep the whole thing a secret.'

'It wasn't too hard.' Pulling out Madeleine's chair, he added with a wry smile, 'Her mind was on other things, wasn't it, sweetheart?'

When, still speechless, she sank onto it, he dropped a little kiss on the top of her head, a gesture that made Eve sigh sentimentally.

As the others resumed their seats, Zoe said to Madeleine, 'I've heard a great deal about you. I understand my darling idiot is hoping to bribe you to sing his praises.'

Seeing the fond, appreciative look she gave Noel, Madeleine found her voice and ventured, 'It doesn't appear to be necessary.'

'It isn't.'

As Noel began to preen himself, she gave him a dig in the ribs with her elbow. 'I know him much too well to be taken in.'

'I say, steady on there.' He looked aggrieved.

Smiling, she added, 'But I still love him,' and earned herself a squeeze.

'Let me see that.' Reaching across the table, Eve took Madeleine's hand and studied the ring. 'Wowee…and then some!

'I must confess that when Rafe and I first talked and he told me how things were and said he needed my help, I was a bit worried. But now, seeing how well it's all worked out, I couldn't be happier…'

What kind of lies had he told Eve to get both her and Noel so effortlessly on his side? Madeleine wondered numbly.

Fairly bubbling over with excitement, Eve added, 'And to put the gilt on the gingerbread, the Starlight Room! The mere idea of coming here to dine took my breath away.

'Though I'm afraid we won't be able to stay and dance. As soon as the meal's over we have to fly. We have first-row seats for *Serenade*, courtesy of Zoe, who is one of the co-writers.'

At a signal from Rafe, the waiter hurried over and, having opened the champagne with a satisfying pop, filled six flutes with the still-smoking wine.

After a toast to, 'The birthday girl,' they sipped champagne while they looked at the menu and ordered.

To Madeleine the whole thing seemed unreal, and, feeling as though she was caught up in some virtual-reality role-play, she chose at random.

When the waiter had gone, Eve and Noel each produced a nicely wrapped gift for her to open.

There was a bottle of her favourite hand and body lotion from Eve and Dave, and a luxurious box of chocolates from Noel and Zoe.

When she'd thanked them all, Dave, a nice-looking man with short brown hair and blue eyes, cleared his throat and glanced around. 'Without wishing to steal anyone's thunder, I've a question I've been going to ask Eve, and as tonight is somewhat special it seemed the right time to ask it.'

Taking her hand and holding it, he said simply, 'Will you marry me?'

'This madness much be catching,' Noel remarked into the momentary silence.

Clearly knocked off balance, Eve stammered, 'But I thought… I—I mean…I wasn't even sure you were happy living with me… Lately you've been so…so offhand.'

'Call it my last-ditch attempt to stay free. Like most males, I suppose, I was wary of committing myself, scared of being tied down.' He smiled quietly. 'But after that last row, I knew if I lost you I'd regret it for the rest of my life. So I went out and bought this…'

Fumbling in his pocket, he took out a small box and opened the lid. 'I'm afraid it won't look much against Madeleine's ring…'

'It's beautiful,' Eve said, her face all soft and glowing, and held out her hand so he could put the diamond twist onto her finger.

'Gosh, it even fits!' she exclaimed in wonder.

'So it should. I borrowed one of your dress rings to make sure I got the size right.'

'Darling.' She smiled mistily.

'Darling yourself.' He leaned towards her to kiss her on the lips.

There was a little burst of congratulations, then Rafe said, 'This calls for more champagne,' and refilled the glasses so they could drink a toast to the newly engaged pair.

On a high, the couples talked and laughed while they ate a superb meal, and if Rafe said little, and Madeleine even less, no one seemed to notice.

Then just as they were finishing coffee, a waiter appeared and murmured that their taxi was waiting.

In a moment, they had thanked their host and were on their feet and ready to leave. Stooping to give Madeleine a hug, Eve said, 'Ring me some time over the holiday and we'll have a good long talk.'

'Enjoy the show.' Rafe shook hands all round as they said their goodnights before hurrying off.

Sitting still as a statue, Madeleine watched them go and felt empty, as hollow inside as a ghost. Now it was too late she wondered if she'd done the right thing by keeping quiet.

Instead of letting them walk away believing everything was fine, should she have pricked the pretty bubble? Admitted how Rafe had treated her? Admitted just how fake her 'engagement' was?

If it had just been Eve and Noel, she might have done. Might have asked for their help. But as things were she couldn't have blurted it out in front of them all. Couldn't have blighted their evening.

Had Rafe been relying on that when he'd set up this birthday dinner?

Or, after the way she'd meekly got into his car at the Denaught, did he genuinely believe she wouldn't leave him?

If it was the latter, it showed a fair degree of arrogance on his part.

For a moment she wished she'd sent it all up in his face. But she couldn't have spoiled Dave's proposal and Eve's moment of glory, her radiant happiness…

'Would you like to dance?' Rafe asked, suddenly a polite stranger.

Squaring her shoulders, Madeleine shook her head. 'But I'd like to know what you told Eve to get her on your side.'

'The truth.'

'She already knew the truth.'

Rafe's green eyes flashed. 'She only knew what she'd heard from you, and that wasn't the truth.'

'If you think—'

He laid a finger on her lips. 'It's high time we set the score straight, but we'll need to go back to the flat and talk openly and honestly.'

'I'm not going back with you,' she said fiercely. If she went back with him she didn't trust herself not to weaken. 'I want to leave.'

'If you still want to leave when we've finished talking, I'll put you in a taxi and pay for a hotel for as long as you need one.

'But first, as it's your birthday, let's have one more dance.'

Rising to his feet, he held out his hand.

After a momentary hesitation, she put hers into it and let him lead her onto the dance floor.

The band were playing an old Jerome Kern tune, a slow foxtrot, dreamy and smoochy, and he held her close, his cheek against her hair.

But while part of her longed to give in to the magic, on-edge and needing to get to the bottom of Eve and Noel's volte-face, she could only be pleased when it was over.

As soon as he'd paid the bill and collected her wrap, they set off back to the flat.

It felt strange to be returning there when she had been so determined not to go back, and she wondered uneasily if she was doing the right thing.

Suppose this was just another trick to get her where he wanted her? He was good at tricks.

Her steps slowed and faltered. 'You promise that after we've talked you won't stop me leaving?'

He urged her forward. 'When you've heard me out, if you still want to leave, I promise I won't stop you.'

She sighed despairingly. What could he possibly say that would alter the situation enough to make her want to stay?

When they reached the flat, he suggested smoothly, 'While I put a match to the fire, why don't you change into something more comfortable?'

It suited her to get changed, and she went through to the bedroom without demure.

Her first act was to take off the ring, the necklace and the earrings, and place them safely in the case. That done, she put the beautiful dress and its accessories in the walk-in wardrobe, and donned the suit, boots and gold earrings she had worn earlier in the day.

If Rafe had been hoping she would change into her

negligee, she thought with a glimmer of humour, he was in for a big disappointment.

When she returned to the living room, a log fire was blazing cheerfully in the wide grate and two glasses, a bottle of brandy and a bottle of port with a paper napkin round the neck were waiting on a low table.

As she hesitated in the doorway, a gleam of irony in his green eyes, Rafe studied her suit and boots, but made no comment.

He'd taken off his jacket and black bow-tie, and the top two buttons of his evening shirt were undone, exposing the strong column of his throat. His sleeves were rolled up to his elbows, showing muscular arms lightly sprinkled with dark hair.

A smut adorned one cheek. As if her glance had made him conscious of it, he raised a hand to brush it away, and finished up with a smear. Without thinking, following her instincts, she reached for a napkin and touched her tongue to the corner to dampen it before wiping away the smear. Then, realising what she'd done, and annoyed with herself for doing it, she took a step backwards and, dropping the napkin onto the table as though it was red-hot, muttered, 'That was stupid.'

'No, it was sweet.' He took the hand that had held the napkin and raised it to his lips.

Flustered, looking anywhere but at him, she sat down in the nearest chair.

A second later, squatting in front of her, he began to remove her boots.

'I'll need them when I go,' she protested,

'*If* you go.'

Trying to regain ground, she insisted, '*When.*'

He shrugged. 'Have it your way, but if you keep them on in here you won't feel the good of them.'

For just a moment she softened at his care and attention, then, reminding herself she couldn't afford to, she frowned at him.

To her surprise he burst out laughing.

Without for a moment intending to, she found herself smiling back.

'That's better,' he applauded. Adding, 'Now then, port and brandy?'

'A small one, please.'

When he'd passed her a port and brandy and poured a brandy for himself, he took a seat opposite and, looking pointedly at her bare finger, said, 'You've taken off your ring.'

'Yes.' Then in a rush, 'I never wanted to wear it in the first place. I don't understand why you insisted on buying it.'

Lightly, he said, 'I believe in doing most things once, and I've never had the pleasure of buying an engagement ring before.'

'You bought Fiona a ring.' There—it was out.

'What makes you think that?'

When she hesitated, he said, 'I thought we were going to talk openly and honestly.'

After a moment, Madeleine admitted, 'She came to the clinic one night and asked to see me. She told me she was your fiancée. That you were engaged…'

'We were *never* engaged.' His answer was categoric.

'She was wearing a ring. A square-cut emerald.'

'Her grandmother gave her a square-cut emerald—a family heirloom, so to speak—for her twenty-first birthday. You can ask Harriet if you don't believe me.'

'Oh…'

'When Fiona told you she was my fiancée, what did you say?'

Remembrance of the hurt and humiliation she had suffered caused a spasm of pain to tighten Madeleine's face. 'I told her I had no idea you had a fiancée.'

'Was she a bitch to you?' he asked quietly.

'Not really. She said she didn't blame *me* in particular. That women threw themselves at you, so it was no wonder you took advantage, and if it hadn't been me it would have been some other woman.'

His green eyes narrowed. 'What else did she say?'

'That now she was home again it had to stop. You were hers. I remarked that if you were that kind of man I was surprised she still wanted you.

'She said, "Oh I want him all right, so if you were thinking of suggesting that I set him free, forget it… For one thing he doesn't want out, and for another, we have a bargain."'

'What kind of bargain?' Rafe asked curtly.

'She told me that her father, who didn't think a woman could successfully run a business, had been concerned about her future, and that he'd agreed to leave the whole of Charn Industries to you if you would marry her and take care of her. She added, "Rafe and I had been lovers for some time, so he was quite happy to make it legal."'

His green eyes glacial, he demanded, 'And you believed that?'

'Wasn't it the truth?'

He slammed his glass down on the table. 'No, it wasn't. Fiona and I were never lovers, and I never made any kind of bargain with my godfather.'

Though it was obvious he was quietly *furious*, she said steadily, 'But you inherited the Charn empire when he died.'

'Yes. Christopher had always intended to leave it to me. But after putting a considerable sum of money in trust for Fiona, he hit a rocky patch, and for the last few years of his life he was faced with severe financial problems.

'By the time he admitted the truth and asked me for help, his "empire" was teetering on the brink of collapse. It was only my financial support that kept it going…'

Was that what Diane had meant when she'd said, 'When Christopher ran into trouble, Rafe stood by him through thick and thin'?

'By the time he died,' Rafe went on flatly, 'I'd put so much capital into it that the whole kit and caboodle virtually belonged to me anyway.'

She had no doubt at all that he spoke the truth.

CHAPTER TEN

DEVASTATED by the realisation that she had been misjudging him all this time, she stared at him in stricken silence.

Seeing that devastation, Rafe bit back his anger and asked, 'Did Fiona say anything else?'

'That you and she would have been married by then and there wouldn't have been a problem if she hadn't been diagnosed with a rare blood disorder…'

'Go on,' Rafe urged.

The scene still engraved on her mind, Madeleine could clearly remember every word. 'She said, 'I've had to spend long periods in a private clinic, undergoing treatment, which meant Rafe was left alone, and as I say, he's a red-blooded man who needs a woman. Any woman… Then I discovered I was pregnant, which made this last treatment more prolonged and complicated, and in the end I lost the baby.'

A white line around his mouth, Rafe said grimly, 'And you believed that baby was mine?'

'W-well…y-yes,' she stammered. All the shock and distress she had felt evident in her voice, she went on, 'I was horrified to think that we'd been lovers while your fiancée went through such an ordeal…'

Sounding incredulous, he demanded, 'You really believed I could treat both her and you so shabbily?'

'I'm sorry…' The words tailed off at the fury on his face.

With a kind of raging calm, he said, 'Fiona was not my fiancée and the baby certainly wasn't mine. It couldn't *possibly* have been mine. There was never anything between us…'

Then what had made Fiona tell her such a tissue of lies? Madeleine wondered, but before she could ask, Rafe went on, 'Or perhaps I should say there was never anything on *my* part. I always thought of her, and treated her, as a much-loved sister.

'Unfortunately she developed a crush on me. I thought that when I went away to university it would die a natural death. But it didn't.

'When I made it clear that there could never be anything between us, that I just regarded her as a sister, she went completely off the rails and had relationships with several different men. Presumably one of them was the father…' He sighed in frustration.

'I'm sorry…sorry I blamed you…' Helplessly, she added, 'I didn't *want* to believe you could treat a sick woman in that way…'

Then, seeing the expression on his face, 'Or are you going to tell me she hadn't been ill, that that was a lie too?'

'The story about the blood disorder was a lie. But she had been ill…if you can call alcohol and drug dependency being ill. The clinics she was in and out of were alcohol- and drug-rehabilitation centres.' Madeleine gasped at his words.

Rafe went on, 'She got in with the wrong crowd, and before any of us realised she was hooked on drugs. It was an absolute nightmare. Each time she left some clinic and came home, we hoped and prayed she was cured. But each time she slipped back into her old ways. Then when her parents tried to get her to go in again for more treatment there'd be terrible scenes.

'For more than eighteen months Christopher was ill and frail, and even before he died Harriet couldn't cope, so it was up to me to take Fiona back and try to get her settled…'

So that was what Diane had meant when she said, 'The whole family were worried sick about her, though Rafe bore the brunt of it.'

'Do you remember the day I was supposed to pick you up to take you to see the Jonathan Cass pictures, and I couldn't make it?' he pursued.

'Yes, I remember. I'd been worried to death in case anything had happened to you. But you were in a strange mood. Though you must have known I wanted some kind of explanation, you wouldn't give me one.'

'*Couldn't*, rather than *wouldn't*.

'That morning I took Fiona back to the Tyler Rhodes Clinic and tried to get her settled in. At first she seemed calm enough, but after I told her I had to leave she became hysterical and violent.

'I couldn't just abandon her. I felt guilty and partly responsible. If I'd been able to love her in the way she wanted me to, things might have been different. Or if I hadn't gone to live with them in the first place...

'When I tried to call your flat to say I'd be late, she snatched the mobile out of my hand and threw it at the wall. Then after a bitter tirade she ran her nails down my face...'

So that was where the scratches had come from.

'It seems that somehow she'd found out about you, and was out of her mind with jealousy. I won't go into details, but that was one of the worst afternoons of my life.'

Feeling ashamed and sorry that she hadn't been more loving and supportive, Madeleine said, 'I wish you'd told me.'

'At the time I felt I couldn't. Though in retrospect I wish I had.'

'If only I'd known the truth I wouldn't have believed Fiona, wouldn't have presumed you'd just been using me and...' Remembering what had happened next, she broke off.

'Sent that email to get your own back?' he suggested bleakly.

'No, not to get my own back.'

His voice rough with anger and frustration, he asked, 'Why didn't you come to me? Why didn't you tell me what Fiona had said? Why, when I came to see what the hell was going on, did you stage that scene with Noel?'

'To save my pride,' she admitted.

'Despite the email, it came as a shock. I could hardly believe my eyes. It made me furiously angry and jealous... Even after Eve told me that you and Noel were like brother and sister, I was—'

'When did she tell you that?' Madeleine broke in.

'When I went to see her at the clinic.'

'What made you go?' Madeleine's voice was soft as she asked the one question that was really important.

'Because of a remark Fiona had made when Harriet mentioned you were coming home, she was convinced that it had been her daughter who was somehow responsible for our break-up. Remembering Noel, I could hardly believe it. But I decided to get to the bottom of things, so I rang Fiona and tackled her about it.

'Though she didn't tell me a fraction of what had been said, she admitted going to see you, admitted that she had claimed to be my fiancée. She said she was bitterly sorry, that she would have confessed sooner if she'd had the nerve.

'After talking to Fiona, I began to wonder about the rest, so I went to see Eve. I presumed she would know the score if anyone did... At first she was distinctly hostile, but when she heard the truth about Fiona things got easier.

'After I'd laid my cards on the table, she opened up and gave me all the information I needed. Including the fact that she was hoping to find a live-in position for you.

'When I told her that Harriet needed a live-in physiotherapist, and was staying with me at the hall, she agreed to help...'

Sighing, he admitted, 'But when I got you there, I didn't handle it very well. In fact that's the understatement of the year. I've been an absolute swine to you. I can't blame you for wanting to go, but I'm hoping you'll stay.'

Madeleine took a deep breath. 'There's something I'd like to ask you.'

'Ask away.'

'It's about Fiona. Diane said she was doing fine, that she'd been given a clean bill of health…'

'That right.'

'But I couldn't help but wonder where she was, what had happened to her…'

'A few weeks after she had been given that clean bill of health she married George Rampling's younger son, Mark, and they went to live in Edinburgh.

'A month ago their little boy was born. No two parents could have been happier, and Harriet and George were absolutely over the moon…'

Dazzled by the light, Madeleine said, 'So that's who they've gone up to Scotland to spend Christmas and New Year with.'

'That's right.'

Watching her face, Rafe asked, 'Does knowing that make it any easier for you to stay? At least for tonight.'

'If I do stay—'

'It will be on your terms,' he broke in quickly. 'I promise I won't try to bulldoze you in any way, and it will give you a chance to think things over. What do you say?'

'Very well,' she said and saw the flicker of relief he couldn't hide.

Getting to her feet, she stifled a yawn. 'I'd like to go to bed.'

'Alone?' he queried.

'Alone.'

Rising, he lifted her hand to his lips. 'Then I'll say goodnight.'

'Goodnight.' She picked up her boots and went.

Rafe had suggested that staying over would provide a chance to think, but, as though both her brain and body had shut down, she felt completely drained and weary, too tired to think.

She changed into her night things like some zombie, and slept as soon as her head touched the pillow.

When she surfaced the next morning, the clock said almost ten-thirty. It was, she realised, Christmas Eve, and decision time.

Before she could begin to think, however, there was a tap at the door, and a second later Rafe's voice queried, 'Ready for some toast and coffee?'

Her heart gave a little leap. Thinking how careful he was being, how circumspect, as though it *mattered* to him, she sat up and answered, 'Please.'

He offloaded a pot of coffee and a jug of warm milk before settling the tray across her knees.

On it, as well as toast, butter and marmalade, was a glass of freshly squeezed orange juice and a perfect hothouse rosebud, its dark red, velvety petals gloriously scented.

The fact that he'd gone to so much trouble touched her heart.

'I was planning to have lunch at the Denaught and fly back to Hethersage Hall this afternoon,' he told her. 'Will you come and spend Christmas there? Simply as a guest.'

When she didn't immediately answer, he suggested, 'Give it some thought while you eat your breakfast.' He turned away, and a moment later the door had closed quietly behind him.

She fought down an urge to call him back.

Having decided he'd made a mistake by bulldozing her, he was being cautious, giving her time, breathing space. She should value that, rather than doing anything impulsive.

While she buttered and ate a slice of toast and drank a cup of coffee, she tried to follow Rafe's suggestion and think.

Though she bitterly regretted not trusting him and ruining

what they might have had, common sense told her that it was no use repining. Nothing could be altered. All she could do was put the past behind her and move forward.

So was she prepared to stay and give him what he wanted? While she loved him, could she cope with knowing he didn't love her?

But she didn't have to make up her mind about that straight away. Spending Christmas at the hall would give her time to think, to decide.

Setting the tray aside, she got out of bed and showered and dressed in record time. Then, putting the rose, the stem of which she'd wrapped in dampened cotton-wool wipes, into her shoulder-bag, she picked up her coat and the case with its precious jewellery, and went through to the living room.

Rafe was standing by the French windows with his back to the room, staring out over the snowy patio. His whole body looked taut, and she could see the tension in his neck and shoulders.

When he turned round slowly and looked at her, she went over to him and handed him the jewel case.

'Does that mean you've decided not to come?'

'No…I…I haven't really decided.'

She saw the flare of hope, before a shutter came down and he asked levelly, 'So the question is, yes or no?'

'You said simply as a guest?'

His eyes on her face, he agreed, 'Yes.'

'Then I'll come.'

His little sigh was audible. 'In that case I'll ask them to bring the car round, and let Jack know roughly what time we'll be back.'

Though there was bright sunshine and a sky of clear, Mediterranean blue, it was a bitterly cold day with a fresh covering of sparkling snow.

Apart from Rafe remarking that it was good flying weather, the drive to the Denaught was accomplished in silence.

After a brief discussion of the menu, and some recommendations on Rafe's part, lunch too was a silent meal.

But where in the past their silences had been comfortable, companionable, now there was a tension between them that stretched like fine wire. Wire that Madeleine wanted to snap.

But she could think of nothing to say.

She was relieved when lunch was over and they were installed in the helicopter and underway. A lot less nervous this time, she would have enjoyed the flight if she hadn't been worrying about the coming hours and days.

In the west the sun had gone down in a blaze of pink and gold, and a blue dusk was just starting to gather as they descended towards the cleared helicopter pad.

Wearing what appeared to be thigh-length rubber boots, Jack was just emerging from the hangar with a gleaming two-seater snowmobile.

When the rotor blades had almost stopped turning Rafe removed his headset and, jumping out, came round to help her out.

'I've a few things to take care of, so Jack will run you back to the house.'

As soon as Madeleine was installed on the passenger seat, Jack handed her a blue helmet. 'If you'd like to put this on, miss… It isn't far, as you know, but I always say, you can't be too careful.'

She thanked him and buckled the strap into place.

When they reached the house the door was opened by a young, round-faced woman with pale blue eyes and sandy hair, who ushered her inside.

'Miss Knight…I'm Annie… I've lit a fire in your flat and left fresh bread and milk in the kitchen. If there's anything else you need, you only have to ask.

'Dinner's at seven-thirty. In the meantime, if you'd like me to bring a nice pot of tea to the living room...?'

'Thank you, Annie, but I think I'll go straight up to the flat.'

As she crossed the hall and made her way upstairs, she felt an odd sense of coming home, as if the old house recognised her presence and welcomed her back.

There was a bright fire burning in the living-room grate, and when Madeleine had put the rose in water and made herself a pot of tea, instead of switching on the light she sat down in the fireglow.

Had she done the right thing in coming back to Hethersage Hall? she wondered. Or should she have been stronger and walked away?

But it was useless to hark back, and too soon to try and think ahead. She would just let go for the present and drift.

The comfort and warmth were soporific, and in spite of her good night's sleep her eyelids gradually closed...

When she awoke, the fire was dying into whitish ash and it was dark apart from a mere glimmer of snowy light coming through the window.

She was just wondering how long she'd slept when the clock on the mantel chimed six-thirty. Time she was getting ready to go down to dinner.

Switching on the light, she went through to the bedroom to shower and change into a midnight-blue sheath, before re-coiling her hair and putting on fresh make-up.

Despite her attempts to stay calm, butterflies were dancing in her stomach as she made her way down to the study and opened the door.

The cosy room was lit by a single standard lamp, and for an instant she thought it was empty. Then she saw Rafe was already there, leaning against the mantel, flickering firelight turning his lean face into a changing mask of bronze and black.

She had the impression that he'd been standing there some time, staring blindly into space.

He glanced up as she came in, and for an instant his face looked taut and tired before a shutter came down and, assuming the role of polite host, he came forward to greet her.

While they had a pre-dinner drink he made polite conversation, and though her heart ached that, having been so close, they should come to this, she followed his lead as best she could.

Though they both tried their hardest, dinner was another uncomfortable meal, and by the time they returned to the study for a nightcap in front of the fire, Madeleine was regretting coming and wondering how soon she could escape to bed.

The curtains hadn't been pulled across the windows and through the diamond-leaded panes she could see that snow was falling.

Into the silence, she remarked, 'It's some time since we had a white Christmas.'

Rafe glanced up from pouring brandy into two goblets. 'The Met Office forecast it.'

'Yes. Noel said so when I was still in Boston.'

'What made you decide to come back to England?'

'When I heard Eve's voice I knew I was homesick.'

'You asked her opinion on whether or not you should marry Alan.' It was a statement not a question.

Madeleine sighed. 'Eve's wise. She said the mere fact that I *had* to ask her opinion proved I didn't love him enough. And of course she was quite right.'

Rafe's eyes met and held hers, as he said quietly, 'I had hoped at one time that you might love me…'

Feeling as though her chest was being constricted, she admitted, 'I did.'

It was his turn to sigh. 'If I'd asked you to marry me then, would you have done?'

She hesitated, before saying in a rush, 'Yes, if I'd been sure you loved me.'

'Oh, yes, I loved you. The instant I saw your face, it was like being socked on the jaw. Rocked back on my heels, I tried to tell myself that what I felt might just be lust, but even then I knew it was love.

'I didn't know you, didn't know what went on inside your head, how your mind worked, what made you happy, what made you sad. I didn't know you had a sense of humour, or that you liked children. I didn't know you had courage and compassion, and not a nasty bone in your body. All I knew was that you were the woman I'd been waiting for. The woman I wanted to marry. I had planned to propose to you in Paris, to take you to the Rue de la Paix to choose a ring...'

Her heart seemed to turn over in her breast.

'That's why I was so devastated when I saw you with Noel. I didn't want to believe it. I might not have, if I hadn't known that all through our relationship you'd been hiding something.'

When she made no attempt to deny it, he went on, 'Every unexplained absence made me wonder if you were seeing another man. Were you?'

'No.'

'Then why all the secrecy? Why wouldn't you tell me where you went?' His frustration evident, he added, 'I still don't know.'

'I went to the Pastures Nursing Home to see my mother,' Madeleine blurted out. 'She'd been in a coma for more than a year. She was injured in the same gas explosion that killed Colin.'

He looked up sharply. 'Why didn't you tell me?'

Her voice unsteady, she admitted, 'Because I felt so guilty...'

'Guilty?'

'Guilty that she was there… Guilty that Colin had died… Guilty that I hadn't really loved him…' Her eyes filled with tears.

Rafe reached out and took her hand. 'Tell me,' he said quietly. 'Start at the beginning and tell me everything.'

When she had herself under control, she began tonelessly, 'Colin was a very nice-looking man and a well-respected tutor. When he first took an interest in me I was flattered.

'I enjoyed his company and what I saw then as his maturity, and, imagining myself in love, I agreed to marry him. Perhaps I was looking for a father figure, I don't know…

'As soon as I got my degree, we were married at a register office. He'd been sharing a small flat with a male colleague, so we moved in with my mother while we looked for a place of our own. Mum and he got on well together, and we were still there when the accident happened…'

'You weren't involved?'

Madeleine shook her head. 'No. I was out shopping.'

'Go on.'

'We'd only been married a short time when I realised I'd made a terrible mistake. I started to feel trapped, and that made me on-edge. We began to have minor quarrels, tiffs over things that didn't really matter.'

Her voice wobbled a little, and Rafe gave her hand a squeeze.

After a moment, she went on, 'On Saturdays, when Mum and I did the week's grocery shopping, Colin used to come with us…'

Rafe raised an eyebrow. 'Most men detest that kind of shopping.'

'He'd been a bachelor for a long time and he'd grown fussy about what he ate… Afterwards we'd all have lunch together at Bennets—the only place Colin would go to.'

'Go on.'

'The explosion happened just before lunch time on a Saturday. If we'd followed our usual routine we would have all been out. But at breakfast that morning, when Colin complained about the marmalade I snapped at him, and we ended up quarrelling yet again.

'I wanted some breathing space, and that must have been obvious to Mum, because she suggested that I went shopping alone while Colin helped her finish the living room she'd been redecorating.

'A new hearth had just been put in, and they discovered afterwards that a gas pipe leading to the log-effect fire had been fractured, which must have caused a build-up of gas behind the tiling. Colin was putting up bookshelves next to the fireplace... Using an electric drill...

'I got back to find the house had been wrecked and Mum and Colin had been taken to hospital. Colin was dead when I got there.'

Rafe saw the numbness of despair on her face.

'So all this time you've been blaming yourself.'

'I was to blame.'

'Don't be foolish,' he said gently. 'It was an accident waiting to happen. If the three of you had gone shopping and had lunch out as usual, it would still have happened sooner or later...'

His rational explanation seemed to help clear her mind, and made her see the scenario differently. For some reason the inevitability of the accident had never occurred to her.

Rafe went on, 'And, when it's too late, a lot of people must discover they've made a mistake and married the wrong person. It's not something to blame yourself for.'

As she felt the weight of guilt easing, he asked, 'What about your mother?'

'She died a few days after we split up.'

'Dear God,' he muttered.

'If she'd still been alive I would never have gone to the States. As it was, I felt I had nothing left. I wanted to get away, to put all the pain and sadness behind me. I soon discovered it wasn't possible…'

'No.'

There was a long silence, before Rafe continued, 'When you went I told myself I was glad. The further away the better. But I found I couldn't let go. I had to know what you were doing, how you were. When I learnt you were coming home, it was with mixed emotions. Then after I'd talked to Eve and discovered that the whole charade had been in response to Fiona's lies, that it had been she and Noel who had suggested the "other man" scenario, at first all I could feel was relief—'

'There's something I don't understand,' Madeleine broke in. 'If you already knew the truth about Noel and me, why were you so horrible to me? Why did you talk about reparation?'

'After the first flood of relief, anger kicked in. I was furious with you for not telling me about Fiona, furious with you for believing her lies, for not trusting me…

'I just went mad. I blamed your lack of trust for all the pain and anguish, for losing us more than a year of our lives…'

If only that were all that had been lost.

'Now the only thing I can do is apologise for the way I treated you…'

If only she *had* trusted him, instead of just becoming an obsession, something he wanted to free himself from, she might have kept his love.

Her eyes sparkled like jewels as tears welled up and splashed down her cheeks.

He rose as if to comfort her, then, as though he'd had second thoughts, he sat down again and passed her a spotless handkerchief.

'Thank you,' she mumbled. She had just finished mopping her face and blowing her nose when she heard the strains of *O, Little Town of Bethlehem*.

Glancing at the window, she saw that a group of perhaps

twelve people had collected. They were muffled up in scarves and gloves and woolly hats, and carrying carol sheets and candle-lanterns.

Turning startled eyes on Rafe, she saw he looked anything but surprised.

'You were expecting them.'

'Yes.'

'Who are they?'

'Estate staff. Most of them worked for the previous owner, and apparently it's become the custom for them to gather on Christmas Eve to sing carols.

'Then they assemble in the hall for dinner and a glass or two of mulled wine, which hopefully Annie will have waiting.'

Taking Madeleine's hand, he drew her over to the window, and they stood hand in hand, listening, while the small company sang their way through all the old familiar carols.

As *We Wish You a Merry Christmas and a Happy New Year* came to an end, the group dispersed.

'Come on,' Rafe said, taking Madeleine's hand and leading her into the hall, where a huge log fire was blazing.

They got to the door just as the knock came. Throwing it open, he welcomed the singers inside.

As they all trooped in, stamping snow off their boots and wellingtons, Annie wheeled in a trolley loaded with a punch bowl full of steaming wine and glass cups with handles. Several plates were piled high with hot mince pies and other festive fare.

'Thank you, Annie.' Taking a long-handled ladle, Rafe filled the cups himself and handed them out, amidst much cheerful talk and laughter.

Rather than just stand there, Madeleine picked up a plate and began to hand round the food.

Catching her eye, Rafe smiled at her.

As she smiled back it crossed her mind that they could have been master and mistress of the hall, following the traditions of the season while their children slept upstairs dreaming of sleigh bells and Santa Claus.

The thought made a lump come into her throat.

By the time everyone had eaten and drunk their fill it was almost a quarter to twelve.

'Well, I'd best be getting back,' one man said. 'I've got to dress up and play Father Christmas for the youngsters.'

'Why dress up?' another asked. 'Surely they'll be fast asleep?'

'Can't take any chances,' the first one replied. 'Last year they spent most of the night wide awake.'

'Well, I don't have to worry. My twins are only eight months old, and both good sleepers.'

'You just wait…'

On that note, with many thanks, and calls of, 'A merry Christmas,' they headed for the door and suddenly Rafe and Madeleine were alone.

'Shall we go back to the living room?' he asked.

Still trying to swallow past the lump in her throat, and tired, despite her earlier sleep, she shook her head. 'It's getting quite late; I think I'll go to bed.'

He nodded in agreement. 'I'll see you up.'

They climbed the stairs in silence.

When they reached the door of her flat she paused, hoping he would take her in his arms, kiss her, ask to stay, do *something*…

'Goodnight.' He raised her hand to his lips, and turned away.

Flattened, she let him go and went inside to get ready for bed.

A glance at the clock showed it was already Christmas Day, but somehow she no longer felt tired, and even when she was tucked up warm and comfortable sleep evaded her.

All she could think was, had Rafe done as she'd hoped, they would be together now.

But, having apologised for the way he had treated her, he

seemed determined to stand back and let her decide the next move.

She wanted to stay. She knew that now. Admitted it. Even though a happy ending was unlikely, she wanted to be with him for as long as possible.

But how could she stay knowing Rafe had loved her and she had killed that love? Her pride balked at staying with a man who merely wanted to use her.

So at the end of the holiday were she and her pride going to walk away hand in hand?

Didn't she owe it to herself?

But it had been *her* stupidity that had caused them both so much pain and anguish.

Rafe had been blameless.

Didn't she owe *him* something?

There was no way she could alter the past, and she might not be able to make up for everything, but she could make *some* reparation.

She got out of bed and, taking off her nightdress replaced it with a robe before going quietly out of the flat and along the dark passage to Rafe's door.

Without knocking she slipped silently into his room, feeling first the smooth floorboards and then the soft brush of a rug beneath her bare feet.

In the snowy light that came through the open curtains she could make out the polished wood of the four-poster and his dark head on the pillow.

She unbelted her robe and let it drop at her feet, then, lifting the duvet, slid into bed beside him.

He slept naked. His breathing was soft and even, his eyes were closed and she could see the fan of dark lashes lying on his hard cheeks.

Supporting herself on one elbow, she leaned to kiss his

lips and saw the gleam of his eyes a moment before his arms went round her.

His voice husky, he asked, 'Do I take it this is my Christmas present?'

'Are you happy with it?'

'It has to be the best I ever had. I hope what I'm giving you comes up to it.'

'What are you giving me?'

Reaching out a long arm, he switched on the bedside light and passed her a small gift-wrapped package. 'Take a look.'

Inside was the bracelet she had admired in Marshall Brand, and with it a chased-gold wedding ring that matched the engagement ring he'd bought.

'Marry me,' he said simply.

'B-but you said I was just an obsession…that you needed to get me out of your system…'

'When I told Eve that I'd never stopped loving you and I wanted you back, she said she was sure you still loved me. It was only when I began to think she was mistaken that I panicked and did and said all kinds of stupid things. *Do* you still love me?'

'Yes,' she said. There would be plenty of time in the coming years to tell him just how much.

'Then answer my question, woman.'

'Well, I might need persuading…'

The words ended in a startled squeak as he rolled, pinning her beneath him. 'How much persuading?'

'Quite a lot,' she said demurely. 'So I hope you're up to it.'

'You can count on me. We'll start with a kiss, shall we, and progress from there?'

'A good start,' she murmured, when he'd kissed her deeply. 'What comes next?'

'This.' He proceeded to demonstrate.

Caught up in the magic he wove so well, she was soon wrapped in black velvet, yet full of heat and light. Glowing. Burning. Incandescent.

His lovemaking culminated in a fire-storm of sensation so intense that she couldn't breathe, couldn't think, couldn't see.

When the fierce sexual heat was replaced by the warmth of belonging and she lay quietly in his arms, he asked, 'How was that?'

'Wonderful,' she murmured. 'You've just upped your chances of a yes vote.'

'I'm glad to be getting somewhere. Of course, to do a *thorough* job of persuading will take some considerable time, but no one can blame us if we spend Christmas Day in bed.'

'No, indeed,' she agreed happily.

TAKEN BY THE TYCOON

BY
KATHRYN ROSS

Kathryn Ross was born in Zambia, where her parents happened to live at that time. Educated in Ireland and England, she now lives in a village near Blackpool, Lancashire. Kathryn is a professional beauty therapist, but writing is her first love. As a child she wrote adventure stories and at thirteen was editor of her school magazine. Happily, ten writing years later, *Designed with Love* was accepted by Mills & Boon. A romantic Sagittarian, she loves travelling to exotic locations.

CHAPTER ONE

THEIR eyes met across the boardroom table and out of nowhere Nicole could feel electricity in the air between them, so hot it almost sizzled. Hurriedly she looked away.

'So, as you can see, gentlemen,' she said as she tried to focus back on her notes, 'the figures are good. If there are no further complications the takeover should soon be complete and RJ Records will be ours.'

There was a ripple of applause around the long table and a lot of satisfied smiles. But Luke wasn't smiling. He was still looking at her with that gleam in his dark eyes as if he could read her mind and look directly into her very soul.

She wished he wouldn't look at her like that. It made her pulses race…it made her hot all over…it made her forget what she was thinking, what she was saying.

'So…' She shuffled the papers in front of her and forced herself to think businesslike thoughts. 'What we need to do now—'

'What we need to do now is adjourn this meeting,' Luke cut across her swiftly, his tone quietly commanding.

Nicole frowned, and was about to tell him that there were a few more important points to run through, but he was already pushing back his chair from the long polished table. 'Thank you for your attention, gentlemen, but I think with our goal in sight we all deserve an early finish tonight. We will reconvene early tomorrow morning.'

Nicole glanced surreptitiously at her watch. It was five-thirty. Not exactly early by normal standards, but compared with the hours they had been working for the last week this was a veritable half-day.

Everyone started to relax and follow the boss's lead, pushing their chairs back from the table. A babble of conversation broke out as the tension of the last few days was put aside. The whole office had been under pressure with work on the proposed takeover.

Nicole gathered her papers and put them back into her briefcase. Across the room she could see Luke chatting with Sandy, his PA. He was leaning against the window-sill, the panoramic view of the Miami skyline spread out behind him. But it wasn't the view outside that held Nicole's attention. It was the span of his shoulders in the charcoal-grey suit...the casual way he had pushed his jacket back to rest one hand against his white shirt, showing the taut lines of his narrow hips.

No man had a right to be as good-looking as her boss, she thought distractedly. Luke Santana was thirty-six and six-foot-two of sheer male perfection. His hair was thick, blue-black, and just a shade too long against his collar, and his eyes were so dark and intense that they seemed to slice into her. He was of Portuguese origin and you could see the continental lineage clearly, even if his accent was some-times more mid-Atlantic. She liked the way he talked, with just an occasional hint of a Portuguese accent, and she liked the way he looked. In fact just glancing at him made her stomach tighten in a strange kind of way. But she was fighting that… In fact she was getting better at dealing with it, she told herself firmly as she turned her attention away from him. At least she was able to maintain a brisk, businesslike veneer around him—even if he made her heart speed up to the rate of an engine in overdrive.

A fellow colleague stopped to have a word with her and then she turned to leave. Luke was standing between her and the door now.

She pushed a strand of long chestnut hair back from her face and tried not to notice how his eyes flicked over her, taking in her slender figure in the white blouse and black pencil skirt.

'The deal seems to be coming together nicely, Nicole,' he drawled.

'Yes, I think we're making good progress.'

He nodded, before adding casually, 'However, there are a few points I think we should clarify, and one figure that I'd especially like to go over again in detail.'

Nicole's green eyes narrowed on him. She had been meticulous in her calculations…how could he not be completely satisfied? 'Which figure were you thinking of?'

'Don't worry about it now. Just make sure you are in here bright and early tomorrow.'

His tone held an abrasive edge, but she was kind of used to that. When Luke wanted something he wanted it then and there. Patience wasn't one of his virtues.

She nodded. 'Of course, boss.'

There was a slightly sardonic gleam in his eye now as he looked at her. 'See you tomorrow, Nicole,' he said.

She smiled and headed for the door.

The corridor outside was silent; she stepped into the lift to head back up to her office and collect her bag.

Before she reached her floor, her mobile rang.

'So, your place or mine?' an arrogant male voice demanded.

Her boss's cool, confident tones made a shiver of excitement race through her. 'I'm not sure I've got time to see you tonight,' she teased huskily. 'I've got figures to redo.'

'So have I…one figure in particular.' Nicole could hear the amusement in Luke's voice, but she could also hear the heat of desire. 'I'll be round at your place in half an hour.'

'Make it three quarters of an hour,' she said, thinking that she wanted time to get ready for him. 'I'll make us something to eat if you like?'

There was a silence at the other end of the phone, covered only by the distant babble of conversation from the boardroom. It was no wonder Luke was a bit surprised. She had never offered to cook for him before. Nicole frowned, surprised by the offer herself. Why had she said that? This was a strictly carnal affair—yes, OK, sometimes he took her out to eat, but that was in the impersonal surrounds of an expensive restaurant, and usually a restaurant where they wouldn't bump into anybody they knew. A home-cooked meal sounded somehow a little…cosy.

'OK, but I'd better warn you…I'm ravenous.' He said the words in a low, rasping tone and she had an immediate mental image of him arriving at her apartment and ripping her clothes off. That was what usually happened. Their time together was always wildly seductive…absolutely frenzied. Just thinking about it made all her senses reel with anticipation.

'I gather you are not talking about food now?' she said with a laugh.

'Got it in one.'

She could hear somebody talking to him in the background.

'Got to go,' he said swiftly. 'See you later.'

Nicole hung up with a frown. Why had she offered to cook for him? She wasn't a particularly domesticated person.

The lift doors opened and she walked through to her office. It was a fabulous space, with its own private lounge area, and behind her desk the Miami coastline sparkled clear and beautiful, like a jewel in the September sunshine. When the Santana Record Company had offered her a transfer out here eighteen months ago she had grabbed the opportunity with both hands. She had been delighted to leave London with its painful memories and start afresh.

During her time in America Nicole had dedicated herself entirely to her work, and it had paid off. Six months ago she had earned herself the position of Contracts Manager. It was no mean achievement at thirty-one. A record label like Santana was part of a hard-hitting business, and in order to rise so high she'd had to brazen it out in the boardroom, pretending to be the cool, invincible, perfectionist Ms Connell. It still stunned her that she had succeeded to convince people that this was the true her. Sometimes she found it amusing that her diminutive five-foot-five slender frame could be in command of anyone.

Everything had been going well. After a painful divorce it had suited her to put work first and relationships second. She had liked the fact that she only had an occasional date. She didn't want to get involved with anyone, had liked keeping everything uncomplicated. And then five months ago Luke Santana had flown into town. He'd been in Europe for the last eighteen months, and apparently they'd only narrowly missed meeting each other in the London office; she'd left for America the day before he arrived. Now he had returned to Miami to negotiate the takeover of another rival record company, RJ Records, and he had chosen Nicole to assist him. Suddenly life had veered off track.

Having an affair with the boss was probably not smart, and she had desperately tried to fight the attraction she felt for him. But from the first moment she had walked into his office and their eyes had met a sort of madness had descended on her.

'Hi, Nicole,' he had said easily as he stood up to shake her hand. 'I've been hearing great things about you.'

Nicole had heard things about him as well; she had heard that he was a ruthless entrepreneur who put the business of making money above everything else. According to the *New York Times* he bought and sold companies as if life was a game of Monopoly. Sometimes he kept the businesses and built them up; sometimes he just ruthlessly tore them apart in a game of asset-stripping. Luckily for her job, his record company was one that he was intent on building up.

Another thing she had heard about Luke Santana was that he had never married and, according to the gossips, had broken more women's hearts than there were days in the year. She had reminded herself of all those things as she had felt tingles of awareness just from his handshake. And because she had been determined to keep her distance she had made sure that around him she was extra cool and businesslike.

Luke had seemed to find this amusing, and a bizarre game of cat and mouse had ensued for a few weeks. The frostier she was, the more charming he became. He hadn't come on to her, in fact he hadn't done anything that could be considered improper…and yet there'd been a sizzling undercurrent that had grown stronger by the day. She'd tried everything to keep her distance—dressed in overly severe suits, scraped her hair back from her face, a sardonic disapproval when he had tested her knowledge of the business to the hilt. She had even told herself that she didn't like him very much—told herself and other people that he was overbearing and far too sure of himself.

But the tension between them—whatever it was—had just seemed to build and build. Then, during a late meeting of the board, her hand had accidentally brushed against his and the feeling had been electric. Such a trivial thing, and yet she'd hardly been able to think straight for the rest of the meeting. Later Luke had accompanied her back to her office to pick up some papers.

'You were very quiet tonight,' he said.

'Well, I've got a lot on my mind.' She found the papers in double-quick time. 'There you are,' she said as she handed them across. 'You'll find everything in order.'

'Yes, I'm sure I will. So, do you fancy having dinner with me some time?' he asked.

'To discuss these papers?'

He shook his head. 'No, to discuss this…'

Then he had kissed her.

The memory of that steamy kiss was enough to make her go hot inside now.

One moment she had been cool and reserved, the next she had melted like an ice-cube in the desert.

He had made love to her right here in her office, and it had been wild and incredible. Never in her life had she experienced such passion! Afterwards there had been a moment when she had been horrified by what she had done—especially when she remembered that he had been prepared for sex and had had a condom with him. But then he had kissed her so tenderly that the feeling had turned to elation.

She had been bewildered by her reaction, had reminded herself that she was a career girl who put emotional entanglements second.

The thought had made her pull away from him. 'I hope you are not going to read anything into this,' she said as she hurried to straighten her clothes and cover her nakedness. 'I've really no inclination to get involved with you. I've no time for a relationship right now.'

It was probably a stupid thing to say to a man like Luke. And certainly when she looked over at him he seemed somewhat amused.

'That suits me fine,' he drawled. 'I'm not cut out for relationships, Nicole.'

'Good. Well, we'll just forget all about this, then…shall we?' Somehow she managed to sound cool and composed, but really she was far from it. All she could think about was getting out of there. She had never felt more embarrassed in her life.

'I don't think so!' His voice was firm as he reached to take her hands away from the buttons on her blouse. 'I'm not finished with you yet, Ms Connell.' There was a playful, husky growl to his words, and she thought for one wild

moment that he wanted to make love to her all over again...
What was even more worrying was the fact that she
wouldn't have been averse to the idea. But he was merely
adjusting her clothing, refastening the buttons that she had
mistakenly fastened crookedly. The touch of his fingers
against her body was erotic.

'I suggest that we have an affair,' he said calmly. 'No
complications, no strings...just perfect sex.'

And for the last few months that was what they'd had.
So far they had managed to keep it a secret, so that it
wouldn't complicate things at work. In public they were
cool and deferential, but in private... Well, in private their
affair was so hot it was on fire.

Nicole had never had a liaison like it before. Casual sex
was something she had never indulged in. But then she'd
had five years in a deeply committed relationship with her
husband, and that had ended badly, so she told herself
there was no harm in having a little fun. She was a thirty-
one-year-old woman, for heaven's sake, and these were
modern times.

Nicole's secretary, Molly, came into the room and put
some letters on her desk. 'I didn't expect to see you back
from that meeting so soon!' she said in surprise.

'Luke called a halt to proceedings and declared an
early finish.'

'Wow! He must be in a good mood.'

'Indeed.' Nicole smiled and reached for her bag. 'So I
suggest you take advantage and finish now, Molly.'

'Great! I'll have time to go down to the florist and sort
out my flowers.'

'Can't be long now to the big day?' Nicole perched

against the edge of her desk for a moment. She liked Molly, a bubbly twenty-five-year-old who was so much in love with her fiancé Jack that it warmed Nicole's heart just hearing about their plans. And in some ways it restored her faith in love as well…a faith that had been badly shaken when her husband had walked out on her.

'Five weeks on Saturday.' Molly's eyes sparkled with happiness. 'In fact…' Molly disappeared back into her own office and then returned a minute later with an embossed envelope. 'I may as well give you your invitation now,' she said with a smile. 'I was going to post it, but I'm on the last minute getting them out anyway.'

'Thanks, Molly.' Nicole opened the envelope and looked down at the pretty card with two hearts interlinked by a gold wedding band on the front. Inside, the invitation was made out to 'Nicole and partner'.

Her first thought was that there was no way she could turn up accompanied by Luke. And then something strange happened…the knowledge seemed to sow a seed of sadness inside her.

With a frown, she pushed the feeling away. What on earth was the matter with her? Her relationship with Luke was just what she wanted, she told herself firmly as she put the invitation into her bag.

Twenty minutes later Nicole was pulling up outside her apartment in her red sports car, laden with bags from the local store. She had rethought her offer to cook for Luke and decided to stop off and buy some appetisers instead—maybe they could have them in bed together later. The idea had grown as she'd walked around the store, and she had got a little carried away and bought champagne and caviar and all sorts of goodies. She felt quite excited as she headed for the lifts. The thought of a whole evening with Luke was blissful.

She had fifteen minutes to spare as she hurried through her front door. Throwing her purchases into the fridge, she headed for the bedroom and had a quick shower before putting on some sexy cherry-red lingerie and a wraparound dress in a matching colour. There was just time to pull a brush through her long chestnut hair and apply some lipstick.

She studied herself for a moment in the mirror. Her eyes were wide and sparkling with anticipation, and there was a healthy glow to her skin. Anybody would think she was in love. The light-hearted thought flicked through her brain and suddenly she froze.

She wasn't in love! She couldn't be in love! It was against all the rules. This was an affair…it was casual sex with a capital C—no strings, no commitment, and certainly no mention of the L word.

So why did her heart go into overdrive when he so much as looked at her? a small voice asked. Why had she felt unhappy that they couldn't attend Molly's wedding as a couple?

The front doorbell rang and she whirled around, her senses pounding guiltily as if she had been caught out in some illegal or immoral act.

She told herself that she was imagining things as she headed to open the door. There was no way she had fallen in love with Luke Santana. She wasn't that brainless. She knew there was no way he wanted a meaningful relationship. One hint of that and he would be heading for the hills at double speed. And anyway, hadn't she promised herself after her divorce that she wasn't going to do love again? It only led to heartache. She liked this casual no-strings approach. Really, she could take him or leave him.

Feeling a little better, she swung the door open.

Luke was leaning against the door-frame. He was wearing the same grey suit he had worn in the office, and he was loosening his tie as if it were cutting into him. There was no other way to describe him other than overwhelmingly sexy. Nicole felt her heart doing its usual dip down towards her stomach.

'Sorry I'm a bit late.' He smiled at her, with that lazy smile that seemed to warm the darkness of his eyes. 'I got caught on the phone.'

Take him or leave him? Who was she trying to kid? she thought distractedly. She was crazy about him…and deeply in love.

'Are you OK?' he asked as he stepped past her.

'Yes, of course.' She pulled herself together sharply. This was a disaster…what the hell was she going to do?

CHAPTER TWO

'WOULD you like a drink?' Nicole headed for the kitchen. 'I've got champagne cooling.'

She opened up her fridge and the array of party food seemed to mock her. She didn't feel like celebrating any more.

Why hadn't she seen the signs that she was falling for him? she wondered. She felt as if someone had just taken the blinkers from her eyes and for the first time in weeks she had clear vision. The signals had all been there, but she had either been too preoccupied or too damn silly to see them. There was the breathless feeling when she was with him, the lack of appetite when she was not. The aching disappointment when he didn't spend the whole night with her after they made love.

And now there was the sudden feeling that she wanted to get to know him on a deeper level. Well, she wasn't going to give in to those feelings. She snatched up the bottle of champagne.

'Champagne? Are we celebrating?' He was at the doorway, watching her.

'Not especially, since the deal for RJ isn't settled yet.' She brought her thoughts firmly back towards work.

'You look lovely, by the way,' he said softly as she walked over to get some glasses.

'Thank you.' She looked over at him and felt herself melt. Luke had a way of looking at her and undressing her with his eyes. He had been doing it in the boardroom this afternoon. And there was something so profoundly sensual about it that it sent her blood pressure soaring. If anyone else had been so forward she might have been annoyed, but with him it really, really turned her on.

All she could think about now was how much she wanted him.

'Shall I open that bottle for you?' He moved to stand behind her, and before she could answer him he had taken the champagne from her hand and was uncorking the bottle. His arms were around her shoulders and she could smell the deliciously provocative scent of his cologne, could feel his body hard and lean against hers. She closed her eyes on a wave of intense desire.

'There.' The cork whizzed out of the bottle and some of the froth sprayed over them. They both laughed, and he put the bottle down to place his hands on her waist and kiss the side of her face. 'I've been wanting to touch you all day,' he murmured.

'Me too…' She leaned back against him and reached up to run her fingers through the dark silkiness of his hair.

His hands moved from spanning her small waist to run upwards over the curves of her body. Immediately her breasts responded to his touch and became hard with arousal. 'You know, you add a whole new and exciting element to opening a bottle of champagne, Nikki.' He murmured the words huskily against her ear and she turned around and melted into his arms.

He liked the way she did that, liked the way she responded to his touch and fitted against him, sinuously inviting yet curvaceously warm. When he had watched her in the boardroom today he had imagined this moment. He had listened as she talked about facts and figures with that brisk efficiency of hers, and he had taken infinite pleasure in the knowledge that later he would be the one to ruffle her calm, cool exterior and arouse her to fever pitch. She was extremely sexy…biddable in the bedroom, yet a force to be reckoned with in the workplace. He found that fascinating, and he intended to explore every inch of her delectable foxy body right here…right now…

His lips ground down against hers, hard and punishing, and she kissed him back with a passion of equal strength. He liked that too.

'Sex is so good between us…' He murmured the words huskily as he trailed red-hot kisses like darts of fire down the side of her neck.

Nicole agreed with him, but inside there was suddenly a traitorous little voice cutting through the waves of passion and mocking her. *You want this to be more than just good sex…*

She pulled away from him, desperately trying to close those thoughts out.

'Are you OK?'

'Fine!' She turned towards the counter-top for a moment. 'I just thought we'd have that drink.' Quickly she rallied herself. She didn't want to ruin their time together with these irrational thoughts. When she looked back at him, she flashed him a provocative look from smouldering green eyes. 'It would be a shame to let it go to waste after the trouble you took to open it.'

One dark eyebrow rose mockingly. 'If you say so…but I did have other things on my mind.'

'So I noticed.' She smiled, then turned away from him. *Sex* was on his mind, while meantime she was filled with these crazy feelings of love. She needed to get rid of them, and quickly. But it was like Pandora's box: the lid was off and all sorts of unwelcome feelings were pounding through her body with insistent force.

Nicole's hand wasn't quite steady as she poured the drink. Luckily Luke didn't seem to notice. He was reaching past her to pick up a designer box that was sitting by the microwave.

'Nice tie,' he said with approval as he took a look inside.

She glanced over and her heart sank. Oh hell! That was another thing she had done…bought him a gift…for no reason at all.

'Yes, isn't it?' It had been very expensive too. Nicole was really thankful now that she had been too busy to give it to him. She had her pride, and she didn't want him to guess that she was falling for him…that would be excruciatingly embarrassing. If he got one hint of her thoughts he would probably pull the plug on their relationship. After all, he'd made his feelings on commitment abundantly clear on more than one occasion. He had even gone so far as to tell her once that marriage and babies were certainly not what he wanted in life. His work came first.

'Who is it for?'

'Just a friend. It's his birthday next week,' she improvised quickly as she turned to pass him his drink. OK, there was no real reason why he should guess what was in her heart just from one gift, she told herself sensibly. But she wasn't going to take any chances. Because the strange thing was that now she had realised the truth it suddenly seemed so glaringly obvious.

He held the glass up and touched it against hers. 'Cheers,' he said softly.

'Cheers.' She took rather too deep a swallow of the champagne and bubbles tickled her nose. This drink was like their relationship, she thought: very pleasurable, but all froth and no real substance. She would do well to remember that if she wanted to continue to enjoy it.

'I thought the board meeting went well today.' Deliberately she turned the conversation back towards the safety of work.

'Yes, you did a good job,' he said quietly. 'I was impressed.'

'I know.' She looked at him teasingly. 'Yet you told me there were further points to clarify and…how did you put it?…one figure in particular that you needed to go over?'

'And I intend to go over it…in fine detail…any moment now…' He drawled the words provocatively. 'But I was playing things carefully. I didn't want people to overhear, put two and two together and realise we are sleeping together.'

He always referred to them as just 'sleeping together'. It had never bothered her before, but today it made her heart thud painfully against her chest. Even the term 'sleeping together' was a bit of an exaggeration for what they had. In reality they did little sleeping, as Luke usually left after they'd made love.

'That would never do,' she said lightly.

'Never,' he agreed, with a wry gleam in his eyes.

It had been Nicole's idea to keep the affair a secret; she really didn't want to be the subject of office gossip. Luke, on the other hand, found the secrecy amusing. It was a game he seemed to enjoy playing.

'Speaking of which…' he continued softly. 'I know you said you'd make dinner, but I think we should put that on hold for a while.'

'Oh, I changed my mind about dinner,' she said airily. 'I thought we'd have nibbles instead…'

'That sounds good…' He put his glass down and then reached to take hers from unresisting fingers. 'I'm all for nibbles.' As he spoke he brushed her hair away from her face and then leaned in closer to nibble gently at her earlobe. The sensation was deliciously intoxicating.

'Now, where were we?' he murmured huskily, and she felt his hands moving down over the curves of her body with bold possession. 'You know, I don't think I can wait one minute longer for you.'

The wraparound dress was easily pushed to one side and his hands found the naked heat of her body. Nicole closed her eyes on a wave of desire. She didn't think she could wait one minute longer for him either. She had wanted him all afternoon. Had longed for the people around them to disappear so she could just melt into his arms.

His lips found hers in a hard, yet sensationally passionate kiss. She kissed him back, loving the warm feeling that melted through her body.

Wrapping her arms around his neck, she lost herself in his caresses. His tongue was inside her mouth now, plundering her sweet softness.

Then his kisses became even more intense, his hands fiercely possessive. She allowed him to untie her dress completely and it dropped to the floor. Suddenly Luke was pulling back from her, and his gaze raked over the slender curves of her body in the sexy underwear. 'Hell, but you're beautiful, Nicole.' He reached a hand out and trailed it softly over the edge of her lacy bra. Immediately her body responded to him; she could feel her breast tightening with need.

It was only four days since they had last made love, yet her body felt starved of his...it was almost as if a fever had taken hold of her and she ached all over.

As he pulled her bra down, exposing the creamy curves of her figure, she felt every sinew of her body glowing and alive with need. His lips moved to nuzzle in against her neck as his hands caressed her curves, then his mouth moved lower, following his hands.

Just as she felt she was going to explode with need he picked her up and carried her through to the bedroom.

They sank down onto her double bed and she started to feverishly unfasten the buttons of his shirt. 'I want you so much,' she said, her voice incoherent with need.

The shirt was discarded and she stroked her fingers lovingly over the smooth breadth of his shoulders. He had a fabulous body...finely tuned, and toned like an athlete's. He was slowly kissing her all over. She loved the way he could be so masterful in the bedroom, yet so incredibly tender at the same time. Her need for him was building up to fever pitch, and as his lips returned to hers again the passion became wilder, less controlled. He pulled her closer and suddenly he was inside her, taking her with hard, driving thrusts yet at the same time stroking her breasts with gentle possession.

The sensations he aroused in her were overwhelmingly intense, but she tried not to give in to them, tried to prolong the pleasure. But the ache of need was building until she felt she couldn't stand it any more. As his lips nuzzled against her she hit dizzying heights, and together their passion exploded into a million splintering pieces of sheer pleasure.

'Wow!' It was all she could say. She was out of breath and her skin was damp against his.

He gave a low laugh and rolled over to lie beside her. 'You can say that again!' There was a gleam of warm amusement in his eyes as he looked across into her eyes. 'That was perfect.'

Nicole wished she could say the same. Yes, she felt physically sated, but there was a raw ache inside her that wouldn't go away… It was the ache of knowing how much she loved him and how futile that love was. This man would never be hers. Trying to claim Luke would be a bit like trying to catch a tiger by the tail. The knowledge hurt unbearably.

For a while they just lay there without speaking.

Her eyes moved over his face. It was such an arrestingly handsome face, she thought. She noticed how his jaw was square and determined, how there was a slight dimple in the hollow of his chin, and how already there were the beginnings of a dark shadow along the olive smoothness of his skin.

Luke reached out a hand and pulled her a little closer to him. She allowed herself to cuddle in against him and he kissed the side of her face. She kissed him back, and then suddenly he was pulling her underneath him and they were making love all over again.

'Where do you get your energy?' she asked him breathlessly when she finally lay exhausted against his sprawled body.

'I don't know. Maybe it's something to do with my Mediterranean roots,' he said playfully. He pushed her silky hair back from her face and looked down at her. She liked the way his dark eyes were flecked with gold, and how they crinkled slightly at the edges when he smiled.

She tried to commit this moment—and him—to memory. And for a precious few seconds she snuggled against him and tried to pretend that they belonged together…that he was all hers. His hand ran down the long length of her spine and then curved around her waist, pulling her even closer.

The shrill ring tone of his mobile phone suddenly broke the relaxed mood. Nicole groaned inwardly and wanted to tell him to ignore it. But she knew better. Work always came first with Luke.

As she had known he would, he reached across and answered it immediately.

'Oh, hi, Amber—how is it going?' Within a second he had pulled completely away from her and sat up in the bed. 'Did you get the figures from Drew? Good. So it's on target, then?'

Nicole lay against the pillows, watching him. It never ceased to amaze her how fast Luke could switch from the warmth of lovemaking to the cool practicality of business. Amber was one of his top accountants who had been at his New York office for the last week.

She wished the outside world would go away… She wished that Luke would look at her and suddenly realise he couldn't live without her…

Now she was being ridiculous! Angry with herself, she tried to close out thoughts like that.

Luke finished his phone call and looked over towards her. 'I'm sorry, Nicole. I'd really better go. I need to do some work at home for the New York office.'

She noticed how his tone was brisk and businesslike. So much for the outside world going away, she mocked herself wryly. So much for her romantic plans for a long evening together and a picnic in bed. She should have known better.

'OK.' With a supreme effort she matched her tone to his. 'I'll make you a coffee while you shower.'

'That would be great, thanks.'

Nicole put on her dressing gown and went through to the kitchen. She didn't really want coffee, but she felt she needed to do something to keep herself busy. Dwelling on this…attraction for Luke was doing her no good! When her marriage had broken up she had sworn she would never let any man get close enough to hurt her again. With determination she had put her life back together, and she had become fiercely independent…self-sufficient. If she gave in to these feelings for Luke now she would be undoing all her good work… breaking all her rules. She was going to have to pull herself together and get some control over her emotions.

When she returned to the bedroom, Luke was just coming out of the *en suite* bathroom. He had a towel wrapped low around his waist and he looked like a Greek god, all muscled perfection with a lean washboard stomach.

He smiled at her and it made her pulses quicken, made

all her firm resolutions waver. 'I made you that coffee,' she said brightly, putting it down on the bedside table.

'Thanks.'

He sat down next to her on the edge of the bed and she noticed how his hair was wet and slicked back, emphasising the lean contours of his face. She wanted to reach out and touch him.

Linking her fingers firmly around her mug of coffee, she forced herself not to, tried to distract her thoughts away from how attractive she found him.

Luke's glance fell on the wedding invitation she had left on the bedside table. 'What's this?' he asked casually as he reached to pick it up.

'Molly invited me to her wedding today.'

'Molly?' He frowned.

'My secretary,' she reminded him. 'You know—'

'Oh, yes…Molly. Attractive girl with blonde curly hair.'

'That's her.' Nicole nodded. She supposed he couldn't be expected to remember all his employees. It was a big firm…and not the only one he owned!

He opened the card. 'The invitation is for you and a partner. Who are you going to take?'

She shrugged. 'I haven't had time to think about it yet.'

'It could have been fun to go together.'

The nonchalant words cut through her. It would have been wonderful to spend time with him openly. 'But we need to keep our affair secret from people at work,' she murmured cautiously. 'Molly might be a bit shocked if we turn up together.'

'Yes, that's the problem.' He laughed. 'And we don't want to blow our little secret, do we? It's far too enjoyable.'

'Absolutely.' She forced herself to smile.

'It keeps things exciting and fun,' he added with a teasing grin.

'Yes, it does.' She took a deep breath and decided to test the water all the way. 'And…after all…it's not as if our relationship is serious, is it?…'

Luke nodded. 'I agree, Nicole. Things are just fine the way they are.'

'I think so too.' *Liar!* a little voice taunted her inside, and desperately she tried to ignore the raw feelings it stirred up.

He put the invitation down and took a sip of his coffee. 'Well, that's OK, then.'

Suddenly she wanted to say, *Actually, no, it's not OK*. But with difficulty she reined in the feeling. She had no right to feel upset. She had agreed right from the beginning that this was a no-strings affair. So she couldn't complain now just because she felt like moving the goalposts.

But the trouble was the more she thought about it, the more upset she felt. With determination, she fought down the feeling.

'So, who will you go to the wedding with?' Luke asked casually.

She shrugged. 'I might just go on my own,' she said airily. 'It can be quite good fun being unattached at a function. You meet more people.'

Luke put his coffee down. 'Well, as long as you come home alone I have no objection.'

The statement made her temper flare. He couldn't expect to have everything his own way! 'Oh, really?' She looked at him with a raised eyebrow. 'I think you'll find you've no right to object to *anything* I might do…'

'Uh-uh.' He shook his head and reached purposefully to take her coffee from her. 'I'll think you'll find I can register my objections very loudly.' Although his voice was playful, his hands were very serious as they moved over her body with firm possession.

And suddenly his lips crushed against hers with a vivid and almost aggressive passion. If he didn't care about her would he kiss her like this? she wondered dazedly. She tried to hold herself back and not surrender to him. But as Luke trailed a heated blaze of kisses down over her face and along the side of her neck she found herself winding her arms around his neck and giving herself up to the moment.

Now he was sliding her further down the bed. 'I thought you had to go and deal with work?' she said breathlessly.

'Yes, I should really go…but first I want you again.' He ripped her dressing gown off with determined hands. 'Right now you belong to me, Ms Connell.' His voice held an arrogant confidence, as did the touch of his hands against her skin as they slid possessively up along the naked slender curves of her hips and waist.

'On the contrary. I belong to no one but myself!' she said firmly, and she wriggled away from him a little.

He pulled her back easily, and a playful struggle ensued before he pinned her against the bed.

He said something to her in Portuguese. It sounded deliciously provocative.

'What did you say?' she murmured.

'I said we'd see about that, my little wildcat.' Luke's voice was teasing and his grip gentle, yet he held her without difficulty beneath him, both her wrists fastened behind her head with just one hand.

He looked down into her eyes and she loved the powerful feeling of intimacy and sensuality that suddenly spun between them.

'God, you are so beautiful…' he said huskily. Then he bent his head and kissed her with a passion that showed her exactly how easily he could stake his claim.

She kissed him back, and the play-acting was forgotten. Luke released his grip on her wrist and their fingers intertwined. His body was hard and possessive against her.

The intimacy between them was so tender, so…warm and loving, that Nicole couldn't equate it at all with the cool certainty that Luke had shown when he'd agreed that it meant nothing.

Since meeting him she had become more alive. He had reawakened her in every way. In fact even her husband hadn't made her feel like this! So how could it not be the real thing?

'You like that, Nikki, don't you?' He whispered the words against her ear.

Like? That was far too weak a word for what Nicole was feeling. She felt as if a burning volcano of need was stored inside of her. When he broke away from her briefly she thought for one horrible moment that he was stopping, but when she glanced around she found he was only reaching for a condom.

As he caressed her, she felt as if she were spinning further and further out of control. He was masterful with her, yet infinitely tender and he made her respond to him without inhibition. By the time he allowed her release from the wildness of her need she felt like crying with pleasure. And all she could do was just cling to him, because she was totally and utterly exhausted in every sense.

Luke watched her as she fell asleep in his arms. Her skin was flushed with heat and her hair was glossy around her shoulders. He allowed one hand to trail provocatively over the smoothness of her back and watched how she smiled in her sleep and cuddled a little closer.

Nicole had stirred a surprising feeling of possessiveness inside him, and that wasn't like him at all. He frowned as he thought about that feeling now. It had probably just been pure desire. He had to admit she turned him on with an incredible force.

And he had to admit that she intrigued him too. What made her tick? he wondered. What drove her?

Watching her in action at the office was a sight to behold. One moment she was provocative and sexy, and the next he'd glimpse this clear-thinking and tenacious woman who could pull off the most audacious of deals when the stakes were at their highest.

She was certainly tough, and she seemed to take emotional issues lightly—in fact she was very much on his wavelength in that respect. She didn't believe in getting bogged down in restrictive relationships, she was career-orientated. And yet at other times he thought he glimpsed an almost fragile vulnerability about her, and then it was gone, making him wonder if he'd imagined it.

When he'd taken her out to dinner the first time she'd told him she was divorced. She had only mentioned it fleetingly, yet he had seen that look in her eyes and noticed how she had quickly moved the conversation back towards the safety of work.

Was she as emotionally tough as she seemed? Or did she hide herself away behind a steely façade?

Luke frowned to himself as he suddenly realised that he was analysing her. Did it matter what motivated Nicole? This was just a light-hearted affair. They shared a lot of laughs, had the same sense of humour. For whatever reason she was a free spirit, like him, and that suited him just fine.

He glanced at his watch, irritated by his introspection. He needed to get his priorities in order—get back to his apartment and phone Amber to make sure the figures were correct on that contract for the New York office.

Very gently Luke eased himself away from Nicole, and, trying carefully not to wake her, he got out of the bed. She stirred a little, but settled back against the pillow without opening her eyes. Stealthily he got dressed. He was just looking around for a pen so that he could scribble a note for her when she opened her eyes.

'You're dressed!' She held the sheet against her body as she struggled to sit up.

'Sorry, I didn't mean to wake you.'

'That's OK.' She pushed the heavy fall of hair away from her face and tried to focus on him. 'Do you have to rush off?' Her voice was sleepy. 'You could stay and have something to eat if you want?'

'Sorry, honey, but you know I've got to go. I told you— I have to get back to my apartment and switch on my computer so I can go through those figures with Amber.'

'Yes, of course.' She drew in her breath and berated herself for asking him to stay. She should have known better. Just because he'd made love to her again it didn't mean he'd changed his mind about leaving. And anyway, this was what always happened…one moment he was curled up with her in bed, holding her tenderly, and the next he was racing to get back to a damn business problem. She'd used to tell herself that it didn't matter, that she didn't care…but she did!

I'm not going to put up with this any more, she thought suddenly. This isn't what I want. With difficulty she remained calm. This wasn't the moment for a confrontation. 'Another time, then,' she drawled.

'Yes, another time.' His eyes flicked lazily over her. It amused him that she was holding the sheet so tightly across her naked body…after all, he'd seen all there was to see.

'How about dinner tomorrow night?' he asked casually as he reached for his tie.

'Actually, I'm busy tomorrow night.'

He glanced over at her, surprised by the refusal. 'OK, we'll take a raincheck.'

'Yes…good idea.' She was sliding back down in the bed now. She stretched and the sheet fell a little lower, down over the curve of her breast.

Surprisingly, Luke found his body starting to respond to the lissom arch of her body, and suddenly he wanted to join her in the bed again. Forcibly he reached for his jacket.

'I hope you get those contracts sorted out.'

'Thanks.' Luke slung his jacket over his shoulder and looked over at her. 'And thanks for a great evening. I've enjoyed myself.'

Nicole couldn't find a light-hearted reply for that. Her heart was beating so loudly she felt it was filling the room with a noise like a bass drum.

'If you are busy tomorrow night we could always just meet up later?' he suggested lightly. 'Take up where we left off tonight?'

Meet up just for sex, in other words. Anger was pounding through her now. 'Actually, I'm going to be out with the girls until late tomorrow night,' she said coolly. In fact she had made no arrangements for tomorrow evening. But she was damned if she was going to make herself available just when it suited him.

He didn't seem to notice her frosty tone. 'OK. Well, we'll leave it until after the weekend, then.'

Nicole made no reply.

'I'll see you tomorrow morning in the office.'

'Bright and early,' she said with mock cheeriness.

He reached and ruffled the silky softness of her hair, and before she realised his intention he bent and kissed her full on the mouth in a sensual and provocative kiss that made her heart beat even faster.

'Bye, Nicole.'

'Bye.' She turned her head into the pillow as the door closed behind him, and then she was left with the silence of her apartment.

Their relationship was sexual and there would never be anything deeper than that between them. She either accepted that or walked away.

She bit down on her lip. As much as she wanted to accept the status quo, she knew now that she couldn't. Her true feelings for him wouldn't allow her. So tomorrow she would finish with him, she promised herself fiercely.

CHAPTER THREE

NICOLE was running late. She hadn't slept well at all. Her mind had been going over and over her time with Luke as she tried to analyse her situation. But analysing emotions was never a good idea…especially in the dead of night, she thought angrily as she straightened the bedclothes. The only thing she had achieved was a feeling of lethargy.

The drawer of the bedside table was open and a packet of condoms stared up at her. Luke was always very careful to use contraception. He had told her quite categorically that he didn't want her to get pregnant. What she hadn't been able to bring herself to tell him was that he had no need to worry about that. Nicole knew she *couldn't* get pregnant. She had longed for a baby when she was married, and she and her husband had tried for a long time to conceive without success. The fault had been found to lie with her, and the agony of the situation had been beyond compare. Ultimately she knew it was what had led to the break-up of her marriage.

She slammed the drawer shut. Yes, she did like the fact that Luke was responsible when it came to making love. But it was quite revealing that the only personal item that he ever left here was a packet of condoms.

When they had first started to sleep together she had suggested that he leave a few things here, like shaving gear and a change of clothes. It had seemed like a practical suggestion to her, and she supposed deep down she had been hoping that if he took her up on it he would stay around with her for longer. But he'd dismissed the idea immediately.

'There is no point, Nicole,' he had said in a matter-of-fact tone. 'My place is only fifteen minutes away. It is as easy for me to go back there.'

And she was losing sleep over the decision to finish with him! Annoyed with herself, Nicole reached to pick up her briefcase and cast a look at her reflection in the mirror. She was wearing a dark pinstripe suit that had a straight skirt teamed with a plain white blouse. Her dark chestnut hair fell in a gleaming curtain, framing her heart-shaped face, and she had done a good job with her make-up. At least she looked the part of the cool, composed businesswoman.

Ahead of her lay a busy day. She had to finish her presentation in the boardroom, and she needed to keep her wits about her and remember her priority was work.

Nothing else matters, she told herself fiercely. You can't rely on a man…you can only rely on yourself in the end. It was a lesson she'd learnt the hard way in the past, and she reminded herself of that fact now as she left for the office.

Her secretary was already in. 'Morning, Nicole. There is a stack of mail waiting for you on your desk,' she said cheerfully.

'Thanks, Molly.' Nicole walked through to her office, switched on her computer and logged in her password so she could check her e-mails. There was one from Luke; by the looks of things he'd sent it in the early hours of this morning.

Why don't you cancel whatever you are doing tonight and come round to my place for drinks? We can continue where we left things last night.

Hell, but he could be arrogant, she thought with a flash of annoyance. Did he think he only had to click his fingers and she'd come running?

She deleted the message without replying to it. Then she turned her attention to the rest of her business correspondence.

She had just finished reading her mail when another e-mail message arrived from Luke.

Morning, Nicole. Do you want to come up and have a coffee with me before we go in to this board meeting?

She wanted to ignore him, but she couldn't really; he was her boss. After a moment's hesitation she replied.

Good morning, Luke. Can't come up. I've got a few things to summarise before the board meeting. See you then.

A few seconds passed and a reply pinged onto the desk.

Just leave whatever you are doing.

Nicole frowned. She supposed that was a command! She sat drumming her fingers onto her desk. Well, if she was going to finish with him maybe now was as good a time as any. It was best to get it over with, she told herself firmly.

Picking up her briefcase, so that she was ready to go

straight to the board meeting afterwards, she headed up to the top floor.

Luke's PA waved her through towards the inner office with a smile. 'He's expecting you, Nicole.'

With a feeling of determination Nicole pushed open the door and went in. This was going to be difficult, but she was going to have to be strong, she told herself resolutely. When she'd got it over with she could take control of her life again.

Luke was sitting behind his desk, talking on the phone; he looked up and smiled at her, his eyes flicking over her slender figure with warm approval.

Immediately she felt her resolve starting to weaken.

'No, Thomas, it's not good enough,' he was saying firmly as he waved at Nicole to sit down in the chair opposite him. 'I won't be a moment,' he murmured, covering the mouthpiece.

She nodded, and tried to focus her attention on the room rather than on him. She'd always thought that Luke's office was more like a suite at a hotel than a place of work. He had everything up here: a lounge with a full bar area, even a walk-in closet with a few suits and shirts hanging up, and a large *en suite* bathroom with a shower and a Jacuzzi.

They had made love up here once. She remembered it now—the way he had undressed her and kissed her all over as he slowly, slowly turned her on to the point where she was just begging him to release her into blissful satisfaction.

Luke put down the phone, and swiftly she closed her mind on that. Memories like that didn't help at all right now.

'Sorry about that.' He smiled at her.

'That's OK.' She smiled back and tried very hard not to be distracted by how attractive he looked.

'And I'm sorry about having to leave so early last night,' he said.

There was a part of her that wanted to say, *You always leave early…* But she held back from that. She knew it would sound too possessive and too revealing, and she had her pride. So she just shrugged. 'I know that business comes first for both of us.' She was pleased at how cool and in control she sounded. 'Did you sort out the figures with Amber?'

'Yes…but we had to come into the office. We were at it until after midnight.'

At what? Nicole wondered distractedly. It didn't help to remember that Amber was a very attractive woman. Flame-haired and slender, with the most amazing blue eyes. *At work*, she told herself fiercely. And even if they hadn't been working it was none of her business. She was finishing with Luke…*remember*?

He got up from his chair and perched nearer to her on the edge of his desk. 'So, as we didn't get around to eating last night, can I make it up to you tonight?' he asked. 'I thought dinner at La Luna?'

La Luna was one of the best restaurants in the area. She had never been there because it was always booked up a long time in advance.

'No. I told you I couldn't make it tonight, Luke.' She brushed at an imaginary crease in her jacket.

'Well, that's a shame.'

Yes, it was. She wanted to accept the invitation; she wanted to forget this notion about finishing with him. If they went out for dinner he would take her home after-wards, and she would invite him in, and then… Swiftly she closed her mind to that. Every time she slept with him she was falling deeper and deeper under his spell, and it was a disaster. The relationship was going nowhere. She had to be strong.

'Actually there's something I need to say to you, Luke.' The words tumbled out hurriedly.

'And what is that?'

Nicole noticed how his tone of voice was huskily friendly.

Her eyes drifted over him, taking in the lightweight suit that looked so good on his broad-shouldered frame. He was wearing a blue shirt beneath, and it seemed to emphasise the almost blue-black intensity of his hair.

'Nicole?' His dark eyes seemed to slice straight through her.

This was one of the hardest things she had ever had to do. In order to take her mind off that fact, she stood up and put a little distance between them. If he touched her...if he kissed her...she would be lost.

'The thing is, this isn't working out, Luke.'

'What isn't working out?' He was half looking towards his computer as an e-mail arrived on screen.

'Us.'

'Us?' He frowned and looked back at her immediately.

'What we have together, Luke...you know...it's just not working.'

'What on earth are you talking about?' He smiled now, as if he thought she was joking. 'Of course it's working. What we have is fabulous.'

'Yes, it has been fabulous,' she admitted. 'But it's time for us to finish it.'

'Why would we finish something when we are both

still enjoying ourselves?' He looked genuinely perplexed. 'We've been having fun together, haven't we?'

'Yes.' She swept an unsteady hand through her hair. That was all she was to him, she reminded herself fiercely. A *bit of fun*. 'But it's run its course, Luke.'

'I don't think so.' He shook his head. 'The sex between us is as hot as ever. Yesterday you were as keen to get out of that boardroom and into bed as I was.'

'Yes.' She really didn't want to think about that right now. 'But now I just think it's time that we end it,' she said firmly.

He looked at her with a raised eyebrow and she could tell he still wasn't taking her seriously. 'Is this because I had to leave earlier than usual last night?'

'No, of course not.' She folded her arms in front of her body, trying to keep herself focused.

'It is, isn't it?' He grinned. 'Come on, Nicole. Last night was unfortunate, but I said I'd make it up to you.'

'This isn't about last night!' How dared he try and talk down to her, as if she were just having some kind of illogical PMT moment? 'Look, Luke, I don't want us to fall out. I want us to remain friends—'

'Good, that's what I want too,' he said calmly. 'So, let's clear the air, and then we can get things back to how they were.'

She bit down on her lip. How could she tell him that the problem was that she didn't *want* to get things back to how they were? She didn't want marriage—she'd had that, and it hadn't worked. But she wanted more from a relationship than he was willing to give. She wanted to be with him in every sense. She wanted to be able to go to parties on his arm, she wanted to spend whole nights with him, whole weekends, whole weeks. In short, she wanted to be more than just a bit of fun…she wanted his love.

'Luke, just take my word for it. It is better for us both if we finish it now,' she insisted. 'Otherwise things could get complicated.'

'I don't see how.' He sounded puzzled. 'We've got the perfect agreement…no complications and we both know where we stand. Where's the problem?'

The coolly impassive question made her blood thunder through her veins. How could someone who was so passionate be so damn detached when it came to real feelings?

Thank heaven she hadn't voiced her real reason for finishing things. He'd have looked at her as if she were mad! And maybe she was. Only a mad person would have fallen in love with a man who had clearly told her up-front that he wasn't cut out for relationships. Well, maybe she should end the affair in terms that he would understand.

'Let me just remind you, Luke, that the terms of our agreement were that we had a no-strings affair…just sex.'

'Yes…?' His eyes narrowed on her.

'Well, we've done that—and now I want to move on.' Nicole surprised herself with the level of brisk certainty in her tone. 'So I think you'll find that *you're* the one going against our agreement by subjecting me to this post-mortem.'

'Don't be ridiculous, Nicole!'

'Oh, I'm sorry. Did you think that the rules of our affair were just there to suit *you*?' Her voice shimmered with sarcasm. 'I thought it was a mutual agreement! Silly me!'

'I'm just asking you what the problem is, that's all.' He grated the words harshly. The phone rang on his desk, but instead of picking it up he leaned across and pressed the intercom to speak to his PA. 'Hold all my calls, Sandy,' he snapped impatiently. Immediately the phone stopped ringing.

Nicole noticed that he could ignore his calls when it suited him. The fact added to her annoyance. She also noticed that his cool, laid-back manner had evaporated. Well, good, she thought heatedly. Maybe she was striking a blow for all those women he had dumped in the past without a backward glance. Luke Santana was far too arrogant and blasé for his own good, and it was about time that someone turned the tables on him and let him know that he couldn't have everything his own way.

With that in mind, she moved to pick up her briefcase.

'Where are you going?' he asked with a frown as he watched her.

'It may have escaped your memory, but we have a board meeting to attend,' she said calmly.

'Of course it hasn't escaped my memory!' He glared at her. 'But that can wait for a minute.'

She glanced round at him with a raised eyebrow. 'I don't think so, Luke. Work comes first…remember?'

With a smile she turned and left the room. But as soon as she stepped from the outer office into the lift her mask of cool bravado started to falter. She couldn't believe that she had finished with him—let alone the fact that she had done it so coldly!

For the last few months she had been on such an incredible high…and it had all been due to him. He'd made her feel amazing; he'd made her glow inside with a feeling of exhilaration. She'd had something to look forward to…something to cherish…and now it was over! What the hell had she done?

With difficulty she swallowed down her emotions and told herself that she had done exactly the right thing.

The lift doors opened and she walked out and into the boardroom. It was teeming with people and buzzing with conversation. Most of the directors were already present, but nobody had taken their seats yet. One of the accountants approached her as she went towards her place at the table

'Ah, Nicole, I wanted to ask you about RJ's sales in the European market…'

She forced herself to concentrate, and strangely the mundane talk about work was soothing…it helped. Slowly her heart-rate was returning to normal. That was until she glanced over and saw that Luke was now in the room. Thankfully he had his back to her, and was talking to one of the directors.

Some people started to take their seats. Molly was refilling the coffeepots at the end of the room. She was going to take minutes for the meeting today. It's just another day, Nicole told herself calmly. A board meeting like millions of others before. Forget about Luke Santana.

He was taking his seat at the top of the table now. Nicole glanced over at him and felt her heart going into overdrive. Hastily she took her papers out and mentally tried to prepare herself.

'When we are all ready…I think we should begin.' His impatient tones cut across the trivial conversation and everyone rushed to take their seats.

And then it was time for Nicole to continue where she had left off yesterday, giving a complete rundown of the RJ Records company and plans for its development once the sale was complete.

Luke watched as she got to her feet. She sounded confident and she looked very together. He couldn't believe that she had just finished things between them. They had been getting on so well…he had really enjoyed making love to her. Just thinking about it now made him lose track of what she was saying, and his eyes drifted over the curves of her body. He liked the way she always dressed in a kind of prim and proper way that somehow managed to make her look even sexier.

Why the hell had she finished things? he wondered again angrily. What was all that nonsense about it being time to move on? He tapped his pen against the papers in front of him and tried to ignore the fact that he'd said similar things to women in the past. This was different… His relationship with Nicole was still red-hot… She knew it…he knew it. So why finish it now?

With difficulty he tried to transfer his mind away from that and back to business. He'd never let a relationship with a woman affect his work, and he wasn't going to start now. He'd just move on, as she suggested. There were other women…

She darted a glance over at him and for a second their eyes met. She had beautiful eyes. Smouldering green, thickly fringed with dark sooty lashes. He didn't want another woman, he realised angrily; he wanted her back in his bed.

Was Nicole seeing someone else? The question flashed into Luke's mind from out of nowhere. It was a possibility. What about the tie that he'd found in her kitchen? She'd told him it was for someone's birthday. At the time he hadn't thought anything about it. But now…

An angry feeling of betrayal seared through him. Then,

annoyed with himself, he shrugged it off. It wasn't like him to think like this. Maybe Nicole was right and it *was* time to move on. Let's face it, he rarely let an affair get past the six-month mark, because he found after that things started to get too heavy. Maybe that was what Nicole was worried about? They had been seeing each other for at least five months now.

But it was a turnaround that *she* had been the one to mention it first. And he didn't like it.

CHAPTER FOUR

WHAT a difference a day made, Nicole thought as she packed her things away ready to leave the office.

This time yesterday all she had been able to think about was getting into bed with Luke and the wild and wonderful effect he had on her. And she had known for sure when their eyes had met that he was thinking along the same lines. Today the relationship was over, and on the few occasions they'd had to speak to each other all hint of warmth and teasing passion had gone from Luke's expression; everything had been completely focused on work.

But what did she expect? she asked herself angrily. Luke wouldn't agonise over their split. In the few seconds he had taken to follow her downstairs into the boardroom this morning he'd probably already lined up another date for tonight.

The thought made her feel desolate.

'Get a grip, Nicole,' she muttered as she headed out towards the lifts.

Molly's desk was empty, as was every office she passed on the way down the hall. It was Friday, and with the urgent work of the week finished most people had gone home about an hour ago. Nicole could have left earlier if she had wanted to, but the thought of her empty apartment and an even emptier weekend stretching before her had not encouraged her to go. It had seemed favourable to bury herself in some paperwork for a while and try to forget it was Friday.

She pressed the button for the lift and then stepped back to wait for it. The only sounds in the building were from the cleaners, who started work when the place was empty. There was the distant hum of vacuum cleaners, a low murmur of voices, and the sound of a radio playing some sentimental love ballad.

Nicole wanted to listen to a love ballad like she wanted a hole in the head. She was about to press the button for the lift again when it suddenly arrived. The doors swished open and to her consternation she was face to face with Luke.

'Oh!' She hesitated. 'I didn't expect to see you. You're working late.'

'That seems to make two of us.' His gaze flicked over her coolly. 'I thought you were going out tonight?'

After a brief hesitation she shrugged. 'I cancelled.'

'I see. Are you getting into the lift or not?'

'Yes, of course.' Hurriedly she stepped in beside him and reached to press the button for the ground floor car park.

There was a moment's silence as the lift doors shut. Nicole was very aware of Luke's eyes on her, and she had never felt more uncomfortable in her life. She searched for something to say to fill the void. 'I've just been filling in that report on the European sales issue.'

Luke made no reply.

'I think we need—'

'Nicole, this is ridiculous!' He cut across her suddenly, his voice calm.

'What is?' Nicole glanced over at him, and as their eyes connected she could feel herself starting to heat up inside.

'You know very well what I mean,' he said gruffly. 'Look, I've thought about what you said this morning and you are right. We shouldn't make heavy weather out of our relationship. But, even so, it seems strange that you are rambling on about European sales and all the while there is an atmosphere between us that needs sorting out.'

'I think we should just concentrate on our work now, Luke.' She looked away from him determinedly. 'I don't really have time for anything else.' She didn't want to get drawn into this conversation. It was an emotional minefield.

'It's six forty-five on a Friday evening, Nicole. I think work can safely take a back seat.'

'On the contrary, I don't think we can afford to be complacent until this deal for RJ is signed.'

His eyes narrowed. 'I'll tell you when we need to concentrate on the deal,' he grated. 'And it's not now. There's no need for you to do any more work on that this evening.'

'Everything has to fit to your requirements, doesn't it, Luke?' She glared at him.

'Well, we managed to fit everything in before,' he said coolly. 'Work and pleasure slotted in together very well, in fact. So what's changed?'

When she didn't answer him immediately, he reached across and to her dismay hit the stop button, causing the lift to grind to a halt between floors.

'What are you doing?'

'We need to talk about what's happened between us.'

'We've said all there is to say.'

'On the contrary, you haven't said nearly enough.' Luke took a step closer. 'I think you owe me a proper explanation,' he said tersely. 'I don't buy all that stuff about work.'

Her heart started to thump against her chest with such violence that it felt like a sledgehammer. 'I don't owe you anything…' She trailed off as he came even closer. 'Luke, I demand that you restart this lift immediately.'

'You demand?' She could see a flicker of amusement in his dark eyes now.

'Yes. I want out of here right now.' She raised her chin defiantly.

'Well, then, the faster you talk, the faster we'll be out of here.'

'There is nothing to talk about,' she said firmly. 'We had an agreement; it was a casual, light-hearted affair. And now it's over. End of discussion.'

He put one hand on the wall at the side of her head and fixed her with a piercingly intense look. 'We were both enjoying ourselves. So why have you finished it?'

'I told you this morning.' It was hard to keep her voice steady and cool. He was too close to her. 'I feel the affair has run its course and—'

'Don't give me all that garbage again, Nicole. I didn't believe it the first time around this morning. I want the real reason.'

'That is the real reason.' Even as she spoke she could feel the sensual awareness twisting between them. He was so close that she could see the gold flecks in his eyes…see the beginning of dark stubble along his jawline. He was so achingly familiar to her. Usually when they were this close she would go into his arms… She longed to do that, to feel his lips pressed close to hers in hungry arousal. 'It's the real reason.' She said the words again, as if by repeating them she could convince herself as well as him.

'So you just woke up this morning and decided suddenly that the affair had run its course?' He sounded scathing.

This was all about his ego, she realised suddenly. He wasn't bothered about losing her…he was bothered because *she* had been the one to finish things. She was probably the first woman who had ever done such a thing, the one that got away, and it was bugging the hell out of him.

'I've been thinking about it for a while, actually.' She raised her chin a little higher and forced herself to hold his gaze. 'Is that so hard to believe?'

'Bearing in mind the steamy passion between us yesterday…quite frankly, yes.'

She tried very hard not to blush…and even harder not to remember what had transpired between them yesterday. 'It was just sex, Luke.'

'No, it wasn't just sex, Nicole.' He said the words with soft emphasis.

'It wasn't?' His words made her heart miss several beats. She felt herself crumble inside as she looked up into his eyes. Had she somehow misread the situation? A ray of hope flared inside her.

'You know it wasn't.' His hand moved to touch her face. The sensations of love and desire that raced through her in that instant were overwhelming.

'So what was it, then?' she asked huskily. She wanted him to say the words…she wanted to hear him say that he cared for her. Even if he couldn't bring himself to mention the L word…a declaration of some emotional intensity would be enough right now. It would be a window of opportunity that would allow her to go back into his arms. And she wanted to do that so badly right now that she ached.

His hand trailed lightly over the side of her face and his eyes were on her lips. 'It was *incredible* sex.'

Nicole felt herself fall from a great height. She flinched away from his hand. Would she never learn? She felt foolish now—foolish to have hoped for even one moment that their relationship had meant anything deeper to him.

Anger burned inside her. 'No, Luke! The real truth is that things were getting stale between us.'

'Really? I hadn't noticed that.' He shrugged. 'There was certainly nothing stale about your responses in the bedroom.'

'Do you have to keep mentioning that?' she asked furiously.

'Well, it *is* relevant,' he said, and looked at her with a raised eyebrow. 'Don't you think?'

'No, I don't. Because the affair is over. And the passion is dead as far as I'm concerned.'

'So the spark between us…whatever it was…has gone?' He clicked his fingers. 'As fast as that?'

'Yes.' She held his gaze defiantly as she tried to convince herself of the fact. 'Now, will you please just restart the lift?'

He ignored her request completely. 'So, if I were to caress you it would have no effect?' he asked quietly.

Her heart missed a beat. 'Luke, I want you to restart the lift!'

A mocking smile played at the corners of Luke's mouth now. 'And if I were to kiss you, you wouldn't want to return the kiss?'

He noticed how her breathing had quickened, how her green eyes had taken on a shimmer of vulnerability.

'Luke—'

He held up his hand. 'Yes, I know—you want out of here.'

She watched with a feeling of relief as he moved back from her and pressed a button, making the lift flare into life.

'So, now we've cleared that up, it's business as usual, then.' He said the words briskly as he looked across at her. 'We'll just forget our little recreational interlude.'

'It's already forgotten.' She tried to sound unconcerned and blasé, but inside she was dying.

The doors opened onto the car park and Nicole wanted to run through them, but she forced herself to walk with dignity past Luke.

'Just one thing.'

His voice made her swing around to look at him, and that was when he caught hold of her and pulled her close against his body.

'I think one last kiss is in order…just to prove to each other that we are doing the right thing.'

'Luke, I—'

Whatever she had been going to say was cut off by the touch of his lips against hers. To her surprise, the kiss wasn't hard or punishing, as the tone of his voice had suggested. On the contrary, it was a gentle assault on her senses. She tried very hard not to respond, her hands stiff by her sides as she willed herself fiercely not to touch him. But the warmth of his caress was so persuasive…so tender…that it made her defences instantly start to collapse. She felt her body starting to weaken, felt her lips starting to soften invitingly as she kissed him back.

It was only as her hands touched against the material of his jacket that she realised she had moved closer. Hurriedly she wrenched herself away. Her breathing was coming in short, sharp bursts; her eyes were wide as they locked on his.

'That wasn't bad, considering the spark has all gone.' Luke's voice was sardonic.

She swallowed hard on a feeling of sadness mixed with fury. 'You shouldn't have done that!' Her voice was trembling now. 'The affair is over, Luke.'

'Of course it is.' He shrugged. 'Relax, there are no hard feelings, Nicole. As you say, the affair would have ground to a halt soon anyway. It was just a bit of fun.'

She folded her arms in front of her body. This didn't feel like fun. This really hurt. But she took another step back from him and just nodded. He was right. If she hadn't finished it, a few weeks down the line he'd have done the deed. At least this way she still had her pride.

The only trouble was that pride seemed a hollow comfort.

'I'll see you next week.' His eyes flicked over her with a look almost of dismissal.

'Yes.' For a second she watched as he headed off towards where his silver Porsche was parked. She was filled with a desire to call out to him, to tell him she had changed her mind and ask could they start over? Hurriedly she fished in her bag for her car keys. She had to remain strong.

Luke was surprised to find that he was filled with anger as he got into his car. It sizzled through him in furious waves. He turned the key in the ignition and the powerful car flared into life. Forget her, he told himself heatedly. She's not worth it. But, even so, anger still pounded through his veins.

No woman had ever acted like this around him before! Maybe that was why he was so incensed, he thought grimly as he swung the car out of his private space and up the ramp into the blinding light of the sun. Maybe she had just dented his ego. Generally *he* was the one who decided when a relationship was over. In fact the last woman to have walked out on him was his mother, and that had been twenty-five years ago, when he was eleven!

He had only driven a block when his phone rang. Pulling over to the side of the road, he reached to answer it.

'Hi, it's me.' Amber Harris's tone was seductively warm.

'Hi, Amber. What can I do for you?'

'I was wondering if you'd like to meet up for a drink to-night?'

The invitation took Luke by surprise, and he didn't answer for a moment.

'You're probably busy, but I just thought I'd ask,' she continued hurriedly.

'Yes, I am busy, Amber.' He found himself fobbing her off. 'I can't make it.'

'Maybe another time?' She sounded disappointed.

'Yes, maybe. Was there anything else, Amber?' Luke continued swiftly.

He listened as she quickly rallied herself and changed the subject back to work.

Why had he turned her down? Luke wondered. Amber was very attractive, and would probably make pleasant company. Not only was he free, he had already made dinner reservations for La Luna tonight—dinner reservations that he had hoped to share with Nicole.

He frowned. Usually he had no qualms about moving

on from a relationship, but strangely the thought of dining with someone else—even someone as attractive as Amber—wasn't firing him with any enthusiasm whatsoever.

Even as Amber was speaking in his mind he was seeing Nicole, and the way she had looked at him a few minutes ago.

Her response to his kiss had held none of its usual dynamism. It had, however, held a curious bittersweet resistance. And that had fired something else inside him… what, he wasn't quite sure. Maybe it was just a sense of challenge?

Whatever it was, he really should just let her go. Should take up Amber's invitation. Trouble was, he didn't want to. He cut across Amber's rambling descriptions of the New York office.

'Look, Amber, I'm going to have to go,' he said impatiently.

'Sure…' She sounded flustered. 'We'll talk later.'

'Yes, I'll look at those last few documents next week.' He closed the phone.

He wasn't ready to move on and date someone else, he thought decisively. What he wanted was Nicole back.

CHAPTER FIVE

THEY were skirting around each other at work, and it had made for an uncomfortable week.

This was what happened when you had an affair with the boss, Nicole thought as she pulled into her parking space at the office with a feeling of dread. Nothing but turmoil ensued.

It certainly felt as if nothing had been going right recently. Not only had she spent the last week trying to convince herself that she was better off without Luke, failing miserably into the bargain, but now she had a particularly nasty bout of food poisoning. She'd been sick all weekend, and it had left her feeling tired and drained. Quite honestly she'd rather have faced the dentist then go and face Luke again for another week of cool, clipped conversations.

And now a third problem was looming. The carefully thought-out business plans for the RJ takeover were in a state of disarray. The owner of the company, Ron Johnson, had failed to sign the contract last Friday.

Nicole had always known that Ron Johnson was unpredictable. He'd built up his business empire with the help of his wife Helen, and since her death just over a year ago he'd been living life as a recluse in the Caribbean, leaving a team of lawyers to organise the sale of his company and becoming more and more intransigent about the terms and conditions under which he would allow his beloved business to leave his possession.

From the outset this deal had been beset with difficulties. Ron's lawyers had wanted to sell to Luke, as his was the highest bid on the table. But Ron had been undecided. He'd had another offer, from a husband and wife team whom he liked, and as he was a deeply religious man he'd said he'd rather sell to them, because he thought they would be more trustworthy and reliable in the workplace.

Nicole found herself remembering the morning a few months ago when Luke had received that news. Their affair had been in full flight, and they'd been working on the first pieces of the jigsaw that would bring RJ Records under their umbrella.

When the phone had rung, and it had been Ron's lawyers *for the fifth time in an hour*, Nicole had had a feeling that more trouble was on its way. They'd already reassured Ron on every aspect of their intentions for the business, but when Luke had heard the latest he'd almost exploded.

'Is the guy *serious*?' he had grated.

'What's the problem?' Nicole remembered she had sat on the edge of his desk and leaned closer.

Luke had flicked on the speakerphone so that she could hear.

'I'm afraid I am serious, Mr Santana. Mr Johnson has deeply held beliefs, and he's also very sentimental about his business. He thinks that a husband and wife team will be the winning combination to look after his company.'

'Well, tell him that *I* run my company with the help of my very trustworthy fiancée,' Luke said sarcastically. 'Tell him anything… In fact tell him we have big plans to turn RJ Records into a family-run business one day.'

'Oh, really?' The lawyer's voice brightened considerably; and the fact that Luke was being completely facetious seemed lost on him. Either that or he had latched on to the statement as a lifeline to push the deal through. 'Well, that might make all the difference, Mr Santana, because I know one of Mr Johnson's concerns is that you might tear the company apart as soon as you acquire it, and sell it off again.'

Luke was struck speechless for a moment.

'I'll tell Mr Johnson about your plans and get back to you,' the lawyer continued briskly. 'I presume the woman in question is the one we have been dealing with? A Ms Connell?'

The lawyer was leading him! Luke glanced over at Nicole with a raised eyebrow. 'Yes, that's the one.'

'Hey! Don't you think you should have asked before using me as your bogus fiancée?' she blazed as soon as the phone call ended.

Luke looked lazily amused. 'It was what you might call a whirlwind decision.'

'Yes, so I noticed—'

'Stop being difficult.' Before she realised his intention he had pulled her down onto his knee and planted a firm yet possessive kiss on her lips. 'It's not a binding commitment…just a temporary stop-gap to please an eccentric millionaire.'

'Hmm…temporary insanity, you mean,' she murmured, distracted by his kiss.

'Well, I can't argue with that… Can you believe that Ron Johnson ever managed to build a business as successful as RJ? Imagine throwing away a deal as big as the one we've offered on some kind of whim! Even his lawyers seem fed-up. That one more or less steered me into a lie!'

'Well, I admire Mr Johnson,' Nicole said staunchly. 'It's not very often that you meet someone who puts ethics above money.'

Luke slanted her a wry look. 'This is just a business deal, Nicole.'

'But it's not just a business deal where Ron Johnson is concerned, is it?' Nicole said. 'He really cares about his company. He and his late wife put a lot of energy into building it up. He wants to sell it to someone with the same moral codes as himself. And he thinks that if he sells it to a husband and wife team it will have a secure future. Whereas if he sells it to you he thinks it could be divided and sold off in little pieces and his workforce could lose their jobs. And, let's face it, he has a point,' Nicole added wryly. 'Because, rather than a warm, family type of man, *you* are an asset-stripping, cold-blooded shark of a businessman.'

Luke shot her an amused look. 'Can I just remind you that this is your fiancé that you are tearing apart?'

'Just thinking laterally,' she said with a smile.

'Well, don't!' He stroked a very sensual caress along the side of her face. 'I'll have you know that I expect loyalty at all times—even from a fake fiancée.'

'Sorry, but I don't know if I can manage that,' she said teasingly.

'Not even with a little persuasion?' He kissed her with a possessiveness that made her heart race.

'Well…on second thoughts I might be open to a little more bribery…' She returned his kisses and wound her arms around his neck.

'So, I wonder if our deal with Johnson is on or off,' Luke said, when they both came up for air.

She smiled and reached up to trail her fingers through his hair. 'Well, put it this way. I hope for your sake that Ron Johnson doesn't read the papers in that remote hideaway of his.'

'Why's that?'

'Because the newspapers refer to you as "The Bachelor Businessman".'

Luke looked amused. 'You are making this up, now.'

'No, it's official: you are a real bad boy. Not only do you break women's hearts, but you also break up companies.'

'It's called asset-stripping, and it is a perfectly legitimate practice.' Luke laughed. 'And as for breaking women's hearts, I think that is a bit of an exaggeration. I'm just not the settling down, pipe-and-slippers type. But I'm always honest and up-front about my intentions.'

'Well, don't shoot the messenger. I'm just telling you what some of the papers say.' Nicole shrugged.

'What kind of newspapers do you read?'

'Quality ones, of course.' Nicole grinned.

'Sounds like it,' Luke said derisively. 'So, the question is: what's a nice girl like you doing with a guy like me?'

'Guess you just got lucky.' She looked at him teasingly. 'Plus, I have to admit I've always been attracted by the element of danger…'

'Ah…now you are talking my language. We seem to have a lot in common, Ms Connell. We both like to take risks.' He stroked a hand along her cheek. 'And we are both free spirits. In fact, I think you are right— I *have* just got lucky. Because you make a great make-believe fiancée.'

It was just a light-hearted remark, but as their eyes connected Nicole felt a brief shimmer of something deeper inside her…a feeling that she immediately dismissed.

Five minutes later they were interrupted by a phone call to tell them that Ron Johnson was willing to go ahead with the deal.

'Thankfully it would appear that Ron reads the financial papers rather than the rags,' Luke said triumphantly as he put the phone down. 'He went for the engagement story.'

'You have no shame, Luke Santana,' she said with a shake of her head. 'Lying without compunction to the poor man.'

'Well, if we are going to be precise, here, it was actually his lawyers who did the lying. And anyway, he's not so poor—he *is* going to get the top price for his business.'

'But he's already a multimillionaire, so maybe the money isn't his real priority.'

'No matter how much money you have, it's still a priority,' Luke said dryly. 'And anyway, haven't you heard that old saying? All's fair in love and business,' he replied with a smile.

'I think you'll find that's love and war,' she corrected. 'There's no mention of *business* in that saying.'

'There is in my book,' Luke said mockingly.

'Well, I think this is a dangerous game,' Nicole warned. 'If Ron finds out that you are lying he will have no choice but to pull the plug on the deal.'

'That is a chance I'll have to take…' He pulled her close with a playful show of strength. 'Now, shall we do something *really* dangerous?' he growled against her ear. 'I feel like celebrating…right here and now…'

Someone was tapping on her car window, and hastily Nicole snapped out of her reminiscences and looked around.

Amber Harris had pulled into the space beside her and come over to attract her attention.

'Oh, hi, Amber.' Hurriedly Nicole reached for her brief-case and stepped out to join her.

'You looked like you were miles away,' the other woman remarked cheerfully as they walked together towards the lifts.

'I was just thinking about all the work I've got lined up for today,' Nicole said briskly. 'I've got a load of new con-tracts to sort out.'

'Tell me about it!' Amber tossed her mane of long red hair over one shoulder as they stepped into the lift. She was wearing a tight little black dress, and it looked fabulous on her. She was more like a top model than an accountant, Nicole thought wryly.

'I'm sorting out figures for the New York office,' Amber said. 'I had to fly there three times last week. I've got to the point where I don't know what city I'm in. '

'That can be very tiring,' Nicole said sympathetically.

'You are not kidding!' Amber pressed the button for the top floor. 'The only thing that keeps me going is Luke. He is just so gorgeous, isn't he?' She leaned back against the wall of the lift and sighed dreamily.

'Yes, very good-looking.' Nicole pressed the button for her floor.

'He's a hard fish to catch, though. I know lots of women have tried to pin him down and failed. But that makes him all the more of a challenge, don't you think?'

'I suppose so.' Had *she* seen Luke as a challenge? Nicole thought about that for a moment and then dismissed it. No, she had originally seen Luke as exciting and fun. She had never set out to want more than that. In fact after her divorce the last thing she had wanted was to fall in love again, and she had thought that being with Luke would be playing things safe emotionally. It was a damn disaster. Life would have been so much easier if she could have just continued enjoying their affair for what it was.

'Anyway, I think he might be on the verge of asking me out to dinner next week.' Amber looked over at her conspiratorially. 'Well, put it this way…I'm working on it.'

Somehow Nicole managed a smile. She was used to women swooning over Luke. And it was none of her business if he chose to go out with someone else now. But even so she couldn't quite get rid of a swirling feeling of loss. *Stop it, Nicole*, she told herself fiercely. *You have to let go of him.*

At least nobody knew about the affair, she consoled herself. Things would be far worse if she were now the subject of office gossip. Swiftly she changed the subject. 'I'm up to my eyes in this RJ Records deal.'

'I heard there are problems with that, and Ron Johnson hasn't signed the contract.'

'Just a blip,' Nicole said with confidence. 'We've had these before with him.'

'Aaron Williams thinks the deal will fold.'

Privately, Nicole was having similar doubts—but she wasn't going to voice them aloud. As long as there was a spark of life left in this deal she was going to fight for it. 'We'll get the company,' she said determinedly. 'It's just a matter of time.' The lift opened on Nicole's floor. 'See you later, Amber.'

Would Luke go out with Amber? Nicole wondered as she walked down towards her office. Every time she thought about it she felt a dart of some dark and horrible emotion twisting inside her.

With determination she turned her attention back towards work. The important thing was finalising this deal with Johnson.

As soon as Nicole sat down at her desk she checked her e-mails. There was nothing regarding the RJ deal. The silence was ominous.

She supposed she would have to check with Luke to find out how he wanted to play things.

Nicole was just reaching for the phone so that she could ring and discuss it with him when an e-mail arrived from him.

You better come up so we can sort this RJ mess out.

No *Good morning, Nicole, how are you?* she thought sardonically as she ran a smoothing hand over her hair and tried to prepare herself for facing him. She could have done without this, she thought as she got reluctantly to her feet. She still felt a bit nauseous; obviously that food poisoning bug hadn't completely gone.

When she walked into Luke's office she found that she wasn't the only one to have been summoned. His lawyer, Aaron Williams, was there, and so was the company's chief accountant, John Sorenson. Luke was pacing around the room like a caged lion.

How was it that Luke could even look sexy when he was

angry? Nicole wondered hazily. He seemed to radiate some kind of forceful energy that was compelling. Maybe it was something as simple as the fact that he looked good in that dark suit. Or maybe it was that attitude of power and dynamism... She didn't know. All she knew was that life would be a lot easier if she were immune to him.

'What took you so long, Nicole?' he asked tersely. 'I've had Ron's lawyers on the phone...' Luke trailed off and looked at her again, his eyes narrowed. 'Are you OK? You look a bit pale.'

'I'm fine,' she lied, surprised he'd noticed.

He looked at her intently for a second, and her heart seemed to skip a beat. *Don't start imagining he gives a damn, for heaven's sake,* she reminded herself fiercely. She angled up her chin a little further. 'I'm fine, Luke,' she reiterated firmly.

He nodded. 'Well, we've got a busy few days ahead of us, so I hope so. This is a crucial time for the business.'

There... All he was worried about was the fact that she might need time off work, and she'd been wondering if he was concerned about her, Nicole thought angrily.

'Anyway, getting back to the matter in hand,' Luke continued speedily, 'the bottom line is that Ron wants to meet with me before he signs the contact.'

'So he *is* going to sign?' Nicole sank down into one of the office chairs.

Luke shrugged. 'Your guess is as good as mine. But we've come this far down the road, so we'll have to go with whatever he wants right now.'

'I've gone over the figures with a fine comb and I think he would be mad not to sign,' John put in heatedly. He was pouring some coffee from a pot that was standing on the desk. 'Do you want a drink, Nicole?'

She shook her head. The mere thought of drinking coffee was making her stomach clench in protest.

With difficulty, she tuned back in to what Luke was saying.

'I don't think it's the money that's the problem. Apparently he wants other assurances, otherwise he's backing out.'

'What kind of assurances?' Nicole asked cautiously. *Was this anything to do with Luke's lie about being engaged?* she wondered suddenly.

'Heaven knows what it is this time,' Luke grated. 'But we are going to have to meet with him today—before the whole deal collapses.'

'Today?' Nicole was taken aback. 'That's too short notice!'

Luke was distracted as she crossed her long shapely legs and sent him a very feisty look from fulminating green eyes. 'It's going to have to be today,' he muttered. 'Talking through lawyers isn't helping. And if we let this drag on any longer we are going to lose the deal.'

'But Ron is virtually a recluse.' She frowned. 'And he lives in a remote hideaway on Barbados, Luke. He won't come here.'

'Yes, I realise that,' Luke said dryly. 'Which is why I've put the company jet on standby.' He glanced at his watch. 'I reckon if we get our act together we can be on the plane and heading off within the hour.'

Nicole started to shake her head. She didn't like the sound of this at all. 'Ron is eccentric, Luke. You know we could go all that way and he might change his mind about seeing us.'

'I don't think that will happen. He said he wants to meet, and he sounded genuine,' Luke said firmly.

'But we'd need a copy of all the paperwork.' Her heart was thumping very uncomfortably now, and it had nothing to do with paperwork and everything to do with the thought of going away on business with Luke. 'And—'

'And Aaron is going to take care of all that.' Luke cut across her swiftly and turned to look at the other man, who was standing silently by the window. 'I'll need it on my desk within half an hour.'

Aaron looked shocked. 'It might take a bit longer—'

'We haven't got longer than that.' Luke cut across him too. 'So I suggest you get a move on.'

'Fine.' Aaron departed from the room, looking immensely agitated.

'And meanwhile I want you to check the figures, John.' Luke turned towards his chief accountant. 'Print out some variations on the theme, in case we have to renegotiate the price.'

'Yes, I'll get right on it.' John swept out of the room, looking as flustered as Aaron.

Nicole couldn't blame them. It wasn't easy to be around Luke when he was in one of these moods. He was a perfectionist, and he didn't tolerate setbacks easily.

There was a tense silence when they were left alone.

'So, what would you like me to do?' Nicole asked hesitantly.

'You better go home and pack enough clothes for a few days.'

'A few *days*!' Nicole looked over at him in surprise. 'This should be an overnight trip at most!'

'I don't know how long it's going to take to sort out. But

we'll have to stay there until we have some kind of handle on it.' Luke perched on the edge of his desk and looked over at her. And despite the seriousness of the situation he couldn't help but feel a certain sense of satisfaction from the words. Maybe at the same time he could get some kind of a handle on Nicole's innermost emotions, he thought suddenly...find out what she was thinking... He'd tolerated this cool, clipped politeness of hers for a week now, and it was driving him insane.

He smiled to himself. 'And *you* are going to have to play the part of my fiancée.'

Nicole felt her face flare with colour. 'Are you joking?'

'No.' Luke's voice was calm. 'This isn't really a joking matter, is it?'

'I told you that you were playing with fire when you lied to Ron!' She glared at him. 'Is this why the deal has stalled? Does he know you fed him a load of rubbish?'

'I've no idea, Nicole,' he said honestly. 'All I'm saying is I am going to need you by my side to play your part. Hopefully it won't take long.'

'I'm not happy about this approach to things, Luke,' she said in agitation. 'I think it's most unprofessional.'

'I'm not wild about it myself, but what can we do?' He shrugged. 'I need you to come with me regardless of the fiancée angle. You've done most of the negotiations. You know this deal backwards.'

He was right. This deal was her baby; she'd nursed it for months. There was no way she was going to cut herself out from it now. 'I'll get Molly to book some accommodation for us, then,' she said decisively.

'No need. I've got a house out there. Accommodation

is the least of our worries.' Luke glanced over as she continued to sit there. 'Is there a problem?'

'Well…' She shrugged. The problem was that this was giving her palpitations! The fact that they would be staying at his house rather than at a hotel seemed to make everything worse. She tried to make herself feel better with the thought that Aaron and John would be accompanying them. But, even so, it seemed much too intimate a situation, given their present circumstances.

'Nicole?' He was watching her with a frown.

Quickly, she rallied. 'I'm finding it hard to get my head around this lie you've told to Ron Johnson, but I don't suppose there is a lot we can do about that now.' She didn't know what else she could say. Telling him she didn't want to stay at his house would sound as if she didn't trust herself when she was around him…which to be honest she didn't. But she couldn't let him know that! She was just going to have to be very strict with herself and dedicate her every thought towards the deal and not him. 'We'll just have to deal with the situation, I suppose. This is too important for us to muck it up now.'

'My sentiments exactly. So at least we understand each other.' His voice was filled with cool authority. 'I'll pick you up outside your apartment in half an hour. Make sure you have all the relevant paperwork with you.'

Nicole stood up and, with a nod, made for the door.

Luke watched her go with a gleam of satisfaction.

Maybe this could all work to his advantage. With Nicole by his side Ron might sign the contract, and at the same time Nicole would be forced closer to him… Which meant he could get past those prickly defences of hers and find out the real reason why she had pushed him away…and in the process maybe he'd get lucky, both in business and in bed.

The thought put a positive spin on the day.

CHAPTER SIX

THERE was no time for Nicole to dwell on the situation. By the time she had driven back to her apartment and thrown things into a case the buzzer was ringing and Luke was telling her impatiently through the intercom that he was waiting downstairs.

She glanced at her reflection in the full-length mirror before picking up her small suitcase. There hadn't been time to change, so she was still wearing the pale blue suit she had been wearing at the office this morning. At least there was colour in her cheeks now—probably due more to agitation than perfect health, But at any rate she no longer looked like death warmed up, so that was something.

The buzzer rang again. 'Yes, I'm coming,' she muttered angrily as she struggled through the door and into the lift with her briefcase and her suitcase.

She hadn't expected Luke to be outside in a limousine! A chauffeur jumped out of the vehicle as she appeared, and took her suitcase before opening the door for her.

She sank down into the comfortable leather seat opposite Luke. 'Sorry to keep you waiting,' she said breathlessly.

'That's OK.' By contrast, Luke appeared to be perfectly

relaxed. He had some paperwork open in front of him and he barely glanced up at her. 'But we *are* cutting things fine.'

'I had to pack and…' She trailed off as she suddenly noticed that they were alone. 'Where's Aaron and John? I thought they were coming with us?'

She had his full attention now. 'What gave you that idea?'

'I don't know…I just assumed…' She took a deep breath and forced herself to sound calm. She didn't want him to realise she was shaken by the fact they were alone. 'I mean, don't we need them? Aaron's legal advice could be crucial. I usually have a team with me when I go on these business trips. Last year when I went to LA I took—'

'Nicole.' Luke looked straight at her, his eyes steely. 'I'm the president of the company. I make the decisions. You don't need anyone else with you.'

She clammed up. When he put it like that, she supposed he was right.

'Now, do you think we could get on with some work? I need you to run your eye over these figures that John has produced.'

Nicole took some of the sheets of paper he handed across to her and tried to concentrate.

For a while there was silence between them as the limousine glided smoothly through the traffic. Nicole finished reading the report and then opened her briefcase to get some paper to make notes. Her glance flicked around the vehicle. She had never travelled in this much style before. Her usual run to the airport was made squashed into a cab with others from the office. This vehicle was enormous, and impressively kitted out with a circular sweep of black leather seats, a mini-bar and TV.

'Do you usually travel like this when you go away on business?' she asked impulsively.

He glanced over at her. 'Yes, of course.'

Stupid question, Nicole berated herself. Luke's whole life was one of luxury.

Home for him was a fabulous apartment in the Art Deco district of Miami. It overlooked the beach and had its own rooftop terrace with a swimming pool. Nicole had only been there a few times, and she had thought the place absolutely beautiful. But she hadn't liked it. The decor was smart and trendy, but geared towards the fact that it was a bachelor pad…and a multimillionaire bachelor pad at that. It had every hi-tech modern convenience you could wish for, and it was coldly impersonal.

She supposed she hadn't liked it because it had reminded her of the things she wanted to forget about Luke. Not only that he wasn't one for putting down roots, but also that they lived in two different worlds. Yes, she was successful enough to be able to rent a beautiful apartment in a nice area, but it was nothing compared to Luke's life. He had houses all over the world…chauffeur-driven limousines…a company jet, for heaven's sake!

Even if he *had* been the settling down type, their relationship probably wouldn't have worked out anyway. He'd have chosen someone from his own social sphere.

He looked up suddenly and caught her watching him, and as his dark eyes sliced into hers it set her heart thundering crazily against her chest. It brought home the fact that she could try and persuade herself all day about why their relationship wouldn't have worked out, but she was still in love with him.

'Would you like a drink?' Luke asked suddenly as he reached to pour himself a coffee from a pot beside the bar. 'There is fruit juice and mineral water if you don't want coffee.'

'I'd love a mineral water, please.' She watched as he reached and opened one of the bottles, then poured it into a crystal glass for her.

'Thanks.' She took the drink from him, being careful to avoid touching his hand. Her eyes looked up towards his, and she knew he had noticed the fact because there was a look of irritation in their dark depths.

'We are not going to have this atmosphere between us for the next few days, are we?' he asked suddenly, his tone derisive.

'What atmosphere?' She tried to ignore the fact that her skin was heating up.

'You seem edgy.'

'Look, as far as I'm concerned this is work as usual, OK?' Her eyes clashed with his across the confined space.

Then he nodded. 'Good. That's OK, then.'

The ring of his mobile phone broke the mood, and Nicole turned her gaze back towards her work with a feeling of relief. He was right. If this feeling of tension were kept up for much longer she would be like a wrung-out dishcloth in no time.

'Oh, hi, Amber,' he said lightly. 'I'm just on my way to the airport now. Did you find that report? That's great. Well, if you would, that would make life easier...' He laughed at whatever she said in reply. It was that lazy, attractive laugh that made Nicole's pulses race. With a frown she tried to bury herself further into her paperwork.

'Yes, OK—I'll see you soon,' he said, and laughed again at what she said.

He obviously found Amber extremely amusing. Nicole was filled with a childish urge to put her fingers in her ears. She really didn't want to hear this. See you soon for what? she wondered suddenly. Dinner…*bed*?

'Yeah, I'll look into that. OK, bye.'

He hung up and silence resumed between them. Nicole glared at her work. She was being ridiculous. Amber worked for Luke. OK, she fancied him like crazy, but despite what she had told Nicole in the lift that didn't mean there was something going on between them. And even if there were it wouldn't last. A few months down the line and Luke would be bored, ready for the next conquest. Trouble was, that fact didn't really cheer Nicole up—because just the thought of Luke kissing another woman…taking her to bed…filled her with a feeling of complete and utter desolation. It was wildly irrational, but she couldn't seem to help it.

She had felt like this when her marriage had fallen apart and Patrick had told her he was leaving her. But she'd had more reason to be upset back then. She'd been married to Patrick for five years, and not only had he been leaving her for someone else but the other woman had been pregnant with his child.

She could still remember the gut-wrenching feeling when he'd told her the news.

To find out that Patrick had had an affair was bad enough, but to discover he was also about to become a father was a double-whammy.

She would never forget the moment he had dropped the bombshell. He'd even had the nerve to tell her that he still loved her. 'The affair only started out as a bit of fun,' he had said sadly. 'A bit of light entertainment. I never meant to hurt you. But the thing is that she's going to have my baby...I can't walk away from her now. I've got to do the right thing.'

The right thing! That was a joke. Nicole had told him that if he had wanted to do 'the right thing' he would never have had an affair in the first place.

She had wanted to throw things at him; she had wanted to rail against the world and him for the cruelty and unfairness. Why couldn't it have been *her* baby? But instead she had conducted herself with cool dignity, picked herself up and carried on with her life. And she'd promised herself that no man would ever hurt her again. It was a promise that she was clinging on to for grim life at the moment.

She bit down on her lip and tried to remind herself of the lessons from the past. She had loved Patrick...or rather she had thought she loved him until he had walked out and she had found out he was really very shallow. Even so, her divorce had devastated her. It had been a sobering lesson on guarding her heart, and most of all on the importance of being independent.

So she had been right to finish with Luke. Especially as her feelings for him were even more intense than anything she had felt for Patrick. She couldn't go through any more pain; she didn't need a man in her life, she told herself firmly.

They were thirty-five thousand feet up in the sky and it felt as if they were nearly as many miles apart, Luke thought irately as he spoke to Nicole for the third time and got a one-word reply.

He glanced across at her. He couldn't see her face; it was obscured from view by the silky curtain of her hair. She'd been sitting like that since take-off, deeply immersed in a report he'd handed her. And although he couldn't fault her behaviour—she was businesslike and courteous—there was something really irritating about the way she had completely withdrawn from him. In the old days when they were working together on reports she would give him a smile or say something amusing. She had a great sense of humour and could usually make him laugh no matter how dry the subject they were immersed in. He missed that.

Luke drummed his fingers on the edge of the table. He had a million and one checks to make before this meeting with Ron. He didn't have time for frivolities. And yet…he found his gaze constantly drifting over towards her.

She had taken off the jacket to her blue suit and was wearing a plain white blouse that was neatly tailored into her small waist. He noticed that her pencil skirt stopped just above her knee. She uncrossed her long legs and then crossed them again. His eyes followed the movement. Then he noticed that her pen had rolled down onto the floor. Before he could pick it up for her she had bent to retrieve it. Her blouse was buttoned low and he could just see the edge of her lacy white bra.

He badly wanted to make love to her again, but he knew this was a game he needed to play carefully. One wrong move and like a skittish colt she might bolt in the opposite direction. Over this last week he had forced himself to bide his time and match her businesslike mood. It was strange, patience wasn't usually one of his virtues, but somehow Nicole was worth waiting for.

No matter what she had said to him about how the spark had gone, how she wanted to move on, he didn't quite believe her. OK, maybe he was being arrogant and over-confident…and maybe she was seeing someone else…he hadn't entirely ruled out the possibility. But he had tasted desire on her lips when he had last kissed her. He was almost sure of it. And now they were going to be alone together… the perfect time to find out what was going on…to get inside her head, sort things out and then hopefully enjoy some passion. Except for one small flaw. She was ignoring him.

He raked an impatient hand through his hair, irritated with himself for dwelling on this now. He should think about this tonight, when business was out of the way. This meeting with Johnson had to be given his full attention. *Snooze and you lose*, he told himself firmly.

He got up and walked over towards the refrigerator at the other side of the plane. 'Do you fancy something to eat?' he asked over his shoulder.

'No, thanks.' She didn't look up.

Luke helped himself to a sandwich and poured himself more coffee. 'Would you like a drink?'

'No, thanks.'

Hell, but she was really irritating him now. He sat back in his seat and rustled through some papers.

'You drink too much caffeine,' she said suddenly. 'That's your fourth cup. I'm surprised you can sleep at night.'

So she had been noticing what he was doing even if she wasn't looking up. 'I never have any difficulty sleeping.' He looked over at her and smiled.

She gave a brief shadow of a smile back, and then returned her attention to her report.

'You should really eat something, you know,' he said.

'I'm not hungry.' She glanced over at him and their eyes met.

'Are you OK?' he asked, with a sudden pang of concern. She hadn't looked well earlier, and now that he studied her she still looked a little drawn.

'You asked me that this morning. And I told you I'm fine.'

'You didn't look fine this morning. You looked like death warmed up.'

'Gee, thanks.'

He smiled at her. 'Just trying to show some friendly concern.'

'I think I prefer you in your usual indifferent and domineering mode.'

'Well, as you have put in a request, a little bit of domineering could be arranged…' He looked at her teasingly.

Nicole tried to ignore the fact that when he looked at her like that she felt her temperature rise to boiling point. She hated herself for being so susceptible to him.

'I think we are getting off track, Luke. We should be discussing our forthcoming meeting, not—'

'You know, Nicole, just because our affair is over, it doesn't mean we can't still be friends.' Luke cut across her suddenly, his voice firm.

The words caused Nicole's heart to thump even more fiercely against her chest. Could you ever really go back to being just friends with someone you had shared such incredible passion with? she wondered. Certainly at this moment, feeling the way she did about him, she didn't think that was even remotely possible. How could you ever truly forget that you loved someone?

'Yes, of course we are friends.' She made herself say the words lightly.

'So why do I detect a frosty tone?'

'There is no frosty tone.' She looked over at him and then, as their eyes met, wished she hadn't. 'I'm just dealing with the situation as best I can,' she admitted huskily. 'Obviously it's a bit…awkward to be away on business with someone…you used to be close with.'

'I don't see why it has to be awkward,' Luke said nonchalantly.

'Well, I suppose you wouldn't,' she muttered, annoyed by his casual manner. 'I suppose you are used to jumping from one relationship to another, but I'm not.'

'But this is *your* choice, Nicole,' he grated.

How had they managed to slide onto such dangerous ground? she wondered in sudden panic. 'Yes, and it's fine. We've both moved on and we've been working well together this last week. As far as I'm concerned there's no *real* problem. You brought the subject up, not me.'

'Because I think if we are to have a good working relationship it's important that we are relaxed around each other. I don't think we should let personal issues get in the way of us doing good work.'

That was all he was ever worried about…work. 'I agree wholeheartedly.' She frowned and looked back at the papers in front of her. 'I just want us to get on and get this situation over with. Then we can go our separate ways and *really* relax.'

'There! That's what I mean! There's that frosty tone

again! You're going to have to watch that, Nicole. We'll never convince Ron Johnson that you are my fiancée if you sound like that around him!'

Her head jerked up at that. 'So that's what this is about!' She glared at him. 'You are not so worried about us being friends as pulling a fast one on Ron Johnson!'

'I am not pulling a fast one on anybody,' he said firmly.

'Yes, you are. You've lied, and in my book that's sharp practice!'

'You agreed to go along with the lie, so you are not so innocent yourself,' he grated sardonically.

'Only because I didn't have any choice in the matter!'

'Well, as I remember it, you didn't put up that much of a fight at the time.' His voice was coolly taunting, and it whipped Nicole's already delicate emotions into a fury. 'In fact as I recall we sealed the agreement with a kiss.'

How dared he throw what had been a romantic moment back in her face? 'Let's just drop this conversation, shall we?' she suggested coolly. 'This is exactly why we can't be friends.'

'Why? Because I'm reminding you of the truth?'

'Because you irritate the hell out of me, that's why!' she flared.

Luke smiled. 'That's better.'

'What's better?' She frowned.

'You,' he said firmly. 'You're back to your old self. That "yes and no" polite act was really starting to annoy me. I get that from everyone else around me. I expect more from you.'

'Really?' Her voice was cool. 'Well, I expect more from you than to throw reminders of intimate moments at me.'

'You can be a real spoilsport, Nicole,' he drawled with a laugh.

'And you can be a real pain in the…neck!'

'So I take it my *let's be friends* suggestion is out the window, then?' he said humorously.

'Oh, don't worry. I'll play my part and be the devoted fiancée around Ron,' she muttered. 'But that doesn't mean I'll like it.'

'I'd never have guessed.'

Luke's calm sarcasm did nothing to make her feel better. 'Well, maybe you should have used some other woman as your fake better half.'

'Maybe I should,' Luke agreed with a shrug. 'But it's a bit late for that. And as you are dealing with the RJ take-over, I'll just have to make do with you, won't I?'

The atmosphere wasn't just frosty now, it was downright arctic. Nicole looked away from him. Silence descended again between them.

The man was impossible, Nicole thought angrily. How dared he say he'd just have to *make do* with her? He was arrogant and insufferable.

Thirty minutes later the fasten seatbelt sign came on and the pilot announced that they would soon be landing. She glanced at her watch as Luke packed away some of his papers.

His arm touched against hers when he leaned across to look out of the window, and instantly she felt tingles of awareness shooting through her in a way that sent all her strong thoughts about how she disliked him into disarray. How was it that no matter how tense the situation got between them she *still* wanted to melt when he touched her? How long would it take her to get over feeling like this? she wondered painfully. *Weeks? Months? Maybe years?* a little voice said mockingly.

'Looks like a nice day down there,' he said easily.

'Does it?' Swiftly she turned away from him and glanced out of the window. Below she could see the sparkling blue water of the Caribbean, and then, as the plane banked, the green swathe of an island fringed with palm trees and golden beaches.

'Beautiful, isn't it?' Luke said.

How could he act so cool when they had just had a blazing row? she wondered. It really irritated her that he could just switch off from feelings; he'd done it when they were together as well…made love to her with fierce passion and then ten minutes later switched from lover to businessman. She hated it.

'Yes, it is.' She returned her gaze down towards the report on her knee, but she was still aware that his shoulder was just touching against hers.

Luke drummed his fingers against the armrest between them. She tried not to notice…tried not to think about the way those hands could rouse her to wonderful heights of passion.

'Shall I put this away for you now?' Suddenly Luke reached and took the report away from her. 'You need to prepare yourself for landing and fasten your belt.'

'Yes, I know that, Luke. But it doesn't affect my ability to read,' she said coolly.

'You've done enough reading. We're on Caribbean time now, so we can be a little more laid back.'

'Not if we want to get around this problem with Ron Johnson,' she reminded him as she snapped her seatbelt shut.

There she was, turning the tables on him again! Reminding him of the importance of work! The fact that she was right annoyed him. Usually *he* was the one who was completely focused. What the hell was the matter with him? he wondered.

He watched as she opened her bag and took out a comb to smooth it through her long, sleek hair. Then she opened a compact and checked her make-up, reapplied the frosty amber colour to her lips.

She had very kissable lips…he thought. This was the problem, he decided distractedly. He needed to get her back in his life and in his bed. Then things would return to normal and he could stop feeling on edge and concentrate properly on work again.

'What time is our meeting?' she asked as she snapped the compact closed and put her bag back under her seat.

'Ron's invited us for dinner at six-thirty.' Luke glanced at his watch. 'We'll just have time to get to my place and change first.'

'Dinner?' Nicole's eyebrows lifted. 'Considering the guy is virtually a recluse, that sounds encouraging. You know he doesn't usually see anybody except his lawyers and the manager he put in charge of the company?'

'Yes, he's an eccentric. But I played on the fact that we are virtually neighbours in Barbados, and it gave me an advantage.'

'Great. Well, hopefully we can get things sorted out quickly. Maybe we'll even be able to come straight back tonight.'

'Maybe.' His eyes held with hers steadily. 'But I wouldn't bet on it,' he said firmly.

CHAPTER SEVEN

THERE was a limousine waiting for them outside the terminal. They sat side by side without speaking as it whisked them down narrow country roads lined with sugar cane.

The mood between them was only broken by the fact that Luke had opened the glass partition to talk to their driver, who was an extremely friendly Barbadian called George. He laughed and joked with them, and Nicole started to relax a little as she looked out at the rolling green countryside.

They stopped when they reached the entrance to Luke's house, and waited for huge electric gates to fold back.

'We are expecting a storm tonight,' George said as he put the car into gear again and they swept on, up a long driveway.

Nicole looked up at the clear blue sky through the tracery of palm trees. 'But there's not a cloud in sight.'

'It's heading in, all right. Should be with us in the early hours of tomorrow morning.'

'I hope it's not a hurricane,' Nicole said lightly. 'I experienced a storm in Miami last year, and it was frightening.'

'I think we are lucky. It *was* hurricane force, but its strength is dropping.' George grinned at her. 'But these tropical storms are as unpredictable as a woman, so you never know.'

The car pulled to a halt and Nicole turned her attention to her surroundings. They were outside a most magnificent period house that was steeped in character.

It was painted white, and had wooden shutters that opened out onto a wraparound veranda. Bright swathes of tropical flowers grew up along the balconies, and behind the riot of colour and greenery she could see white wicker furniture, placed to look out over a garden that sloped gently down towards the sea.

Nicole let out her breath in a sigh. 'Wow.' It was all she could say.

Luke slanted an amused look over at her. 'I take it you approve?'

'Who wouldn't approve of this? It's idyllic.'

George opened the door for them and they stepped out of the air-conditioned car into the heat of the day.

There was a lazy tranquillity about the place, a silence that was infinitely soothing. The only noise was the gentle wash of waves against the shore and the occasional drone of a bee amongst the old-fashioned climbing roses.

They walked up into the shade of the veranda as the front door swung open and a woman in her mid-fifties greeted them. Her ample frame was squeezed into a bright floral dress and she had a round, smiling face. There was something warm and friendly about her, and Nicole immediately liked her.

'Welcome home, Mr Santana,' she gushed. 'I have everything ready for you.'

'Thanks, Deloris.' Luke reached and shook the woman by the hand. 'I'd like you to meet my business associate, Nicole Connell,' he said smoothly. 'Deloris is my house-keeper, Nicole, and a fine job she does too. I don't know what I'd do without her.'

The woman beamed with pleasure. 'Anything you need, Ms Connell, don't hesitate to ask me.'

They followed her into the house across a wide hallway with polished wood floors. Nicole glimpsed a very elegant drawing room to her left, before proceeding up the wide curving staircase.

'I've put you in the guest suite, Ms Connell,' Deloris said as she opened a door along the landing with a flourish.

Nicole walked past Luke into a large bedroom with a wooden four-poster bed. French doors were open out onto the veranda, and Nicole could see the bright blue of the Caribbean Sea. 'This is really lovely. Thank you.'

'I'm glad you like it.' Deloris turned towards her employer, who was standing just outside the doorway. 'There have been a few phone calls for you, Mr Santana.'

As Deloris reeled off a seemingly never-ending list of names, Nicole perched herself on the edge of the bed. She felt a little tired… In fact she felt like lying down. It was probably the heat; there didn't seem to be any air-conditioning, just the overhead whirl of the ceiling fans.

Deloris finished with her list of messages and then moved on to ask about requirements for dinner.

'We are going out, thanks, Deloris,' Luke said easily. 'Mr Johnson is sending a boat for us.'

'A boat?' Nicole looked over at him in surprise as the housekeeper left them.

'Yes. Apparently the only way to access Ron's house is by boat. He's a bit manic about security, it seems.'

'Well, if we are travelling by boat, I suppose I better put some flat-heeled shoes on, then.' Nicole kicked off her high heels and rubbed her foot absently.

Her skirt had ridden up a little. Luke followed the line of her body with narrowed eyes. 'Nicole?'

'Yes?' Her hair swung back as she looked over at him, her green eyes wide and questioning.

Luke hesitated. What the hell was he going to say to her? *Don't rub your foot like that...it's turning me on?* It sounded crazy...even to his ears. 'Never mind,' he grated impatiently. 'We haven't got long, so get a move on, will you?'

Then he was gone, closing the door very firmly behind him. Tonight, after they'd sorted out business, he would seduce her back into his bed, he promised himself. And order would be restored in his life.

When Nicole went downstairs twenty minutes later she followed the sound of Luke's voice and found him in a large study with doors that were open onto the garden.

He was sitting behind a desk with his laptop computer open in front of him. 'Bear with me for a moment,' he said, covering the phone as Nicole walked in. 'Nicole, do you remember how we access the files for RJ's accounts?' His eyes flicked over her as she walked closer, taking in the white slim-fitting trousers and the crossover black and white top. She looked smart, and yet sexy at the same time. How did she manage to do that? he wondered absently as he pressed another key to try to get the screen he wanted.

'Here.' She walked behind him and leaned over. He

could smell the scent of her perfume, sultry like a summer's day. 'We hid the files under a code…remember?'

As he watched she keyed in the code, and instantly the right file opened.

'Thanks. I'd forgotten we'd done that.' He picked up the phone again and resumed his conversation. But out of the corner of his eye he was watching Nicole as she walked around the room. She picked up a photograph of his father that was sitting next to the bookshelves. And then admired a watercolour painting that hung over the fireplace.

'This house isn't at all what I expected,' she said idly once he had hung up.

'And what *did* you expect?' Luke asked as he leaned back in his chair.

She was looking at a porcelain figurine now, which was on the windowsill. 'Well, the décor in your apartment in Miami is kind of… I suppose, at the risk of sounding rude, it's clinical…in a very stylish way, of course,' she added hastily.

'Clinical?'

'Yes…you know. Impersonal—as if everything in it isn't really your choice, it's been designed for you.'

'That's because it *was* designed for me,' Luke said with amusement. 'I paid an interior designer. I haven't got time for décor, Nicole. I'm too busy running my businesses.'

'Yes, I know.' She looked over at him. 'But this place is more of a home, somehow.'

'It was my home for a while,' Luke said with a shrug. 'My parents moved here from Portugal when I was nine.'

'I didn't realise!' Nicole looked around again with renewed interest. 'It must have been an idyllic place to grow up.'

'It was OK.' Luke glanced at his watch.

'So where are your parents now?' she asked.

'My father is dead and my mother lives in France.' Luke stood up. 'We better sort out a few last-minute details on this deal and make tracks. We don't want to be late for Ron.'

'No, of course not.'

She noticed how when the conversation veered towards something personal he only gave the briefest information and then quickly moved on. It had always been like that with him. Luke had never talked about his childhood, or shared any secrets from his past with her. And when she thought about it that hurt. They had snuggled up together in bed in the most intimate way and Nicole had longed to talk to him…really talk to him…get to know him on a deeper level. Yet he never had truly opened up to her. Yes, he'd held her after lovemaking, and he had made her feel special. But then, just as she had begun feeling closer to him than to any person in the world, he'd always pulled away…talked about business…talked about practicalities…never emotions…

She watched as he walked over towards one of the cupboards and took out a wooden box. 'What are you doing?'

'You need an engagement ring.' As he spoke he was emptying out the contents of the box on his desk.

Some old costume jewellery spilled across the leather top.

'Where did you get all that?' she asked curiously.

'It belonged to my mother.' He opened some more drawers in the box and searched around before pulling out a velvet case. 'Ah, here we are.' He opened the lid and Nicole could see a square-cut diamond ring glinting in the sunlight.

He took it out, and then to her surprise tossed it casually in her direction. 'Here—try it on for size.'

She only just caught it. 'This looks very expensive,' she said as she looked down at it.

'Well, I think Ron will expect to see a nice ring on your finger.' He nodded towards it. 'Go ahead, try it on.'

With a feeling of extreme trepidation she slipped it on. 'It's a fraction too big.' She was about to take it off again, but before she could Luke walked across and took hold of her hand to look.

'It seems fine to me. I think you'll get away with it.'

The touch of his hand against hers made her heart start to beat with uneven heavy strokes against her chest. 'Is this charade really necessary, Luke?' she muttered as she pulled away from him.

'Maybe…maybe not. But I'm damned if I'm going to let this deal slip away just because of some quirky idea that Ron Johnson has.' Luke's eyes held with hers, a serious expression in their velvet dark depths. 'So every little helps, and this certainly can't hurt, can it?'

'That's a matter of opinion, Luke. If Ron knows you've lied to him it could hurt a great deal. And as everyone knows you are a professional bachelor, the game could be over already.'

'Well, if that's the case we'll just persuade him that I've had a change of heart.' He shrugged. 'Let's face it, it happens. Stalwart bachelors do sometimes bite the dust, fall in love and change their mind about marriage. I could have looked into your eyes and had a lightning change of character.'

'It might be more believable if you told him you'd had a brain transplant and then fallen in love,' she said derisively.

He smiled at that. 'Well, I'll grant you neither of us are the settling down type, are we? But Ron doesn't need to know that.'

She didn't answer him.

He looked at her teasingly. 'Come on, Nikki. If we do this right it'll probably swing the deal for us.'

Nikki... He had only ever called her that when they were making love. He'd whisper it in her ear... 'That was so good, Nikki...you turn me on so much...'

Just thinking about those words and the way his hands had run with silky softness over her skin made her melt inside. 'OK...OK—I said I'd do it!' She raked a hand through her hair as she tried to make the memory go away. 'But you'll have to tell the lies because I'm not going to.'

'That's OK.'

He smiled at her, that lazy lopsided smile that she knew and loved so much. She'd have done anything for him when he looked at her like that....which was really worrying.

'Thanks, Nicole,' he said softly.

'Never mind thanking me, let's just get this show on the road.'

Fifteen minutes later they were on a speedboat, skimming across the turquoise bay. The feeling was exhilarating; Nicole could taste the spray of the water on her lips and feel the warmth of the breeze against her face.

As they rounded a headland the boat slowed, and in front of them a long white beach shimmered in the evening sun. A residence stretched along its perimeter like a luxury hotel. It was ultra modern and built on two levels. It even had its own private marina at one end of the beach and an outdoor cinema with a huge screen.

'This is it—Easter Cottage. Ron's place,' Luke said as the boat drew up alongside one of the wooden jetties.

'It's the most spacious cottage I've ever seen,' Nicole said in amusement.

'Yes—if you've got to be a recluse this is the place.' Luke laughed.

As the boat docked Luke jumped off and then held out a hand to help her ashore. She would have liked to ignore the offer, but the breeze was picking up and the boat was rocking about. So, slinging the strap of her leather briefcase over her shoulder, she swallowed her pride and placed her hand in his. Unfortunately she lost her footing as she transferred her weight from the boat and ended up stumbling against him.

For a moment he held her close against him with a steadying hand, and she was achingly aware of the lean power of his body and the familiar tang of his cologne.

'Are you OK?' He bent his head and his voice sounded deep against her ear. If she moved just a fraction, her lips would be close to his.

'Yes…sorry…about that.' It took all of her self-control, but she made herself pull sharply away from him.

'Don't apologise.' He smiled at her. 'We've got an audience, so it's good to look close.'

Nicole slanted a glance past him and saw a grey-haired man of about seventy-five standing by the top of the jetty. He was smartly dressed, in a navy blue blazer and white slacks, and he was leaning on a walking stick. He waved the stick in salute as they turned to walk closer.

'Good to see you, Ron,' Luke said as he reached to shake the man's hand. 'I'd like you to meet my business associate and fiancée, Nicole Connell.'

'Delighted.' Ron smiled at her. He had very bright blue eyes that were filled with a quiet intelligence. 'You remind me of someone,' he said suddenly as his gaze moved over her face searchingly.

'Well, I know we haven't met before, Mr Johnson.' Nicole smiled at him. 'Although I do feel I know you after all the research I have put into your company.'

'Call me Ron, please,' he insisted. 'Come on up to the house. And we'll talk in comfort.'

The inside of Ron's house looked like something out of a movie set. Persian rugs covered smooth marble floors and the views out across the Caribbean from large picture windows were spectacular.

They sat in the conservatory, looking out towards the sea.

'You've got a great place here, Ron,' Luke said as he accepted a glass of iced tea from a member of staff.

'Yes, I like it. Helen and I had planned to retire here together this year but then she got ill and…it wasn't to be.'

'You must miss your wife a lot,' Nicole said with sympathy.

'Yes, it's been hard living without her.' Ron shrugged. 'But life goes on, and I have tried to keep her memory and her wishes alive—which is why I'm being very careful about whom I sell my company to.'

'You've spent a lot of time building your business up. It's understandable that you want the best deal,' Luke said with a nod.

'Not just the best deal, the *right* deal.' Ron leaned forward in his chair and looked at them earnestly. 'Which is something my lawyers don't seem to comprehend.'

'Well, the only time lawyers get emotional is when they send out their invoice,' Nicole said wryly.

Ron looked over at her and laughed. 'Exactly right, Nicole.'

'I understand your concerns, Ron,' Nicole said gently. 'In fact I think it's wonderful that you care so much about your company and feel loyalty towards your staff. Everything nowadays is so geared to profit that the important things, like loyalty and integrity, seem to have gone by the board.'

'That's right. You see, not everyone gets that.' Ron put his glass of iced tea down with a thump. 'I've been trying to get that point across to my lawyers for the past five months, but they can't seem to see it.'

Luke leaned back in his chair with a smile and watched Nicole at work. She was incredible; she practically had Ron eating out of her hand.

'Shall we go through the points that are causing you concern one by one?' Nicole started to unfasten her briefcase.

'Let's have dinner first,' Ron said. 'And you can tell me a little bit about yourselves.'

'Yes—OK.' Nicole put the briefcase down again. 'There's not much to tell, though, Ron.'

'Now, that can't be true.' Ron smiled. 'You and Luke must have lots of plans for the future.'

'Yes…lots…' Although she smiled, Luke knew Nicole well enough to know that she was rattled. She didn't want to lie to the man…she liked him.

'Where did you two meet?' Ron asked as he settled himself back in his seat.

'Well, I've worked for the Santana company for a while now. But I didn't actually meet Luke until I transferred from the London office out to Miami.'

Luke reached across and took hold of her hand. 'And what Nicole is too shy to tell you is that it was love at first sight,' he told Ron smoothly.

Nicole glanced over at him and felt her heart starting to go into overdrive. Did he have to go OTT? It was too…discomforting…

Ron nodded. 'That was how it was with Helen and I. The moment I saw her I just knew she was the one. Some things just feel right, don't you think?'

'Absolutely.' Luke's fingers stroked over Nicole's hand in a caressing and tender manner. 'I knew the moment I set eyes on Nicole that we were destined to be together. And the strange thing was that before that moment I'd been adamant that the bachelor life was for me.'

The gentle caress of his hand against hers was sending electrical darts of awareness shooting through her entire system. With difficulty she forced herself not to pull away, conscious that it might look bad, but she desperately wanted to. It was pure torture having Luke touch her, look into her eyes and say those things.

'So, have you set a date for the wedding?' Ron asked with a smile.

'Not yet,' Nicole answered firmly. 'We've got a few things to sort out first.'

'What sort of things?' Ron asked.

'Well…' Nicole shrugged; she was starting to feel out of her depth. 'This deal with you, for one. You know what it's like, Ron.' She smiled. 'We haven't got around to getting a house together yet. We've been so busy trying to put everything into order at work. There are a lot of responsibilities in running a company, as you well know.'

Ron nodded. 'Helen and I worked together, and I remember it was sometimes hard in the early days. But a word of advice, Luke. You better pin this lady down, and quickly. Nothing is more important than that!'

'You're right, Ron.' Luke squeezed Nicole's hand. 'That's exactly what I intend to do.'

CHAPTER EIGHT

'YOU were absolutely fantastic.' Luke whispered the words in her ear. His arm was around her shoulder and he squeezed her closer.

For a moment Nicole wanted to give in to the temptation and just lean against him. It was so wonderful to be close to him…and yet so painful at the same time.

They were in the boat heading back to Luke's place and the deal was signed. Nicole could hardly believe it. For five months they had been wading through red tape, and now suddenly it was over.

'I never thought he'd sign tonight!' Luke's tone was ecstatic.

'Neither did I.' She waved towards Ron, who had come down to the beach to see them off.

'You know what swung it…you telling him that we couldn't set a date for our wedding until the deal was settled! It was pure genius, Nicole. From that moment on he was putty in our hands.'

Nicole didn't reply. She was pleased the deal was signed, but as hard as she tried she couldn't summon Luke's enthusiasm. She didn't feel good about the lies they had told. She'd really liked Ron…and deep down there was a curl of guilt that wouldn't go away when she thought about how they had deceived him. Luke had played his part very well too…in fact so well that if she hadn't known better even *she* would have been convinced that he had fallen for her at first sight.

The boat pulled out across the bay and the velvet darkness of the night closed in around them. And as the lights from Easter Cottage faded Nicole forced herself to move away from Luke. Instantly she felt bereft. It would have been so easy just to stay in the circle of his arms. All evening he had been looking at her provocatively, teasing her and talking to her with velvet warmth in his voice, and it had played havoc with her emotions. All right, she knew it had been all an act for Ron's benefit…but even so she had ached inside for it to be real. And she really hated herself for that weakness.

Although it was a warm night, she shivered.

'Do you want my jacket?' Before she could refuse the offer, Luke had taken his jacket off and draped it lightly around her shoulders.

'Thanks.' She smiled at him.

'We'll open a bottle of champagne when we get back,' he said softly. 'Have a celebration.'

'Don't you feel in the slightest bit troubled about the lies we've just told?' she asked suddenly in a husky whisper.

He smiled at her. 'Nicole, all Ron was really worried about was that his precious company is in safe hands, and it is. So, no, I don't feel guilty.'

'And you will build RJ Records up, as you agreed?' she asked him sharply.

'Yes, you know my plans, Nicole.'

'I also know that in six months' time you could change your mind and tear the place apart if it suited you.'

'None of us can see into the future. But my intentions are good where that company is concerned.' Luke turned so that he could look into her eyes. It was strange, he never usually worried about what people thought of him, but he did care about Nicole's opinion. 'I may not be sentimental when it comes to business, Nicole, but I made Ron a promise and I intend to honour it.'

Nicole inclined her head. Yes, Luke *did* have integrity in business. The only intentions that were a sham were the ones he had feigned for her, she thought suddenly. And maybe that was what was really eating away at her. He had lied so convincingly about that. All that stuff about it being love at first sight, when he didn't even believe in love.

'Well, that's all right, then.' She tried to gloss over the feelings.

'Yes, it is.' He smiled at her. 'We've done it! We've pulled off the deal of the century.'

She smiled back and tried to push everything else out of her mind. He was right. The deal was done and Ron was happy. It was the culmination of months of work and it was time to celebrate.

'And you did a great job.' He leaned across and whispered against her ear, 'I couldn't have wished for a better fake fiancée.'

'Not bad for someone you were just *making do* with,' she reminded him with a raised eyebrow. And maybe she was reminding herself of that comment as well…anything to help keep her barriers up.

He smiled. 'You know I didn't mean that. You just wound me up.'

'No, *you* wound *me* up,' she said firmly.

'But we are friends again now, so it doesn't matter,' he said huskily.

She looked into his eyes.

'We are friends.' He reached out and touched the side of her face. 'Because you know that's important to me, don't you?'

The touch of his skin against hers made her tingle inside with hungry awareness.

'Yes.' She looked away from him, her heart beating uncomfortably. 'Just friends.'

To Nicole's relief they reached the shore just then, and the engine of the boat was cut. Luke stood up and took hold of her hand to help her out onto the jetty. She noticed the flash of the diamond ring on her finger as the moonlight caught it.

As she waited for him to join her on the beach she played absently with the ring, twisting it around her finger. They could never be just friends…it was an impossibility. The tug of sensuality was still there between them, twisting insidiously like a serpent ready to pounce. She reckoned he knew that as well as she did. Maybe he'd even been playing on it this evening. She had a feeling that, like a hunter, he was always ready for the kill…waiting, biding his time…

And it would be so easy to let her guard down. When he touched her she felt an ache inside that was so deep it was scary.

Flashes of lightning lit the night sky as the boat pulled out to sea again.

'There's a storm moving in,' Luke said as he turned to walk with her up the beach and into the garden.

'Yes, guess our driver today was right.' She took a deep breath of the warm night air. It was scented with jasmine. The garden looked ghostly and unreal, the crooked shadows from the moonlight distorting the bright colours, turning everything to silver and black. There was a feeling in the air of suspense…as if the flowers and the parched earth were longing for the rain. Or was thát feeling of tension just inside her? she wondered as she darted a glance over at Luke and found his eyes were on her.

'Let me give you your jacket back.' She handed it over to him and watched as he slung it casually over his shoulder. Hell, but he was far, far too good-looking, she thought nervously. 'Oh, and before I forget you better have this…' She took the engagement ring off and held it out towards him.

'Give it back to me later.' He waved a hand dismissively and changed the subject. 'I still can't believe how well tonight went. Ron was completely bowled over when you came out with all those details about the company's structure, you know. You were brilliant. Just the right amount of business, teamed with just the right amount of fictional wedding day dreaminess.'

The engagement ring seemed to burn mockingly against her skin as she put it back onto her finger. 'Thanks. All part of the fake fiancée job,' she said lightly. 'You weren't so bad yourself.'

In fact, if she were being honest, Luke had been very, very impressive. He had a brain like a steel trap, she thought wryly, and yet he could be so utterly charming. Good fun as well. Over dinner they had relaxed a little, and he had told amusing anecdotes about the recording business that had really made her laugh. She had found herself just watching him, just drinking in the lean, handsome contours of his face, the dark intensity of his eyes…the sensuality of his lips…and she had wanted him so badly that she had ached.

Luke laughed. 'We are a good team, Ms Connell,' he said roguishly.

'Break open that champagne, Mr Santana,' she said, with equal flippancy.

Luke reached and took hold of her hand. 'How about we get back together again?'

The question came so quickly on the heels of their banter that it caught her by surprise.

'Luke, don't!' She pulled her hand away from his.

'Don't what?' He came to an abrupt halt beside her.

'Don't spoil a successful evening,' she said gruffly.

'I thought I was putting the perfect end to the perfect evening,' he said. 'We could have a *real* celebration, for old times' sake…'

'*Don't*, Luke.' She shook her head.

'Don't what? Don't tell you that I want you?'

Luke stared down at her. Her eyes looked almost jade-green in this light and filled with a vulnerability that seemed to kick him inside. Women never usually made him feel like this, but she brought out a strange feeling of protectiveness inside him. 'You know I'd never do anything to hurt you.' He said the words softly.

'I know.' She looked away from him. Little did he know that he *could* hurt her so…so easily…she was just too vulnerable where he was concerned.

'Hey, you know I'm not trying to get heavy here,' he said with a smile. 'We've had a real buzz out of clinching this deal, a real surge of adrenalin. And I think we should go further and really—'

'Stop it, Luke.' She cut across him fiercely. 'I want us to be businesslike and—'

'To hell with businesslike.' Luke reached for her then, and suddenly his lips were on hers. The kiss was hungry and intense and she couldn't fight it…didn't want to fight it. After an initial stunned resistance she was melting against him and kissing him back. And it was good, so good, that she felt her legs going weak beneath her, felt her whole body surging with pleasure.

'That's better!' He pulled back from her for a moment and looked down at her teasingly. 'We are so good together, Nicole…how did we drift apart this last week?'

She shook her head. 'I don't know…I just know that we shouldn't be doing this.' Her voice was a hoarse whisper in the silence of the night.

'Why?' He held her tightly. 'We are both single. We're not hurting anybody. And it feels so right when we are together, doesn't it? How can that be wrong?'

She couldn't answer that. How could she say that she loved him? He'd probably laugh. Or at the very least he would mock her.

His mouth found hers again, and softly plundered her sweetness. 'You excite me so much.'

Nicole tried very hard to pull back.

He just wants you back in his bed to satisfy his ego, she told herself fiercely. *Don't give in…don't…* But even as she was telling herself that, her body was traitorously betraying her. She was winding her arms around his neck and kissing him with a passion that was overwhelming.

For a long while they didn't talk. They were just lost in the pleasure of being back in each other's arms.

A low growl of thunder tore through the air and suddenly large raindrops started to splatter down over them. They broke apart, startled.

'Let's get out of this!' Luke took hold of her hand and they ran towards the house. But before they could get there the rain became even heavier, drenching down over them in a torrent. It was so heavy that it made Nicole gasp, and it almost obscured the house from view.

They were both out of breath and laughing as they reached the shelter of the veranda. 'Wow—look at us! We are soaked!' Nicole pushed her wet hair back from her face and glanced down at her clothes, which were sticking to her body now.

'And you still look fabulous,' he said mischievously. 'The wet T-shirt look really suits you.'

She felt a dart of embarrassment as she noticed how revealing her top was now. 'I better go and get out of these things.'

He put a hand on her arm as she made to move past him. 'I'll come and help you.'

The playful seductive tone made her pulses race in disarray. The sensible side of her was telling her that she shouldn't have kissed him, shouldn't have allowed herself to be drawn back to him. She was still leaving herself wide open to be hurt. But there was another voice inside as well, a very insistent voice that was reminding her how wonderful it was to make love with him…reminding her how much she wanted him…right now.

'Luke, nothing has changed.' She forced herself to listen to the sensible facts.

'Of course things have changed. We've got RJ; the strain of the deal has been lifted from both of us.' He reached out and touched her face. 'I know how hard you've worked on that, Nicole, and I know it's been very highly pressured.'

He was right, it *had* been high pressure, but she would rather have gone through that a million times over than go through this torment of loving him and wanting him.

'We can relax now.'

If she relaxed now she would be back to where she started…

He traced a finger softly over her trembling lips as he looked deeply into her eyes. 'I've really missed you, Nikki,' he said as he bent closer and his lips burned across her skin. 'I've missed your sensuous body…your laughter…the spark as our eyes meet across that boardroom table.'

'Luke…' Before she could form any coherent words he had covered her lips with his. His kiss was sweet, heart-rendingly tender. She had wanted him so much, for so long, and the feelings of temptation were now overwhelming…

How was it he was able to turn her on like this? She breathed deeply, trying to block out the need…but at the same time she was putting her hand in his and allowing him to lead her into the house and up the stairs to bed.

The heat of the night was intense. Nicole threw back the sheets on the bed as she listened to the storm that was raging outside. Brutal roars burst through the night air and the darkness of the room kept exploding with violent flashes of lightning.

Tomorrow they would go back to Miami and she would forget her weakness…forget that she had just spent another incredible night in Luke's arms. She squeezed her eyes tightly closed. And she *would* forget it, she told herself firmly. Because it meant nothing.

The words ran like a reassuring mantra through her mind…except that they weren't working. How could she forget something so blissfully wonderful? How could she pretend that it meant nothing when she loved him with every fibre of her soul?

Nicole turned in the bed as another flash of lightning lit the room. Luke was next to her, the sheets low on his waist. Their eyes met across the pillow and she realised he wasn't asleep either. He reached out a hand and stroked it up over her shoulder, then raked it through the thick darkness of her hair, pushing it away from her face. The touch of his hand was possessive and sexy…and it made her heart skip several beats.

'You are incredible in bed…' He smiled that half-smile that turned her on so much.

'I'm not sure what the correct response to that should be…' She smiled back at him. 'I was always told to accept a compliment gracefully, but *thank you* sounds a bit…odd, under the circumstances.'

Luke laughed a deep throaty laugh that stirred her. Then he caught hold of her hand and turned the palm upwards towards his lips to kiss it. The feeling was curiously tender.

She felt a strange reaction in the pit of her stomach, as if her heart had somersaulted down and then bounced back up.

'I don't know why we keep ending up back in bed together.' She conjured the words almost like a protective shield. 'Because it doesn't mean anything.'

He looked over at her with a teasing gleam in his eyes. 'You analyse everything too much…' He reached for her and pulled her into the warmth of his arms. 'There are times for thinking…and times when it's good just to go with the moment…give yourself up to the feeling within.' As if to prove his words, his hands moved silkily over her body.

She closed her eyes on a wave of ecstasy. He kissed her neck and then her shoulders, and a shudder of pleasure rippled through her.

A low growl of thunder tore through the air and seemed to echo the feelings of wild pleasure inside her as he rolled her over and took her one more time…

CHAPTER NINE

SOME hours later, when Luke opened his eyes, dawn had broken outside and rain was pounding heavily against the house like a continuous rolling drum.

Scenes from the night flashed through his consciousness. The way Nicole had put her hand in his and allowed him to lead her upstairs…the way they had frantically torn their wet clothes off…hardly able to wait for each other.

He had her back! An intense feeling of satisfaction raced through him—and it made him frown. His first thought should have been the satisfaction of the business deal yesterday, and yet it seemed to pale into insignificance next to the fact that he had succeeded in getting Nicole back into his arms.

Luke turned and watched her as she slept so peacefully beside him. She looked so beautiful. Her glossy dark hair had dried in curls and her skin was clear and milky-white. He noticed how long and dark her lashes were next to her skin, how the gentle curve of her sensuous mouth moved in a half-smile.

She was beautiful, and she was his again. He could relax now, get his priorities in order. He should probably make a phone call and organise the company jet to get ready to take them back to Miami. His task here was accomplished and there were a few loose ends to tie up at the office. Plus he had business to take care of at his New York office. His mind drifted ahead as he thought about what he had to do.

Nicole's eyes flickered open and connected with his. 'Hi.' She smiled sleepily.

'Hi.' He smiled back. 'How did you sleep?'

'OK…' She stretched languorously. 'How about you?'

'Best night's sleep in a week,' he said honestly.

She turned onto her side, her eyes moving over him contemplatively. 'You know, I think this is the first time we've ever woken up in the morning with each other.'

'Is it?' He looked amused, and immediately she wished she hadn't said that.

'Anyway, I suppose we should get up.'

'I suppose we should.' Luke put his hand on her arm as she made to turn away. Suddenly, despite all his earlier practical thoughts he found himself loath to let her go. 'But we do have a lot more catching up to do,' he reminded her.

'What sort of catching up had you in mind?' she asked huskily.

'Well…' He pretended to think about that for a moment, then he leaned a little closer and kissed her lips softly. 'This kind of catching up…' He breathed the words softly. The caress was gentle and sexy and infinitely pleasurable, and she found herself moving closer, winding her arms around him.

He was the one to pull back from her, and he looked deeply into her eyes for a moment. 'That was some kiss…'

'Yes.' Her heart was racing almost violently against her chest. He was right; it had been incredible—so tender and warm that it had almost seemed to sear her soul. *She loved him so much.*

'I told you the spark hadn't gone between us.' His words held an almost smug sense of satisfaction. 'What was all that nonsense about anyway?'

Alarm bells started to cut through the pleasurable mists of Nicole's thoughts. He sounded so pleased with himself…and he made it sound as if she was some kind of errant teenager he'd pulled back into line again.

'I told you what it was about,' she said numbly.

He shook his head and moved away from her. 'Well, I guess we were both under a lot of pressure with the RJ deal.' His voice was brisk. 'But things are back to how they were between us now, and that's all that matters.'

Back to how they were. Nicole could feel her body tense at those words. Obviously he assumed that because she had slept with him again that things were back on the same footing as they had been before. As far as he was concerned his ego was sated and the one that had got away was tamed.

She watched as he started to pick his clothes up from the floor, and felt a mixture of emotions. There was a part of her that wanted to say, Yes, it's great, things *are* back the way they were—because she had hated this last week without him and last night had been so wonderful. But the other part of her was angrily reminding her that things could never go back to how they were. She loved him too much for that. Even now, watching him throw his clothes on and talk in that brisk, businesslike tone, she was filled with a feeling of *déjà-vu*, and a certainty that this wasn't what she wanted. What she wanted was for him to come back into the bed and tell her he had real feelings for her… but that just wasn't going to happen.

'All in all, it's been a very successful trip.' He glanced over at her playfully, before continuing, 'I've got some loose ends to tie up in the office when we get back to Miami, and then I've got to squeeze in a trip to the New York office before the weekend. But I'll be back on Saturday. So I think our plan should be to get together on Saturday night.' He glanced over at her, and again there was that teasing, sexy expression in his dark eyes. 'For a little more catching up,' he added huskily. 'I'll book a table at Romano's—'

Hell, but he was so arrogantly self-assured. He could have at least asked if Saturday was convenient. 'Actually, Luke, I don't think that is a good idea.' She said the words quickly, before she could change her mind. She would have adored going out with him, and there was a part of her that wanted to say, Why not? Let's just leave things as they are. But she knew in her heart that she couldn't afford to allow things to drift. Nothing had changed. She would just be storing up trouble for herself if she allowed the affair to continue in the same vein, knowing how she felt.

He looked over at her. 'Well, if you don't want to go to Romano's, we could go to Luigi—'

'No, you misunderstand.' She reached for her dressing gown and got out of bed. 'I mean that things *aren't* back to how they were.'

Luke frowned.

'Last night was great…but it was a one-off.' She forced herself to sound coolly in control, but it was light years away from how she was feeling. 'We both got a bit carried away; it was a celebration after a tough deal. You said as much yourself,' she reminded him.

'Yes, I did.' Luke glared at her. He didn't need her reminding him that things were not serious! He felt as if he had just been kicked in the solar plexus, and it was not a feeling he was used to where women were concerned. 'I also made it clear that I wanted things back to how they were between us.'

'Well, it's not what I want.'

'I don't believe you,' he grated. 'Last night was more than a one-off.'

He was rewarded by a glimpse of complete vulnerability in her green-gold eyes. She wasn't as sure as she sounded.

He moved towards her. 'I realise you've been hurt in the past, Nicole, but—'

'This isn't about the past.' She cut across him forcefully. 'It's about the future.'

'So are you seeing someone else? Is that it?' Luke forced himself to ask the question, and as he did he felt an anger inside him that surprised him. If she *was* seeing some other man he wanted to physically get hold of the guy and throw him out of her life…

'No! There's no one else!' Her voice shook vehemently.

He felt a bit better at the strength of her denial. 'So are you worried the relationship might get too serious? Because I can tell you now, Nicole, that's not my style. I don't do commitment.'

Her lips twisted wryly. Did he really think he needed to point that out? She felt like saying something sarcastic, like, *You don't say?* But she controlled herself.

Instead she forced herself to shrug and then glance at

her wristwatch. 'Actually, Luke, we really don't have time for this.'

'Oh, yes, we do.'

Deep down Luke was telling himself to just drop this now. He honestly didn't believe in analysing relationships. And if she wanted to make this just one last fling…well, he should let her. It didn't matter! Except that when he looked over at her it *did* matter…damn it!

'Look, why don't I take you out for dinner at the weekend and we can just talk…clear the air?' He sounded as if he was begging! Luke was angry with himself; he had never lowered himself to beg a woman for a date! His father had done that with his mother, when their marriage had been on the rocks, and it hadn't worked. In fact it had just made things worse.

Nicole shook her head. 'We'll never just talk…' Her voice held a slight edge. 'We'll just go to bed together and things will be the same.' And what good would talking do anyway? she thought inconsolably. One hint of the word *love* and it would all be over anyway.

Luke watched with a feeling of complete frustration as she coolly glanced at her watch. 'It's almost eight-thirty. What time do you think we should set off back to the airport?'

'For heaven's sake, Nicole…' Luke trailed off as he noticed she suddenly looked stricken. 'What's the matter?'

Nicole was looking down at her hand. There was no ring on her engagement finger! Panic zinged through her. Where on earth was Luke's ring? She didn't remember taking it off. 'Luke, I don't know how to tell you this…' She looked over at him, her eyes wide with distress.

'What?' He took a step closer.

'I think I've lost your mother's ring!'

'Oh! Is that all?' He shook his head impatiently.

'What do you mean, *Is that all*?' She stared at him. 'It was beautiful and it belonged to your mother!' Hastily she turned and started to search on the bedside table, and then along the floor by the bed. In one way, although she was horrified to have lost something that wasn't hers, it was a relief to have something else to focus on instead of the empty, aching feeling inside her.

'Nicole, you won't have lost it.' Luke's tone was nonchalant. 'You'll have taken it off and put it somewhere. We've got other things to concentrate on right now.'

She shook her head. 'I don't remember taking it off.' She raked a hand distractedly through her hair as her mind ran back over the events of the night, trying to place when she had last seen it. 'I definitely had it in the garden, because I tried to give it back to you.'

'Nicole, just forget about the ring for now.' She was really bugging him. Why wouldn't she just talk to him?

He wanted to take hold of her and force her to look at him, but before he could say or do anything further she was heading for the door.

'I'm going to go and search downstairs. It might be lying on the veranda.'

Pulling her dressing gown tightly around her, she searched the stairs on her way down, and then she looked around the hall. There was no sign of the ring.

She stepped outside onto the veranda. Despite the rain that was thundering down it was pleasantly warm. For a moment she leaned against the railing and took a deep breath of the morning air. She should never have slept with Luke last night; it had just made everything worse. She had been so weak…but she really hadn't been able to help herself.

With determination she forced herself not to dwell on emotions and just search for the ring. A black cat had taken shelter from the storm and was curled up on a cushion on one of the large wicker armchairs. She looked up curiously as Nicole searched under her chair and around the plant pots.

There was no sign of the ring.

Nicole was just debating whether to brave the rain in her dressing gown and look along the garden path when the front door opened and Luke followed her outside. He had changed and put on a pair of light blue jeans and a white T-shirt. She had never seen him dressed so casually before. The look suited him, made him look younger, and emphasised his lean hips and broad shoulders.

She tried not to be distracted by how handsome he looked. 'I'm sorry, Luke, I haven't found it.'

He took in the look of strain in her eyes. 'I told you not to worry,' he said calmly.

'Of course I'm worried!' She ran a hand abstractedly through her hair. 'I'm starting to think it might have fallen from my finger when we were running through the rain last night.'

'We'll look later.' Luke shrugged. He knew Nicole was genuinely upset about losing the ring, but he sensed there were other emotions teeming behind those beautiful eyes. 'Why don't you sit down and I'll make us some coffee?' He hesitated. Before following her downstairs he had told himself to act coolly and not pursue the issue of seeing her again. But she looked so…captivating… He felt he needed to know exactly what was going through her mind…in depth. He frowned; it wasn't like him at all! He didn't usually need to know what women were thinking. He didn't usually care to analyse emotions. But he cared about Nicole…more than he wanted to admit even to himself. He cared about what she was feeling, what she was thinking…

Before he could stop himself he was adding, 'We really need to talk.'

'Believe me, Luke, talking isn't going to help,' she grated. Then she let her breath out in a sigh. 'And, anyway, I need to find your ring.'

'The ring really isn't that important,' he muttered angrily.

Nicole had been concentrating on scanning the floor of the porch, but she looked up with a frown. 'Of course it's important. It belonged to your mother; I'm sure it's of great sentimental value apart from anything else.'

He shook his head. 'My mother took anything of any real value to her away from this house many years ago.'

The harsh sound of his words made Nicole pause. 'What do you mean?' Despite the fact that she was so anxious about the jewellery, he had her full attention now.

'I mean that my mother was a very calculating and cold woman.'

'Was she?' Nicole was totally taken aback now. 'That's not a very nice thing to say, Luke.'

He smiled at that. That was so typical of Nicole. She was so straight…so decent. 'No, but unfortunately it's the truth.' He shrugged. 'Look, if you really want to know, my parents split up when I was eleven. My father had lost all his money on a bad business deal. He nearly lost the house…nearly lost everything. And my mother…well, let's just say she liked a certain lifestyle, if you know what I mean.' His voice grated derisively. 'She walked out on the marriage. Found herself a richer guy who could keep her in the style to which she had grown accustomed.'

'And what about you?' Nicole asked quietly.

'What about me?'

'Did she take you with her?'

'Don't be silly.' Luke's mouth twisted in disdain. 'An eleven-year-old child certainly didn't fit with her new life.'

Nicole looked over at him and suddenly a lot of things fell into place. This was the reason Luke had a complete aversion towards getting tied down into a relationship, why he concentrated on business above everything else. 'I'm so sorry, Luke,' she murmured gently. 'That must have been awful for you—'

'Hey, I don't need or want your sympathy.' He cut across her quickly. 'I only told you because you're so worried about that damn ring. In all honesty my mother probably did me a huge favour when she walked away. It taught me a thing or two about relationships…and about the importance of keeping your eye firmly on business.'

'It was a hard lesson to learn at eleven.' Nicole shook her head.

'Children are resilient.' Luke shrugged. 'It was my father who really suffered. He was able to rally himself after losing his business…but I don't think he ever really got over losing his wife.'

'He never remarried?'

Luke shook his head.

'And what about your mother?'

'Oh, yes, Adrianne remarried.' Luke's lips twisted wryly. 'Three more times, to be precise. And each time to a wealthy older guy... It never ceases to amaze me how stupid men can be where a beautiful woman is concerned.'

Nicole noticed that there was no bitterness in his tone, just a mocking irony.

'So, you see, the ring is of no importance at all. It probably isn't even worth that much either—because, knowing Adrianne, she would have had it valued. Certainly all the jewellery that was in the safe went with her.'

Nicole wanted to reach out to him, put her arms around him. But she knew such a move would just make him annoyed, so she forced herself to stand where she was. 'Do you ever see her?'

'Yes, we've met a few times. It's all very civilised.' He looked as if the subject was now boring him. 'So, let's forget foolish notions about that ring...it's of no sentimental value at all, OK?'

'OK, but I'd still like to find it,' Nicole insisted.

The door opened behind him and Luke's housekeeper walked out onto the veranda. 'There is a phone call for you, Mr Santana,' she said politely. 'It's Ted Allen from your New York office.'

'Tell him I'll ring him back,' Luke grated distractedly. The last thing he wanted now was a business discussion.

'He said it was urgent,' Deloris murmured apologetically. 'Something about a crisis with a new contract?'

Luke hesitated. 'OK. Thanks, Deloris. Tell him I'll be along in a minute.'

The door swung shut as the housekeeper went to do his bidding.

'Sounds like you might have to go straight to New York.' Nicole tried to remain stoical.

'Maybe…'

'If so, I can always take a scheduled flight back to Miami and deal with the loose ends from the RJ deal.'

For a second Luke's eyes moved over her slender figure. She looked very tantalising in the white silk dressing gown, her hair flowing like liquid silk around her shoulders. She also looked fragile, like a china doll that could break very easily. Yet she was talking about business in that damn practical tone. No other woman he had ever met had given him these problems. She was an enigma, and she was driving him totally demented.

'Never mind about that…or the blasted ring,' he grated. 'Let's talk about us, shall we?'

'Us?' She looked at him through narrowed eyes.

'Yes…' For a moment he hesitated. Had that sounded a bit heavy? 'We have fun together, Nicole,' he said firmly. 'And it's not as if either of us is looking for something more…so what's the problem?'

'The problem…?' Nicole took a deep breath and her eyes moved gently over Luke's face. His expression was intensely serious. She had never seen him look like that before.

Maybe they had reached a place where only the truth would now suffice? 'All right, I suppose…if you must know…I've never really been a casual relationship type of girl…' The words just tumbled out. 'I've enjoyed what we have had,' she added huskily, 'but deep down I'm a bit old-fashioned, I guess.' She tried to make a joke, but it fell flat. Luke was now staring at her as if she were speaking with a forked tongue.

Maybe the truth hadn't been such a good idea! 'Hey, don't look so worried. I'm not saying I want to make things deep and meaningful with *you*,' she backtracked swiftly, trying to cloak her feelings and protect her pride. 'I know *you* are not into commitment. What we had was just a fling. I know that. But I need to move on now.'

When Luke still didn't say anything, she continued swiftly, 'So, you see, talking isn't going to help.'

'I see.' Now Luke looked totally disconcerted. 'I didn't spot that coming.'

'Neither did I, to be honest.' Nicole forced herself to sound casual. 'Anyway…' she said crisply. 'You go and take your phone call. And I'll go and pack my bags.'

Somehow she managed to smile, and with her head high she moved past him and back into the house.

Her heart was racing against her chest. She felt sick. She shouldn't have said all that!

But after he had told her about his mother, somehow she just hadn't been able to lie to him any more in that flippant tone. She had thought it was better to be honest.

Big mistake! As soon as she had seen the perplexed look on his face she had known she had stepped on a landmine! At least she had thought on her feet and he didn't know she had fallen in love with him. That would have been too embarrassing. She needed to leave herself with some dignity.

Nicole sat down on the edge of the bed. Suddenly she was feeling very ill. What was causing that? she wondered. Emotional upset? She couldn't still be suffering from food poisoning…could she?

She sat for a few moments longer, but instead of feeling

better she started to feel worse. The queasy feeling intensifying, she dashed for the sanctuary of her *en-suite* bathroom.

Half an hour later, as she lay weakly on the bed, she found Luke's ring lying under the sheet. It must have fallen off when they were making love. She turned it in her hand, watching how it sparkled in the morning light. At least she now knew why Luke was so determined to avoid any lasting intimacy.

Not that it changed anything, she thought sadly. With determination she got up. There was no point lying here trying to question things. She should shower and change and pack her bag.

A little while later Nicole went back downstairs. She had dressed in a pale blue summer dress and her hair and make-up were perfect. She was determined that there would be no chink in her armour when she faced Luke.

He was making another phone call; she could hear his crisp, businesslike tones drifting down the hallway from the study.

'Would you like some breakfast, Ms Connell?' Deloris appeared from the kitchen.

The mere thought of eating made Nicole's stomach turn in disapproval. 'No, thanks, Deloris, I'll just have a glass of water.'

Luke looked up as she appeared in the doorway. 'I've decided that Ted Allen is totally useless when it comes to anything urgent!' he grated as he put the phone down. 'You were spot on. I *am* going to have to get to New York straight away!'

She smiled. 'You just like to be in control,' she observed softly.

For a moment Luke leaned back in his chair. She was right. In fact she knew him very well…maybe better than any woman before. The knowledge added to what she had said earlier and intensified the feeling of disquiet inside him. Nicole wasn't the sort of woman you just had a fling with. *Why hadn't he seen that before?* He frowned. Maybe he *had* seen it, and he had just ignored it because it was too disconcerting. He didn't want a serious relationship… the very words were an anathema to him.

'Yes, you're right; I *do* like to be in control. And I can't trust Ted Allen to sort this out on his own.' He forced himself to concentrate on the business in hand. 'The fact is that I'll probably be stuck out there for a week at this rate.'

'That's no problem. As I said, I'll deal with the remainder of the paperwork for RJ.'

She was fabulous, Luke thought as his eyes drifted over her. So cool and poised and yet inside so decent and— He switched his thoughts off abruptly and stood up. 'I've managed to get you on the next available flight to Miami. It leaves at midday.'

'That's good. Will your driver be able to take me to the airport, or shall I get a taxi?' she asked briskly.

'My driver will take you.' Luke sat down on the edge of the desk and looked over at her. 'About what you were saying earlier…' he began cautiously.

'Listen, Luke, we don't need to go through that again.' She intersected him hurriedly. She really didn't want to talk about anything personal now. She was holding herself together on the slimmest of control lines as it was. 'As you said yesterday, we're friends and good work colleagues.'

Luke frowned. 'Yes…yes, we are,' he agreed in a firm

tone. 'And when I get back to Miami maybe we can still have dinner?' He folded his arms.

She shook her head and swallowed. 'Not a good idea, Luke.'

The silence between them seemed loaded with some kind of emotion that twisted inside Nicole, inflicting even more pain.

'Your taxi is here, Mr Santana.' Deloris appeared in the doorway.

'OK—thanks, Deloris.' Luke glanced at his watch. 'I've got the company jet waiting, so I'd better go, Nicole.'

She forced herself to smile brightly at him. 'Yes—you have a good flight.'

As Luke stood up and walked over towards her she could feel herself tremble inside.

'You take care of yourself.' He touched her face lightly, and for a moment looked into her eyes. Then he was gone.

CHAPTER TEN

NICOLE returned from Barbados and threw herself into her work. On her first day back a bouquet of flowers arrived for her. It was hand-tied and magnificent.

'Gosh, they are really beautiful,' Molly said as she handed them across to her.

'Yes…' Nicole's heart thundered hopefully as she buried her face for a moment in the sweet peppery scent. Maybe Luke had gone to New York and had a rethink… Maybe he missed her… Cutting her thoughts abruptly, she opened the accompanying card.

Thanks for everything. Luke.

She stared at the card in utter disappointment. But in reality it had been absurd to expect anything else.

'Got an admirer?' Molly asked inquisitively.

'No, they're just from Luke, thanking me for my work on the RJ takeover.' She handed them back to her secretary. 'You deal with them, will you?'

'Yes, of course. How lovely of him!'

'Yes…lovely.'

After that she tried very hard not to think about Luke at all.

A week went by, and apart from one phone call from him to check on the loose ends from the RJ deal there was no further contact. According to the gossip around the office he seemed firmly ensconced in the New York office and might be there for some time.

Probably just as well, she told herself firmly as she remembered their stiltedly polite telephone conversation. If speaking to him were difficult, then seeing him would be even worse. Yet, no matter how many times she told herself that, she still missed him.

In spite of the fact that she no longer had to worry about the RJ deal, things were pretty hectic in the office. Nicole had a lot of work to do on new contracts, and her days seemed to be getting longer and longer. So she supposed it wasn't strange that she should feel tired, but what was strange was the fact that she was still suffering from nausea.

She had been so sick this morning that she had hardly been able to drag herself into work. And by mid-morning she felt so bad that she had to phone the doctor for an appointment.

'Will you cancel my appointments from three-thirty onwards tomorrow?' she asked her secretary as she brought some mail in for her. 'I've got a doctor's appointment and I'm not sure how long I'll be.'

'OK.' Molly glanced over at her with sympathy. 'You do look very pale.'

'I feel a bit better at the moment, actually.' Nicole went through her correspondence with a brisk efficiency. 'But this seems to be the pattern. I think I'm feeling better and then, whoosh, it's back again the next day.'

'My sister is like that at the moment. But then she's pregnant.' Molly laughed. 'It's not morning sickness, is it?'

'I think that's one thing I can definitely rule out,' Nicole said firmly. 'Did you manage to get Bob Tate on the phone, by the way?' she asked as Molly headed back to her own office.

'Yes, he said it was all in hand. And the recording studio is booked for the day.'

'Great.'

'Oh, and by the way,' Molly added casually, 'Luke is back from New York. I've just seen him in the corridor.'

Nicole tried not to react to this piece of information, but it rippled through her in shock waves. Luke was back! Just knowing that he was in the building filled her with a sense of excitement…and a sense of sadness as well. He'd obviously walked right past her office and hadn't even come in to say hello. But then why should he? She had made it clear that she wasn't going to sleep with him again, and he'd probably moved on. All that talk about being friends was rubbish.

With determination she continued with her work. But it was difficult to concentrate now. She longed to see him…

Although she had tried not to think about him since returning home, in reality he had filled her mind. She remembered the look in his eyes when he'd told her about his parents splitting up. She imagined him as a vulnerable eleven-year-old in that house in Barbados, abandoned by his mother, imagined his loneliness and his feeling of helplessness as he watched his father fall apart.

No wonder he was so focused on business and so flippant with women. Nicole felt for him. She really did. But the worst thing she could do was to feel sorry for him. Luke didn't want her sympathy, and she had to remember that.

Even so, she itched to pick up the phone now and make up some excuse to speak to him. She clenched her hands and forced herself not to do any such thing! If their last telephone conversation were anything to go by it would only be a stilted and wooden exchange anyway.

By five o'clock she couldn't stand it any longer and packed up her papers. 'I'm going to finish this paperwork at home, Molly.' She put her head around her secretary's door.

'Not feeling well?' Molly asked with concern.

'No, not really.' It was as good an excuse as any, Nicole thought as she headed down towards the lifts. In fact she felt all right. At least she didn't want to throw up—and for the first time in ages she felt hungry.

As there was nothing in her apartment to eat, she stopped off at the local store and as usual hurriedly shoved a few things in a basket. As she stood by the till, waiting to be served, she glanced down at her purchases and was struck by how strange they were. She never usually ate chocolate ice cream, or pistachio nuts or olives…

Heck, if she ate the combination that was in that basket, she would *deserve* to be sick tomorrow!

It's not morning sickness, is it? Molly's teasing words flashed through her mind.

Now she came to think about it, her period *was* late. *But she couldn't be pregnant.* It wasn't possible. And anyway, she and Luke had always made love responsibly.

It was her turn to be served and she moved to put her

basket on the counter. *Except there was that one time a while ago, when they'd had an accident.*

The memory zinged into her mind and she felt herself freeze. *No, she couldn't be...* But even so she heard herself saying to the assistant, 'I've forgotten something. Could you put my basket to one side, please? I'll be back in a minute.'

'Sure.' The basket was removed, and Nicole found herself walking down the aisles towards the pharmacy.

She stood for a while in front of the pregnancy testing kits. There had been a time in her life when she had bought those regularly. And the results had always been negative. She couldn't look at them on the shelf now without remembering her many disappointments. What were the chances of her being pregnant after one accident when she had spent so long trying for a baby with her husband?

It would probably be a waste of time even trying a test. But even so... Just to eliminate the possibility from her mind she reached and took one of the boxes off the shelf.

When Nicole got back to her apartment she made herself something to eat and then finished off the paperwork from that afternoon. But even as she was ploughing through her work she was conscious of that test kit, waiting for her in the bathroom cabinet.

By nine o' clock she couldn't put it off any longer...

'Yes, I can confirm that your test was correct. You are pregnant, Nicole. Probably about six weeks, I would say.'

The doctor's words thundered through Nicole's mind as she left his surgery and got into a cab. But she still could hardly believe it.

Last night when she had done the test and it had been positive, she had convinced herself that the result was a mistake.

All that time of trying, longing to be pregnant…and suddenly it had just happened, when she least expected it. She had said that to the doctor and he had just smiled and shrugged. 'Sometimes that is the way it happens.'

Nicole stared sightlessly out at the Miami streets, at the bright sunshine reflecting on the glass windows of the Art Deco buildings.

She was still in a state of shock.

'You might have been very tense and stressed when you were trying for a baby before,' the doctor had said nonchalantly. 'And this time you were relaxed. That can make a difference.'

She had certainly felt relaxed around Luke. The chemistry between them had been much more powerful than it had ever been with Patrick. In fact if she were really honest she had never felt the same depth of emotion for Patrick as she had for Luke. Yes, she had loved him…but it had been a different kind of love. She had found herself trying to please Patrick, and had felt that she'd never really succeeded because he had always made it clear that it was her fault they had no family.

They had got to the point where nothing she had done was right. She remembered she had suggested they adopt and he had been furious. The idea had been completely abhorrent to him. She realised now that their relationship had been hollow…Patrick had only truly loved himself.

Luke, on the other hand, had been a wonderfully considerate lover. He had also been responsible enough to mention the morning after pill when that condom had broken, she reminded herself fiercely.

'Don't worry about it,' she had murmured as she watched him getting dressed to leave. 'I'll deal with it.'

The words echoed in her mind now. *She really had meant to deal with it.* But that day had been doubly hectic. There had been numerous meetings, there'd been people bombarding her from all sides with e-mails and questions, and by the time she'd got to the end of that day she had felt as if her head was exploding. The morning after pill had been the last thing on her mind. And if she were honest she hadn't really worried about it at all. She hadn't felt she needed to take that pill because the fact was that she had been married to Patrick for five years and for eighteen months of that time they had been desperately trying for a baby…with no success.

But now here she was…pregnant. It was like a miracle.

Butterflies of excitement stirred inside her. She knew that she was on her own and this wasn't an ideal situation. Luke didn't want any kind of commitment, and a child was the biggest commitment of all! But she had longed for a baby for so long that she couldn't help but feel thrilled.

Her baby would not have a father, but she had enough love inside her to make up for that. She knew she would cope…knew she would make a good mum.

But what should she say to Luke? The question caused the butterflies to flutter a little more fiercely inside. He would be furious!

Maybe the best thing to do would be to hand in her notice and go back home to England without telling him about the baby. She had a friend in London who had started her own business, and she had talked in the past about offering Nicole a job. Plus, she would have her parents around for support. They would be over the moon to be grandparents.

All things considered, going home was probably the most sensible thing. If she left the company Luke wouldn't need to know that he was a dad. She would just never see him again.

The thought caused regret to ricochet inside her. But she quickly buried it.

Leaving without telling him she was pregnant was the best thing all round. He'd only be furious when she told him how much she wanted the baby. It could turn into a very unpleasant situation, with him blaming her for not taking the morning after pill. There was no point in even having that conversation. She didn't need Luke anyway. She was an independent modern woman and she would manage perfectly on her own. This was *her* baby.

The taxi pulled up outside her office block and Nicole got out. As she walked inside and got into the lift she was still planning her future. Back in London she could find a lovely downstairs apartment… That would be easier with a pram…

'Ah, there you are, Nicole.' Molly's friendly tones cut into her daydreams.

Nicole took a hasty step back and looked in through the open door of her secretary's office. To her surprise, her eyes met directly with Luke's. The connection caused a jolt of electricity to sizzle through her.

He was perched on the edge of Molly's desk, and it looked as if they'd been having a relaxed conversation. 'Hello, Nicole,' he said quietly.

'Hi.' She tried very hard to gather her scattered wits. 'I didn't expect to see you.'

'I got back from New York yesterday.'

She nodded. 'Good trip, I hope?'

'Yes, it was fine.'

There was silence for a moment and as she looked at him Nicole could feel the ache of missing him like a tangible force.

'Anyway, Luke, I've got rather a lot to do, so I'd better get on…' She was suddenly desperate to get away.

'Actually, I wanted a word with you.' Luke stood up. 'We'll talk in your office.'

'Oh…OK.' She shrugged. Even though she sounded casual her heart was turning over. Being around him was so hard…especially now, with her secret burning inside her. 'I think I've got ten minutes…haven't I, Molly?' She glanced pointedly over at her secretary.

Molly looked at her blankly. There were no appointments in the book because Nicole had asked her to cancel everything for the rest of the afternoon. So really she could spend whatever time she wished with Luke.

'My next appointment is due in about ten minutes, isn't it?' Nicole prompted her sharply.

'Oh…yes!' Molly finally took the hint and nodded.

'I thought so,' Nicole continued briskly. 'Come through, Luke.'

She led the way into her office and then, closing the door behind them, made her way round to sit behind the safety of her desk.

In contrast to how *she* was feeling, she noticed how relaxed Luke was as he sat opposite. He was wearing a dark suit and a pale blue shirt that was open at the neck, and he looked impossibly handsome. Just looking at him made her heart race a little faster, made her remember what it was like to lie in his arms and be held close.

'Before I forget, Aaron Williams has had some trouble with one of the contracts I need to deal with…' Nicole flicked through some paperwork sitting next to her and tried to focus on business. 'Yes, here we are…it's for the new group we want—'

'I'll go up and talk to Aaron about it later.' Luke cut across her. He leaned back in his chair and fixed her with that steady look that she found so unnerving. 'Molly tells me you've just had some time off to go to the doctor,' he said suddenly. 'I'm sorry to hear that you've been ill.'

'Oh, that! It was nothing.' Nicole waved a hand airily and hoped her voice was steady. 'I feel much better now.' She imagined that she could feel Luke's dark gaze burning into her, and that he knew the truth… Which of course he couldn't possibly… But even so she could feel her temperature rising.

Didn't he deserve to know the truth? a little voice suddenly asked inside her. Did she really have the right to keep the fact that he was going to be a dad from him?

Hastily she cut those thoughts dead. *He wouldn't want to know…*

'Well, I'm glad to hear it.' Luke smiled. 'But if you need some time off work, that's not a problem,' he added.

'Luke, I'm fine.' Was it her imagination, or were his eyes moving almost searchingly over her features? Hastily she changed the subject. 'So…was there something *about business* that you wanted to talk about?' She forced a bright and efficient tone into her voice and glanced at her watch.

When she glanced back at him, she could see a glint of impatience in his dark eyes.

'Listen, Nicole, you can drop the pretence,' he grated suddenly.

'What pretence?' She felt the colour drain from her face.

'I know the truth.'

The blunt words made Nicole's heart stop beating for an instant. She stared at him in horror. How could he know? She'd only just found out herself! 'What are you talking about, Luke?' Her voice came out in a croak.

'I'm talking about the fact that you have no appoint-ment. I've just looked in your diary, for heaven's sake!'

'Oh!' She felt her breath come out in a rush, felt almost weak with relief. 'Well, I *am* busy, Luke. I've just taken a few hours off, and the work doesn't go away.'

'Yes…whatever.' Luke cut across her, his voice harsh. 'Look, I've got a few details to discuss with you. But as you are so obviously overstretched we'll discuss them later.'

'Yes, if it's not important business, then that would be better.' Nicole grabbed the opportunity.

'Fine, I'll ring you later.' His eyes seemed to cut into hers.

Nicole nodded. Then watched as he turned and walked out of the room. He closed the door with a firm thud behind him.

Nicole bit down on her lip. This situation wasn't good. And the longer she left it the worse it was going to get, she told herself sensibly. The only thing she could do was to give in her resignation. And she would have to do it straight away.

With determination she turned towards her computer, opened a new blank document and started to type. She would get Molly to bring it upstairs just at the close of day.

CHAPTER ELEVEN

IT WAS six-thirty and Luke was still sitting at his desk. He was furious with himself. Nicole was starting to become an obsession, he told himself angrily.

All the time he had been in New York he hadn't been able to get her out of his head. All week he had thought about her…her beautiful body…her soft skin…her eyes…her smile… And every woman he looked at he'd compared with her and found them lacking. When he had phoned her to talk about the remaining aspects of the RJ deal it had been pure torture, because he'd had to force himself not to let the conversation veer towards anything too personal.

It had been the same yesterday. As soon as he had got back into the office he had gone down to her floor to see her. And then he'd stopped himself. Because he didn't have any business to discuss with her. Anything he said to her would have been of a personal nature. And that wasn't right. Nicole was off limits, he'd told himself. She was in the past.

She wanted to move on to something more serious and he just wasn't cut out for that kind of a relationship. He was the carefree bachelor type, for heaven's sake. He liked to enjoy himself!

Trouble was, he wasn't really enjoying himself. In desperation he'd gone out on a date last night, to try and clear Nicole out of his mind. But the strategy hadn't worked. He hadn't been able to find any enthusiasm for the woman… and yet she had been gorgeous and entertaining and more than willing to go to bed with him. So why had he turned her down? Why had he gone back to his flat early, alone and morose?

So today, unable to bear it, he had breezed down to Nicole's office. All right, he didn't want a serious relationship—but that was OK, wasn't it? Because she had made it clear she didn't want one with *him*…just with someone else. So why couldn't they just continue to see each other until the time when she *did* find someone else?

It seemed a simple enough option…and they *had* agreed that they were going to be friends…

Except, once again, Nicole was treating him with cool disdain.

And she'd looked so pale. Maybe he should have insisted that she took a few days off. She had been working very hard.

Now he was worrying about her! The woman was driving him crazy. How on earth was he going to get her out of his system?

There was a tap at his door and Sandy, his PA, came in. 'I'm going to get off now, Luke,' she said with a smile.

'Yes, of course. Sorry, Sandy, I didn't realise you were still here.'

'That's OK; I was doing a bit of catching up. Oh, and Nicole's secretary brought these up a while ago.'

She put two letters down onto his desk.

'Thanks, Sandy.' Luke picked them up and opened

them. The first was a memo on the details of the trouble-some contract that Nicole had mentioned to him earlier. His eyes flicked over it with little interest.

The second was Nicole's letter of resignation. Luke stared down at it in complete and utter shock!

Nicole had luxuriated in a long, relaxing bath, and now she was curled up on the sofa in her dressing gown, listening to some music. She'd lit some candles along the mantel-piece and she was enjoying some ice cream. All things considered, she felt quite good.

True, she had just given up her dream job. But she was pregnant…and that was the one thing in life that she had always wanted. So she had no real regrets.

She'd had no choice anyway. She couldn't stay here and work for Luke whilst having his child…it would be too awkward a situation. And if she had asked to be transferred to the London office that wouldn't have worked either, because Luke would have found out about the baby through the grapevine. And, all right, he couldn't force her to have an abortion…but he could make life very difficult. Plus there would be the torture of seeing him…watching as he got on with his life and dated other women. She didn't think she could bear it. Today when she had seen him in the office she had just ached for him…

Swiftly she turned her mind away from that and tried to think positively. You couldn't have everything in this life, and being back in London would have its compensations. Her parents would be nearby, and there was the opportunity of another job…it would be fine.

She didn't need Luke.

She stretched and turned on one of the lamps next to her, and then picked up a magazine on pregnancy that she had bought on her way home from work.

The shrill ring of the front doorbell shattered the silence.

Nicole looked up with a frown. Who could that be? she wondered. As she was in her dressing gown, and not expecting anyone, she decided not to answer it. She continued to read.

The bell rang again, and then a few seconds later someone rapped loudly on the door. Maybe it was one of her neighbours, Nicole thought suddenly. Maybe there was something wrong...it sounded quite urgent. Putting her magazine down, Nicole tightened the belt of her dressing gown and went to investigate.

She opened the door a couple of inches and peered out.

Her eyes widened in surprise when she saw Luke standing on her doorstep. 'What on earth are *you* doing here?'

'I think you know!' He put one hand against the door and opened it wider, then strode past her into the lounge without even waiting to be asked. 'We need to have words.'

'This really isn't a good time.' She ran after him in consternation.

'No?' His eyes flicked around the room, taking in the low lighting and the candles, and then lingering on her. She looked fabulous in that black silk robe; it dipped at her neckline, giving just a hint of the firm curve of her breast. Her hair was tousled and sexy, her skin held a flare of heat over her high cheekbones, and her eyes sparked with green fire. 'Are you expecting someone?'

'No! I'm having a relaxing evening.' She glared at him angrily. 'Not that it's any of your business!'

She was right—it wasn't any of his business. Luke tried to calm down, but he was filled with anger. He watched as she moved towards the sofa and straightened the cushions. It looked as if she was hiding something behind one of them.

'Look, I realised this isn't a good time—but there never seems to be a good time, does there? I tried to talk to you this afternoon, but you were too busy.'

Nicole crossed the room and turned the music off. 'What is this about, Luke?'

Her calmness really infuriated him. 'Why the hell didn't you tell me that you wanted to quit your job when we spoke earlier?'

'Oh! You've received my resignation, then?' She ran her hand down over the silk of her robe.

'Yes, of course I've received it!' He glared at her. 'Why didn't you tell me to my face this afternoon that you wanted to leave?'

'I thought it was more professional to put it in writing.' She moistened her lips nervously. 'And, as you have just pointed out, I was very busy this afternoon. It wasn't a good time.'

He looked at her through narrowed eyes. 'So why do you want to leave?'

'Luke, I don't really want to discuss this right now.'

'Well, I do.' He took a step nearer.

She sat down on the sofa. 'I want to go back to London.'

'Have you been offered another job?' Luke moved and stood in front of the fireplace, glowering at her.

She felt as if she was being interrogated, and she didn't like it. 'You know what, Luke? That really isn't any of your business.' She said the words quietly. 'I've behaved in a businesslike way, I've given you the required amount of notice, and that's all that should matter.'

'Well, I think I deserve more!'

'Why?'

The calm question threw him. 'Well, because we had more than a businesslike relationship, for one thing…and for another I thought we were friends.'

'It's nothing personal.' Nicole had to look away from him now, because her cool composure was cracking a little. Who was she kidding? *Nothing personal?* This was as personal as it could get. 'I just think it's time I went home.'

The silence in the room suddenly seemed so heavy that she could hear the clock ticking on the mantelpiece as if it had been magnified a hundred times.

'And you couldn't tell me to my face?'

Why did he keep harping on about that? Nicole raked a hand impatiently through her hair. 'I told you…I thought it was best to keep things on a businesslike footing.'

'OK.' Luke leaned one hand against the fireplace. 'So let's cut to the chase, shall we? How can I persuade you to stay?' he asked briskly. 'How about a pay rise? And I'll throw in some shares…'

He sounded so calm and confident. Luke always got what he wanted, she thought as she looked at him, but not this time. She shook her head. 'This isn't about money, Luke. This is about what is best for me in the long term.'

'Is this because you haven't been feeling well?' he asked suddenly. 'Are you all right?'

The sudden deep concern in his tone was nearly her undoing.

'I told you, I'm fine.'

'But you haven't been feeling well, have you?' His voice held a sudden note of insight. 'Maybe what you need is a break.' He stepped away from the fireplace and came to sit next to her on the sofa. 'I've got a house down in Key West. It's really beautiful down there. Why don't you take a trip, have a week off, laze by the pool in the sun and just think about things?'

'Thanks, Luke.' She shook her head. 'But that's not going to help.'

'It might do you good.' He smiled at her. 'And at the end of the week I could jump on the company jet and come down and see you. We could just chill out together and talk.'

His gentle velvety tone was infinitely sexy, and as she looked into the darkness of his eyes she was almost tempted to say yes. But what would it solve? She would just be prolonging things. And when she went back to work nothing would have changed except for the fact that her pregnancy would be further advanced.

There was no time to put things off, she told herself. She shook her head. 'Thanks for the offer, Luke, but I've made my mind up.'

'And there's nothing I can say to make you change it?'

She shook her head.

'I see.' Luke's glance moved from her towards the coffee table. He noted the tub of ice cream, and there was a china dish of pistachio nuts, some black olives and a bowl of cherries. 'That's a strange combination.'

'What?' Nicole felt herself stiffen.

'The food.'

'I'm just unwinding, Luke.' She shrugged. 'I think you should go now.'

He transferred his attention back to her face. But he made no attempt to move. He was only inches away from her, and she could see the flecks of gold in the darkness of his eyes.

'I don't want you to go back to London, Nicole.' He said the words quietly, and there was a deep sincerity in them that melted her heart. She didn't want to go either. She would have given anything to just lean a little closer and go into his arms. To give up all pretence of being strong and in control…

This was the father of her child. The words echoed inside her. Maybe if she told him the truth…

'Apart from anything else, you are invaluable to the company here.'

His words were like a cold splash of water. Luke's main concern was always business. Nothing would ever change that. 'Well, you know what they say, Luke. No one is irreplaceable.' She moved further away from him.

'So they say.' His eyes raked over her face. 'Are you leaving because of our relationship?'

The softly asked question ricocheted through her. 'What relationship would that be?' she muttered flippantly.

'You know what I mean.'

She shook her head. 'You think everything revolves around you, don't you, Luke? Honestly, sometimes you can be insufferably arrogant.'

He smiled at that. 'Just checking.'

Fleetingly she was lost in that smile. Sometimes when he looked at her in a certain way…like now, for instance…

she felt a sudden flare of longing that overwhelmed everything else.

'Well, now you've checked I think you should go.' She forced herself to say the words.

Instead of moving, he leaned back against the cushions of the sofa. 'Aren't you going to offer me a drink before I go? That's not very hospitable of you, Nicole.'

'Yes, well, I'm not feeling particularly hospitable.'

'I'll just have a coffee, and then I'll get out of your way.' He didn't budge.

She stared at him. Heavens, but the man was infuriating.

He raised an eyebrow and gave her that mocking smile she knew so well.

Obviously he didn't care that she didn't want him here. She shook her head. 'One coffee and then I want you to go,' she warned him shakily.

'Thanks. Black, no sugar…in case you've forgotten.'

'I hadn't forgotten.' She turned and went into the kitchen.

It was damn ironic that when she had wanted him to hang around here he wouldn't, and now that she wanted him to go he was making himself comfortable on the sofa! Nicole wished she'd thought to hide that pregnancy magazine before she opened the front door. She'd managed to shove it behind one of the cushions, but it was hardly the safest of places.

Nicole switched on the kettle and got some cups out of the cupboard. Then she stood and tried to compose herself. She would chat politely with him and then show him the door…no distractions…that was final. And she was doing the right thing not telling him about the baby.

As soon as Nicole disappeared into the kitchen Luke

searched behind the cushions to find what she had hidden. He really didn't know what he had expected to find, but it certainly wasn't a magazine about pregnancy! He stared at it, completely dumbfounded. Then his gaze moved towards the table and the strange combination of food. He felt a rising sense of what could only be described as panic. It was the same sensation he had felt when he had read Nicole's resignation, and it was a whole new experience for him.

Was *this* why Nicole was leaving? His mind flicked back to what Molly had told him today about Nicole being ill…then there was her trip to the doctor.

Had she lied to him when she had told him there was nothing wrong? With a feeling of grim determination he stood up and went through to the *en suite* bathroom off her bedroom. His eyes raked along the shelves; there was nothing there apart from the normal beauty products and bath foams. He didn't really know what he was looking for, just some other conclusive proof, and as he glanced at the open bathroom cabinet there it was. An empty box for a pregnancy testing kit.

Nicole was pouring Luke's coffee when he appeared behind her in the kitchen doorway.

'So…interesting choice of reading material.'

His dry tone made her swivel around.

He was leaning against the doorframe, watching her through narrowed eyes. 'Care to explain?' Although his voice was light, one look at his face made her stomach start to knot with dread.

'Sorry?' Instinct told her to play this very carefully. Best to pretend she didn't know what he was talking about. 'Explain what?'

Luke took a step further into the room and to her consternation tossed the magazine down on the kitchen table with a less than good-humoured thud.

'Oh, that!' Nicole glanced down at the glossy page, with its picture of a pregnant mother, and cringed. What on earth had possessed her to buy that? 'It's not mine. A friend left it behind last week.'

She could see anger in the darkness of his eyes now. And as he stepped further into the room Nicole took an instinctive step back.

'I suppose this isn't yours either?' The box from her pregnancy testing kit followed the magazine down onto the table.

'Where the hell did you get that?' To her dismay her voice wasn't at all steady now.

'It was sitting in your bathroom cabinet.'

'How dare you go through my things?'

He just looked at her with dark, disdainful eyes. 'You've lied to me!' He came closer.

'Luke, you are scaring me!' Without realising it she had backed into the countertop behind her and couldn't get any further away from him.

'Only for the fact that you are *pregnant*… I'd say good.'

For a fleeting second she wondered if she could still lie her way out of this, tell him the box wasn't hers either. But, judging by the harsh expression on Luke's face, she would probably just make things worse. He wasn't going to be receptive to any more lies.

Luke watched the shadows flicking through her green eyes. 'Haven't you got anything to say?'

She raised her chin a little higher. 'You've no right to come round here, prying into my life!'

'Well, it's a damn good job I did!' he growled. 'Because you *had* no right to keep this from me. I presume it's my baby?'

'Of course it's your baby!' Nicole swallowed hard on a knot of anger and tried to keep her nerve.

'So how many weeks pregnant are you?' Luke demanded.

When she didn't answer him immediately he put one hand on the counter behind her, effectively trapping her.

'Six weeks!' she answered hurriedly.

He pulled back and looked furious. 'Six weeks and you didn't mention anything!'

She raked an unsteady hand through her hair. 'I've only just found out. I had it confirmed by the doctor today. I didn't tell you because it wouldn't have served any purpose.'

'Oh, really? And you decided this all by yourself?'

Nicole tried to ignore the cutting sarcasm in his tone. 'Yes.' She angled her chin up firmly. 'I don't want you to concern yourself with this, Luke. It's my business and I'll take care of it.'

'Take care of it?' His eyes narrowed on her face. 'Are you thinking—?'

'No, I am not!' She cut across him, her eyes wide with horror as she realised he was about to mention termination. 'I want this baby with all my heart.' Her voice trembled slightly.

'I see.' He seemed to relax for a moment, and then he started to pace up and down beside her.

'What I'm saying is that it's *my* responsibility,' she added tersely.

'So what are you telling me? That you made medical history and conceived all by yourself? You better think again about that.' Luke swung around to face her again and his voice was very cold now. 'Because, if my memory serves me correctly, six weeks would just fit in with the night when a wild episode in your bed led to my suggesting the morning after pill.' He noticed how the pallor of her skin suddenly flared with incriminating colour. 'I take it you didn't follow my advice?'

A long silence stretched between them. She could feel Luke's eyes boring into her with deep intensity.

'Nicole, I asked you a question.' He took a step closer, and now he was so near that he was within a whisper of her. She could feel the heat from his body, smell the scent of his cologne. It brought back memories of their last night together... She remembered how he had made her feel...how he had caressed her, held her, stroked her.

'Nicole?' The coldness of his tone was a million miles away from the passion of that night.

'No.' Nicole made the admission huskily. 'No I didn't take your advice.'

'So you deliberately went against my wishes,' he said calmly.

She didn't answer him...couldn't answer him.

'Have you just used me as a sperm bank?'

The angry question shocked her. 'No! No, Luke—of course not!'

He coldly watched the play of emotions in her eyes. 'Well, from where I'm standing that is what it looks like. And I am not happy about it, Nicole.'

She looked horrified. 'Luke, really! No matter what else you might think, I didn't plan for this to happen!'

'So, as a matter of interest, why didn't you take that pill?'

The calm question made her temper flare. 'Because I didn't think I could get pregnant. So I didn't worry about it.' She glared at him, her eyes over-bright with emotion. 'My ex-husband and I tried for a long time to have a baby. It's what eventually broke us apart…' Her voice wobbled precariously. 'He now has a two-and-a-half-year-old little girl. So I never thought in a million years that when we had one little accident I would get pregnant. How could I, after all that time of trying…of hoping? So how dare you talk to me like this? How dare you accuse me of something so…so…?'

He reached out a hand and touched her arm, but she shrugged him away. 'I have every right to be angry, Nicole.' Although he said the words firmly, his tone was softer now. 'You should have told me!'

'Told you what? That I thought I couldn't get pregnant?' Her voice trembled. 'That was really none of your business. We were having sex, Luke, not a relationship.'

'Don't be sarcastic, Nicole.'

As she looked up she could see a pulse ticking in the side of his jaw, and his eyes were dark with fury.

'I meant you should have told me that you were pregnant.'

'There was no point.' She held his gaze firmly.

'No point?' He looked as if he was having difficulty reining back his temper again. 'I'm the baby's father. Of course there was a point! We need to discuss this.'

'There is nothing to discuss. I'm not going to have an abortion, Luke, and that's final.' Her heart was thundering against her chest so hard it was making her feel ill. 'I told you. I want this baby.'

He stared at her for a moment. 'It sounds like you've got everything all worked out.'

'Yes, I have.' She held his dark gaze steadily. 'I didn't plan it…but I've had time to think about it and work out what I'm going to do. All I'm saying is that *you* don't need to worry. I don't want anything from you…either emotionally or financially. I'll be absolutely fine. That's why I didn't tell you.'

'And I take it this is why you are going back to London?' He asked the question in a low, calm tone, yet for some reason it made a shiver of consternation race down her spine.

'Yes.'

'I don't think you've thought this out at all, Nicole,' he said furiously. 'How do you think you are going to manage on your own, with a baby and no job?'

'I'll get another job. No problem there.' She glared at him, her chin held high. 'I will be perfectly fine on my own.'

She probably *would* find herself another good job, Luke thought bleakly. He'd employ her again like a shot! He forced himself not to think like that. 'If you don't mind my saying so, that sounds very idealistic…and it is probably great in theory…but the reality is going to be very different, Nicole. And very difficult.'

'Don't lecture me, Luke. I'm the one having the morning sickness; I'm the one who can't even have a cup of coffee any more without wanting to throw up. I'm well aware of the realities.'

'No, you're not. This is just the start.' Luke's eyes raked over her face. 'This is the easy bit. You are going to be alone with a baby. You don't have a home. You don't have a job. Babies are expensive—they need feeding and clothing, not to mention all the necessary accessories. And if you are going to go back to work full-time it'll be very tiring. Who will help you when the baby cries at night and you are so bone-weary you feel you can't drag yourself out of bed to look after him?'

'I'll manage perfectly well—'

He cut across her. 'Then there is the question of schooling, of giving him or her the best start in life. You'll have to do everything alone…*you* will have all the responsibility.'

'And I'll enjoy it,' she said mutinously. 'If you are trying to scare me, it's not working, Luke.'

'And one day your child will turn around and ask about his father. Then what will you say?'

'I'll say…' Nicole faltered.

'Yes?' Luke held her eyes with determination.

'I'll cross that bridge when I come to it, Luke,' she said crossly. 'It's years in the future, and as long as my child knows that he or she is loved that's all that matters.'

'Very commendable…'

'I don't want to listen to this negativity!' Nicole was furious now.

'I'm just pointing out that, contrary to popular belief, being a single parent is a tough job.'

'I know what you are doing, Luke. You're trying to jolt me into thinking about getting rid of my baby, but it's not working.' She tried to push past him but he put a hand on her arm and wouldn't let her go.

'If you don't mind, I've had enough of this. I want you to leave.' She stared up at him in fury.

'But I *do* mind.' In contrast to hers, his voice was perfectly calm.

'You see, this is *exactly* why I didn't want to tell you

about the baby in the first place!' Her voice was vehement. 'I knew you would be like this.'

'You haven't given me a chance to say what I think.'

'On the contrary—I've just listened to your opinions at length.' Her eyes flashed fire at him. 'I didn't expect you to be pleased…in fact I didn't expect anything from you… so I'm not disappointed. Now, please take your hand off my arm—you are hurting me.'

He released her immediately and watched as she rubbed her skin as she walked away.

'I'm sorry, Nicole. I didn't realise I was hurting you.' He ran an impatient hand through the darkness of his hair. 'But you can't just leave things like this.'

'Watch me,' she said firmly.

Their eyes clashed across the room.

'I want you to go,' she reiterated.

For a long moment he said nothing, just looked at her in a deeply contemplative way. 'I didn't mean to upset you.'

'I'm not in the slightest bit upset,' she said quickly, but even as she was fervently denying the fact she was aware that deep down inside she felt very emotional. 'I'm furious with you for speaking to me the way you did…but that's about it.'

'You can't blame me for being angry—'

'Yes, I can—because I haven't done anything wrong.' She held his gaze defiantly. 'I certainly didn't deliberately set out to get pregnant *with you*.'

Luke held that gaze for a moment, then shrugged. 'But the fact is you *are* carrying my baby—and I had to drag the information out of you.'

'Come on, Luke, it wouldn't have made a blind bit of difference to you if I'd told you directly. We would still have had that conversation about how you think I won't be able to manage. The fact is you want me to get rid of the baby. But I've got news for you, Luke. You are not in control of this situation. I am.'

She put her hand on her hip and met his eyes squarely. 'I am having this baby and I will manage just fine. So you don't need to concern yourself about it.'

Luke watched her through narrowed eyes. She probably would manage very well on her own. She was determined and clever and self-sufficient enough to manage anything. 'But the fact is I *am* concerned,' he said quietly.

'Only because this is not what you want! We could go round in circles like this all day. I want you to go.'

As Nicole turned to leave the room she suddenly felt dizzy, it was just a fleeting feeling, but she had to reach out and grab hold of the table.

'Are you OK?' Instantly Luke was by her side. And when she didn't answer him straight away he put a steadying arm around her shoulder. 'Come on, you better sit down. I'll help you through to the other room.'

'I'm OK, Luke.' She shrugged him away angrily. 'I'm not an invalid!'

'I know that, but you do look very pale.'

'Don't pretend that you give a damn, because I'm not that stupid!' She looked over at him, her eyes wide and glimmering a fierce gold-green.

'Of course I care about you!' His reply was instant and vehement. 'You know I do!' he added gently.

Their eyes met and she felt a deep pang of regret. Maybe he did care about her. But not enough. Not in the way she ached for him to care.

'Come on, let's get you onto the sofa.'

She flinched away from his helping hand. She couldn't bear for him to touch her. It just made the raw pain of wanting him all the worse.

'Just go away, Luke.'

He stepped back from her, an expression of deep consternation in his eyes. 'Shall I phone for a doctor?'

'Don't be ridiculous.' She looked over at him and despite everything she smiled. 'I know what's wrong with me…remember?'

He smiled back.

Suddenly she was aware of tears prickling at the back of her eyes. Furious with herself, she drew herself up and headed for the front door. 'You'd better go.'

Luke hesitated for a moment before following her.

'Are you going to be OK?'

'Of course.' She glared at him. 'I'll be wonderful.'

'Take the day off work tomorrow.' He paused by the door, his voice brisk and businesslike. 'And then, when you've rested, we'll talk. That way we'll both have had a chance to calm down and think logically about the situation.'

'I am thinking logically,' she told him quickly. 'And I'm not going to change my mind, Luke. I'm having this baby.'

'But we still need to talk about it.' He said the words tersely. 'I *am* involved in this, whether you like it or not!'

With that he turned and left.

CHAPTER TWELVE

NICOLE spent a sleepless night, tossing and turning, trying not to think about Luke. But scenes from their confrontation kept replaying through her mind. His accusation that she had used him just to have a baby! How dared he? She had been shocked to find she was pregnant…shocked and more than a little scared. Yes, it was something she wanted…but it was something she had given up on a long time ago, when her marriage had broken down.

Then there had been Luke's negative comments about how she wouldn't be able to cope with a baby on her own.

Sadness vied with anger inside her. She tried to focus on the angry thoughts; it seemed easier to cope that way. She couldn't wait to get away from him, she told herself firmly. But even so she kept remembering his voice, and the look in his eyes as he'd told her that he cared about her. Her ex-husband had said something similar to her, she reminded herself. Just before he left her for another woman.

It was a relief when dawn broke and she could get up. Despite Luke's order that she take the day off, she got ready to go into work. She didn't want to sit around thinking about things. It was better to keep busy. So, almost in a defiant mood, she showered and dressed in a pale pink dress that skimmed her figure in a flattering way.

She scanned her appearance critically before leaving the apartment. Her hair was sitting perfectly, and even though she hadn't slept much she looked pretty good. She ran a hand soothingly down over the flatness of her stomach. It was still hard to believe that she was pregnant. A quiver of excitement cut through her anxiety about Luke. It didn't matter what he said…nothing could take away the pleasure of the fact that she was having a baby.

With a smile, she picked up her briefcase and headed into work.

Molly looked surprised when she walked into Nicole's office and saw her. 'I thought you were taking the day off!'

'What gave you that idea?'

'Luke just sent me a memo telling me you would be off for at least a week.'

'Did he?' Nicole felt a prickle of annoyance. 'We've obviously just got our wires crossed. I've no intention of taking time off.' She reached for the pile of mail waiting for her in the in-tray. 'Hold all my calls for a couple of hours, will you, Molly? I've still got some catching up with this paperwork from yesterday.'

'OK.' Molly smiled at her. 'You look better.'

'Actually, yes, I do feel better.' Nicole smiled as she suddenly realised she'd had no morning sickness today.

It was a hectic morning, as usual, and Nicole was glad of the fact—glad that she could bury herself in faxes and e-mails and not have to think about anything else.

At ten o' clock Molly put her head around the door. 'Luke is on the phone. Shall I put him through?'

Nicole hesitated. Part of her wanted to say no…but then Luke might think that she was hiding away from him. She needed to brazen this out as best she could, she told herself. 'Yes, put him through.'

With a supreme effort of will Nicole snatched up the phone and forced herself to sound briskly businesslike. 'Good morning, Luke, what can I do for you?'

'Now *there* is a loaded question!' He sounded amused.

Nicole had expected him to sound annoyed. She'd been unprepared for that deeply attractive husky tone.

'I thought I told you to take today off?' he continued.

'Luke, if I feel I need some time off I'll ask you for it,' she answered calmly. As she was speaking to him she filled in a report, trying to distract herself from thinking…from feeling.

'You are very stubborn,' he muttered. 'How are you feeling this morning?'

'Absolutely fine, thank you.'

'So, no sickness today, then?'

She tapped her pen impatiently against the desk. 'No, I told you, I feel great.'

'And no dizzy turns? I was worried about you after I left last night.'

Nicole frowned… Like hell he was. She wasn't going to be taken in by this note of concern. She knew damn well that his main worry was probably the fact that she was going to go through with this pregnancy.

'No. Now, I really better go. I've got someone waiting for me on the other line—'

'I'm going to book a restaurant for us to have lunch. So make sure you keep a few hours free from twelve-thirty onwards.'

'I'm not going to have lunch with you, Luke,' she said firmly.

'Yes, you are.' His voice was equally firm. 'I've come to a decision, Nicole, and we need to talk about it. I'll meet you down in the lobby at twelve-thirty.'

The line went dead. What did he mean, he had come to a decision? Nicole put the phone down with a frown. There were no decisions for him to make. She was leaving and she was having the baby.

She tried to concentrate on her work but it was difficult now. That sentence kept rolling through her mind. Maybe he was going to give her the name of some abortion clinic? Her mouth tightened in an angry line. Well, whatever he was going to say, she supposed she would have to meet him.

By the time twelve-thirty came around, Nicole was feeling extremely uneasy. She checked her appearance in her vanity mirror and reapplied her lipstick. Then, picking up her purse, she strolled towards the lifts. It would do Luke good to be kept waiting, she told herself. She wanted him to know that *she* was in control of this situation.

Even though Nicole had given herself a stern pep-talk about how she didn't care what Luke thought, and how she just wanted to be far away from him, her emotions seemed to give a weird flip of pleasure as she saw him standing in the lobby waiting for her.

He was just too handsome for any woman's peace of mind, she thought as her eyes drifted over the lightweight suit he was wearing. Not only did he dress stylishly, he had a fantastic body as well.

'I was just starting to think you weren't going to show.' He turned and smiled at her.

He also had the sexiest eyes of any man she had ever met, she thought distractedly.

'Well, I've got to eat.' She shrugged and tried to keep her voice flippant. 'So I thought I might as well listen to what you had to say.'

'Good decision.' There was a mocking gleam in his dark eyes which made her think that if she hadn't come down here he'd have gone up to her office and collected her physically.

Trying to ignore that disturbing mental picture, she turned to walk outside with him.

Luke's silver Porsche was parked directly outside and he had left the roof down. 'I thought we might as well get a few rays of sunshine while we are out.' He opened the passenger door for her and watched as she settled herself comfortably in the deep leather seat.

After the air-conditioned cool of the office, it was pleasant to sit in the sun, with a gentle breeze wafting over her as they drove down towards South Beach.

'You look lovely, by the way.' He glanced over at her as they stopped at traffic lights.

'Thanks.' She tried not to be pulled into the dark seductiveness of his gaze. Luke found it very easy to be charming, and she didn't want to allow herself to be lulled into a false sense of security.

'Did you sleep well last night?' he asked nonchalantly.

'Luke, will you just drop this phony interest in my well-being? It's annoying me now,' she said tightly as she looked away from him again.

'I'm asking because I am genuinely concerned for your health…and the baby's health,' he added softly.

She glanced back at him with a frown.

'Don't look at me with that suspicious light in your eyes.' His lips twisted in a mocking smile. 'I'm not an ogre, you know.'

'I never said you were.' Her heart twisted painfully. 'But I know you are not concerned about the baby.'

'That's a bit harsh, Nicole.' He changed gears and accelerated away from the lights with a grim expression on his face. 'I admit that maybe I could have handled the news that you are pregnant better. But it did come as a bit of a shock.'

Her swirling feeling of suspicion grew inside. Luke sounded conciliatory, and that wasn't usual.

'It came as a shock to me as well.'

'I know.' He nodded. 'I shouldn't have flown off the handle and accused you of deliberately getting pregnant… it was wrong of me.' He glanced across at her.

Something about the way he had said those words…the way he'd looked at her…made her feel incredibly vulnerable somehow. But she knew he was probably just trying to soften her up so that she would agree to whatever he wanted. She'd seen him in action enough times to know that he was very clever at getting his own way and that she shouldn't underestimate him! Nor should she underestimate the power he seemed to hold over her senses either. Because, at the same time as she was telling herself these things, she was drawn by that silky note of gentleness.

'Well, let's just forget about that, shall we?' she said hurriedly. 'I know you don't particularly trust women, so I suppose it was grist for the mill.'

He frowned, and seemed to think about that for a moment.

'I suppose you are right. I do have trust issues.' He shrugged. 'And, from what you told me yesterday, so do you.'

'I don't know what you are talking about,' she said firmly.

'Come on, Nicole. You told me about your ex-husband, remember?'

'That's all in the past—'

'Yes, and the past is what shapes us, isn't it?' He glanced over at her with a raised eyebrow. 'You know, sometimes I used to look at you and see this really vulnerable light in your eyes. I used to wonder about it…used to wonder if I had imagined it. But now I know I didn't.'

She shifted uncomfortably in her seat. 'Luke, this has nothing to do with our situation now—'

'Yes, it does.' Luke pulled the car over to the side of the road. 'You've been hurt a lot, and I certainly don't want to add to that.'

'You won't—because I won't let you!' she assured him crisply.

He smiled as he met her gaze. 'Maybe it's time we both lowered our barriers a little,' he said softly. 'We don't just have ourselves to think about now. There's a child involved.'

Luke could see the wariness in her eyes as she looked across at him. 'Come on, let's go and get something to eat,' he suggested lightly. 'We can talk honestly, try and relax a bit…OK?'

Nicole found herself nodding. OK, she would try and lower her barriers a little, she told herself. But not too much…Luke had too powerful an effect on her for her to risk that. If she weren't careful he would be taking over. The thought made apprehension spiral inside her.

Luke got out of the car and gave his keys to the valet attendant. Then, putting a hand at her back, he allowed her to precede him up onto the pavement. The restaurants at this point on the promenade were lined up together, and tables and chairs spilled out over the pavements under brightly colored awnings.

The buildings were all Art Deco in design, and the whole ambience was one of stylish sophistication.

Luke led her towards a restaurant that had its own courtyard garden. A band was playing salsa music at the back, and a few couples were dancing next to the swimming pool.

They sat under the shade of a parasol amidst a riot of greenery. Nicole had a clear view out across the road towards the wide sweep of white beach.

A waiter came over and Luke ordered drinks.

'Just a mineral water for me.' She smiled at the waiter and accepted the menu that was passed across to her.

As she glanced down at it she tried to pretend that she was interested in the food. But really all she could wonder about was why Luke had insisted on taking her out to lunch…and what motive lay behind that charmingly laid-back smile that he flashed across at her as their eyes met.

'It's lovely here.' She tried to relax a little.

'Yes…' Luke leaned back in his chair and his eyes drifted over her contemplatively.

'And the band is good.' She tried not to be aware of his gaze on her and instead looked over towards where the group were playing.

'The music reminds me of the first evening I took you out,' he said suddenly. 'Do you remember?'

'Yes, of course.' She smiled. 'We had dinner together

and then on the spur of the moment had a few dances at that Cuban salsa club next door to the restaurant.'

'Considering neither of us could dance, we did pretty well.'

Nicole laughed. 'Well, there were so many people on that small dance floor and the place was so dark it didn't really matter, did it?'

For a second she had a flashback to that evening. She remembered how they had laughed, and how in the end Luke had just taken her into his arms and they had smooched the night away. She had been oblivious to the crowds after that; all she had been aware of was his hard, lean body next to hers, the touch of his hands against her skin. She had hardly been able to wait until they could get out of the place so they could be alone together.

Their eyes met across the table, and she felt herself blush with the heat from that memory.

'We've always had good fun together,' he said softly.

'Yes…' Nicole looked away from him. She was relieved when the waiter brought their drinks at that moment. Remembering good times wouldn't help now, she told herself.

As soon as they were left alone again she quickly tried to switch the conversation onto safer ground. 'By the way, did you have a chance to look into the problem with that contract I mentioned yesterday?'

'We are not talking business this afternoon, Nicole,' he said firmly. 'It's off-limits.'

Her eyes narrowed on him for a moment. 'Well, I was only asking—'

'Save work for the office.' He cut across her briskly. 'We have more important things to concentrate on.'

'More important than work?' She couldn't help the sarcastic note that crept into her voice. 'You must be worried, Luke. Because in my experience *nothing* is more important than business where you are concerned.'

'Well, maybe…like yours…my priorities have just been given a good shake-up.'

'I'm sorry for that, Luke,' she flared. 'I certainly didn't mean to shake up your well-ordered world—'

'No, you just meant to run away without telling me the truth.'

She glared at him, her heart thumping rapidly against her chest.

The waiter arrived at that moment to ask if they were ready to place their food order. Nicole looked back towards the menu. The atmosphere was tense and horrible now, and she wasn't in the slightest bit hungry. This situation was too uncomfortable…She chose the first thing off the menu. All she wanted to do was get this lunch over and get away.

Luke, on the other hand, took a little more time over his selection, and chatted amiably with the waiter.

He was too relaxed, Nicole thought suddenly. She had observed him in times of conflict over business and had found that the more laid-back he seemed the more on your guard you had to be…because there was usually some surprise plan waiting around the corner.

The notion made her very uneasy. Nicole reached for her glass of water and took a sip. She was starting to become paranoid, she told herself sensibly. What plan could he possibly have? *She* was in the driving seat. This was her baby, and he couldn't make her do anything she didn't want to.

'You seem very on edge, Nicole,' Luke remarked as they were left alone again.

'I suppose that's because I *am* on edge. I know you are not happy with this situation…and I'm wondering why you've invited me here. Maybe we should just cut to the bottom line and you can tell me,' she said shakily.

'I've told you what I want. I want us to talk honestly.' He held her eyes steadily. 'And I don't want us to fall out.'

'That's easier said than done.'

'Not if we meet each other halfway.'

'Halfway?'

'Yes, and sort things out in a cordial fashion.'

'You make this sound like just another business deal gone awry.' Her lips twisted in a half-smile.

'I was hoping we could agree on things without becoming too emotional.'

There it was again. That pragmatic, relaxed tone…

'God forbid we become emotional,' Nicole grated sarcastically. 'That would go completely against everything you stand for, wouldn't it, Luke?'

She watched his eyes darken angrily. 'I mean I don't want us to argue. I was trying to be civilised.'

'You weren't being very civilised yesterday, when you told me I wouldn't be able to bring up a child on my own.'

'I said it would be difficult,' he corrected her quickly. 'And anyway, I thought we'd agreed to put yesterday behind us.'

She shrugged, and glared at him mutinously. 'I just hope you are not going to mention the word *termination,* Luke. Because I'm going to get up and leave if you do—'

There was a look of horror in Luke's eyes now. 'You really think I'd say something like that to you?'

'I thought…' She brushed a hand unsteadily through her hair. 'I don't know, Luke…'

'God, no!' He looked over at her earnestly. 'Nicole, can we start again?' he asked suddenly, his voice husky. 'This conversation isn't going quite as I'd planned.'

For a second she was completely disarmed by that tone in his voice and that look in his eye. 'What way had you planned it?' she asked shakily.

'Oh, I don't know.' He shook his head. 'I've been awake all night, thinking.' He reached across and took hold of her hand.

The touch of his fingers against her skin set her pulses racing in chaotic disorder.

'You have?' Nicole looked at him in surprise. Luke never lost sleep about anything.

'Yes.' He met her gaze firmly then. 'And I'm worried about you.'

'Worried!' She felt a jolt of disappointment and pulled her hand away from his. She didn't want him to be worried about her!

'Nicole, I can't let you go back to London and deal with this on your own.'

'Well, you are just going to have to, Luke.' She didn't know how she kept her voice so calm, because inside she was a seething mass of furious regret. 'Because I don't *need* you to worry about me!' She glared at him.

'Maybe not…but I am just the same.' He raked a hand distractedly through his hair.

'I can assure you that I will be fine.'

'You can't assure me of anything, Nicole,' he said harshly. 'You are running away back to England!'

'I'm not running away!' She sat straighter in her chair. 'I'm thinking about what is best for my child.'

'*Our* child,' he corrected her quietly.

Nicole looked across at him, her emotions racing wildly.

'I've thought about it long and hard,' he said softly. 'And I can't let you go. This child is my responsibility as well as yours. I want you to stay here in Miami with me.'

CHAPTER THIRTEEN

FOR a long moment Nicole was so stunned that she couldn't find her voice to answer him. Luke, however, didn't seem to notice. He was talking about the fact that they were both responsible for this precious new life and they had a duty to do their very best for it.

It was the word *duty* that finally snapped her back into some kind of sanity. 'I'm sorry. But this isn't going to work.'

Luke had been in the middle of telling her that in his opinion a child needed two parents. He trailed off and looked at her through narrowed eyes. 'What's not going to work?'

'This.' She waved a hand airily between them. 'This show of...of concern is all very noble. But I am not hanging around in Miami while you salve your suddenly acquired new conscience and play duty dad. So you can just forget it!'

Luke shook his head. 'You misunderstand, Nicole. I'm not trying to salve my conscience. I want to do my best for this child. I want to make sure that you are financially secure. I want to look after you.'

'And I don't want to be looked after.' She cut across him coolly. 'You know, Luke, when my ex-husband was leaving me he told me that his new girlfriend was pregnant. He also told me that he still had feelings for me. That he didn't really want to leave. But he felt that he had to do the right thing by his child.'

'Nicole, I know you've been hurt, but this situation is different.'

'No, it's not. Because do you know what I felt when he said those things?' She fixed him with a clear and penetrating gaze. 'I felt sympathy for his girlfriend…and I thought that if she had an ounce of sense she would send him packing as soon as he landed on her doorstep.'

'Would you have had him back?'

Her eyes opened wide. 'You must be joking! I wouldn't have had Patrick back if he'd been gift-wrapped.'

Luke smiled. 'Good. Because he sounds like a complete jerk—'

'Whereas *you* sound absolutely so damn perfect?' She looked over at him and shook her head. 'Luke, I've got news for you. I don't want a father for my baby who is just sticking by us out of duty.'

'But I've thought about it, and it's what I want to do,' Luke said seriously.

'I'm sure it is right at this moment. But it won't work. What are you going to do? Take an hour off every week to bounce the baby on your knee and then run back to your precious business for your real commitment?'

'I think I can do better than that.' Luke's voice was terse.

'And how's a baby going to fit in to that contemporary hi-tech apartment of yours? Not to mention the fact that it's going to play havoc with your social life. And do you think a baby seat will fit in the back of that Porsche?'

'Very funny,' he grated.

'Yes, it is—isn't it?' Nicole held his dark gaze for a moment. 'Because the truth is that after a few months of playing duty dad you'd be bored to tears. The baby would get in the way of your jet-set lifestyle and your glamorous women.'

'You are wrong about that, Nicole,' Luke said quietly.

'No, I'm not.' She took a deep breath. 'But you were right about one thing. We are both products of our past. I'm older and wiser and I'm certainly not going to get tied… however tenuously…to the wrong man again. And you…' She met his eyes steadily. 'You are an emotional desert, Luke.'

Before Luke could say anything to that she was pushing her chair away from the table. 'Thanks for the invitation to lunch, but I think I've just lost my appetite.'

'Nicole, don't go!' But he was talking to himself. She was walking away from him, out onto the street.

Luke wanted to rush after her, but at that second the waiter arrived with their food. He was forced to waste precious minutes trying to explain that they wouldn't now be eating and asking to have the bill. By the time he followed Nicole out of the restaurant there was no sign of her.

Fury rushed through his entire body as he glanced up and down the crowded street and then across the road towards the beach. He had made a complete and utter botch of everything. With a grim feeling of utter frustration he took out his mobile phone, brought up Nicole's number and dialled it.

Nicole had planned to jump into a cab and dash back to the office. But when she got outside the restaurant she suddenly couldn't face going back to work. Instead she found herself crossing the road and walking back in the direction they had come, cutting across a strip of parkland towards the beach.

She sat on a wall and looked out across the wide sweep of white sand. It was a perfect day. The sun was beating down from a clear blue sky and the waves were crashing in against the shore, with just a hint of a breeze rustling through the palm trees.

Would she never learn? Nicole wondered angrily. For a while, when Luke had looked at her across that table and made it clear that he wanted their baby, she had felt a rush of happiness that had almost overwhelmed her. In those precious few seconds she had pictured them as a couple… as a family. It was amazing how many pictures of the future you could fit into a few seconds…and how blissful those images could be. Blissful—but foolish!

As if Luke could ever be a family man!

Her phone rang, and she took it out of her handbag and flipped it open. Luke's name was flashing on the screen.

She disconnected and put the phone back in her bag again. There was no point talking.

But what about the fact that he wants to try and do the right thing? a little voice cut through her unhappiness. Didn't that count for something? Did she really have the right to make the decision to march off back to London? They had made this baby together…it wasn't just her decision to take…was it?

She swallowed hard on a lump in her throat. But how could she stay here knowing that she loved him? Watching him play dad at a distance would be torturous. For the preservation of her sanity she needed to leave.

The phone rang again. It would be him…she knew it would be him. She tried to ignore it.

Would allowing him to play dad at a distance be better than nothing at all? That persistent little voice inside her was rising in volume, cutting through all her strong thoughts.

She fished the phone out of her bag again and opened it. As she had known it would be, Luke's name was on the screen.

He would be a terrible dad, she told herself. He'd always put business first…and he'd always have a different beautiful woman on his arm. And there lay the crux. Was she fleeing back to London because she couldn't face the fact that she wasn't going to be in his life? And, if so, was that selfish? Shouldn't she be putting her baby's needs first?

Maybe Luke would make a terrific dad! How did she know? Didn't Luke deserve a chance to prove himself?

The phone rang and rang, and suddenly she couldn't stand it any more and answered it.

'Nicole…thank God.' His voice was fervent. 'Look, I'm sorry. How can I put this right?'

The lump in her throat grew. This didn't sound like the Luke she knew.

'I don't know,' she murmured honestly.

'Where are you?' His husky voice tore at her emotions.

'I'm…I'm across the road…by the park.'

'OK, stay where you are. I'm on my way.'

With a frown, Nicole snapped the phone closed. This was probably a mistake. She was feeling vulnerable, and it wasn't a good idea to talk in this state. What she should have done was head back to the office and bury herself in work until she had regained some strength.

She put her phone away and stood up to leave—and that was when the first pain struck her in the stomach. She didn't dare to move for a moment, and she waited with apprehension to see if it would return. A few seconds later it was followed by another, sharper pain.

She sat back down on the wall and put a hand to her stomach in alarm.

'Nicole?'

She looked up and saw that Luke was beside her, but his voice seemed to be coming from a long way off. She felt dizzy now.

'Honey, are you OK?' He crouched down beside her and looked at her with concern.

'I think you'd better get me to the hospital,' she whispered, as another pain stabbed through her. She was really frightened now. This couldn't be happening! She was losing the baby…she could feel it… A sob rose in her throat.

Afterwards, the memory of getting to the hospital was all a bit of a blur to Nicole. She remembered that Luke had taken charge, and that his calm manner had been soothing. He had started to help her to walk and then, as the pain came back, he had swept her up into his arms and carried her.

In a matter of minutes he had hailed a passing cab.

Now Nicole was in a private room as a nurse took her details and they waited for a doctor. She couldn't believe that this was happening! She had felt so well this morning! Was it her fault? Had she done something wrong? Worked too hard? Maybe if she had taken the day off, as Luke suggested?

The doctor came into the room and spoke to her before

starting an examination. Nicole closed her eyes and prayed that her baby would be all right.

Luke was pacing up and down in the corridor outside. The smell of antiseptic and the bright neon lights dazzled him. He couldn't remember ever feeling this helpless before. Nicole had asked that he wait outside while they were examining her, and he had respected her wishes, but he just wanted to be with her, to do something.

He whirled around as the nurse came out of the room. 'How is she? Is the baby OK?'

The nurse looked over at him with sympathy. 'We don't know yet if Nicole has lost the baby. Dr Curran has suggested that we do an ultrasound scan to see exactly what is going on.'

'And how long will that take?' He frowned.

'Not long. There is a coffee machine at the other end of the corridor, and some comfortable seats if you'd like to wait down there,' she told him.

Luke shook his head. 'I'd like to be with Nicole while she is having the scan—'

'Yes, of course…Nicole has asked for you. I just meant for you to wait while Dr Curran is finishing the examination. Give us a few more minutes and then I'll bring you in.' She hurried away again, and once more he was left to pace up and down outside.

It felt like for ever before they told him he could go inside. Nicole was lying on the bed, propped up by a few pillows; she looked so fragile that his heart ached for her. Her hair was so dark against the pallor of her skin, and her large green eyes were misted with anxiety.

He went straight across to her and took hold of her hand.

Nicole was so glad to see him that she could feel tears welling up inside her.

'So, how is the patient doing, Dr Curran?' he asked.

'Nicole's pain has stopped, so that is something.' The doctor pushed her glasses further up her nose as she studied some notes. 'I am having difficulty finding the baby's heartbeat. But we'll know more when we do the ultrasound.' She put the notes down suddenly and looked over at them both with a serious expression on her face. 'I'm afraid miscarriages are common within the first weeks of pregnancy. It's a risky time.'

'Are you saying you think Nicole has lost the baby?' Luke's voice was grim.

'I'm saying that it's a possibility.' She looked from one to the other of them. 'I am sorry, but I feel I should prepare you for the worst…just in case.'

Nicole felt a lump rising in her throat. She wanted to cry, but the tears seemed lodged deep inside, like a dam waiting to burst.

'Are you going to do the ultrasound now?' Luke asked.

He sounded so calm, Nicole thought. Just like he did when he was in the office, sorting out an unexpected problem. She listened as he asked questions and the doctor explained the procedure.

'Thank you, Doctor.' Luke nodded.

'You're welcome.'

The door closed behind her and they were left alone.

'It doesn't sound good, does it?' Nicole's voice was shaky.

Luke perched on the side of the bed and looked at her gently. 'The doctor was just preparing us for the worst. But that doesn't mean the worst has happened.'

'I don't want to lose my baby, Luke.' She whispered the words unsteadily. 'I want this child so much…'

'I know, honey.' He stroked her hair back from her face with a gentle hand. 'But let's think positively.'

She noticed how ashen his face was, how his eyes were filled with an intensity of pain. She had never seen Luke look like that before, and it shook her. Suddenly she realised that he was trying to keep calm for her, and that this was tearing him apart too!

Tears trickled down her face as she realised that he was hurting every bit as much as she was.

'Don't cry, Nicole!' He put an arm around her, and the next moment she was pulled close against his chest. 'Let's remain positive about our baby, hmm…? Let's not cross bridges until we have to.'

His voice was husky and deep and infinitely soothing. She leaned against him, grateful for the support, loving the feeling of closeness, the familiar tang of his cologne…the warmth of his body. She closed her eyes and tried to draw strength from him. 'Luke, I'm so sorry.'

'Sorry for what?' He stroked her hair tenderly. 'You haven't done anything wrong.'

'I said horrible things to you at lunch!' She squeezed her eyes tightly closed.

'I think I deserved them.'

'No, you didn't!' She pulled back and looked at him through eyes that burnt with feeling. 'You told me you wanted our baby, and I…I didn't realise just how much you meant it!'

'Yes, I did mean it. But I can understand you being wary of my motives. After all, I have always enjoyed life in the fast lane, without commitments.' He shook his head ruefully. 'You're right about me. I have been an emotional desert.'

'I really shouldn't have said that,' she murmured.

'Yes, you should—because it's the truth.' He took hold of her hands. 'And I've deliberately tried to keep myself that way as well…it seemed safer, somehow.'

'I know that feeling.' She bit down on her lip. 'I felt the same after my marriage broke up. Told myself that I wasn't going to get emotionally involved ever again.'

'Yes, but you are a nicer person than me. Because you couldn't keep that way of life up. You are warm and loving and you wanted more—which is why you finished with me. And I don't blame you, Nicole.' His lips twisted ruefully. 'I've been so blind… I just didn't see the truth… Or maybe I just didn't want to see the truth until it hit me.'

Nicole swallowed hard. 'And now you realise how much you want to be a father…that you're ready for that commitment—'

'Not just that…'

She looked at him with puzzled eyes.

'Nicole, from the first moment you walked into my office you changed my life.'

'I did?'

He nodded, and wiped a tear away from her face with a tender hand. 'I thought I had my life all in order until the day you walked into my office and into my life, with your fabulous green eyes and your fiery spirit. I was totally…totally captivated. And since that day everything I thought I knew about myself has been thrown into chaos.'

'It has?' Nicole was looking at him in bewilderment.

He nodded. 'Oh, I've tried to pretend that it hasn't…in

fact I've been too cussedly stubborn to even listen to my own heart! When you finished things I was devastated. But I told myself it was just an affair and I'd get over it….and then I realised that I wasn't just going to get over it.' He gave a grim laugh. 'And when you told me that you wanted a deeper and more meaningful relationship I was quite frankly in a complete tailspin.'

She smiled shakily.

'I've accused you of wanting to run away back to London. But *I've* been the one who has been running away, Nicole…' His voice held a deep, raw sincerity that touched her to the core. 'I've been running away from my own emotions, running away from myself… And when you put in your resignation I realised that. I was devastated at the thought that I'd lost you. Because without you I'm nothing. You make me a better person…you make my life complete…'

Her heart lurched crazily and she just couldn't find her voice to say anything.

'And then I found out you were pregnant. I was in a state of shock…not only because I'd found out I couldn't bear to lose you…but suddenly I found that I wanted the whole package. I want you and the baby…and I want it so much that it hurts.'

She swallowed down her tears.

'This is what I meant to say to you over lunch. But of course old habits die hard and I found myself hiding behind all kinds of excuses to keep you here…' He shook his head. 'And now look at me…blurting all this out at the wrong time. I have made a complete mess of things.'

'It's not the wrong time.' Her voice was groggy with tears.

'It is. But I'm going to say it anyway... I love you, Nicole, and I think I have from the first moment I set eyes on you. I've just been too stupid and too stubborn to face it. And now I can't face the thought of life without you. If we lose our baby...' His voice cracked slightly and he smiled. 'Sorry...I just need you so much, Nicole, and I'm begging you to give me a chance to prove myself to you. I want us to face this situation as a couple...'

Nicole put her arms around him and just held him. 'I want that too.' She whispered the words fervently. 'More than you'll ever know.'

'Really?' He pulled back from her. 'Because I know that before you found out you were pregnant you wanted to get out of our relationship and find someone else...someone who didn't have all my hang-ups...'

'I want *you*, Luke...' Her heart was thundering against her chest. 'That's why I finished things. Because I love you and I didn't think you would ever return that love.'

She saw the look of hope in his eyes. 'So...no matter what the outcome of this scan is...we'll face it together?'

She nodded.

'Nicole, will you marry me?'

Nicole was so stunned that she couldn't say anything for a moment. 'Luke, I—'

'Don't say no!' He placed a finger over her lips. 'I know this is the wrong time, but I have to say this now. I love you so much. Just give me a chance to prove to you that my feelings are genuine.' He watched as a tear trickled down her cheek.

'Don't cry, sweetheart, please. It just breaks my heart.'

'You shouldn't be saying this.'

'I know. But if our baby is all right and I ask you later, it will seem like I'm only asking you because we are having a child. And if the news is bad…God forbid…' His voice was grim now. 'Well, at least something good will have come out of this situation.'

'Luke, you don't know what you are saying.' Her voice was husky with the weight of her emotion. 'If we've lost this baby you might be committing yourself to someone who can never give you a family. I couldn't get pregnant with Patrick…this child might be my last chance.'

'We'll take that a day at a time, Nicole…a step at a time.'

She shook her head. 'I can't marry you, Luke. I'm sorry, but I can't go through all that again.' Her voice cracked huskily. 'I can't go through the pain of not being able to give you what you want. I've been through that once before with Patrick, and it was…unbearable…' She looked up at him with wide eyes. 'I suppose that was the reason I tried to keep my emotions switched off when we started our affair. I was scared of falling in love all over again, scared of the same thing happening…'

'The same thing *isn't* going to happen—because I'm not Patrick,' he said gently. 'And I love you.' He gripped hold of her shoulders and looked at her. 'I love you…I need you…and as long as I have you I can face anything else.'

'And you still want me even though…if I lose this baby…I might not be able to give you another one?' She looked up at him with wide green eyes.

'I want you with all my heart, Nicole,' he murmured. 'And if we lose this child we'll face it together…comfort each other…grieve together…and then try again—maybe adopt. There are ways around the situation.'

She shook her head. 'I can't think about this now, Luke,' she said brokenly.

Luke hesitated. He wanted to press her further, but she looked so distraught. 'OK…we'll leave it for now.' He wrapped his arms around her and for a moment they just held each other. 'Just know that I'm here for you.' He stroked her hair. 'And I always will be. No matter what.'

His words made her melt.

The door opened and the nurse came in.

'It's time to take you down for your scan now, Nicole.'

The fear instantly returned, but Luke caught hold of her hand. She could feel his strength and his love in that touch, and it helped.

Nicole would never forget those next few moments as they wheeled her through to another room and a different doctor appeared and introduced herself.

There was silence as the doctor started the procedure. Nicole looked at the expressions on the doctor's face as she looked at the screen that would show her baby.

'Is everything OK, Doctor?' It was Luke who asked the question, and his voice was tense.

The doctor didn't answer straight away; she was too busy staring at the screen. Then she smiled. 'I can see your baby…and, yes, everything appears to be fine.'

Nicole hadn't realised how hard she had been holding her emotions in check until then; she felt weak with relief and just buried her face in her hands.

Luke reached and took her into his arms. 'It's OK, honey…everything is going to be all right now.'

The doctor smiled at Luke as she got up from her seat beside them and left them alone.

EPILOGUE

A WARM fragrant breeze drifted across the turquoise water of the Gulf of Mexico and rustled the palm trees outside the bedroom window.

Nicole stood and watched as the early-morning sun played over the water. She loved being down on the Florida Keys.

'What are you thinking about?' Luke's voice jolted her from her contemplation.

'Just how lovely it is here…' She looked around at her husband, who was lying in the four-poster bed; the sheets were low on his abdomen, showing his fabulous torso to advantage. Nicole felt a flare of desire just looking at him.

'I thought you were asleep.' She smiled.

'No, I was lying here admiring your sexy silhouette in that white nightdress.'

She blushed and he laughed. 'Amazing—I can still make you blush even after twelve months of marriage…happy anniversary, darling.' He held out a hand to her and she went back to bed, slipping in beside him to melt into his arms.

'Happy anniversary.' She kissed him, and for a long time they were lost in each other's embrace as passion flared.

'I love you so much.' She breathed the words against his

skin. 'And I just want to say thank you for a wonderful year…' She pressed her lips against his chest and kissed him fiercely.

'Hey, it's just the start of many wonderful years to come.' He squeezed her closer. 'Marrying you was the best deal I ever closed.'

She looked at him wryly and he laughed. 'I don't mind saying that you were the hardest deal to break as well.' He shook his head. 'Negotiations have never been so tough.'

Nicole laughed. She had made Luke wait for a while into her pregnancy before capitulating to marriage. It hadn't been that she was trying to play hard to get, or being deliberately difficult. She had just been wary of marriage. Living with Luke would have suited her.

But Luke had pursued her with dogged determination. He had sent her flowers and gifts and declared his undying love, and had told her that nothing less than total commitment would satisfy him.

She smiled to herself now as she thought about the change in Luke. They had almost had a role reversal after his declaration of love. She'd been the wary one and he'd been so…sure.

'You didn't need to send me all those presents…' She kissed him now. 'Because the best thing you ever did was to give me Thomas.' She whispered the words huskily.

As if on cue their baby gave a gurgling cry in the cot next to the bed. They both rolled over to look in at him.

Thomas Santana was ten months old now, and was the most beautiful baby boy. He had jet-dark hair and eyes like Luke's and he had a smile and a sunny nature that melted their hearts.

'Hello, my darling.' Nicole sat up and reached over to pick him up and bring him into the bed between them.

Every day when she woke and looked at Thomas she marvelled at her little miracle, and gave thanks for the fact that although it had been a difficult pregnancy she'd had Luke by her side, supporting her and being strong for her.

'So, what shall we do today?' she asked. 'A bit of gardening, perhaps, or—?'

'Never mind the garden…' Luke said firmly. 'You, me and Thomas are off to Barbados this afternoon, for two sun-drenched and relaxing weeks.'

Nicole looked at him in surprise. Luke had been due to go back up to Miami first thing tomorrow, leaving her here at the Key West house. 'I thought you had some important meetings lined up at the office this week?'

He smiled at her. 'I've delegated.'

'Have you?' Nicole grinned. 'These really are changed days!'

'Well, we never did get around to going away for our honeymoon, did we?'

Nicole shook her head. They'd had to cancel their trip because she had been ordered to take things easy for the rest of her pregnancy and it had meant a lot of bed-rest.

'And, as I recall, at the time I did promise you a golden beach and as much ice cream as you can eat…and a promise is a promise, Mrs Santana…'

THE TYCOON'S PROPOSAL

BY
LEIGH MICHAELS

Leigh Michaels has always been a writer, composing dreadful poetry when she was four years old and dictating it to her long-suffering older sister. She started writing romance in her teens and burned six full manuscripts before submitting her work to a publisher. Now, with more than seventy novels to her credit, she also teaches romance-writing seminars at universities, writers' conferences and on the internet. Leigh loves to her from her readers. You may contact her at PO Box 935, Ottumwa, Iowa 52501, USA or e-mail her: leigh@leighmichaels.com.

For Alexandra, who knows why

CHAPTER ONE

LONG BEFORE THE banquet was over, Kurt was feeling restless. Why couldn't people just say thank you and leave it at that? If he hadn't wanted to donate all that equipment he wouldn't have done it. So why should he be required to sit at a head table and smile for what seemed hours while everyone from the university's president on down expressed their appreciation?

As if she'd read his mind, his grandmother leaned toward him and whispered, "Most people who donate things enjoy the public recognition. You look as if you have a toothache." She gave an approving nod toward the podium and applauded politely.

Kurt hadn't noticed until then that yet another speaker had finally wound to his interminable conclusion. He rose, made the obligatory half-bow toward the speaker, gave the audience another self-deprecating smile, and hoped to high heaven that they were done.

Apparently they were—or else the audience had finally had enough too, for most of them were on their feet. "At last," he said under his breath.

"It's only been an hour," his grandmother said. "You really must learn some patience."

Now that it was almost finished he could begin to see some humor in the situation. "I didn't hear you saying anything about the need to be patient while I was getting myself established in business, Gran. In fact, I seem to remember you egging me on by saying you wanted me to hurry up and get rich enough to buy you a mink coat."

"What I said," she reminded him crisply, "was that I wanted a mink coat and a great-grandchild before I died, and since I was perfectly able to buy my own mink coat you should concentrate on the great-grandchild."

He suppressed a grin at how easily she'd stepped into the trap. "Well, these people have been telling you all evening how great your grandchild is. So the way I see it, now that you know I'm perfect you have nothing left to complain about."

She smiled. "And here I thought you brought me tonight only because you couldn't decide which of the young women on your list deserved the laurels."

She wasn't far wrong about that, Kurt admitted. He could think of half a dozen women who would have been pleased to attend this event with him—unexciting as it had turned out to be. But that was part of the problem, of course. *Invite a woman to a party and she understands it's just a date. Invite her to a boring banquet in your honor and she starts thinking you must be serious.*

His grandmother was looking beyond him. "Don't look now, but here comes another one."

And if you take your grandmother to the banquet instead, he thought, *the hopefuls start coming out of the walls.*

From the corner of his eye, he spotted a woman coming toward them. This one was blond—but only the hair color seemed to change; they were all young, sleek, improbably curvy, with perfect pert noses. It was as if someone had put a Barbie doll on the copy machine and hit the *enlarge* button.

There had been two of them before they'd even sat down to dinner—fluttering over to enthuse about how wonderful he was to make such a huge contribution, obviously thinking that the way to any man's heart was through his ego. If Kurt had started the evening with any inclination to think himself special—which he hadn't—that would have been enough to cure him.

"Time to get out of here." He offered his arm to his grandmother.

Outside the banquet room, a few people were milling about, buttoning winter coats and wrapping scarves before leaving the warm student union for the wintry outdoors.

"There's a chair," Kurt said. "And isn't that your friend Marian? You can talk to her while I get your coat."

The cloakroom counter was busy, and only one attendant was on duty. When they'd arrived the crowd had been trickling in and there had been two people manning the cloakroom. Now that everyone wanted to leave at once there was just one. Bad planning, Kurt thought.

Several young men were clustered at one end of the counter. Kurt recognized some of them as the athletes who had helped to demonstrate the equipment he had donated for the student union's new gym before all the dignitaries had trooped up to the banquet room to start the congratulations. Kurt looked past them and saw why they were hanging around—the attendant on duty was female, young, and not at all hard on the eyes.

He fidgeted with his claim ticket as he waited his turn, and he watched the young woman. She wasn't conventionally pretty at all. She was far too thin for her height, he thought. Her eyes were much too big for her face, and her auburn hair was cropped shorter than many men's. And the anonymous uniform of a server—black trousers, boxy white tuxedo shirt, bow tie—did little for her slim figure. But she was stunning, nevertheless, the sort of woman who drew gazes, and attention, and interest.

The athletes were certainly interested. Every time she came back to the counter with a coat, one or more of them had a comment. Some of the remarks she ignored, some she smiled at, some brought a quip in return.

She's leading them on, Kurt thought. Not that he cared whether she flirted with the customers, as long as she continued to work efficiently through the crowd. He eyed the small glass jar which sat discreetly at one end of the counter, hinting that tips would be welcome. It was half full of bills and coins. No doubt the occasional flirtation increased the evening's take.

Before long the foyer was emptying out, but the athletes were still hanging on. "When do you get off duty?" one of them asked the attendant.

"Hard to say," the young woman said. "With all these people to take care of, it might be another hour."

"I'll hang around for a while," the athlete said. "You'll need a ride home because it's snowing."

"No, thanks. I like snow. Besides—" She checked the number on a ticket and went to the farthest rack to get an overcoat.

By the time she came back the athlete had apparently thought it through. "I know. You've got a boyfriend to come and get you."

She flashed a smile. "What do you think?"

"I'll save him the trouble," the athlete offered.

The young woman held out a hand for Kurt's claim check, but she didn't look at him because she was still studying the athlete. "Tell you what," she said. "I'll give you a phone number. Call in an hour—just in case he hasn't shown up."

The athlete was practically salivating. He grabbed for a discarded napkin that lay on the counter and thrust it at her. She scribbled something and pushed it back.

"Is this your cell phone?" the athlete asked. "Where are you from, anyway? This isn't a local number."

She didn't seem to hear. She looked up from the ticket she held and smiled at Kurt. "Be right back."

Now he understood what had drawn the athletes. She might

be skinny and big-eyed and boyish, but when she smiled—even that polite, almost meaningless smile of acknowledgment—the room instantly grew ten degrees warmer. Or maybe it wasn't the entire room which heated up but just the men in her general vicinity. That would certainly explain why the athletes' tongues were all hanging out.

There was something almost familiar about that smile....

But then, practically everything Kurt had seen in the last few days had given him a sensation of déjà vu. It was because he was back on campus, that was all. It had been a long time since graduation. And there were a lot of memories—good and bad—to dredge up...

She was gone for quite a while, and he started to wonder if she was ever coming back. Kurt leaned against the counter and crossed his arms, and the young men, after a few wary glances in his direction, moved away.

She returned with his grandmother's mink and his own dark gray cashmere overcoat. "Sorry to take so long. I had the mink tucked away clear in the back, where it would be safer. It's too beautiful to risk." She ran a hand over the fur before she passed it across the counter.

Kurt laid the mink down and put on his own coat. "I seem to have driven away your admirers."

"Oh, that's all right," she said lightly. "If they'd hung around here much longer they'd have gotten me in trouble with the boss."

"I hope I didn't discourage the young man from calling."

"Probably not." She didn't sound excited at the possibility. "I hope he likes listening to the time and temperature recording in Winnipeg."

He wasn't surprised that it hadn't really been her number she'd handed out. But why had she admitted it to him—a complete stranger?

Three guesses, Callahan, he told himself. *Because she's*

after bigger game, so she's making sure you know the athlete's not important.

No wonder he'd had that flash of thinking she looked familiar. One predatory feminine gaze was pretty much like another in his experience.

Her fingertips went out to caress the fur, still draped across the counter. "Careful where you leave that. We get a soft drink spilled every now and then around here, and I'd hate to see that beautiful coat get sticky." She looked up at him through her lashes, with something like speculation in her gaze.

She's debating what kind of approach will be most successful, he thought. Well, maybe he'd make it easy for her.

He picked up the mink, and then turned back as if struck by an afterthought. "I wonder…." He did his best to sound naive. "If *I* asked for your phone number, would you pass me off with time and temperature in Winnipeg?"

She looked at him for a long moment and her eyes seemed to get even bigger.

Calculating my bank balance, no doubt.

"Wouldn't dream of it." She reached for his claim ticket, which was still lying on the counter, flipped it over, pulled a felt-tipped marker from her pocket, and wrote a number on the back side. "Here you go."

It certainly wasn't the time and temperature in Winnipeg, Kurt saw, because she hadn't added an area code. Not that he'd expected anything else. Now she had connected him with the expensive coat, there was no doubt in his mind that she had given him a real number.

Still, he had to admit to a trickle of disappointment, because somehow he'd expected more subtlety from this young woman.

So much for subtlety. He wondered how long she'd wait for him to call. Too bad that he'd never get to find out.

He dropped a substantial tip into the glass jar, and didn't look back as he crossed the lobby to where his grandmother was talking to a white-haired dowager. "I'll meet you here for lunch tomorrow, Marian," his grandmother said. "And perhaps you can bring that young friend of yours to tea sometime in the next few days? Kurt's staying with me through Christmas, you know."

Kurt held his tongue until they were outside, protected from the falling snow by the awning as they waited for the valet to bring his car around. The street was already covered, with soft ruts starting to form in the traffic lanes. Flakes the size of quarters were falling slowly and almost silently. "Marian's young friend is a female, of course," he said.

"Now, what would make you say that, dear?" His grandmother looked meditatively at the street. "Falling snow is almost hypnotic, really. It's such a relief in weather like this to be in the hands of an exceptionally good driver."

"What big fibs you tell, Granny," Kurt said dryly.

His Jaguar pulled up under the awning. As he reached into his pocket for a tip for the valet his fingers brushed the claim ticket. Maybe he should give that to the valet, too, he thought. No—the kid might think he'd been handed a reward, and no inexperienced young guy deserved the kind of trouble that woman represented.

Kurt decided he'd tear the ticket up and throw it away when he got home. Or maybe he'd keep it for a while, just as a reminder of how careful a guy needed to be these days. Not because he'd ever be tempted to use it.

The ticket slid from his fingers and drifted downward like one of the snowflakes. The small card was warm from his pocket, and the first huge flake which collided with it melted instantly and blurred the ink. He dived after it, and his dress shoe slipped on an icy spot, almost careening him headfirst into a drift.

Even as he was scrambling to keep his balance in the snow he told himself it was stupid to care whether he could still read a number that he had no intention of calling. But it burned itself into his brain anyway, as he picked up the ticket and carefully blotted the snowflake away. The handwriting was strong, clear, and neat, with each numeral precisely formed. And there was a nice sequence to the numbers, too. A memorable sequence.

An *odd* sequence, he thought as he slid behind the wheel. Maybe it was even a little too rhythmic. *Five-six-seven-eight*.... Wasn't that just a little too handy a combination to be real? It sounded more like an aerobic dance routine than a phone number.

"Was there something you needed to go back for, dear?" his grandmother asked. "Or are you just planning to sit here and block traffic for the rest of the evening?"

Kurt stared at the ticket still cupped in his palm, and then he reached for his cell phone, angling it in the light from the entrance canopy so he could compare the keypad with what the young woman had written down. The corresponding letters leaped out at him. *Five-six-seven-eight*.... He started to laugh.

It looked like a phone number, all right, but he'd bet it led only to a mis-dial recording. Because surely no phone company would deliberately give a customer that particular series of numbers.

The ones which corresponded to the words GET LOST.

Lissa smothered a yawn and tried not to look at the clock posted high on the foyer's opposite wall. The banquet was over, and most of the crowd was gone, but her nerves were still thrumming from the encounter with Kurt Callahan. She couldn't let down her guard yet, however; she had to stay in the cloakroom until the very last garment was claimed or turned over to Lost and Found once the security officers declared that the building was completely empty of guests.

The double doors of the banquet room opened and one of her co-workers emerged pushing a full cart. She looked hot and tired, and Lissa wished she could go lend a hand. Though the work was harder, she'd much rather draw dining room duty than tend the cloakroom. She'd rather be busy than sitting around doing nothing. The time went faster, the tips were usually better, and there was no opportunity to think…

She glanced at the glass tips jar. Not much in it tonight, except for the nice-sized bill Kurt Callahan had pushed through the slot. A big enough bill, in fact, that she half regretted giving him a fake phone number. Not that she would have given him a real one under any circumstances, because Kurt Callahan was the epitome of trouble; she'd learned that lesson long ago. But she could have just told him no.

She hoped he wouldn't actually call. No, she amended, what she really hoped was that the owner of the number wouldn't take offense if he did. She really should have checked out whether that number was actually assigned to a customer…

But then she'd never needed a backup before, because the time and temperature in Winnipeg had served her well through the years. Until tonight—when she'd blurted out the truth to Kurt Callahan. But why had she told him about her ploy? To show off how clever she was? To very delicately let him know that she hadn't been trolling for a date with the athlete? To hint that she needed such stratagems to hold off the vast numbers of men who clustered around her? To point out that even though he wasn't seriously interested in her other men were?

She smothered a snort at her own foolishness. As if any of that would matter to him. A man with his success, and the good looks to match—hair so dark it had had a bluish cast under the artificial lights, blue-gray eyes, a chiseled profile, and a dimple in his cheek which peeked out at the least expected moments—wouldn't have any doubts that he was attractive to any woman still able to breathe.

Maybe she *did* hope he'd call that number. It would do him good to have his ego trimmed back a bit. And if she could be the one to do it… *Somebody has to start a trend,* she thought.

Besides, if she'd coldly refused to give him the information he wanted, he might have started to wonder why. No, this way was better—he wouldn't call, and so he would never have reason to question why the woman in the cloakroom was immune to his charm. He'd probably never give her a second thought.

Her long evening shut up in the cloakroom should have meant plenty of time to finish reviewing her notes for the next morning's political science final. Of course it hadn't quite happened that way. Despite her best efforts, she hadn't been able to concentrate. A dozen times she'd started to study, only to find herself straining to listen to the speeches coming from the ballroom instead.

Well, it was too late to go to the library. She'd walk straight home instead, look over her notes again, then get some sleep. And once her last exam was past, and she had worked her only remaining dining room shift tomorrow, the semester would officially be over and she would have no other obligations until after January first.

No obligations—but also no income. For with school out of session the student union would close as well.

Lissa bit her lip. She had enough cash tucked back to survive two weeks without a paycheck—and the idea of two weeks of freedom, with no timeclock to punch, no boss to answer to, was sheer heaven.

A crash made her jump and look toward the banquet room. Another of the dining room attendants had misjudged and rammed a cart loaded with the last debris of the banquet—coffee cups, water glasses, crumpled linens, and a few odd baskets of dinner rolls—into the edge of the door. An awkward stack of half-empty glass dessert plates wobbled on the corner of the cart.

Lissa swung herself up onto the cloakroom counter and across, jumping off just as the stack of dishes overbalanced. She slapped her hand down on the top plate, stopping the disaster but splashing leftover creme caramel over the front of her own white shirt and the waitress's. "Sorry about making such a mess, Connie."

"No problem. I'd rather wash out a shirt than clean glass shards out of the carpet. I think that stack will stay in place now."

"Now that I've squashed the plates together and spread dessert all over the foyer, you mean?" Lissa cautiously lifted her hand. Caramel and custard oozed between her fingers. "Maybe I should just lick it off."

"I wouldn't advise it—those things never taste as good as they look."

Lissa reached for a crumpled napkin and tried without much success to wipe the sticky sauce off her fingers.

Their supervisor appeared from the banquet room. "What's the holdup, girls? And why aren't you in the cloakroom, Ms Morgan?"

"There are only two coats left, and no one seems likely to claim them at this hour," Lissa said. "So I was giving Connie a hand with the cart." She didn't climb over the counter this time; she very properly went through the door and back into the cloakroom.

"Connie needs to learn to manage on her own." The supervisor eyed the glass tip jar. "You seem to have done rather well this evening. The contributions of young men, by any chance? Perhaps I should make it clear, Ms Morgan, that the cloakroom is not a dating service. If I hear again about you giving out your phone number…."

"Yes, ma'am." Lissa didn't bother to explain. She suspected her boss would not see the humor in Winnipeg's time and temperature. And right now she didn't even want to think about how the supervisor might have heard about the whole thing.

"All the guests have gone. Lock up the rest of the coats, and then you may punch out," the supervisor said.

Lissa was relieved to be outside, away from the overheated

and stale atmosphere of the banquet room. Now that traffic had died down the snow was getting very deep—though she could see a pair of plows running up the nearest main street, trying to keep the center lanes clear. She slung her backpack over her shoulder, took a deep breath of crisp air, let a snowflake melt on her tongue, and started for home.

Though it was only a few blocks, it took her almost half an hour to struggle through the snow, and by the time she reached the house she was cold and wet. There were still lights on upstairs, but the main level was mercifully dark and relatively quiet. With a sigh of relief she unlocked the sliding door which separated her tiny studio apartment—which in better days had been the back parlor of a once-stately home—from the main hallway.

The fireplace no longer worked, of course, but the mantel served nicely as a display shelf for a few precious objects, and in the center she'd put her Christmas tree. It was just twelve inches tall, the top section of an artificial tree which had been discarded years ago, stuck in a makeshift stand. There were no lights, and only a half-dozen ornaments, each of them really too large for the diminutive tree. But it was a little bit of holiday cheer, a reminder of better days, a symbol of future hopes….

She frowned and looked more closely. There had been a half-dozen ornaments that afternoon, when she'd gone off to work. Now there were five. On the rug below the mantel were a few thin shards of iridescent glass where the sixth ornament, an angel, had shattered.

Someone must have slammed a door, she told herself, and the vibration had made the angel fall. But she knew better. The fact that there were only a few tell-tale slivers meant the ornament had not simply been broken, but the mess had been hastily swept up.

But no one was supposed to be in her room, ever.

Lissa's breath froze. She spun around to the stack of plastic crates which held almost everything she owned and rummaged through the bottom one, looking for her dictionary. In the back of it, under the embroidered cover, was an envelope where she kept her spare cash. She'd tucked it there, secure in the thought that no other occupant of the house would be caught dead looking up a word even if they did invade her privacy to snoop through her room, as she had suspected some of them might be tempted to do.

The envelope was still there, but it was empty. Someone had raided her room, searched her belongings, and walked away with her minuscule savings. All the money she had left in the world now was in her pocket—the tips she'd taken from the glass jar before she left the student union tonight.

She had to remind herself to breathe. Her chest felt as if she was caught between a pair of elevator doors which were squeezing the life out of her.

You've survived hard times before. You can do it again. There would be a check waiting for her when the union reopened after the holidays, pay for the hours she'd worked in the last two weeks.

But in the meantime, to find herself essentially without funds and with no immediate means of earning any....

Maybe, she thought wryly, she should have given Kurt Callahan a real phone number after all. At least then, if by some wild chance he had actually called her, she could have hit him up for a loan, for old times' sake....

By the next afternoon the snowstorm was over, though the wind had picked up. In the residential neighborhood where his grandmother's three-story Dutch Colonial house stood, some of the alleys and sidestreets hadn't yet been plowed. The driveway had been cleared—the handyman had been busy since Kurt had left that morning—but in places small drifts were beginning to form once more, shaped by the wind.

He parked his Jaguar under the porte cochere at the side of the house and went in.

From the kitchen, the scents of warm cinnamon and vanilla swirled around him, mixed with the crisp cold of the outside air. Christmas cookies, he'd bet. He pushed open the swinging shutters which separated the kitchen from the hallway and peered in.

His grandmother's all-purpose household helper was standing on a chair, digging in a top cabinet which looked as if it hadn't been opened in years. As he watched, a stack of odd pans cascaded from the cabinet, raining past Janet's upraised arms and clattering against the hard tile floor.

He offered a hand to help Janet down, and started gathering up pans almost before they'd stopped banging. "Why are you climbing on a chair, anyway? I thought I bought you a ladder for this kind of thing."

"It's in the basement. Too hard to drag it up here. That's the pan I need, the springform one." She took it out of his hand. "Everything else can go back."

If only all of his store managers were as good as Janet at delegating responsibility, Kurt thought, the entire chain would run more smoothly. He gathered up the remaining dozen-odd pans and climbed up on the chair to put them back. "Is Gran home from her lunch date?"

"Not yet. She and Miss Marian always have a lot to talk about."

Including, Kurt remembered ruefully, planning a tea date for him and Marian's "little friend." As if he couldn't see through that for the matchmaking stunt it was. No wonder Gran had been helping to hold off the procession of women at the banquet last night…

"There's fresh coffee," Janet said.

Kurt got himself a cup and carried it and a couple of cookies into the big living room. The sun had come out, and it reflected off the brilliant whiteness outside and poured into the house.

The arched panel of leaded glass at the top of the big front window shattered the light into rainbows in which a few dust motes danced like ballerinas.

The enormous fir tree in front of the house swayed in the wind, and a clump of wet snow fell to the sidewalk just as a small reddish car turned the corner and pulled into the driveway. Kurt stared. That was certainly his grandmother's car, but why she would have taken it out in weather like this—

The side door opened and shut, and he met her in the doorway between hall and living room. "What the devil are you doing driving around in this snow?" he demanded.

"The streets are perfectly clear now, dear. We're used to snow in Minneapolis, and the road crews are very good at their job."

"It's freezing out there, Gran. The wind chill must be—"

"A man who climbs mountains for fun is worried about wind chill?"

"Not for myself," he growled. "For you. You could get stranded. You could have a fender-bender. Just last night you were telling me how much you appreciated having a good, reliable driver."

"Very true. It's quite a fine idea, in fact. Would you hang up my coat, dear? And ask Janet to brew a pot of tea." She dropped her mink carelessly on the floor and walked into the living room.

Kurt bit his tongue and started for the kitchen. Just as he pushed open the swinging shutters to call to Janet the side door opened again, and he had to jerk back to prevent his toes from being caught under the edge. Cold wind swirled in, and a feminine voice called, "Mrs. Wilder?"

"I'm just across the hall," his grandmother answered from the living room. "Come on in."

A face appeared around the edge of the door. A heart-shaped face with very short auburn hair ruffled around the ears and cheeks reddened by the wind. The young woman from the cloakroom.

Kurt stared at her in disbelief. "Where did you come from?"

She didn't answer directly. "I didn't expect you to be here. I mean—right here. I didn't bang the door into your nose, did I?"

Finally things clicked. What was wrong with him that it had taken so long to make the connection? "I should have known Marian's 'little friend' would turn out to be you," he grumbled. No wonder she'd looked at him that way last night. She'd been speculating, all right—wondering what his reaction would be when he finally figured out who she was. "Is that why you pulled all that nonsense with the phone number last night? So I'd be surprised when you turned up here?"

She flushed suddenly, violently red. "Look, I'm sorry about the phone number. It was a stupid trick, and if someone took it as a prank call—"

"I didn't have to dial it to figure out the joke."

"You didn't? Then I honestly don't know what you're talking about. All I did was drive your grandmother home from the student union."

He rubbed the stubble on his chin. "Why?"

His grandmother crossed the hall to the stairs. "Kurt, you said yourself just now that I shouldn't be driving in weather like this, so Lissa drove me home." Her voice faded as she reached the top of the staircase.

Kurt stared at the young woman again. "You're *not* the friend of Marian's that Gran invited to tea?"

She shook her head. "Sorry to disappoint you. Are you talking about Marian Meadows? I know who she is, but that's all."

"Then what are you doing here?"

"I'm trying to tell you, if you'll just listen. Actually, I'm glad to find that you haven't gone back to Seattle yet."

"You've done your homework, I see. Not that it's hard to find out where I live."

Her gaze flickered, and he felt a flash of satisfaction at disconcerting her. But she didn't explain, or defend herself. "Maybe you can convince your grandmother to see a doctor," she went on. "I didn't get anywhere when I tried."

His attention snapped back to her like a slingshot. "Doctor?"

"She had a dizzy spell. She'd had lunch at the restaurant in the student union. Mrs. Meadows left, and Hannah—"

"You're on a first-name basis?"

"Your grandmother stayed to finish her coffee. When she stood up, she almost passed out. I tried to get her to go to the emergency room, but she insisted she was fine to come home."

"So you grabbed the opportunity to drive her out here."

"She was going to drive herself," the young woman protested. "Why not just put her in a cab?"

"She didn't want to leave her car there to be towed by the snowplow crews. Will you quit yelling at me and think about it? I'm betting that's just like her."

She was right, Kurt admitted. His grandmother was perfectly capable of refusing to see a doctor, and of insisting on not leaving her car unattended, of driving when she shouldn't. And she was behaving oddly—she didn't normally fling her coat onto the floor.

"Thank you for bringing her home," he said quietly. "I'll take it from here."

But the woman didn't budge. She looked almost uncomfortable.

Kurt wondered why she didn't just go. Was she waiting for some sort of payment? Or did she have something else on her mind?

He frowned as he remembered the flash of familiarity he'd felt last night. He'd dismissed that as the look of a woman on the prowl. But had it been more than that? He tipped his head to one side and looked closely. Tall, slim and straight, red hair and big brown eyes, and a smile full of magic… What had his grandmother called her?

A few random words swirled in his brain and settled into a pattern. *Magic smile. Lissa. You've done your homework....*

"Calculus class," he said softly. "You're Lissa Morgan."

It was no wonder, really, that he hadn't recognized her last night. There was nothing about this slender, vivid woman with the huge brown eyes which even resembled the lanky, awkward girl who was stored in his memory—the one with frizzy carrot-colored hair straggling to the middle of her back. The freshman frump, some of his fellow students had called her—dressed in oversized shapeless sweaters and with her face always buried in a math book.

And yet there was one thing which hadn't changed. He'd seen it last night when she'd smiled, and that was why she'd looked familiar, despite all the surface changes. Because the only other time that she'd ever smiled at him....

That was long ago, he told himself. *Another lifetime, in fact.*

Still, no wonder he'd been itchy around her last night. No wonder he'd picked at her, egged her on, found fault with everything she did. His subconscious mind must have recognized her, despite all the changes in her looks.

"So you're still hanging around the university?" he said. "I figured by now you'd be head actuary for some big pension fund or insurance company or national bank. Or an engineer somewhere in the space program. Or—no, I have it. You must be working undercover at the student union, checking for fraud. Because I'm sure a woman with the brainpower you've got would never be satisfied with just running a cloakroom."

Her jaw tightened, and he thought for a second she was going to take a swing at him.

"She's not running a cloakroom," his grandmother said from the stairway landing. "Not anymore. Kurt, Lissa is my new driver. Only I'm going to call her my personal assistant, because it sounds so much nicer. Don't you agree?"

CHAPTER TWO

IF HANNAH WILDER had pulled the stair railing loose and hit her grandson over the head with it, Kurt couldn't have looked more dazed. Under other circumstances, Lissa thought, she might have enjoyed watching him turn green. She wondered whether it was Hannah's announcement or his past coming back to haunt him which had caused Kurt's reaction.

Then she almost snorted at the idea. As if Lissa Morgan popping back into his life after all this time could have any such stunning effect on him. Frankly, she was surprised that even her name had jolted his memory loose. Any guy who would make a bet with his buddies on whether he could get the most unpopular girl in the class to believe that he was interested in her—and prove it in the most intimate of ways—just so they could all laugh at her for the rest of the semester because she'd been taken in by his charm, wouldn't bother to remember the details six years later.

Unless she'd been an even funnier joke to him than she'd realized. Unless she'd been an even easier conquest than he'd hoped for.

Which, of course, she had been. Stupid—that was the only word for her back then.

He'd been a senior in college, taking advanced math for the

second time to fill out his requirements, struggling to get his grade point far enough above the danger level so he could graduate in a couple of months. So when he'd asked her—only a freshman, but the most advanced student in the class nevertheless—to tutor him, there had been no reason for Lissa to think he might not be telling the truth about his motives….

Stop it, she thought. That was all over. Her days as the frump were long past. If anything, she should thank Kurt Callahan, because in a convoluted way he'd inspired her to lose the frizzy hair and the bulky sweaters and make herself into an entirely new woman….

Yeah, right, she thought dryly. *Keep talking, Lissa, and maybe you'll convince yourself that a one-night stand with him was a good thing.*

Still, she wasn't about to let herself overreact now; she was bigger than that, and running into him again wasn't going to change anything.

So what if he was even better-looking now than he'd been in college, with his crisp black hair and unusual blue-gray eyes, his youthful arrogance mellowed by time and success into something more like self-confidence? It didn't matter to her anymore.

But why couldn't that encounter last night have been the end of it? She'd been proud of the way she'd handled herself in the cloakroom standoff. She hadn't lost her temper or embarrassed herself. She hadn't even needed to publicly rub his nose in the facts in order to feel good about telling him to get lost. But now that she was face to face with him once more…. Now that he had remembered her….

Hannah's offer had seemed so simple on the drive from the student union to her house. And it was so perfectly logical. *You need a job,* Hannah had said. *And I need some help for a while. We can be a team.* What difference did it make whether the woman offering to hire her was Kurt Callahan's grandmother? He wouldn't know anything about it.

Only here he was—in the flesh. And what nice flesh it was, too, Lissa thought. Today he wasn't wearing a suit, but khakis and a polo shirt, and the clothing showed him off nicely. He was tanned and athletic without being showy—no overdone bulges of biceps. In fact, he was perfectly proportioned, without a flaw anywhere to draw the eye. He might be a little more muscular than he'd been six years ago, a little more imposing. But even then he'd been pretty much perfect—strong and hard and clean and intoxicatingly attractive.

In short, she admitted, he'd been simply intoxicating. He'd acted on her senses like a rich old brandy, sweeping away every inhibition, every fragment of common sense…. He'd used his charm, he'd used *her,* just so he could win a bet.

What a shame it was that Kurt Callahan's flaws were on the inside. He hadn't had a conscience six years ago, and she doubted very much that he'd grown one since.

Well, she'd just have to work around him, that was all. Surely he wouldn't be staying in Minneapolis for long—a man with his responsibilities? And Hannah's plan was not only simple, logical and sensible, it was the best deal Lissa was likely to find.

How it had come about, however, was nothing short of fantastic, when Lissa stopped to think about it. She'd simply been doing her job, taking care of two elderly lunch patrons. She'd seen them many times before in the union's dining room—they were simply Mrs. Wilder and Mrs. Meadows, and she treated them as she did every other patron.

Then Mrs. Meadows had left, and Hannah Wilder had sat still a little longer, drinking her coffee and chatting as Lissa cleared the table and brought her receipt. And then she'd got up from her chair, reeled, and almost fallen….

Lissa still didn't quite understand why she'd actually told

Hannah about the money which was missing from her room. More than twelve hours after the discovery she'd still been a bit dazed over the realization that she'd been robbed, of course. But why she'd actually confided in Hannah—who had enough problems of her own just then—was beyond her.

However, Hannah had asked her to sit down for a few minutes and keep her company while she recovered from her spell of lightheadedness. And then she'd looked straight into Lissa's eyes and said, "What's troubling you, my dear?"

It was the first time in months that anyone had treated Lissa with such obvious personal concern. One thing had led to another, the words had come tumbling out…and here she was.

"Driver?" Kurt said.

Lissa pulled herself back to the moment.

"Personal assistant," Hannah corrected. She came down the last few stairs, holding tightly to the railing. "If you insist on discussing it, Kurt, let's go back into the living room and have a seat."

Kurt was instantly beside her, offering an arm. "I'm sorry, Gran—I forgot you weren't feeling well."

"It was only a momentary weak spell, and it has passed. I got up too suddenly, that's all. I'm certainly not an invalid."

Lissa couldn't stop herself. "But if your blood pressure is likely to behave like a jumping jack, you shouldn't be driving."

Kurt shot a look at Lissa. "I can't disagree with that—though it sounds self-serving when it's *you* who's saying it. I suppose you're the one who suggested the whole plan?"

"The only thing she suggested was that I see a doctor," Hannah said placidly. "I don't think the idea of a driver would have occurred to Lissa at all. Since she doesn't have a car herself, she doesn't think in those terms."

Kurt was starting to look like a thundercloud. "You don't have a car? Do you even have a driver's license?"

"All students do," Hannah put in. "I understand there's some rule about not being able to go into a bar without one."

You're not helping matters, Hannah. Lissa put her chin up and looked squarely at Kurt. "I have a perfectly valid driver's license, and not just to use as proof of my age so I can go out drinking."

"When's the last time you were behind the wheel of a car?"

She'd been hoping he wouldn't ask that. "I suppose you mean before today? A while."

His eyes narrowed.

"All right, it's been—maybe three years. I don't remember."

"Great. Add up the two of you, and we still have a mediocre, inexperienced driver."

Much as she wanted to, Lissa couldn't exactly argue with that. Between the unfamiliar car and the slick streets she'd been nervous, on edge, and too cautious for their own good, creeping along at a snail's pace in fear of losing control. But at least she knew her limitations.

"They say you never forget how," Hannah added helpfully. "Or were they talking about bicycles?"

Kurt rubbed the back of his neck. "Gran, it's a wonderful idea for you not to drive anymore. But since Janet doesn't drive either, it would be much better to sell the car and use the money for taxis. The car's probably only worth a few hundred dollars, but that's a lot of taxi rides."

With all his money, Lissa thought, he could buy Hannah her own private limo service. Instead he was suggesting she sell her car and tuck the money away in a taxi fund? "I didn't realize you had such a cheap streak, Kurt."

He shot a look at her. "I'm not the one with the cheap streak."

"I hate to wait for a ride," Hannah said. "In fact, I hate taxis all the way around—they smell. And a cabby won't walk you into a doctor's office."

"That's why you have Janet."

"Janet's no steadier on her feet than I am these days." Hannah laughed lightly. "You should have seen us trying to buff the hardwood floor in your room before you came, Kurt—we must have looked like the Three Stooges on ice. Well, two of them, at least."

"Why were you buffing…?" Kurt closed his eyes as if he were in pain. "Never mind. How often do you even leave the house?"

Hannah began ticking points off on her fingertips. "The hairdresser, the massage clinic, physical therapy, the doctor, the pharmacy, the grocery store, the bank, my broker, the—"

"All right, I take your point. What about a limo service? They don't smell."

"I'd still have to wait around for someone to come and pick me up. And it would be expensive, because I go out at least once a day. I deliberately split up my errands and appointments so that every day I get some fresh air and exercise."

"I can afford it, Gran."

"Waste is waste, no matter who's paying for it."

Kurt shot a look at Lissa. "See? I told you I'm not the one with the cheap streak."

"I'm not cheap," Hannah said. "I just like to get value for money. So if you're worried about Lissa getting off too easily, don't. She'll have plenty to keep her occupied, helping me out."

"Gran, you can't have it both ways. If you're saying now that you're ill enough to need someone right beside you all the time, then surely a personal nurse would be a better choice?"

"Oh, no." Hannah took a deep breath and let her gaze wander around the room, as if she'd rather look anywhere than at him. "I don't need a nurse. Just an extra pair of hands and a strong set of legs. I wasn't going to break the news to you just yet, Kurt, but I suppose it's time to tell you."

Here it comes, Lissa thought. She hadn't quite believed it

herself when Hannah had told her. Not that it was any of her business, but she felt like ducking behind the couch to avoid the worst of the explosion when Kurt heard the news.

"Tell me what?" Kurt sounded wary. Almost fearful.

"I've decided to give up the house," Hannah said simply. "I'm just not up to taking care of it anymore, and neither is Janet."

"Then hire a housekeeping service."

Despite her best efforts, Lissa couldn't keep her mouth shut. "Perhaps you could stop snapping out orders and just listen for a change?"

Hannah was smiling. "Thank you, Lissa dear. It's really no wonder that the women he dates have such a short shelf-life, is it? I can't blame them for getting tired of it."

"I'm only trying to help!" Kurt's voice was almost a bark.

"In such a typically masculine way, too," Hannah murmured. "Your grandfather used to do the same thing—as soon as I complained about something he would tell me precisely how I should solve the problem. It was really quite annoying, and I never managed to break him of it… At any rate, I have a house-keeping service already. It's not the work I'm concerned about, Kurt, it's the responsibility."

Kurt frowned.

"I'm tired of writing out a list for the housecleaning team and making sure they follow it. I want someone else to think about the weeds in the flowerbeds and the leaves in the gutters, and whether the draperies in the guestroom need to be replaced or just taken down and sent along to the cleaners."

Kurt rubbed his finger along the bridge of his nose. "I see. You're talking about moving into some kind of retirement community, I suppose, where they do all that stuff for you? I'll see what's available, and—"

"You mean you'll assign someone on your staff to see what's available? Anyway, I've already looked. I know where I want to go. It's a very nice apartment complex which provides all the assistance anyone could want—and doesn't bother people when they don't want help."

Kurt shrugged. "All right, Gran. Whatever you want to do."

The gesture looked as if it hurt him, Lissa thought. Clearly this was a man who didn't enjoy being left out of the loop.

"When are you planning to do this?"

"Well, that's a bit more difficult. I can't just lock the door and walk off. This house holds many years of memories to be sorted out, and only I can do that. But Lissa's going to be my hands and feet while I get the job done—starting tomorrow. I'm going to go upstairs for a nap now, so you just entertain yourselves for a while, children."

As her footsteps retreated up the stairs, Kurt turned to Lissa. "If you think you're going to walk in here and get away with this—"

It was clearly time to take a stand. "Get away with what? I'd say Hannah's the boss, and you're not—so what she decides goes, Kurt."

"Maybe I can't contradict her orders. But I can darned sure try to make sure she's safe. Put your coat on."

"Why?"

"Well, we're not going to go build a snowman. Before I let you start chauffeuring Gran around, you're going to have to pass a driving test. Scare me, and you flunk. Got it?"

She would have told him to jump headfirst into a snowdrift, except that Lissa knew some practice behind the wheel would be a very good idea—and she figured if she could drive safely with a frustrated Kurt riding shotgun, then she wouldn't be putting Hannah into any danger at all. And if his backseat driving got to be unbearable, she mused, she would just slam the passenger side of the car into a tree somewhere and walk home....

"Watch out for that truck," Kurt said, and Lissa pulled her attention back to the street.

Hannah's car was small and light, and as the afternoon waned and traffic grew heavier the packed-down snow which remained on the streets grew ever more slippery. But, after a false start or two, Lissa's confidence began to come back, despite the silent and glowering male in the passenger seat next to her.

Maybe Hannah had been right after all, she thought, and driving a car—like riding a bicycle—was a skill which never quite vanished from the subconscious mind. If it didn't bother her to have Kurt either issuing instructions or seething not quite silently—like a pasta pot just about to boil—then she could handle normal traffic along with Hannah's chatter with no trouble at all.

"Well?" she said finally, after a solid hour of negotiating everything from narrow alleys to eight-lane freeways. "Since I haven't smashed either you or the car, and you haven't grabbed for the steering wheel or the brake in at least twenty minutes, I'm going to assume that the test is over and take you back to Hannah's house."

"Not quite. Parallel park in front of that diner up there."

"Parallel park? Nobody ever has to actually *do* that."

His level look said that she would do it or else, so Lissa sighed and took a stab at it. Two tries later she was quite proud of the result. "Good enough?"

"Shut the car off. Let's have a cup of coffee."

"I'm honored at the invitation, but—"

"Don't be. This is the only way we can talk without Gran interrupting."

"We've been riding around for an hour," Lissa protested, "and you haven't had a word to say the whole time. So why should I—?"

"I wasn't going to risk taking your attention off the road. Come on." He slammed the car door and kicked at the wad of snow and ice which had built up behind the front wheel. "Looks like this thing could stand some new tires. Would you like coffee, tea, or hot chocolate?"

She settled for tea and refused a piece of apple pie to go with it. Kurt surveyed her over the rim of his coffee cup and said, "All right, what's really going on here? How did all this happen?"

Lissa sighed. "I didn't stalk your grandmother, if that's what you're suggesting. It just happened to be my table she chose at lunchtime. There aren't all that many of us working at the union, you know—not as regulars in the dining room, at least. It's also the last day before the holidays, so a lot of the kids who work there have already gone home for Christmas."

She waited for him to ask why she wasn't going anywhere for Christmas. But he didn't.

"Look," Lissa said, "I'll tell you exactly what happened. Mrs. Meadows left because she had an appointment of some sort, and your grandmother stayed to finish her coffee. I cleared the dessert dishes, she wished me a Merry Christmas, then she got up from the table and started to sway. I helped her back in her chair and offered to find a doctor. She said no, but would I just sit down with her for a minute, so I did. Then when she felt better she asked if I'd walk her out to her car. When I found out she was planning to drive herself home, I suggested she take a cab, and—"

"And she offered you a job? Just like that?"

"She's not quite that fast a worker," Lissa admitted. "It took her maybe ten minutes in all."

"Why?"

"Ask her. How should I know why she offered me a job?"

"I will. But what I really want to know is why you took it."

"Because I need a job—"

"But *why* do you need a job? You were the math whiz of the

entire campus—why aren't you a chief financial officer at some big corporation by now?"

All the plans she had made and the dreams she had dreamed…. Lissa had thought she'd come to terms with all the losses and the delays, but it wasn't until now—when Kurt Callahan asked the question in that slightly cynical tone—that she realized how much it hurt that after so long she was still marking time.

"Did you get caught with your fingers in the till, or what?"

Lissa bristled. "No. I'm still here because I had to drop out for a while. I have one more semester to go before I finish my degree."

He went absolutely still. "Why, Lissa?"

"Why should it matter to you? It's long over with." Then she bit her lip and said quietly, "I'm still here because my father got lymphoma and I had to drop out and take care of him in the last year of his life. That cost me my scholarships, because walking out in the middle of a term doesn't sit well with the financial aid people around here. I worked for a while, and saved money to come back, but I was just getting up to speed again when I got pneumonia. That knocked me down for months. I couldn't keep up with classes, so I had to quit again."

He seemed to be waiting for something else. Finally, when the silence drew out painfully, he said, "That's nasty luck."

Was there a hidden meaning in his tone? She told herself it was pointless to try to analyze. "Yes, it was."

"But hardly anything new for you. You dropped out of that calculus class, too."

"Noticed that, did you?" Lissa said dryly. "I'm amazed you were paying attention."

"Dammit, Lissa, I tried to talk to you, but you wouldn't listen. You wouldn't even stop walking down the hall, much less let me apologize. And then before I knew it you were gone—"

"So what would you have said you were sorry for? Not making love, I'll bet."

"No," he admitted. "Not that."

"Then what? Getting caught? Making sure everybody in the class knew you'd won your bet?" She saw curiosity flicker in his eyes, and she took a deep breath and reminded herself that it didn't matter anymore. The last thing she wanted to do was let him think she still cared. She'd buried those feelings long ago. "One-night stands happen, Kurt. I was quite a little more innocent than you were, that's true, and it annoyed the hell out of me that you'd told everyone in class I slept with you—"

"I didn't tell them."

"Oh, really? Then how did they know? I don't recall them being in your room observing."

A smile tugged at the corner of his mouth. "Lissa, a brass band could have marched through my room that night and you wouldn't have noticed."

Heat swept up her throat, over her face. "The point is, it's over. There's nothing to be gained by dissecting what happened." *Though at the time I'd have liked to dissect you.* "I believe, before we got sidetracked a few minutes ago, that you were asking why I need a second job. Right now my budget's unusually tight, so—"

"Couldn't you make more at some other kind of job, instead of working at the union?"

"Possibly. But waiting tables isn't a bad income, really. Most of our clients are alumni, and the tips are usually generous. Besides, the hours are flexible, and I don't have to waste any time commuting. I can work an hour here and there and fit partial shifts in between classes. If I had to go all the way across town to a job I wouldn't make any more, even if I got a higher rate of pay for each hour I worked."

"Because it would take so long to get there, especially since you don't have a car. I see. Still, I wouldn't think you'd have gotten in over your head financially, wizard with figures that you are."

"It's hard to pay tuition and medical bills at the same time. Pneumonia's not cheap, and I didn't have any health insurance after my dad died."

"Perhaps some financial planning advice—"

"There you go, problem-solving again. I'm sure your banker would be tickled pink to handle my portfolio, because I've usually got about fifty bucks to my name." She was irritated enough not to stop and think before she went on. "I'd saved up enough to get through a couple of weeks with no income—but then I was robbed last night."

His eyebrows went up. "Are you all right?"

"Oh, yes—thanks for asking. I wasn't held up at gunpoint or anything. I'd left my extra funds in my room—only I obviously didn't pick a good enough hiding spot." She knew she sounded bitter, and probably stupid, too. She waited for him to say it.

He didn't. "Did you call the police?"

"No. It wouldn't do much good. It was cash, and there's no way to prove that any specific twenty-dollar bill was mine once. Besides, if I'm right about my suspicions, and the thief *is* someone else who lives in the house—"

"You think your roommate robbed you?"

Why had she told him anything at all? Of course it had seemed safe, because he'd never been known for tenacity back in their college days. Quite the opposite, in fact—at least when it came to studying. But now he seemed to be like a bulldog with a bone, and it was too late to back out without explanation. "We're not what you'd call roommates," Lissa said reluctantly. "Or even housemates, for that matter. It's more like a boarding house. Seven individual bedrooms, shared kitchen and bath. Reporting it would only make things more difficult in the future. Nothing would be safe."

He nodded. "You always were pragmatic."

"You don't have to make it sound like a disease. In some situations there aren't any good choices, Kurt. You just deal with it and go on, that's all."

He didn't answer, but he pushed his apple pie away as if he'd lost his appetite.

Puzzled at the response, Lissa went on. "Anyway, to get back to the point—your grandmother got that much out of me and then she went all quiet. The next thing I knew—"

"She'd manufactured a job for you."

"You mean she made it up from nothing? I don't think so. If she's going to move out of that house, she really does need help. There must be closets everywhere. Unless you're planning to stick around to pack boxes…?"

Kurt gave a little shiver.

Lissa went on coolly, "Yeah, what a surprise. You're too busy, right?"

"I'll hire a crew."

"She doesn't want a crew, she wants me."

"Maybe she thinks she does—right now."

"And what does that mean? If you're threatening to discredit me by telling her what happened between us all those years ago I suggest you think again, because you won't exactly come off as Mr. Pure of Heart yourself. Anyway, someone will have to do the work, so why shouldn't it be me?"

"How long do you think it will take?"

"I have two weeks free until school starts up again."

"Surely you don't think that job can be done in two weeks? And if you start dragging things out of dark closets and then abandon her—"

"Hello? What was that you were telling your grandmother earlier about not being able to have things both ways? Neither can you, fella. At any rate, I figure within two weeks Hannah will either have decided that she's too fond of her house to leave it, or she'll have gotten tired of sorting and decided to call an auctioneer and get it over with in a hurry."

He stared at her as if he were seeing her for the first time. "So in the meantime you're just going to let her pay you for humoring her?"

"I intend to do whatever she asks me to. You know, it might not be a bad plan for you to follow, too. Humoring her, I mean, instead of arguing with her all the time." *And maybe you could see your way clear to cutting me a little slack, too.* She'd probably better not hold her breath, though.

She looked at her watch. "I don't mean to rush you, Kurt, but I have things to do. And, since your hair hasn't turned white yet, I'm going to assume I passed the driving test."

"We're not all the way home yet. And I'm in no hurry to get back in that car. I felt like I was riding around in a tomato soup can."

"Well, it's not my fault that your grandmother drives a compact. If you're used to the Jaguar I saw parked outside the house—"

"Don't even daydream about driving my car. Buy her some new tires first thing, all right? Give me the bill for them." He stood up and pulled out his wallet.

Lissa sat very still, her tea mug clutched between her hands. "Then you're withdrawing your objections?"

"No. But since she seems set on the idea, I'm putting my objections on hold."

At least he wasn't still threatening her. Quite sensible of him, she thought. "Fair enough." Once back in the car, she turned on the radio and hummed along with Christmas carols as she drove. She thought Kurt was looking even more like an approaching rainstorm. "What's the matter?" she asked finally. "You don't like 'Jingle Bells'?"

"Not when it's played on accordion and banjo, thanks. Where did you find that station?"

"I didn't choose it, it was already tuned in. Why doesn't your grandmother have a Christmas tree?"

"Tradition. It goes up one week before Christmas."

Lissa calculated. "That's tomorrow."

"Enjoy the job," Kurt said. "I'd help, but I'll be at the grand opening of my new Twin Cities store."

"Oh, that's what's keeping you here." Lissa parked the car right behind the Jaguar, under the porte cochere.

"The grand opening runs through the weekend." Kurt walked around to her side and opened her door. "Aren't you coming in?"

"No, I'm just dropping you off."

"Wait a minute. You're taking Gran's car? Do the words grand theft auto mean anything to you?"

She looked out over the dull red finish on the car's hood. "Not *grand* theft, surely? Now, if I was taking *your* car, then I could understand you saying—" He started to growl, and Lissa thought better of pursuing the argument. "She told me I could."

"You're planning to commute using Gran's car? And what other employee benefits have you talked her into providing?"

"Not to commute, exactly." Her gloved hands tightened on the wheel, and she looked up at him through her lashes, waiting to enjoy the explosion she expected. "I'm just taking it today so I can load up my stuff." She paused for just a second to let the news sink in, then added gently, "And of course I need to talk to my landlady as well—to give notice that I'm moving in with Hannah."

And before he could open his mouth Lissa put the car in reverse and backed out into the street.

The sense of freedom was incredible. Traffic on the outbound streets was a disaster, but nobody was trying to get downtown this late in the day, and the little car buzzed along easily. For the first time in years Lissa wasn't simply enduring Christmas carols, she was enjoying them. With the dim prospect of two weeks of living on macaroni and noodles now erased from her calendar, life was definitely looking up.

Of course there was the little matter of Kurt Callahan lurking in the background. But once his grand opening was past he'd be going home, and that interference would be gone as well. With him out of the way her peace of mind would be restored, and she and Hannah could get down to some serious digging and sorting…for a while, at least.

The nerve of the man, threatening to tell Hannah what had happened between them all those years ago. Of course he wouldn't actually do it, because *he'd* be the one who ended up looking bad. Still….

Lissa had thought she was long over the sting of the single evening she'd spent with him. Even in the cloakroom last night she hadn't entirely lost her perspective. But that had been before she'd had to deal with him on such a personal level, and now all the feelings had come flashing back: the frustration and the anger, the hurt, the desolation and—yes, the attraction too. Because he *had* been attractive, even to a frump of a freshman who'd known perfectly well that he was far beyond her sphere. A *dumb* frump of a freshman, Lissa reminded herself, who had bought the tale of his needing tutoring—which had certainly been true, as far as it went—and who had gotten in way over her head. And only when it had been too late had she found out that the whole thing had been the result of a bet, with the entire class in on it. That the single night which had been so magical to her had meant less than nothing to him.

You dropped out of that calculus class, too, he'd said.

Well, he was almost right. She'd stuck it out for a while, hoping it would all blow over and everybody would forget that stupid bet. But though the professor had kept order in the class-room, the teasing before and after class hadn't ceased. After a while she'd made herself so sick over it that she'd skipped the rest of the lectures and turned in her work at the professor's office. Only the fact that she was such a promising student had kept her from finishing up with a failing grade.

Just one more thing that Kurt Callahan was responsible for....

The steps up to the front of the boarding house were still buried in eight inches of snow, though a couple of trails had been broken by people going in and out. Lissa picked her way carefully up to the porch and let herself into the hallway. The landlady was standing outside the room which had originally been the front parlor, arguing with the tenant who was supposed to pay part of his rent by shoveling the walks.

Lissa unlocked her own door, then cleared her throat.

The landlady turned her head. "What do you want?"

Lissa debated. It wasn't smart to announce that her room would be unoccupied for a while—but she couldn't simply disappear for two weeks without letting the landlady know, either. "I just wanted to let you know that I'm going away for a while."

The woman looked at her suspiciously. "How long a while? You going to pay for January in advance?"

Lissa couldn't pay in advance if she wanted to. Not on the proceeds of last night's tips. "I'll pay for January when January comes," she said firmly. "Just as I do every month."

The front door opened again, and she saw the landlady's eyes widen as she spotted the newcomer. Lissa looked around to see who had come in, and her heart sank.

CHAPTER THREE

KURT STAMPED HIS feet on the doormat and cast a long look around the dim hallway of the boarding house. The wallpaper was peeling, the glass in the door rattled as he closed it, the floorboards creaked under his feet, and the air smelled of burned popcorn.

Lissa looked over her shoulder. "Fancy meeting you here. I suppose Hannah gave you the address?"

"She sent me over to help so you'd be finished moving in time for dinner."

The landlady stopped yelling and bustled over. "Did you say you're moving?"

"I'm not giving up the room," Lissa said. "I'm just picking up the stuff I'll need for a couple of weeks."

The landlady folded her arms across her ample chest. "If you want me to hold the room, you'll have to pay ahead of time for January. Otherwise, how do I know you'll come back?"

Kurt stepped between them."You trust her—the same way she trusts you not to put the rest of her stuff out on the curb the minute her back is turned."

The landlady gave him the same stare she would a bedbug and went on, "And don't expect me to return your deposit if you do give up the room, because there's a hole in the wall." She returned to the front parlor and went back to haranguing the other tenant.

"Home sweet home," Lissa said. "The hole in the wall was there when I moved in."

Honestly curious, Kurt asked, "Why do you put up with this?"

"Because it isn't for much longer, and because living cheaply now means I won't have so much debt to pay after I get my degree."

"But you can't want to come back here, after you were robbed."

"Well, that's rather beside the point, isn't it?" Lissa pushed a door open. The sliding panel squeaked and stuck, and she gave it an extra shove.

In some situations there aren't any good choices, she had said. *You deal with it and go on.*

It was starting to look to him like she was an expert at dealing with things and going on. Nursing a sick father, getting pneumonia herself….

She'd had a streak of hard luck, there was no doubt about that, but he couldn't help but wonder if there was even more to the story than she'd told him.

Kurt followed her in. She flipped on every light in the place—such as they were. How she managed to get dressed in this gloom, much less read or study, was beyond him.

His gaze came to rest on the mantel, where a little Christmas tree stood bravely in the center, drooping under the weight of five too-big ornaments.

Damn. He didn't want to feel sorry for her…but he did.

"You pack," he said. "I'll carry."

The trouble was, Lissa had no idea what to pack. Clothes weren't a problem—her wardrobe was limited, so she figured she'd just pile everything into a crate and take it along. It was all the other things she wasn't sure about.

All the other things. What an all-encompassing, grandiose statement that was, Lissa told herself, considering how few material goods she actually possessed. Everything she owned would fit in the back of a minivan with room to spare.

Kurt came back from his third trip out to the car and raised an eyebrow at the half-empty crate Lissa was contemplating. "What's the holdup?"

"I'm trying to decide what else to take."

He looked around, as if he had no idea what she could be talking about.

She had to give him a little credit, though—Kurt hadn't said a single disparaging word about her surroundings, her belongings, or the fact that her luggage consisted of plastic crates and not the monogrammed leather bags his crowd probably carried.

"Besides clothes, what could you possibly need?"

"Books, maybe. I wonder if I'll have time to start studying for my spring classes."

"Those would be the classes that won't start until January? You already have the books?"

"Some of them. Picking up one or two at a time is easier on the wallet than buying them all at once."

He looked startled, as if he'd never thought of that before.

His expression made it perfectly obvious, Lissa thought, that budgeting for textbooks had never been a problem for Kurt Callahan. "It's sort of like putting money in the bank," she said. "Buying what you need ahead of time, I mean."

"So if you had invested all your cash in math books rather than just leaving it lying around, you wouldn't be in this spot."

"It wasn't lying around, it was hidden." *Just not well enough.* "And if I'd bought all my books with it I'd still have had a problem—namely, what I was going to eat for the next two weeks."

"Speaking of eating," Kurt suggested, "Janet promised

prime rib for dinner, and I like mine rare. So can we hurry this project along?"

Lissa's stomach growled at the mere suggestion of rare prime rib. Or, for that matter, medium or well-done prime rib; it didn't matter, because it all sounded the same to her. Delicious, in a word.

"Just grab everything you might need, and let's go."

"Everything?" she said doubtfully.

"Sure. That's really what's bothering you, isn't it? You're wondering if the vandals around here will pop in to inspect whatever you've left behind and destroy it if it isn't of any value to them."

She couldn't argue with that, since it was exactly what she'd been thinking. It was the reason she'd hesitated to tell the landlady that she'd be gone at all. If word got around that she wouldn't be back for a couple of weeks she might as well leave the door standing wide open.

Still, her pride was nicked at the idea of dragging out the detritus of her life in front of him.

In front of *anyone,* she corrected herself. It wasn't specifically Kurt she was sensitive about. She didn't like letting anyone see the pathetically few sentimental things that remained to her.

Kurt strolled over to the mantel and picked up a textbook from the political science class she'd just finished. "What are you taking next semester?"

He was actually trying to make things easier for her—making conversation to cover her discomfort. If she had half a brain, Lissa thought, she'd be grateful. Instead, she was unreasonably annoyed—as if he'd come right out and said that he realized she had reason to be embarrassed, so he would do the proper etiquette thing and pretend not to notice. As if etiquette and good behavior were a big consideration with him!

She gathered up a couple of bags of books and kept her voice level. "Accounting theory, auditing, organizing information systems, advanced database programming—"

"What do you do for a hobby? Write the computer code for the federal government to calculate income tax?"

"I could," Lissa said calmly. "In fact, I have. Not the government's software, but a sample package for a small corporation. That was last year, in my tax practicum." She pulled a ragged box from under the bed.

Kurt ran a hand over the back of his neck. "I'm curious— do the words *pizza and a movie* mean anything to you? You notice I'm not even talking about anything as elaborate as going to a basketball game or a dance."

She shrugged. "I don't have the time or money for entertainment."

"Everybody needs to relax. And you can't tell me those guys hanging around the cloakroom last night wouldn't buy you a pizza. That looks like a very old quilt."

"Congratulations, you win a prize." She shook her head and started to push it back. "Nobody would steal that."

"What is it, honestly. Your security blanket?" He took the box out of her hands. "If it's really old, somebody might just pick it up. Better take it."

"Hannah's got enough of her own old stuff to deal with."

"It's a big guestroom. She and Janet are probably getting it ready for you right now, putting in all the little touches to make it feel like home. You know, scented towels, fresh flowers, robe and slippers laid out, a chocolate mint on the pillow…."

Lissa looked around the drab little room. "That *will* make it feel just like home," she said dryly. "And in case you're trying to hurry me along by pointing out that I'm supposed to be relieving Hannah of household duties, not creating more work for her—"

"The idea had crossed my mind."

"Yes, and I already feel guilty about being here instead of helping out. But so should you—I caught what she said about waxing the floor for you." She got her single good dress from the closet and folded it carefully atop a crate. "Why aren't you already in the guestroom, anyway?"

"Because she keeps it for guests," Kurt explained, with an air of long-suffering patience. "She always has. I have my own room up on the top floor, reserved from the time when I was a kid and went to visit her for the summers."

"Every year? You mean, like all summer?"

"Yeah."

"And she put you in the attic?"

"Hey, I liked the attic. It was better than being at home." Then, as if he realized too late what he was saying, he seized the crate from her arms and walked out.

So maybe Kurt's life hadn't been so privileged after all. Well, that was certainly something to chew on some night when she couldn't sleep, Lissa thought.

She picked up another crate and followed him out to the Jaguar.

The steps were still piled with snow, but the front-room tenant was picking at the sidewalk with irregular thrusts of a ragged-edged snow shovel.

"Good exercise," Kurt commented as he walked past. "The repetitive arm motion builds the biceps—and that gets the girls' attention every time."

The tenant rolled his eyes. "So maybe *you* want to clear the sidewalk?"

"Oh, no," Kurt said pleasantly. "I already have my girl's attention, you see."

The tenant looked at Lissa as if he'd never seen her before. And perhaps, she thought, he hadn't—she'd certainly done her best to remain invisible around the boarding house. But suddenly a warm gleam of appreciation crept into his eyes.

She set the crate into the back of the Jaguar. "Gee, thanks," she said. "Now I suppose when I come home I'll have him on my doorstep asking for dates. You know, Kurt, if I wanted someone to advertise my good points I'd ask. But you wouldn't be the salesman I chose—so don't hold your breath."

He raised his eyebrows. "Advertising your good points? I was just trying to hurry him along to finish the sidewalk before one of us slips on the snow and falls down."

When they went back inside, the landlady was hovering suspiciously in the doorway of Lissa's room. "It sure looks like you're moving out," she accused. "The only things you've left are junk."

Lissa swallowed the retort she'd have liked to make—something about the landlady knowing junk when she saw it, since that was all the woman owned—and reached for another crate. This one was full of office supplies, and when she laid a board across the top, it served as her desk. She decided to leave the board behind. The landlady had finally moved on, and she decided to distract herself. "What is it with guys anyway?"

"Let's not start with the philosophical questions, Lissa."

"I'm serious. Why do men always seem more attracted to a woman after someone else has shown an interest in her? Even—" She bit her tongue. *Even in calculus class,* she'd started to say. The other young men had certainly looked at her with more interest after Kurt's tutoring session—at least in the few classes she'd managed to sit through before she'd cut and run.

"We want to make sure that other hunters agree that the quarry's worth going after, I suppose."

"Charming," Lissa muttered. "It's like being singled out as the meatiest mammoth in the herd."

Two trips later, the sidewalk was in much better condition.

The shoveler paused to smile at her and lick his lips, and Lissa shuddered as she slid behind the wheel of Hannah's car.

Two weeks, she told herself. *I don't even have to think about it for two weeks.*

It was amazing how much stuff the woman thought she needed for a two-week stay, Kurt thought. Okay, he was responsible for her bringing the security blanket, but most of the rest had been her own idea. It had taken them far longer to load up all of Lissa's belongings than Kurt had expected it to, and when he carried in the first crate he was greeted with the scent of prime rib and fresh bread drifting through the house. At the top of the stairs, the guestroom sparkled, complete with robe and slippers laid out across the antique coverlet which covered the brass bed.

"There's no chocolate on the pillow," Lissa said. "And no fresh flowers."

He blinked in surprise. What an ungrateful little brat she was—to *complain!*

Then he saw the dazed look in her eyes as she looked around, and he took a minute to assess for himself the differences between Hannah's guestroom and the dark little hole they'd just left. Even at dusk on a winter afternoon the guestroom was bright and cheerful, airy and full of color and warmth, while he'd bet that at high noon on a sunny summer day the boarding house would look gloomy.

In fact, the only thing in the guestroom which wasn't particularly colorful was Lissa herself. She was still wearing the stark white tux shirt and black pants from her waitress shift earlier in the day, though she'd taken off the bow tie. And even her hair looked a little subdued—as if she were tired from head to foot.

I can work an hour here and there and fit partial shifts in between classes.

No wonder she was exhausted. But he thought it would be

wiser not to share the suggestion which trembled on the tip of his tongue—that she might look better after a nap. Instead, he said mildly, "Well, the garden's covered with snow, and you had the car, so she couldn't go to the flower shop. I guess you'll have to do without the flowers."

"I just meant…." She shook her head. "I was being silly. This room is stunning. Those must be the drapes she thinks need to be replaced."

He could hear the incredulity in her voice, and he had to stop and think what she was talking about. Oh, yes—Gran had said something about drapes in the midst of that litany of reasons why she wanted to sell the house. "I guess so. She did say guestroom, I think. But they look fine to me."

Lissa sighed. "Me, too. Better than fine, in fact."

"I'll go bring up another load." Kurt paused in the doorway. "You might want to change clothes before dinner. I caught a glimpse of silver in the dining room on my way up the stairs, so I think it's a dress-up occasion."

By the time he'd brought up the rest of her things Lissa had vanished into the bathroom. He stacked the last of the crates neatly along one wall of the guestroom, retreated to the attic bedroom to change his shirt, and went downstairs.

Janet and Gran had pulled out all the stops. The dining room table was laid with the heaviest and best of the silver flatware, and an old-fashioned epergne stood in the center, filled with oranges and apples and kiwi.

Hannah was sitting up very straight on a velvet chair in the living room, next to a flickering fire. She was wearing something lush and purple, with a row of sparkly clear stones around her neck.

She was staring out the front window, and for a moment Kurt thought she hadn't heard him come in. "Gran?"

"Oh, hello, dear. I assume you got all of Lissa's things moved?"

"Yes." The question left him feeling a bit uneasy. *All of Lissa's things....* "Everything she could possibly need for a couple of weeks, anyway. You're not expecting her to stay longer than that—right?"

"How could she stay here, Kurt, if I'll be moving out myself?"

His grandmother's eyes were unusually bright, and Kurt wondered if she'd been sitting there staring into space, thinking about her move. Maybe even winking back a few tears. Lissa just might be right after all. If Gran was already having second thoughts....

Maybe we didn't need to pack up so much after all. A few days and Lissa might be headed straight back home...in a manner of speaking. Well, when it came time to shift it all back, he'd gladly pay a mover.

"Can I get you a sherry?" he asked.

His grandmother smiled. "That would be lovely, dear."

He was standing at the sideboard in the dining room when he heard the creak of a stair. Third one from the bottom—he remembered it well from trying to sneak in after his curfew, before he'd learned how to climb the oak tree and swing over the rail of the attic balcony to let himself in.

He poured a second sherry. It probably wasn't the drink Lissa would choose—he suspected she'd rather have a beer—but if she was going to live under his grandmother's roof for a couple of weeks she'd better at least be introduced to the sherry ritual.

He turned toward the living room, saw her standing at the foot of the stairs with one hand still on the newel post, and stopped dead.

There was nothing outstanding about the dress Lissa wore—neither the cut nor the fabric shouted for attention, and he'd bet it had come from an anonymous designer and a discount rack. But the deep rich color fell somewhere between ordinary blue and ordinary green, and ended up not being ordinary at all. She didn't look like a faded photo anymore—she was once more vivid and brilliant and stunning.

And the cut—commonplace though it would probably look on another woman—was anything but common on Lissa. There was still no doubt in his mind that she was too slender. But when she was clad in something more feminine than the tux shirt and black pants she wasn't at all the stick he'd expected. The way the dress draped around her body drew his gaze upward to a slim, straight neck, and downward to slim, straight legs. And then he lingered over a whole lot of soft and gentle curves in between.

Soft and gentle curves she hadn't had six years ago. He'd have remembered those, just as clearly as he remembered the way she'd slowly come to life as he'd kissed her…the way she'd sparkled as he made love to her…the way she'd made him catch fire….

You wouldn't have heard a brass band that night either, Callahan.

He must have made some kind of a sound, for his grandmother looked over her shoulder at him. "My goodness, dear, I thought for a moment you were choking."

No, Gran, only acting like those guys at the cloakroom counter last night. He handed his grandmother a glass, holding another out to Lissa. "Would you like sherry, Lissa?"

"Yes, please." Her fingers brushed his as she took the crystal glass, half full of amber liquid, and Kurt felt something shift deep inside him, like the first warning tremor of an earthquake. She wasn't even smiling at him, but the lights in the room seemed to dim in comparison.

The woman was dangerous, he told himself. She always had been—even more so when she looked the most innocent. And, if he was smart, he wouldn't let himself forget it.

* * *

Maximum Sports' newest and biggest store had already been open for business for several weeks, in order to take advantage of the enormous potential offered by holiday gift-buying. But the formal grand opening celebration had been put off till this week—both for the sake of making a bigger splash and so Kurt could be present.

There were thirty-seven stores, and he hadn't missed a grand opening yet—though now that they were considering selling franchises it might not be quite so easy to keep up the pace. Still, even after thirty-seven times, Kurt enjoyed the thrill of cutting the ribbon to formally unveil a new location. This was the fun part of his job—talking to employees who were excited about the new store, listening to customers as they exclaimed over the variety and style of the merchandise, and watching as golf clubs and snowboards and bicycles surged through the checkout lines.

And, of course, he enjoyed personally demonstrating a few of the things that made Maximum Sports so different from other sports outfitters.

In his position halfway up the climbing wall, he braced himself for a brief rest and looked down at the crowd watching his progress. The wall was sixty feet tall, and though climbing it wasn't exactly a challenge on the same level as Mount Everest, it was no walk on the beach. He was at the point now where the wall began to curve back over his head, making the rest of the climb similar to dangling over thin air while scrambling up an overhanging knob of rock.

Nobody to blame but yourself, Callahan, he thought. The climbing walls in most of the stores had been built with beginners in mind, and even this one had a couple of easier sections. But he'd designed this bit himself, based on a particularly challenging outcrop on a mountain he'd climbed in Peru last year. It should be a piece of cake after defeating the original.

He looked out over the crowd. Mostly young women, he saw. *What a surprise.*

A flash of red hair caught his eye, but it wasn't Lissa. There was no tiny gray-haired lady beside her. Where were they, anyway? Cracked up somewhere on the freeway? He should have known better than to rely on her driving skills....

His toe slipped from the foothold and the crowd gasped. Half were frightened, Kurt thought, and half were anticipating the possibility that the head of Maximum Sports might end up splattered at the bottom of the climbing wall. Which was why they had the rule that no one could be on the wall without a safety harness and a trained belaying partner.

He got his breath back and moved on before the crowd could lose interest and wander off.

He didn't see Gran and Lissa come in, but twenty minutes later, when he reached the floor once more, his grandmother was chatting to the weight-lifter lookalike who was paying out Kurt's safety ropes. "We simply couldn't keep him on the ground as a youngster," she was saying. "He climbed out of his crib before he was ten months old, and he climbed up the bookshelves in the library when he was two. And then there was the time he tried to fly off the garage roof with a kite in each hand...."

"Learned my lesson on that one," Kurt said.

"What? How to build a bigger kite?" Lissa murmured.

He shed the harness—not his favorite piece of equipment, since it tended to be warmer than was comfortable. "You finally got here, I see. You missed the best part."

She was still looking up at the wall. Her hands were buried in the pockets of her coat—the same oversized, old-fashioned man's wool tweed overcoat she'd been wearing yesterday. On her slender frame it managed to look like a fashion statement rather than a castoff.

Kurt mopped his forehead with a towel. "How much of the demonstration did you watch?"

"Enough," Lissa said. He looked more closely; she seemed to be a little pale around the edges. "That's what you do for fun?"

"I'd rather do it on real mountains, without all the safety ropes. But, since Minneapolis is smack in the middle of the flat-lands, I take what I can get. I suppose your reaction means you don't want to give the wall a try?"

"You got that much right. I'll stick to writing tax software, thanks."

"Just as well—because all of today's slots are already reserved anyway. Where have you been, Gran? I thought you were coming over first thing this morning."

"We were busy with the Christmas tree."

Kurt frowned. "I expected you'd wait for me to help put it up."

"You sound like a disappointed six-year-old. Anyway, it's not up yet," his grandmother said. "We were just trying to find one."

"What's wrong with the tree you always use?"

"I decided to have a real one. I've always wanted a live tree, but Janet thinks they're a fire hazard. This year I decided to set my foot down and buy one anyway—but you have no idea how hard it is to find a nice-sized tree."

"That's too bad," he said. "Of course, it *is* getting pretty late in the season."

"So when will you be home? We need a man to get it balanced properly."

"I thought you said you couldn't find one."

"It just took longer than I expected. I think we've looked at every tree for sale on this side of the city," his grandmother said proudly. "I was just about to suggest that we go out in the country and find a tree farm, but we finally found what I wanted. It'll take all of us to get it wrestled into place, I think."

He shot a glance at Lissa, who seemed to be studying a

display of ropes and crampons. She looked guilty—there was no other word for it. "How big is this tree, exactly?"

"I figure we'll need to use every ornament in the house if we decorate it properly," his grandmother said. "Which is lovely, because then when the tree comes down after the holidays I can sort all the decorations out and set aside a boxful for each member of the family—the special things that will have memories for them. There are at least a dozen ornaments somewhere that you made in grade school. You used to send me one for Christmas each year. Remember?"

"I've done my best to forget. How did you get this thing home? Tie it on top of the car? That must have been a sight."

Lissa shifted her feet. "Well, that's something we should probably talk about."

He groaned. "I suppose you want me to take charge? All right—tell me where it is."

She looked doubtful. "Are you offering to pick it up in the Jaguar?"

"Of course not. The store has delivery trucks."

Lissa looked around. "At the rate people are buying treadmills and weight benches, we might get a delivery by New Year's Day."

"I'm the boss. They'll do what I tell them."

"And you're so good at bossing, too," his grandmother said warmly. "At any rate, don't concern yourself about the tree—we've got that all figured out. Now, let's get out of the way and let him go back to being the boss, Lissa."

"I'll walk you out," he said. "I could use a little fresh air after that climb, anyway."

The crowd made navigating difficult. Hannah dawdled behind for a while, looking at sports socks on an end cap, and then, making up her mind, hurried ahead of them toward the checkout lanes with some merchandise in hand.

Kurt felt like the first skier on a run after a big snow—it was exhausting just to break a trail through the crowd.

They reached the entrance, and Kurt leaned against one of the granite pillars just inside the main doors. A woman—not much more than a teenager—who was just coming in from the parking lot spotted him, flicked a hand over her hair, batted her eyes, and shifted course to come straight toward him.

"They start young, don't they?" Lissa murmured. She leaned against the pillar next to him and eyed the young woman, and to Kurt's utter amazement the woman flushed pink and veered off toward camping goods.

"How did you do that?" he asked.

"Do what? All I did was look at her. I think she just got cold feet when you glared. About this Christmas tree, Kurt." She sighed. "I think Hannah saw my little tree yesterday when you carried it in. It was right on top of a crate, and I think that's what gave her the notion."

"Oh—of course." He remembered his own reaction to seeing that pathetic, straggly little artificial tree with its five too-big ornaments. Gran, sentimental old darling that she was, would have felt even more strongly that anyone who could cherish such a bedraggled little tree deserved a real one.

"So if you want to blame me," Lissa said, "I guess you can go right ahead."

"Oh, what the hell?" he said. "It's her last Christmas in the house—she should have whatever she wants."

His grandmother came up to them, triumphantly waving a shopping bag emblazoned with the penguin which was Maximum Sports' mascot and logo, and he pushed the door open for her.

Lissa shot a look up at him. "I'm really glad you feel that way," she murmured.

Kurt's veins prickled—and not just because of the cold wind. There was something about her tone…

He scanned the parking lot, looking for the small, faded red car, and blinked in astonishment as his grandmother stopped beside a very different vehicle. A dark green and obviously spanking new sport utility vehicle. And on top of it, neatly bound with rope and tied down tight with bungee cords—

It wasn't the tallest pine tree he'd ever seen, but it was certainly the longest he'd ever encountered in a horizontal position. At least he thought it was—but his eyes seemed to be freezing solid in the brisk wind so he wasn't quite certain what he was looking at. "Gran, what's this?"

She smiled merrily. "Isn't it nice? They call it a sieve, or something like that, I can't think why. Have you got the keys, Lissa? I'll put this stuff in the back."

"An SUV," he said faintly. "You bought an SUV just so you could get your tree home, Gran?"

"Of course not," she said indignantly.

Kurt gave a small sigh of relief. That sounded more like his grandmother. Renting the vehicle for the day, or borrowing it from a good-hearted neighbor, would make a great deal more sense than actually buying it.

"We'll be hauling all kinds of stuff as we clear the house out," his grandmother said, "and it would have been simply too hard for Lissa to get big boxes of things in and out of that little car. So I decided to make it easier on her."

His jaw had dropped, and now his tongue was starting to freeze.

"Besides," his grandmother went on, "the nice salesman gave me a whole lot more money for my car than you thought it was worth, so trading ended up being much more sensible than just selling it for taxi fare. And you did tell Lissa to buy me new tires, so—"

Kurt sputtered, "Dammit, Lissa, you told her about the tires?"

She sounded defensive. "Well, you didn't actually say I shouldn't mention it. And I thought if she understood that you really would like to do something for her—"

Kurt couldn't even find his voice.

Hannah said, "You thought I'd turn down the gift if I knew about it, didn't you? But Lissa was very convincing that I should let you make things easier for me." Hannah opened the passenger door and stood back to show it off. "Isn't this nice? See how the little board slides out automatically, so I have a step? Don't forget to give him the bill, Lissa." She climbed up into the SUV and firmly closed the door.

"The bill? You mean the bill for the—?"

Lissa was very convincing that I should let you make things easier for me.

Lisa looked at him with a gleam in her eyes that made him long to choke her. Then she pulled a sheaf of paper out of the pocket of her overcoat.

Kurt muttered, "Gran *would* be the one person on the planet to get confused about the difference between *a set of tires* and *a set of wheels.* I didn't intend to buy her a whole—"

"Remember?" Lissa chided. "You said you're not the one who has the cheap streak. Well, here's your chance to prove it. And from now on when you ride with me you won't feel you're in a tomato soup can!"

CHAPTER FOUR

IT HAD TAKEN Lissa most of the afternoon to feel truly warm again after being out in the brisk wind so much of the morning. Shopping for a Christmas tree, wandering through the dealer's entire assortment of SUVs, and then standing in the parking lot discussing both purchases with Kurt had left her chilled to the bone.

So she wasn't at all surprised when Kurt came into the living room late in the afternoon and without a word went straight to the fireplace to hold his hands over the flames. He'd been out in that parking lot without even a coat when he'd still been perspiring from his stunt on the climbing wall. It would be no wonder if he was feeling the after-effects of that knife-edged wind even hours later.

The room felt different to Lissa the moment he walked in—though it wasn't so much the gust of cold air he brought with him as something far less tangible. The tang of testosterone, she told herself wryly, watching him out of the corner of her eye from her cross-legged position on the carpet almost under the Christmas tree. The air seemed to sparkle with the power of his presence.

He'd changed out of the stretchy, close-fitting climbing gear he'd been wearing in the store that morning and into a bulky sweater and wool trousers. She preferred him in street clothes, she decided, because the hardness and strength of his body weren't quite so blatant. That didn't mean he was easy to ignore, of course—the man still moved like a well-oiled machine. But at least every muscle wasn't obvious, as it had been this morning, reminding her with his every twitch that once—just once, so long ago—she had stroked those muscles and luxuriated in the warmth and power of his body....

It was a one-night stand, she reminded herself rudely. *A bad soap opera, not classic literature. Get over it.*

"Have a cup of tea," she suggested. "It's a fresh pot."

Kurt turned his back to the fire, as if to baste his spine in warmth. "I'd rather have a stiff Scotch."

Lissa shook her head. "Alcohol doesn't warm you up, it only fools you into thinking you're comfortable." She reached for another box—this one simply marked *Xmas decorations*— and wondered what was likely to be in it. She'd already unearthed a *papier-maché* nativity set, a collection of angels which took her breath away, and an assortment of Santa statues which could outfit a gift shop at the North Pole.

"I'm more interested in its pain-killing properties. The fire's taking the edge off the cold, but it would help my attitude immensely if you weren't playing 'Let It Snow' in the background."

Lissa considered turning up the volume. Instead, she got up and poured him a cup from the still-steaming teapot. "Here. At least drink this first. It'll warm you up *and* improve your mood. If anything can."

"Watch out, Lissa. Someone might think you're concerned about me."

She sank down beside the stack of boxes once more. "I've had pneumonia, and I wouldn't wish it on my worst enemy. Of course, you *deserve* to get at least a good old-fashioned cold. Standing in the parking lot in your shirtsleeves like that, even if you hadn't still been soaked from doing your stunt on that wall thing—"

"That *wall thing* is one of the most popular features of my stores."

"Popular, maybe. Profitable, no way. It can't possibly be, after you pay the insurance costs."

"I have a perfectly good team of accountants, Lissa, so anytime you're finished imitating a professional you can stop analyzing my business."

She felt herself color with irritation. All right, maybe she had been showing off a bit, making it clear that she knew a few things about profits and losses—but did he have to clip her quite so hard just because she didn't have a set of letters after her name yet?

"The wall draws people in to watch or to climb," he pointed out. "And once they're in the store, they usually buy something."

"Of course I know profit isn't the only motive for offering a service. But—never mind." She shifted a particularly heavy box, deliberately turning her back to him.

"I see you got the tree set up without my help."

Lissa didn't even look over her shoulder at him. "The handyman was here to finish clearing the snow off the walks, so your grandmother enlisted him." She took a deep breath of pine scent. The tree's fragrance was gradually filling the room as the branches relaxed in the warmth.

"This was the biggest one the two of you could find, right?"

"It's a little larger than I thought it was," Lissa admitted. The spread of the tree's lowest limbs took up almost half the width of the room.

Kurt drained the teacup and went to pour himself a drink from the cabinet in the dining room. "Want a glass of wine or something?"

Lissa shook her head. "Sorting out these boxes is making me dizzy enough, thanks."

"Where's Gran, by the way? I thought decorating this tree was her pet project."

"Well, she's pretty good at delegating the parts she doesn't want to do. I don't suppose *you'd* want to work on untangling the strings of lights?"

"Good guess."

"Hannah would like the lights to be on so she can start decorating after her nap."

"Then you have your job cut out for you. She's taking another nap?"

"What's wrong with a nap every afternoon? She's had a busy day. When we were looking for just the right tree she was inexhaustible—but an eighty-year-old woman can't keep up that pace forever."

"And then there was the SUV to buy," Kurt said. "Why did you let her do that, anyway?"

"*Let* her?" Lissa's voice was an incredulous squeak. "I'd have liked to see *you* stop her, once she got the notion in her head!"

He went straight on without apology. "That's the big question, you know. Just how *did* she get the notion in her head?"

"All I told her was that you wanted her to have new, safe tires, and you'd make it part of her Christmas gift. In fact, I asked her if she wanted me to take care of it so she wouldn't have to bother. She said no, she'd talk to her favorite mechanic to get some advice about what sort of tires would be best for her car. Of course as soon as she set foot in the dealership—"

"The salespeople were on her like vultures, I suppose."

"They didn't exactly take advantage of her," Lissa said reluctantly. "All the salespeople were busy, in fact—so she wandered around, looking at all the tires in the showroom. Then her feet started to hurt and she decided to sit down inside an SUV, and when she spotted the friendly little running board sliding out to help her climb in she fell in love."

Kurt groaned.

"Then it was just a question of which color she wanted. We

had to look at every one they had in stock so she could decide. I didn't realize there were so many colors. If you're worried about the money—"

"I'm not." His voice was clipped.

"Well, I wouldn't blame you if you were," she said with mock sympathy. "It can't be cheap to start up yet another brand-new store, and when you've got a whole chain in expansion mode—"

"I'm not in any financial difficulty, but thanks for your concern."

"I'm very glad to hear it. Anyway, what I was just going to tell you is that Hannah was only joking about you paying for her new car."

"And I suppose that's why you handed me the bill?"

"Obviously you still haven't looked at those papers. If you had just listened to me this morning instead of shoving everything in your pocket and walking away—"

"Are you nuts? If I hadn't walked away I'd still be standing there. Only by now I'd be imitating an ice sculpture."

"It would be the perfect job for you," Lissa muttered. "If you'd stuck around for thirty seconds longer I would have told you that she wrote a check for it."

Kurt's eyebrows had raised a fraction. "She paid the entire amount?"

"All except the tires. She seemed to think that was a really good joke." She lifted the lid off the heavy box and peered inside. "You wouldn't happen to know why Hannah would have spray-painted a bunch of bricks bright red and packed them up with the Christmas stuff, would you?"

Kurt shrugged. "Not a clue."

Lissa stacked the bricks neatly to one side, set the box into the pile of empties, and dragged the next carton over in front of her. "And that's another subject, you know. Keeping that sort of money lying around in an ordinary demand deposit account makes no sense whatsoever when she could be earning interest on it."

"Oh, I don't know. A checking account seems a whole lot smarter to me than keeping cash in an envelope in a boarding house."

"I'll do my best to remember that next time I have a small fortune to invest. My point is, she could be earning a lot more in a money market fund than in an ordinary checking account."

"Now that it's spent," Kurt said, "it doesn't seem to matter much where she had it stashed. In an envelope, under her mattress, at the bank—what's the difference? What's she going to do with a vehicle like that in a retirement village?"

"Take all her friends out for joyrides, I suppose."

"Who's going to drive? Are you planning to extend your two weeks into permanent employment?"

Lissa felt a little stab of regret. Two weeks—and one of her precious fourteen days of freedom was already nearly gone. "Of course not. By then she'll have seen a doctor, and maybe with an adjustment in her medication she'll be able to drive again."

"Oh, that would be a real relief," he said dryly. "Gran at the controls of a sport utility vehicle—"

"Well, you have to admit she'll be safer in the SUV than in the tomato can, no matter who's behind the wheel."

"That's true," he conceded. "I'm not convinced there's a penny's worth of difference between the two of you when it comes to driving skills."

She shot a narrow look at him over the box she'd just opened, which seemed to be full of garishly colored needlepoint Christmas stockings.

"Retirement villages provide transportation," Kurt said. "Buses and vans and wheelchair lifts and all that stuff. The residents don't have to drive at all."

"Maybe, but I can't quite see Hannah scheduling her massage

times to fit the bus driver's schedule. Maybe she really bought the SUV because she's planning to have you take her mountain climbing? There's plenty of room for the gear in the back, plus four-wheel drive so you can go off-road and rough it."

"Gran? Don't be ridiculous."

Lissa shook out a ruffled lace tree skirt which had been crushed under the needlepoint stockings and pretended not to look at him. "You didn't seem to want her to move into a retirement village anyway. What's your plan? That she move in with you instead?"

She was a little surprised that he didn't react to the bait. Instead he planted one hip against the arm of the couch, right above where she was working, and meditatively swirled his drink.

"You're looking a little flushed," she said. "Are you feeling all right? Because pneumonia can really—"

"You can stop trying so hard to convince me you had pneumonia, Lissa."

She was startled. "What? Why would I lie to you about—?"

"I'm convinced. Your background check said it was quite a case you had."

She gritted her teeth. "You ran a background check on me?"

"Sure." His tone was casual. "I do it with all employees— of course I'd want to know that my grandmother's personal assistant wasn't a felon on the run. Why does it bother you so much that I looked into your past, anyway?"

She swallowed hard. "It doesn't bother me, exactly. It just took me by surprise."

"Sure it did. You know, Lissa, it makes me wonder—if there *is* something you want to hide, what might it be? You were so eager to tell me why you had to drop out—your father being ill, your pneumonia. I couldn't help but wonder if the real story was just a little more."

"Like that wouldn't be enough," Lissa muttered. "So what were you expecting to find?"

He rattled the ice in his glass and said, very clearly, "A baby."

The silver glass ball she'd just picked up slipped from her hand and shattered on the floor. *What on earth had given him that idea?* "You mean…like…*your* baby?"

"The possibility occurred to me. The way you disappeared from that calculus class…and talk I heard from people who'd seen you around the university —"

"Your pals from class were spying on me, I suppose?"

"It's not a huge campus, Lissa. But they just thought you looked miserable. It didn't occur to me that you might actually have been ill. Or pregnant. Anyway, I'd forgotten all about that till—"

"Fine time to be thinking about it now. This baby you're postulating would be five years old," she said.

"Yes, and I feel bad about that. But I didn't know that you'd dropped out of school. I had no reason to be suspicious back then."

"So why now?"

He hesitated. "Yesterday, when you started talking about how in some situations there aren't any good choices, I started to wonder exactly what you meant."

"And because of that you thought I was telling you I'd had your baby?" Her voice was tart. "And what did you think I'd done with this supposed infant?"

"Given it up for adoption, I suppose."

"And what would you have done about it now?"

He looked down into his glass. "I don't know."

Lissa's heart twisted just a little. "Well, I hope you're satisfied that it never happened."

"You had a father with lymphoma, followed by a bad case of pneumonia."

Lissa shrugged. "Exactly what I told you."

The doorbell chimed, and Lissa pushed a box aside and got to her feet, groaning a little as her knees protested at the length of time she'd been on the floor.

As she pulled the door open, the bells on the wreath she had hung there jingled gaily.

Hannah's friend Marian was standing on the wide front porch, her fingertip already pushing the bell a second time. "Sorry," Marian said, not sounding as if she meant it. "Janet's getting hard of hearing, you know. What on earth are *you* doing here? I barely recognized you out of uniform." Her gaze drifted over Lissa's jeans and sweater.

"I'm helping out a bit, Mrs. Meadows," Lissa said coolly.

"Oh, yes, of course. I heard Hannah had a fainting spell after I left the restaurant the other day, so I came to check on her." Marian brushed past Lissa, already taking off her hat. "Goodness, it's cold out there."

Lissa took the hint and stepped back politely. "Would you like a cup of tea? Mrs. Wilder is having a nap, but I expect she'll be downstairs soon. Kurt's here."

Marian looked past her, as if to check out what Lissa had said, just as Kurt appeared in the pillared archway between the living room and the foyer. "In that case I'll come in. It's too bad that my little friend couldn't come along today. I guess you'll have to wait for that treat, Kurt."

She sounded, Lissa thought, as if she was denying a five-year-old a ride on a carousel. *Little friend?* How corny could the woman get, anyway?

Marian bustled past Kurt into the living room and stopped dead. "What is going on in here?"

"Just some holiday decorating," Lissa said. "I hope you won't mind if I keep right on working after I pour your tea."

"Not at all." Marian didn't even look at her. "In fact, I'll pour, and Kurt and I will just sit down here at the other end of the room, where we'll be out of your way."

"Sorry, Marian," Kurt said smoothly, "but I'm helping Lissa untangle the lights. Since she was good enough to volunteer to

help decorate, I couldn't possibly leave her to face the conse-
quences if it isn't all done by the time Gran wakes up."

Not that it was exactly a compliment, Lissa thought, to know
that he'd rather be on her end of the room unpacking boxes than
drinking tea with Marian….

The man had seriously entertained the notion that she'd had
his baby? After six long years, what had made him contemplate
the possibility now?

"But help yourself to tea," he went on cheerfully. His voice
dropped to a murmur that tickled Lissa's ear. "Quick—where
are the lights?"

I should ignore him. But Lissa used her foot to push a box
toward him. "As long as we're talking about weird hypothe-
ses…do you also believe the moon landing was a fake?"

"I had reason to be suspicious, Lissa."

"Because I told you I'd dropped out for a while? Honestly…." She took a deep breath and decided it would be
prudent to change the subject. "Never mind. I had no idea you
were such a coward, by the way."

"Coward? Me?"

"Yes—running from a simple thing like Marian's 'little friend.'
And she isn't even here to run from—that's what's so hilarious."

"Better to squelch the whole idea up front. The only thing
worse than an elderly matchmaker is a pair of them."

"I suppose that's true. Is this the little friend you had mixed
up with me?"

Kurt lifted the lid of the box and heaved a huge sigh. "Next
time look for an electrical engineer to do this job." He dug both
hands into the box and pulled out a gnarled mass of dark green
wires and small multicolored bulbs. "And if you're expecting
me to admit that I'd rather Marian's friend *had* been you—"

"Heavens, no. I wouldn't want you to break your long-stand-
ing record and actually be flattering to me."

Marian was coming back toward them, cup in hand. "I had no idea you knew Hannah so well that you'd volunteer to give up your Christmas break to help her." Her voice took on a cool edge. "Or is this a chance to earn some extra money?"

"Actually," Lissa said sweetly, "I haven't been acquainted with Hannah all that long. It's Kurt I've known forever, so of course I'm happy to lend a hand wherever I can to help his grandmother."

"I'm quite sure of *that*." Marian's voice had gone icy.

From the foot of the stairs, Hannah said, "Marian, how delightful of you to drop by! Rae didn't come with you?"

"No, darling, because I didn't expect Kurt to be here this afternoon. But we could stop by tomorrow, if the two of you will be free."

"Don't count on it," Kurt said under his breath. "There must be twenty strands of lights in here." He found a plug and untangled enough cord to reach the outlet. Just three of the tiny bulbs lit up. "We've known each other forever, hmm? I think all those Christmas carols are starting to rot your brain."

"Hey, I'm not the one who's into conspiracy theories." Lissa turned back to the box she'd just opened, which seemed to contain nothing but crocheted snowflakes. The starch which stiffened them had yellowed with age. "And even you have to admit it does feel like forever. Besides, it would be foolish for me to pretend I've been Hannah's friend when all Marian would have to do is ask and she'd find out differently."

The bigger question, Lissa asked herself, was why she'd said anything at all. So what if Marian Meadows took a swipe at her? Why on earth had she implied that she and Kurt were pals, and had been forever?

They'd never been friends, though once—for a painfully brief span of time—she'd thought they might be more than friends. Much more. But that had been only an illusion, and he'd stripped it from her as quickly and painfully as an adhesive bandage peeled off skin. So what had inspired her to say it now?

Janet had appeared with a fresh pot of tea and a plate of cookies still warm from the oven. She set them on the coffee table at the far end of the room, and the two women settled down on the couch there. Though Lissa wasn't trying to overhear their conversation, Marian's slightly shrill voice made it impossible to ignore her.

"I hope your new helper is working out well," Marian said. "I wouldn't have thought of hiring her, myself. But it makes perfect sense. As a waitress, she's used to this sort of work—fetching and carrying and general picking up. Though it must be very uncomfortable for her, having to be a hanger-on at someone else's holidays."

Kurt seemed to be talking to the box of tangled wires. "I bet the woman's a lousy tipper."

"Not *lousy*, exactly," Lissa felt compelled to say. "She's very correct and proper. Fifteen percent, right down to the penny."

"Charming. Just the sort of woman I want to know better—and her *little friend,* too. I've got it. Let's drag out the decorating till tomorrow, and when she and the pal show up for tea we can be gone buying new lights."

She must have looked at him oddly, because he went on, "I'm not talking about some sort of date, you know. It's only to buy lights."

"Oh, I'm glad you clarified that. Thanks for the invitation, but I'm simply dying to meet Rae."

"If I felt safe leaving you here to talk to Rae, I'd go get the lights by myself."

Lissa set a stack of snowflakes aside. "Besides, Hannah would never approve. Wasting money on lights that will only be used once? How foolish."

"I'm paying—it'll be worth it to be able to throw these

away. After Christmas she can hang them all over her SUV if she wants." He raised his voice. "Gran, you don't mind if I buy all new lights for the tree, do you? Untangling these is a waste of time, and you don't have enough anyway."

"You can do whatever you want, dear. But you'll need to get them tonight, so we can have the tree nice and neat for tomorrow when Marian's bringing Rae. So run along, both of you, and take care of it right now." Hannah smiled. "You can take my new sieve if you like."

The look of chagrin on Kurt's face made it difficult for Lissa to smother a laugh. "Next time," she managed to say, "you might try selling her on tinsel instead of lights. That goes on *after* everything else."

It didn't take Lissa choking on her own amusement to let Kurt know he'd been had once more—and it was no consolation at all to know that this time he'd pretty much done it to himself.

"All right," Kurt said. "Let's go." He dragged Lissa's coat out of the closet and warily eyed the keyring she pulled out of her pocket. "I'm sure not riding with you. We're taking my car."

"That's fine with me. This is your errand anyway—I was only hired to do your grandmother's running around. In fact, there's no reason for me to go at all." She started to slide out of her coat.

Kurt grabbed her arm. "I want to talk to you. But not where the pacemaker generation can overhear."

"What about? If you're still going on about this baby—"

"No."

"You believe me?" She wanted to put an end to it.

"Let's say I believe in the background check."

"Oh, that's a comfort." She subsided, and let him usher her out the side door. "So what's this about, really?"

"Lights."

"Honest? Well, you should have seen that one coming a mile away. Now what are you going to use for an excuse to be gone at teatime tomorrow?"

"I'll think of something." The Jaguar skidded sideways as he pulled out into the street just a little too fast for the road conditions.

"You're sure you don't want to take the SUV? You'd have better traction on slick streets with those new tires."

Kurt shot a look at her.

Lissa bit her lip as if to hold back a smile, and sank into the smooth leather seat of the Jaguar. "I was only trying to be helpful," she murmured. "So what did you want to talk to me about?"

"The lights were a bad idea."

"No kidding."

"If I avoid Marian's little friend tomorrow, they'll just set up another time."

"Not that you have an inflated opinion of how far someone will go to meet you, of course. Sorry—I didn't mean to interrupt. You're probably right. Marian doesn't seem the sort to give up easily."

"If I'm not there at teatime, they'll stay for dinner."

"And if you miss dinner…." She sounded almost thoughtful, except for the tang of laughter in her voice. "You know, it might be interesting to see if they'd actually turn up for breakfast."

What was it going to take for her to treat this seriously? "I have a better idea. I'm going to meet What's-her-name—"

"Rae."

"As scheduled tomorrow. Only *you're* going to be with me."

She sounded wary. "With you…how?"

"I'll be polite and civil and obviously not intrigued by Rae because I'm interested in someone else. You, to be precise. You've already laid the groundwork by telling Marian we've known each other forever. So when she and the pal show up tomorrow we'll go into our more-than-friends act—"

"Wait a minute. *More than* friends? I didn't even say we were friends, much less—"

"That's the beauty of it. She'll be up all night, working out the possible interpretations, and by tomorrow she'll be easy to convince that her little pal doesn't stand a chance with me as long as you're around."

"And you think *my* brain's rotting?" Lissa shook her head. "I can't imagine why you think that would work."

"I got the idea at the store this morning, when you ran off that woman at the door."

Lissa stared. "I did what?"

"You took one look at her and she veered off course like a bad torpedo."

"But not because of anything *I* did. There's nothing to say she ever really intended to come over to you."

"She did. I know."

She looked at him thoughtfully. "How many warehouses does it take just to store your ego, Kurt?"

"The point is, I don't know how you waved her off, and I don't care. Just as long as you do it again tomorrow."

"By scaring Rae into a retreat? Honestly, Kurt, why you suddenly think you need a bodyguard to protect you from Rae—"

"If you want to know what's in it for you, Lissa...."

"Oh, yes, please—tell me what the reward is here." Lissa tossed her head back against the seat, and soft-looking hair met soft leather. The static electricity made a few of the auburn strands stand up straight. His fingertips itched to smooth them back in place.

Almost too late he realized what he was thinking and drew his hand back to a safe distance.

Watch it, Callahan. It's a good idea you've got—as long as you remember that she's dangerous. It's not smart to play with dynamite, but if you use it carefully....

"You're hoping your grandmother gets annoyed and fires me, aren't you? Well, I'm not playing along. Because I have a better plan."

"I'm listening."

"Actually, it's your plan—just without me. All you have to do is be cool and polite to Rae tomorrow and see what happens. It's one day, Kurt. What's the big deal?"

"What about the rest of the week?" He pulled up at a traffic light and looked over at her, taking just a bit of malicious pleasure in the dismay which gleamed in her eyes.

"The rest of the week?" she said lamely. "You told me your grand opening would be over on Sunday."

"And it will. But surely..." The light changed and he eased the Jaguar into the intersection. "Surely you didn't expect me to go home and leave my grandmother to celebrate Christmas all by herself. Did you?"

They bought all the lights they could find in two different stores, but they were still arguing about Marian's friend and what to do about her when they returned to the house. Lissa was chilled by the weather but heated by the discussion. She was so absorbed that she didn't even see the extra car parked under the porte cochere until Kurt stopped the Jaguar just short of the bumper.

"Where did that come from?" she asked.

"Considering the emblem on the front, I'd say Japan," Kurt said dryly. "It's not Marian's, because it wasn't there when we left."

"No doubt Rae's lying in wait for you, right inside the door."

"I wouldn't put it past Marian. What about it, Lissa?"

"You mean The Great Friendship Escapade? You've never been particularly good at being straightforward with women, have you? Maybe it's time you had some practice."

"What in the hell does that mean? If you'd have just listened to me back then—"

"To what? You justifying how you hadn't *really* made a bet with your friends that you could get me to go to bed with you?"

"I didn't."

"Oh, please—let's not start arguing over definitions. It's over. Your friends took care of letting me know where I stood, so you didn't have to. And that's exactly what you're trying to do again. Only instead of me being the dupe this time, you want me to run interference for you. Well, I'm not interested. Deal with Rae yourself." She dug a pile of boxes from the back seat. The wrappings were slick, and the boxes seemed to want to slide off to every point of the compass.

Kurt had an equally large and awkward stack, but he managed to get them tucked under his arm so he could open the side door of the house. Rather than put the boxes down to take off her coat, Lissa went straight to the living room to dump the new lights under the tree.

Kurt was barely a step behind her when she crossed the threshold and saw the new addition to the tea party. Only now it was more of a cocktail party, she realized, with crystal glasses and clinking ice rather than teacups, and three people forming an uneven triangle—Hannah and Marian on the couch, and standing nearby, one hand braced on the mantel….

Lissa blinked in surprise. Then she realized what had happened—what must have happened—and tried to push down the bubble of laughter which was threatening to explode deep inside her.

"There you are, Kurt," Marian said. "I've been so eager for you to meet my young friend that I decided not to wait till tomorrow in case you couldn't be here after all." She pointed at the young man standing by the mantel. "This," Marian went on proudly, "is Ray."

CHAPTER FIVE

LISSA BIT HER tongue as hard as she could, trying to turn her gasp of amusement into a cough or a gulp. But nothing could stop the delight she'd felt when she saw the look on Kurt's face as he caught sight of Ray.

It was all she could do to get herself out of the room before she lost control completely. "I must go take my coat off," she managed to babble. "It's awfully warm in here." She bent to set down the lights under the tree, but the boxes slipped and sprayed out of her hands. Lissa didn't stop to pick them up; as it was, she barely made it to the foyer before she doubled over, clutching her tummy and trying to hold back a shriek of laughter.

Kurt had made such a mighty effort to avoid being matched up with Marian's little friend—and then Ray turned out to be a *guy*. No wonder Marian had made it sound as if she was promising a little boy a playmate!

Lissa held onto the newel post and tried not to howl—there was, after all, only a pillar, a thin wall, and the crackle of the fire to block any sound she made from the guests' ears.

Kurt was only a few steps behind her. "What in the—?"

"If you could see yourself," Lissa gasped. She slid out of her overcoat and draped it over the bannister.

"Would you stop?" Kurt said. "This isn't funny."

"Well, it might not be from your perspective, but it's pretty hilarious from where I'm sitting." She suited the action to the words, sinking down on the lowest step. "All the effort you went to, trying to manipulate me into helping you, and not a bit of it was necessary!" She tried to gulp back another laugh, but the effort went wrong and she began to cough instead.

Kurt dropped down beside her and slapped her lightly between the shoulders.

Lissa pulled away. "Hey, you don't have to beat on me."

"I'm just trying to keep you from choking to death now so I can have the joy of strangling you with my own hands later." But he stopped patting her back.

"You can't possibly blame *me* for this," Lissa argued. "I'm not the one with such a tremendous ego that I jumped to conclusions. You really should get over yourself, Kurt. The very idea that women are standing in line to be noticed, scheming to be introduced—"

Kurt heaved a sigh and leaned back, elbows propped on a stair. "Enjoy yourself."

"Oh, I will. It never even occurred to you that Ray might be a guy, did it?"

"I don't recall you expressing doubts on the subject, either."

"The look on your face when you saw him—" This time she didn't even try to swallow the peal of laughter which bubbled up inside her.

Before it could quite reach the surface, however, Kurt's arm closed around her shoulders and pulled her off balance toward him. Suddenly, before Lissa realized what he intended, his lips brushed hers lightly and then settled into a firm kiss which, along with robbing her of any desire to laugh, took away the little breath control she still maintained.

His touch burned through her sweater, scorching her skin as easily as if she were wearing nothing at all. His mouth against hers was neither gentle nor soft. It was uncompromising, almost demanding—though not harsh.

For an instant time seemed to fold in on itself, and she was back in his room at the fraternity house. She was curled up on his bed because there was no other place big enough to spread out textbook, notebooks, scratch paper, calculator, and all the tools of the mathematician's trade. She was shifting around to get comfortable, trying to find a position that would support her back and still keep the books at an angle where both of them could see. Finally Kurt draped an arm around her shoulders and pulled her up next to him, propped against the pillows at the head of the narrow bed. She'd tensed at the idea of being so close to him, half-lying together on the single bed, and he'd joked about how rigid her muscles felt and then turned back to the problem she'd been demonstrating. He'd been so casual about it that he hadn't seemed to even notice that his arm was still around her. And it hadn't occurred to Lissa that he might have other plans….

Not until midway through her explanation, when she'd realized he wasn't looking at the notebook any longer but at her. As she'd stumbled to a halt he'd kissed her, and then, eyes narrowing, said that since it was clearly her first kiss he'd be happy to give her some pointers. And he'd kissed her again, very slowly and sensually, just to demonstrate step by step how it was done.

He'd been wrong and right, all at the same time. It had not been her first kiss, but it had been the first one that mattered. The first one that had warmed her, curled her toes, made her insides go mushy. The first one she hadn't wanted to end….

This time the kiss was different—not tentative, not exploratory. But it evoked the same rush of sensation in her, the same heat, the same intensity that had made her want, on that long-ago night, to learn just as much as he could teach her.

Get a grip, Lissa, she told herself. *Just because last time it ended up being a whole lot more than a kiss doesn't mean you want it to this time, not after last time.*

Still, it took more effort than she liked to admit to protest. Fighting off attraction, she had to admit, took just as much attention as did wallowing in it. But first she had to get control of her body—how had she ended up lying sprawled across the stairs, anyway? She planted her hand against Kurt's chest to push him away, and felt as if she'd succeeded only in welding them together with the heat he'd stirred deep within her.

Which simply proved, she told herself, that she had the normal range of hormones. It sure didn't have anything to do with Kurt himself, because she'd learned that lesson long ago.

"Knock it off, Callahan." Despite her best efforts she sounded breathless. "I thought I'd made myself clear that—"

From a few steps above them, a sultry feminine voice said, "I do so hate to interrupt such a touching scene, but if you'd excuse me so I could get through…."

Lissa's head snapped back so sharply that she felt the crack as a muscle popped in her neck. A few steps above them stood a dark-haired beauty, looking impossibly tall from this angle.

There hadn't been anyone in the hall or on the stairs when Lissa had come out of the living room. Even though she'd been caught up in her amusement she remembered looking around to be certain it was safe to laugh. So how had this woman managed to come down without her hearing anything?

Stupid question, Lissa told herself. *You were a bit preoccupied just now.*

Lissa slid to one side of the stairs, and Kurt stood up. "Sorry to be in your way—Miss…?" he said.

"Oh, I quite understand. Seizing the moment and all that." The brunette slinked down the last few stairs and, once at floor level, smiled up at him and held out a languid hand. "I'm Mindy Meadows. Nice to meet you. I suppose you'll be coming back to join the party sometime, so I'll go in to sit with my mother now." Without a glance at Lissa, she drifted off into the living room.

"Mindy Meadows?" Kurt said slowly.

"Marian's daughter? Not her little friend."

"The precise relationship doesn't make much difference. I will now accept your apology."

Lissa was aghast. "*My* apology? For *what?*"

"For not taking all this seriously, for starters."

"Oh, come on, Kurt. Like you can't avoid unwanted attention. If there are really so many women after you, why hasn't one of them nailed you yet?"

"And for assuming I was wrong about Ray—"

"You *were* wrong about Ray!"

"I erred in details, not in substance."

"Gender's a bit more than a detail. Stop trying to change the subject. Whatever you were trying to prove with that kiss, give it up. You're not going to get anywhere."

He sat down beside her once more. "Really? I thought I'd gotten quite a long way." His gaze roved over her with a warmth that made her want to slap him. "I certainly proved that it would be no great hardship for you to play along and pretend. But if it makes you uncomfortable…."

Something warned her not to agree.

"Then I'd have to wonder why."

"Because you don't need protection."

He shot a look toward the living room, as if he could see Mindy through the wall.

"You're doing it again, Kurt—acting as if there couldn't possibly be a woman in the world who's indifferent to you."

"Mindy doesn't fall into that category."

"I suppose your psychic powers tell you that? Well, I'm not going to indulge you." She pushed herself up from the step. She was still a little wobbly, she noted. "I'm going back to the party. Since I'm *not* going to be playing the role of your girlfriend, I might as well get a closer look at Ray."

* * *

Lissa had less than no interest in Ray. All she really wanted to do was escape—or perhaps go jump off Kurt's climbing wall at the mere idea that he could affect her so much with a kiss.

But of course that hadn't just been a kiss—not an ordinary kiss. It had brought back memories she'd tried for six years to suppress, of the kiss that had changed her life.

It had not been her first kiss, but it had been the first one that mattered. The first one that had warmed her, curled her toes, made her insides go mushy. The first one she hadn't wanted to end....

So of course it hadn't ended. Lissa took full responsibility for that fact, because she could have stopped him if she'd really wanted to. She could have swatted him across the chin and walked out.

Instead, she had let the kiss go on, deeper and deeper, long past enjoyment and into hunger. Hunger that she had thought—if she'd been thinking at all by then—was shared. She'd let herself believe that it was as important to him as it had been to her.

By then she'd had no control left at all. She not only couldn't have stopped him, she couldn't stop herself. And so for the first time in her life she had let her inhibitions be stroked away by a man's touch on her body, and she had let Kurt Callahan make love to her.

Ultimately, a long time later, she'd come back to her senses. She'd been embarrassed to find herself wrapped around him, clinging, almost begging. Mortified at the idea of being naked and exposed where his roommate might walk in. Ashamed by the depth of a passion she'd never suspected she possessed. Abashed to remember everything she'd done and everything she'd let him do. Disconcerted to realize that the thing she wanted most just then was to do it all over again.

And horrified by the stunned expression on Kurt's face.

It had taken her a while to realize that he was just as dazed as she was, but for entirely different reasons. Like an idiot, she'd asked what he was thinking—and when he'd said something about her being a whole lot different than he'd expected, the shock in his voice had brought her back to earth with a bang.

It had become apparent that he, too, had gotten much more than he'd bargained for—but in a whole different way. He was, she'd thought, clearly afraid that now he wouldn't be able to get rid of her.

"I guess I'd better be going," she'd said, and when he hadn't argued the point she'd pulled herself together and made her escape. She remembered being quite proud of the fact that her voice hadn't even trembled as she'd stood in the doorway of his room and said she'd see him later.

She'd gone to calculus class the next day, still sensitive about how much of herself she'd revealed to him, braced to greet him with cool civility, as if none of it had happened. If it hadn't been important to him, then she'd make sure he understood that it hadn't been important to her, either.

But before she'd even made it to the lecture hall the whispers had started, and the truth had quickly become clear. He had placed a bet on her…and it was plain that his bet had paid off. So when she'd come face to face with him at the classroom door at the end of the lesson, she'd cut him dead and walked away.

It had hurt for a while. Quite a while, if she was honest. But in the end she'd chalked it up to experience. She hadn't just gotten a college credit for that calculus class, she'd earned the equivalent of a graduate degree in human relations.

But it was long over. Not important anymore. And now—well, now she'd positively enjoy watching Kurt get caught in the same kind of manipulation he'd created for her.

* * *

The innocence of the woman, Kurt fumed, not to see with a glance what Mindy Meadows was. Or perhaps Lissa had seen the woman quite clearly and was simply looking forward to the show.

Kurt swore under his breath and reached for Lissa's coat, still draped across the bannister, to hang it up. The wide oak boards at the foot of the stairs where their feet had rested were wet with the half-melted snow they'd tracked in. No—snow that *he'd* tracked in. Lissa had kicked off her shoes the instant they'd come in the door; he remembered thinking that she was acting as if she felt right at home in his grandmother's house.

At any rate, he'd better mop up the mess before Janet saw it, or there would be hell to pay. He took off his own shoes, hung up the coats, and went to the kitchen for paper towels.

Janet was rolling out pastry, muttering under her breath. "'Just make a few snacks for the guests,' she says. If I'd known she was going to have a party I'd have laid in supplies. I'm the one who'll look bad if I can't come up with something fancy."

"Don't try. Put out stale pretzels and maybe they'll go home early and give us all a break." He pulled a wad of paper towels off the roll.

Janet glowered. "Live Christmas trees, spur-of-the-moment decorating parties…. Mrs. Wilder never did this sort of thing before that woman came. She's bewitched, your grandmother is— that's what's going on. She's not acting like her normal self at all."

Bewitched….

That was putting it a little strongly, of course. But there was no denying that Lissa had a strange effect on people. Even Kurt himself.

Not that he was completely crazy where Lissa was concerned. He had good reason for proposing a truce and a mock courtship. A mild flirtation, the occasional longing look, perhaps a meaningful clasp of the hands—that would be enough to ward off approaches by the Mindys of the world. Lissa had proved it, in the store just this morning.

But then she'd laughed at the whole idea—a laugh which was no less musical and infectious even when she'd been practically choking herself to hold it in—and he'd lost all sense of proportion. He'd certainly never intended to do anything like what had actually happened in the front hall just now. Stretching her out on the staircase as if it were a bed…as if he were still a randy frat boy with a girl in his room and a necktie on the doorknob….

Janet was looking at him keenly. "What's she been doing to you?"

"Nothing at all," Kurt said airily.

You're a liar, his conscience whispered. *Ever since you saw her again, you've been wondering whether she really did kiss like an angel all those years ago. And now that you know, what are you going to do about it? Start trying to find out if she still makes love that way, too? Hardly.*

"Well, you'd better keep your head, or you'll wake up one morning and not know what hit you. I'm talking about things like lawyers."

The change of direction was so unexpected that Kurt started to laugh. "How did lawyers get into this?"

"I don't know," Janet said primly. "I just heard that woman suggest to your grandmother that the next step she needed to take was to talk to her lawyer."

Well, he'd always suspected that Janet listened at keyholes. Nevertheless, the whole idea sobered him. What the hell did his grandmother need to discuss with a lawyer, anyway? And even if she did, why would Lissa be the one suggesting it? She was a juvenile accountant, not a budding attorney.

Janet slapped the pastry down on a baking sheet and waved it at him. "You're between me and the oven."

Kurt wiped up the puddle at the foot of the stairs, tossed the paper towels into the nearest wastebasket, and headed for the living room.

Though he was walking as he did when in the woods—trying not to make a sound because it startled the animals—it was apparent that Mindy had been watching for him. The instant he saw her face she was already starting to smile in his direction. He wondered if she had a crick in her neck from keeping her head turned toward the doorway all the time he'd been gone. And, as far as that went, how could he possibly have thought that the way Lissa had looked at him that night at the cloakroom counter had been a predatory gaze? Here was the real thing, and there was no comparison.

Mindy was on one side of the tree, holding up a glossy ornament and looking past it toward him. She was probably checking out her reflection from the corner of her eye, Kurt thought. Making sure there wasn't a crumb stuck to her upper lip.

But it was the tableau on the other side of the tree which captured his attention. Ray was holding two bright red bricks in each hand, displaying them triumphantly like a weightlifter. The guy was posing for Lissa, and, sure enough, she was soaking it up. He wondered if she was really attracted or if she was doing it just to get his goat—to pay Kurt back for that kiss in the hallway.

"They're for the stockings, dear," his grandmother was saying.

"Bricks?" Lissa sounded doubtful. "I thought that was coal."

"Not to put *in* the stockings. The bricks are to weigh the tops on the mantel, so the stockings won't come tumbling down when Santa fills them."

Lissa looked thoughtful, as if the idea of a stocking packed so full that gravity might have an impact was something she'd never contemplated before.

Was that shadow in her eyes just a trick of the light, or did she really look sad? Kurt wondered if she even owned a Christmas stocking. If, in fact, she'd *ever* had a stocking....

Don't even start thinking of that pathetic little tree and how woebegone it looked, he told himself. *You'll only get yourself in deeper trouble.*

The *maître d'* in charge of the hotel dining room greeted Kurt soberly. "We don't see enough of you these days, Mr. Callahan. Your grandmother has her favorite table. Would you like me to show you over?"

"No, thanks—I remember." Which was not exactly a feat, considering that he'd been coming to Sunday brunch here with his grandmother for years on his summer visits. Certainly since he was old enough to appreciate ice cream sundaes with all the trimmings, even if he hadn't yet learned to enjoy crab, sushi, quiche, or a good many of the hotel's other specialties. What astounded Kurt was that even if he turned up just once a year the *maître d'* called him by name. Did the guy have a notebook of mugshots tucked under the reservations calendar?

He forgot the *maître d'* as he approached the table. His grandmother was nowhere in sight, but Lissa was sitting with her back to him. Beyond the arched curve of the chair he could see only that she was wearing some kind of black sweater thing that hugged her figure. Her hair, short as it was, was upswept today, in a style that might have made anyone else look like they'd stuck a finger in an electrical socket. Lissa, on the other hand, looked as if she were wearing a flaming tiara. And between the hair and the high collar of the sweater a bit of the back of her neck, porcelain-ivory and delectable, peeked out and seemed to beckon to him.

Kurt wondered what she'd do if he slipped up behind her and dropped a kiss on that tempting spot just above her nape. Shove a seafood fork into him, most likely. In any case, it wasn't as if Marian and Mindy and Ray were around, needing to be impressed, so he'd be far better off keeping his hands—and lips—off. Besides, he had things to talk about with this young woman, and kissing the nape of her neck would only distract him.

Lissa looked up. "You're a bit late. Busy at the grand opening?"

"It's even crazier than yesterday was." He pulled out a chair beside her. "Actually, I'm surprised you're on time, with the mess you were in when I left this morning."

"Oh, it's still a mess. I just walked out and left it. That's the only house I've ever seen which has a linen closet the size of a bedroom."

"Wait till you get to the attic. There are built-in cedar-lined chests up there. What does she keep in the linen closet, anyway?"

Lissa gave him a gamine grin. "Linens, of course. There are towels in every color of the rainbow—and most of them have never been used. She still has the ones she got for her silver wedding anniversary. Did you know they used to package towels wrapped up in coordinating satin ribbon inside the boxes, with little bows and everything?"

"Towels come in boxes? I figure I'm doing well if they get onto the rack instead of the floor."

"If I find any that are already mildew-colored, I'll save them for you," Lissa said dryly.

"Very thoughtful. Where's Gran?"

"Trying to decide whether she's going to have breakfast first or just start with the seafood, I think."

"Good. I want to talk to you."

"Kurt, if you're going to start up that business about Ray and Mindy again—"

"Nope. I want to talk about lawyers. Why did you suggest to Gran that she needs one?"

Lissa hesitated and looked past him. Kurt was almost disappointed. He'd expected her to have an easy answer, even if—*especially* if—it wasn't quite a real one.

His grandmother had paused beside the table, resting a hand on his shoulder to keep him from rising. "I saw you come in, Kurt, but the chef was telling me how he makes his remoulade, and I didn't think I should just walk away in the middle of such an impassioned and poetic description."

She'd seen him come in? It was a very good thing, then, that he'd suppressed that urge to kiss Lissa's neck. Not that it had been anything more than a fleeting thought, he reassured himself. He'd never seriously contemplated acting on it.

"Don't just sit there—let's eat," his grandmother said cheerfully.

"What's it going to be?" Kurt asked. "Breakfast or seafood?"

"Neither. It occurred to me that life is short, so I'm going straight for the dessert bar and see how much I can pile on a plate." She marched off across the ballroom.

Kurt got himself a Belgian waffle, loaded with cream and picture-perfect fresh strawberries and blueberries. Lissa, he noted, had filled a plate with steamed seafood. It was probably not the sort of thing that came her way frequently, he thought—and told himself not to let sympathy get in the way of good sense. He looked over his shoulder and, not seeing his grandmother, started in again. "Tell me about the lawyer, Lissa."

This time she didn't even pause. He was annoyed with himself for giving her time to think. He'd handed her an opportunity to come up with a good story.

"Maybe you didn't know that your grandfather's name is still on the deed for the house? Hannah's isn't."

Kurt choked on his coffee. "It can't be. He's been dead for thirty years."

"It probably hasn't been any trouble all this time, but I thought she should get legal advice before she tried to dispose of a house that she technically doesn't own. It will be easier to work out the fine points beforehand rather than when there's someone impatiently waiting to move in."

He couldn't exactly argue with that. Still…. "You know, I can't quite see that subject coming up in casual conversation."

Lissa shrugged. "She thought it might be a problem, so she asked me."

"Then why hasn't she done something about it before now?"

"Because it was too much trouble. Haven't you noticed how good she is at starting projects and then not finishing? There are half-made crafts and half-knitted sweaters all over the house, and— Here she comes."

His grandmother had been as good as her word. Kurt had never seen so much whipped cream on one plate. He ate his waffle slowly and thoughtfully. Janet had said the lawyer had been Lissa's idea, but from Lissa's description it sounded as if his grandmother had been the one to broach the subject. He wondered which was closer to the truth.

When Hannah finished the last bite of her peach cobbler and went back for seconds, Lissa watched her go out of sight and then said calmly, "I also suggested that she get legal advice and talk to an accountant about setting up a trust for Janet. But apparently by the time we got to that subject Janet had stopped listening."

"You knew she was eavesdropping?"

"I wouldn't call it eavesdropping. She was clearing the breakfast table at the time."

So Janet hadn't been listening at the keyhole after all. And if Lissa had been talking openly, knowing quite well that the housekeeper was there—well, that put an entirely different light on things.

Unless she was far more cunning than he'd given her credit for…. "A trust for Janet?" he asked.

"To provide some security for her in retirement."

"Janet's retiring?"

"What did you expect her to do?" Lissa said dryly. "Sign up at the employment agency for a new position?"

"No, I expected her to go with Gran."

Lissa shook her head. "In the retirement village everything will be provided. Hannah won't need a housekeeper or a cook—that's the whole point of the place—so Janet would be like a fifth wheel."

"So Gran *is* going to a retirement village? The last I knew you were insisting that she intended to move in with me."

"Perhaps she thought with Mindy around she'd be in the way."

"Don't threaten me with Mindy. I'm going to get something else. Should I bring you another plate of crab and shrimp, or would you like them just to wheel the cart over here?"

She didn't take offense. "I am being a bit of a pig, aren't I? I think I'll have a salad next, and then one of those cream puffs that Hannah obviously liked so well."

"Have two—they're small." When he returned with a plate of rare roast beef and all the accompaniments, his grandmother was nowhere to be seen. Kurt looked around in puzzlement. "Gran didn't go back to the dessert table for thirds—did she?"

"She hasn't come back at all." Lissa's eyebrows drew together. "I was watching for her while I was at the salad bar. I thought she'd probably just stopped to talk to a friend, but I hadn't realized how long she's been gone. Kurt, what if she's had another dizzy spell?"

"Possibly brought on by an overload of whipped cream," Kurt said dryly. "I doubt it. If she'd collapsed, we'd have heard the uproar."

"But if she felt faint and got herself to the ladies' room…." She was out of her chair. "I'll check."

But she'd taken only a couple of steps when the *maître d'* approached, a folded sheet of stationery in his hand. "Mr. Callahan, your grandmother asked me to deliver this to you."

"Does she need help?" Lissa asked anxiously.

Kurt opened the note. "Apparently not. She says she needs to do some shopping and she'll take a taxi home when she's done."

"I thought she was dead set against taxis?"

"Only when it suits her purpose, I suspect. She goes on to say: *And if you're wondering why I don't have Lissa drive me, it's because it's Lissa I'm shopping for. Have a good time, children. And don't miss the peach cobbler.*" He dropped the note on the table. "No wonder she had dessert first."

"I wonder where she went. I could still catch her, maybe."

"If you can figure out where to look. There must be a half-dozen department stores and a couple of hundred shops within six blocks of here. Relax and enjoy your salad. She doesn't want you."

"She hired me to drive her around."

"Apparently you get a day off for good behavior. What's the matter, really? Don't you like gifts? For somebody who's as nuts as you are about Christmas—"

"Not from her," Lissa said. "I mean—of course I like to get things. But she doesn't need to buy me anything. She's already given me a wonderful gift."

He was taken aback for an instant. Then he realized that of course she didn't mean anything material. He couldn't help but wonder, however, exactly what it was that Lissa saw as the "wonderful gift" Gran had given her. He listed the possibilities in his head. Two weeks away from that frightful boarding house, a salary which he suspected would be far above her normal pay, an old-fashioned Christmas with food and decorations galore….

"What did she give you?" he asked idly. "The SUV?"

Her gaze froze him in his chair. He wondered how anything as friendly and warm as her eyes could turn to icicles without warning.

"Thanks for reminding me," Lissa said. "Since I have a vehicle at my disposal, I don't have to stick around for this sort of treatment. And I have an errand to run. Excuse me, please." She pushed her salad away.

Kurt put out a hand. As his fingers brushed her wrist he could feel the surge of her anger like an electrical charge. "Stop. Lissa, I apologize. I shouldn't have said that."

She stayed in her chair, but she looked like a bird perched on a wire, ready to fly. "You've already had one chance to be nice today. Why should I give you another one?"

He looked at her with the most endearing expression he could manage. "Because I'll bring you a cream puff."

Lissa laughed. "You're an idiot."

"Yes. But I'm a charming one. What's the errand?"

She had relaxed enough to pick up her fork again. "I've got the first load of sheets and towels to drop off at the homeless shelter downtown."

"That's in a rough neighborhood."

"Not much worse than the one I live in."

He frowned. "And those people are addicts and ex-convicts—"

"Who know perfectly well that they have to behave or they'll get thrown out."

"It's the ones who *aren't* in the shelter who worry me. Driving a brand-new expensive SUV through that kind of territory is asking for trouble."

"At least I don't have to worry about a flat tire," Lissa pointed out. "And before you start ragging on me because I was originally planning to take Hannah along this afternoon, believe me—she'd have been under orders to stay in the car with the doors locked."

Somewhat to his surprise, that aspect hadn't occurred to him. He finished his roast beef. "I'll go with you."

She looked startled. "That's not necessary. You have a car here."

"I'll come back and pick it up."

"I was going to stop at my place for a minute. It's almost on the way."

"So we'll stop."

"You need to get back to work."

"This store will run all next year without me in the building. It can survive for an hour right now. But one thing's non-negotiable."

She looked doubtful.

"I'm driving," Kurt said. "Do you still want that cream puff, or are you ready to go?"

CHAPTER SIX

LISSA COULDN'T BELIEVE she'd agreed to let him come along. What had happened to her, anyway? Had a mere couple of days of the softer life made her less resilient, less self-sufficient? Surely she wasn't afraid. She walked all over campus and through a less than stellar neighborhood at all hours of the day and night. Why hadn't she just told him she could handle this by herself?

At any rate, if she'd felt the need for a bodyguard Kurt wouldn't have been her first choice. Oh, his muscles were impressive, and so was his agility—if she'd needed a reminder of that, seeing him on the climbing wall would have done the trick nicely—but he wasn't the bruiser type. He so obviously preferred charm to brawn as a method of getting his own way….

It might be amusing, though, to see how he handled himself in a squabble. Not that there was going to be one.

She also had to admit that it was also just plain nice to have an extra pair of hands as he supervised the unloading of the SUV while she filled out the donation forms. The whole thing took less than fifteen minutes.

As they pulled away from the shelter, Lissa said, "You see? I didn't need a bouncer along after all."

"Maybe not. But there's no telling what might have happened if I hadn't been there."

"Are you in training for the Olympic competition for largest ego, or what?"

"There's a medal for that?"

"I wouldn't doubt it—and you don't even need to practice. You're a shoo-in."

His smile made her want to reach out and flick a fingertip across the dimple in his cheek. "What are you going to tackle next?"

Lissa found herself frowning. "I'm not sure. Hannah hasn't given me any kind of agenda, and she seems to have gotten distracted by the whole Christmas thing. She spent the morning putting together Christmas baskets for me to mail tomorrow. And she wouldn't even have thought of the linen closet if I hadn't finally tackled her and demanded that she put me to work."

"It just occurs to me to wonder—if the linen closet's empty…."

"It's not, actually. There's another whole load to take to the women's shelter."

"Gran owed *two* entire carloads of sheets and towels? Do you want to take care of that right now?"

Lissa shook her head. "I know the director, so I'll take things there tomorrow—I don't get a chance to talk to her very often anymore. Besides, you can't help with that one because they don't allow men on the premises."

"Why not?"

"Because so many of the women are there because of violent men, that's why."

"Oh. Of course. Where is she coming up with these charities? Throwing darts at the phone book? Or is it you who's making the list? If you know the director—"

"I know lots of people—and there is the little matter of matching up what Hannah has to give away with what clients can actually use."

"Well, that should keep you entertained for a while. If the

linen closet's going to be empty, does this mean I can't have clean sheets for the rest of my stay?"

"Of course you can," Lissa said heartily. "You can wash the ones that are on your bed anytime you like. Washer and dryer are in the basement."

He slanted a look at her. "Don't make the mistake of thinking I can't do my own laundry."

"But will your things still be the same color when they come out of the washer as when they went in? Seriously, Kurt—when was the last time you were in that basement?"

"I don't know. A few years, probably."

"Well, neither your grandmother nor Janet should be running up and down those stairs. I tried to stop Hannah from taking a load of laundry down this morning, and she said she'd been doing it for as long as she could remember and she intended to keep right on."

The silence stretched out. Lissa had almost concluded that Kurt wasn't going to answer, when he said, "She intends to keep on? You think she's starting to waver about moving?"

"Maybe," Lissa said slowly. "It's one thing to give away sheets and towels you've never taken out of the box, but from here on the decisions will only get harder. It may take her longer than I expected. You're sure you don't mind stopping by the boarding house?"

Kurt shook his head and turned toward her old neighborhood.

He might not mind stopping, Lissa thought, but *she* certainly minded. If she hadn't forgotten her address book in her hurried move she wouldn't have gone anywhere near the place. Not until she had to.

In fact, she realized the instant they walked in, though the boarding house hadn't changed at all, spending two days away from the gloomy atmosphere had made it seem even worse than usual. Dark and dingy, the hallway smelled of one of the residents' sausage and garlic lunch. She tried to hold her breath while she dug for her key.

"What are we picking up?" Kurt asked.

"Just my address book. I'll only be a minute. You can wait outside if you like." She pushed the sliding door open.

She remembered perfectly well pulling boxes out from under the futon she used as a bed, and then pushing them back. Perhaps she hadn't put them away as neatly as she'd thought. But as surely as the broken Christmas ornament had told her that someone had invaded her privacy before, the twinge in Lissa's gut told her that it had happened again.

"What's the matter?" Kurt asked.

"Somebody's been in here, looking around. It's not important." She was talking to herself as much as to him. "There's nothing left worth stealing."

"That doesn't mean it's not important to you."

"I guess when I come back I'll put a padlock on the door for when I go out." She dug through the pile of books on the end of the mantel and found her tattered address book. "Come on, let's go. I'll deal with this later."

But Kurt didn't budge. "Get your stuff. All of it."

"What?"

"Don't leave anything behind."

"You're being a little high-handed again, aren't you? It's really not your business—"

"Is the furniture yours?"

She glanced from the futon to the one worn chair. "No, thank heaven."

"Then we don't have to have it put into storage. We'll take the rest of your things today, so you don't have to come back here."

"And where do you suggest I go in a couple of weeks, when the new semester starts? At least this place has a window."

He wandered over to look. "And such a view. An alley and a

row of trash cans. Tell you what, Lissa—I'll pay the rent on an apartment for you."

Lissa frowned at him, not quite sure what she was hearing. "Why?"

"You're graduating in the spring, right?"

With a sudden flash of wry humor, Lissa said, "Well, I've learned the hard way not to count on anything. But that's the plan, yes."

"Then I'll pay your rent till you graduate."

Big as the offer looked to her, it was peanuts to him. *So don't go getting crazy, Lissa—it's not like he's offering to set you up in a love-nest.* "So what's the catch? I suppose in return you want me to play games for Mindy's benefit."

"You really think that would be enough?" His voice was almost a drawl. "Six months' rent is a tidy sum. What are you offering in exchange?"

She noted that his dimple was showing, and she couldn't decide whether to be relieved that he was teasing or annoyed that he was laughing at the idea of them being lovers—at least for anything more than a one-night stand. "I'm not interested in having an affair with you, that's for sure."

His eyebrows raised slightly. "I don't recall offering one. But if that's what you'd like, Lissa…." His voice had gone low and soft, with a rough edge.

This was how he'd sounded that night. She'd never forgotten, and when she heard that tone again quivers started to run through her body, reminding her of emotions and sensations that were far better left buried. She tried to ignore them. "Now if you'd forget about the apartment and hire me to do an internship at your store instead…."

"What for?"

At least now he was taking her seriously, she noted. The dimple had vanished. "Because in order to get a good job when

I graduate I need to have experience in the field. But most internships are unpaid."

"And you can't afford to give up the job you have now."

She held out both hands, her gesture encompassing the dingy little room. "It's because I insist on being surrounded by such luxury, you see."

"Yeah, if you'd just cut back on your standard of living…."

"And I can't do both jobs and keep up with my classes, too. So—"

"I've got it. If you share a place with someone…."

"Like who? You?"

"There you go again—tempting me. And you say you're not interested in an affair."

"Kurt, the only way you'd be interested in a roommate is if there was a revolving door on your bedroom."

"Damn, you have good ideas." He sobered. "All right, Lissa. Here's the deal. Originally, you thought that within two weeks Gran would change her mind about clearing out the house. I'm raising the stakes. You get her to settle down to this project and get it over with, and I'll fork over your rent for the next six months. And I'll think about that internship."

Was he serious about giving her a job? Lissa shook her head in disbelief. "You want me to have the whole house cleared in two weeks? I don't think it can be done."

"Nope. I want her to make that decision you're so sure she'll reach—either to keep the house and leave everything right where it is or call an auctioneer. I really don't care which she ends up doing."

"Because either way she'll be done with it?"

"Yes. All I care about is that she not kill herself by trying to clear out all the debris she's collected in sixty-odd years."

"Isn't there anything in all that so-called debris that you care about, Kurt? Souvenirs? Mementoes?" She was honestly curious. "You spent every summer in that house when you were growing up—isn't there a single thing there you want?"

"Now that you mention it…."

Suddenly she realized that he was standing closer to her than she'd expected. He was right behind her at the mantel, so close that she could feel the warmth of his chest against her spine. His hands skimmed her shoulders and moved down her arms, and he turned her to face him.

"One thing does come to mind," he said softly.

He was so close that there was barely room to take a breath. So close that she couldn't even smell the sausage drifting in from the hallway anymore, only the light scent of his after-shave. She couldn't stop herself from looking at his mouth. She couldn't quite suppress her quick intake of breath as she looked. And she couldn't prevent the very tip of her tongue from running along her upper lip.

His eyes narrowed. Slowly, and very deliberately, he lowered his head.

She felt like bacon being held over a hot griddle—feeling the heat, knowing that very soon she would be sizzling out of control. A little shiver ran through her.

"What was that?" he whispered. "Not revulsion, I'm sure. Are you scared? Or eager?"

She opened her mouth, not quite knowing what she'd say. But before she could try to form words he took advantage of what must have looked like willingness and kissed her.

His caress was soft, almost tender. The very gentleness of it fed her hunger, made her want more—and, as if he tasted her desire, his kiss grew more demanding. His hands slipped to her back and drew her closer, until she was melting against him, meeting him kiss for kiss.

What are you doing? Lissa asked herself.

She'd been so certain that she could handle him now, that

their single night together had been an anomaly, that she'd only been so vulnerable to him back then because she was young and inexperienced. Even that stolen kiss on the stairway didn't really count in the equation, she'd told herself, because it had taken her by surprise. But once warned she had been on her guard. He shouldn't be affecting her like this.

But all he had to do was touch her, and she went to pieces like a tarpaper shack in a hurricane. Obviously she wasn't as experienced as she'd thought she was.

And, just as obviously, he was even more so. But the most terrifying part about that, she realized, was that when he was kissing her she didn't care that Kurt's women came and went with about the same frequency as the daily newspaper. She only cared that right at this moment his attention was entirely focused on her.

Maybe the moment is enough....

Hardly aware of what she was saying, she murmured, "We're not in college anymore, Kurt."

"And that's the real beauty of it," he whispered against her lips. "No more confusion. No more games."

No more bets....

"Just two people who know what they want."

With the last of her strength Lissa managed to break free. "Yes—and I also know what I don't want. I don't want this."

Kurt smiled. "Sure, Lissa," he said softly. "You just keep telling yourself you don't—and maybe someday you'll make yourself believe it. Now, let's get your stuff gathered up."

She didn't have the energy to battle him, and in any case, taking a few more of her belongings didn't mean she wasn't ever coming back. So, almost meekly, Lissa helped to load the rest of her possessions into the SUV. Then she dropped Kurt off to pick up his car and went straight back to Hannah's house, hoping to have all her things unloaded and safely tucked away in the guestroom before Hannah returned from her shopping trip. There was no sense in upsetting her hostess—which the news that Lissa was all but officially homeless was quite sure to do.

It took seven trips for Lissa to transfer all the stuff from the SUV upstairs. By the time she'd finished, the guestroom, with its solid furniture and luxurious drapes, looked like a warehouse.

As she came down the stairs the doorbell rang. Hannah was standing on the front porch, her eyes bright and her arms full of gift-wrapped boxes. "I couldn't reach my key," she said cheerfully. "In fact, I couldn't get to my wallet to pay the driver, so the poor man's still waiting out there for me to come back. Put these under the tree, will you?"

Lissa juggled the boxes into the living room, where the lights were gleaming on the Christmas tree. By the time she had them neatly stacked Hannah had come back from paying the taxi, dusting her hands together. "Did you and Kurt have a nice brunch?"

"You scared us to death, you know, disappearing like that."

"But not for long, I hope. I just asked Henry to wait until I was safely out the door before he delivered my note."

"I think he gave you an extra-long headstart. It looks as if you finished up your shopping list."

"Don't you want to know which ones are yours?"

"Which *ones?* Plural? Hannah—"

"And now I'm ready for tea." Hannah smiled and dived into the pile of packages. "I got Janet a gadget that's just too good to save for her stocking. She can use it while she's cooking the Christmas turkey."

Just what we need. One more gadget to clear out when it comes time to tackle the kitchen. "I'm sure she'll be thrilled," Lissa said.

There were two voices in the kitchen, pitched softly but still quite audible. One was Janet, of course; the other was deeper. Lissa hadn't seen the Jaguar outside, so Kurt must have come in while she was making the last trip upstairs and settling her belongings.

Lissa paused for an instant just outside the swinging door. It had been difficult enough to work with Kurt after that kiss this afternoon, loading up the SUV and then taking him back to the hotel. To face him in front of an audience....

Well, there was no help for it. She put her hand on the door just as Janet spoke.

"She brought in a lot more stuff today," the housekeeper said. "Strange-looking stuff."

"I know." Kurt's voice was casual. "There was a problem with the place she lives in."

"Kurt's home already," Hannah said, and the voices in the kitchen stopped abruptly.

Hannah greeted Kurt with a kiss on the cheek and handed Janet a long thin box. "It's a special fork," she said. "It reads the temperature instantly when you stick it into a roast or a turkey."

"The old-fashioned way is good enough for me," Janet muttered. "Sit down. I'll get you some tea."

Hannah pulled out a chair at the kitchen table, opposite Kurt. Between them, stacked on the gleaming oak surface of the table, were a dented stockpot, a rusty cookie sheet, and a glass cake pan with a big chip out of the corner. "What are these for, Janet?"

"They're things we don't need anymore," the housekeeper said.

"And neither does anyone else, I'd say." Hannah sounded quite cheerful about it. "Isn't that cake pan likely to explode if it's heated again, with that crack in it? Put them in the garbage, Janet, not the donation pile."

Lissa was just concluding with relief that Hannah's hearing

hadn't been quite good enough for her to distinguish the words they'd overheard, when Hannah went on, "What's the problem with your apartment, Lissa?"

It was Kurt who answered. "The thieves hit again."

"Oh, no, my dear! What did they take this time?"

"Nothing," Lissa said.

"But of course you don't feel secure leaving your possessions there." Hannah pushed the stockpot aside so Janet could set a cup of tea in front of her. "You brought all your things, of course? Good. You can stay here just as long as you like."

Kurt shifted in his chair. "You won't be here, Gran."

"Oh, Kurt, I won't be ready to move anytime soon. I've been just too busy with other things. Lissa can drive the sieve to her classes when they start up again, and then we can take our time with the cleaning." She sounded delighted.

Kurt's gaze met Lissa's. The message in his eyes was quite clear—*Remember our deal.*

Lissa smothered a sigh. Suddenly the next couple of weeks didn't look quite so much like a holiday. And as for the chance of an internship—she might as well kiss that goodbye right now.

Maximum Sports was not nearly as busy on Monday afternoon as it had been over the weekend, though the crowd was still respectable. Lissa couldn't believe the sheer size of the place; she and Hannah had obviously covered only a fraction of it on Saturday. But then, she recalled, almost the first thing which had caught her eye that day was Kurt hanging off the ridiculous wall—and after that she'd barely seen anything else until he was safely down.

Only because it would have been too awful if he'd fallen and gotten hurt in front of his grandmother, she told herself.

Again this time her gaze went straight to the wall, but since it was apparent that neither of the climbers was Kurt—one seemed to be no more than a child, the other was very blond—she relaxed and went looking for him.

Twice she had to stop a salesclerk to ask for directions, and she felt as if she'd walked a mile or two before she finally found Kurt at a kiosk toward the back of the store, flicking through pages on a computer screen. Figures and code numbers scrolled by at a pace almost too fast for her to see.

"Hey," she said. "Figuring out how good the grand opening sales were?"

He looked up. "It's hard to tell, with Christmas mixed in."

"Well, math never was your strong suit. Want me to take a look?"

He surveyed her for a long moment without answering.

It had been a careless offer, and not one she had expected him to take up. But the long stare made Lissa feel defensive. "I am almost an accountant, after all," she pointed out. "And I'm not some corporate spy. Even if I saw something valuable in your data I wouldn't know who to sell it to."

Kurt pushed his tall stool back from the computer. "Be my guest."

It took Lissa a couple of minutes to untangle the details—things like how sales were reported and compared with the remaining inventory, and how the thirty-seven locations were coded. "It looks as if this store took in the most cash over the last seven days, but the Denver one is the most profitable."

"It's the oldest." His eyebrows had gone up. "You could tell that in just a few minutes?"

"It shouldn't have taken that long. I could simplify your reporting system."

"That's what you want to do for an internship?"

Lissa's nerves were thrumming—was he actually considering it? She forced a careless-looking shrug. "Depends on what you need."

"I'll keep that in mind. How did the battle end this morning?"

"The one over the breakfast table, about the pots and pans? I'd call it a draw. Janet insisted she needs to keep every item in the kitchen in order to cook a holiday dinner, and Hannah told her that after Christmas either Janet will clean out the cupboards properly or Hannah will send me in to do it."

"Good. Gran's getting serious about the cleaning out."

"Well, I couldn't say that, exactly. I offered to start on the attic this morning and she gave me a shopping list instead. That's why I'm here."

"Too bad. It doesn't sound like you're going to get your internship, does it?" He didn't sound sorry at all. "Unless—"

"*Not* interested."

"But you didn't even listen," he complained.

Lissa took a deep breath. This was going to be even tougher than she'd imagined. "Kurt, would you loan me some money?"

"Gran gave you a list of things to buy and no funds to do it with?"

"Of course not. But I'd like to get her something nice for Christmas, and until she pays me I don't have enough cash."

"Then ask her for an advance on your wages."

"So I can buy her a present? That would be tacky, Kurt."

"What's the difference between asking her for an advance against your first paycheck and asking me for a loan till you get paid? It's the same money."

She had to admit it was an excellent question.

"And you're supposed to be the accounting whiz." Kurt shook his head, almost sadly.

Lissa bit her lip and looked straight at him. "All right, I confess—no matter what I do, it's tacky. The trouble is, I don't have any more family heirlooms to pawn."

His gaze drifted over her. "I wouldn't be so certain of that."

Lissa glared at him.

"You still have that quilt."

The sudden change of direction left her speechless for an instant. "I'm surprised you remember the quilt. What's it worth to you?"

"I'm the one who doesn't appreciate heirlooms, remember?" He pulled out his money clip. "Keep the quilt. How much do you need?" He peeled a couple of bills out of his money clip.

"Not that much. And I'll consider the quilt to be security for my debt."

"I suppose I'll end up hiring you just so I can garnish your wages instead of ending up the owner of a quilt I don't want," Kurt grumbled.

She folded the money and pushed it deep into the pocket of her jeans. She should be feeling relieved that he hadn't made it hard on her, she thought. And yet…she knew that he'd read her mind and knew perfectly well what she was thinking. She'd expected him to proposition her in return for the loan. More in a teasing way than as a serious suggestion, of course. Instead, he'd shifted course like an America's Cup racer before the wind.

Because, though teasing her was fun, he wasn't about to let things get serious. Well, that certainly told her where she stood.

Kurt looked past her and stifled a groan.

Lissa looked over her shoulder to see Mindy and Ray coming toward them.

Mindy kissed the air in the vicinity of Lissa's cheek and sidled up to Kurt. "I've never been in one of your stores before," she gushed. "But I should have expected it would be just like you—you're so big and strong and impressive and solid."

And looking slightly sick to the stomach at the moment, Lissa would have added.

"I'm dying to try the climbing wall," Mindy went on.

I'll just bet you are.

"In fact, it took us so long to find you that by the time I get into my gear it'll be my turn on the wall. Would you like to come and join me?"

To her amazement, Lissa realized that it wasn't Kurt whom Mindy was inviting, but her.

"The guys can watch us," Mindy went on.

"Sorry," Lissa said. "I have some shopping to do. In fact, I must be going—goodness, is that the time? I'll see you all later. I know—maybe we should all go out for dinner one night."

She couldn't stop herself from looking over her shoulder as she walked away. Kurt was watching her.

No doubt he was renewing his vow to strangle her, she thought, and with her good humor restored, she went off to look for the first item on Hannah's list.

Kurt watched as Lissa walked off. The vintage coat she wore was oversized for her, but it did nothing to hide her femininity. The coat swayed along with her hips, every bit as intriguingly as if she'd been wearing a fancy ballgown with a hoop skirt, and he'd bet that she knew it. At the very least she obviously realized he was watching her, for she not only looked back at him, but actually had the nerve to wink just before she went out of sight between two racks of fishing equipment.

Now, there's a fitting description, Kurt thought. *She's just one more lure, mixed in with the rest of the bait.*

Except he knew better. She wasn't just one more lure. She was the top of the line.

He'd known from the beginning that Lissa Morgan was trouble. Even before he'd actually recognized her he'd realized that much. And why he hadn't had the sense to run....

You did run, he reminded himself. *Well—almost. It wasn't your idea for her to actually move in.*

Still, he could have kept his distance. Instead, he'd managed to get himself even more entangled as the days went on. What had he been thinking?

Either she would succeed in her mission, and he would owe her an apartment, or she wouldn't—which meant she'd probably be hanging around Gran's house whenever he happened to be in Minneapolis. He wasn't sure which was worse. Her staying at the house, he supposed. Because he could rent her an apartment, pay for it in advance, and never set foot in it. Except he had his doubts it would be quite that easy to avoid her.

Because you don't want it to be easy, his conscience whispered.

Ever since Lissa had made that crack yesterday about the possibility of them having an affair, he hadn't been able to get the idea out of his mind. Not that he hadn't had a few unseemly thoughts even before that—but having his grandmother in the bedroom just under his had kept those pretty much under control. But the idea of an apartment, where the neighbors didn't care and there was no elderly bright-eyed woman to wonder what was going on…. Yes, as fantasies went, that one was a whole lot more interesting.

Mindy was watching him, he realized, with her eyes narrowed. Well, if she'd gotten the message that he was too interested in Lissa to pay attention to her that was all to the good. Especially because he hadn't had to say it, or do anything much to create the image. Or even talk Lissa into cooperating.

"Yes?" he said, as if he was having to pull himself back from a far country. "You said you'd reserved a climbing time? You'd better not take a chance of missing it. There's usually a waiting list for cancellations."

"I'll stick around," Ray offered. "I'd like to talk to you, Kurt."

"Sorry, I'm busy right now, or I'd love to chat. And you don't want to miss Mindy on the climbing wall—I bet it'll be quite a show." He shook hands with Ray.

"You mentioned dinner," Mindy said abruptly.

I didn't, Kurt wanted to point out. *Lissa did—and that's an entirely different thing.*

"It's a lovely idea, Kurt. Let's do it tonight. You're free, right, Ray?"

The question was careless, as if Ray's main responsibility was to be at Mindy's command. It didn't surprise Kurt that she'd want an extra man hanging around. The Mindys of the world were like that. But they usually weren't quite so obvious about it. Surely she didn't think Kurt would be jealous? Or perhaps she was just making sure that he realized that she wasn't serious about Ray. As if it would make a difference to him whether she was or not.

"Dinner?" Mindy said again.

"I'll have to check whether Lissa's made other plans, so—"

"It was her idea," Mindy pointed out.

And I'm going to get her for it, too. "Dinner," he agreed. "You choose the place."

Mindy named a restaurant. "They have the best lobster Newburgh I've ever eaten, and they can always fit me in with a reservation."

"Fine," Kurt said. "We'll pick you up at seven." Then he went back to staring at the computer terminal—not studying the inventory this time, but figuring out how to get even with Lissa for landing him with Mindy and Ray for an entire evening.

CHAPTER SEVEN

FILLING HANNAH'S SHOPPING list wasn't the end of the job, of course. When she got home, Lissa found her employer at the small table in the middle of the library, humming a carol as she wrapped boxes. "Oh, good, you can take over," Hannah said. "I believe my ankles are swelling, so it's past time for a break."

Lissa stacked her purchases neatly at the end of the table. "Swollen ankles? You assured me you'd see a doctor, Hannah."

"And I will. But swollen ankles are nothing unusual for me."

"This week."

"Well, I don't know when I'll be able to go in. It'll be hard to get an appointment right now—with the holiday so close, you know." Hannah nodded firmly, as if to deny there could be any disagreement with her point of view, and went off.

Relatively sure that—having gotten the last word— Hannah wouldn't come back for a while, Lissa wrapped her gift first. It was a small package, and she took particular care that it be beautiful.

She had done almost no Christmas shopping for years— student budgets being what they were, she and her friends had long ago opted to give themselves a present by making Christmas a gift-free zone. It was funny, though, how quickly the knack came back—folding the heavy paper to make a crisp crease, keeping everything square and tight, curling the ribbon and adding just the right color bow to finish off the presentation. The stack of wrapped boxes grew steadily.

She made a trip to the living room to deposit the finished gifts under the tree, and realized that instead of sitting with her feet up Hannah was in the dining room, digging in the bottom of a built-in cabinet. The table was already stacked with old-fashioned pink vinyl cases—some round, some square.

Lissa went in to see what was going on. One of the cases had been unzipped and the top folded back. She peeked in to see a stack of glossy china plates—the color of heavy cream, rimmed with gold, with a soft pattern of pink roses at the edges.

They'd been using china for every meal—no inexpensive pottery for Hannah—but nothing to compare with this. "It's beautiful," Lissa said.

"It's my wedding china. I don't use it often, but I wanted to get it out for Christmas."

Lissa had no trouble hearing the part Hannah hadn't said. *Since it might be the last time.*

Hannah sighed. "I'd forgotten how much of it there is, and how much room it takes. I don't know what I'll do with all this."

Lissa looked at the long table, almost covered with vinyl cases. There must be enough china laid out there to serve sixteen—and it looked as if Hannah had all the extra pieces as well. She saw soup plates, serving bowls, coffeepots, cunning little covered dishes, even a cake stand. Hannah was quite right; there would not be room in the average retirement apartment for half of this.

But the answer was obvious—wasn't it? "I'm sure Kurt will want it," Lissa said. "After all, it's a family heirloom."

Hannah gave a genteel little snort. "Kurt lives in a shoebox," she said tartly. "And his idea of a nice plate is what you buy in the freezer section of the supermarket with the food already on it. He has no room or desire for anything sentimental."

"He won't always feel that way," Lissa argued. "He'll settle down someday."

"May I live so long. After the way his parents—" Hannah broke off. "It's been sixty years since I chose this pattern, and I haven't broken so much as a nut dish. Take my advice, Lissa— when you buy your china, get extras of everything. It's almost a guarantee that you'll never drop a single piece."

"I'll keep that in mind," Lissa said dryly. *When you buy your china....* As if that day would come anytime soon. She let the silence drag out until she couldn't bear it anymore, and then she tried to keep her voice casual. "What were you saying about Kurt's parents?"

Hannah didn't look up from the china. "Hmm? Oh, nothing—I was just talking to myself. Perhaps you're right. Someday he'll slow down enough to notice that women aren't just for entertainment, and material things aren't just junk."

The sadness which underlaid Hannah's tart tone tugged at Lissa's heart. But her sympathy was mixed with another sensation—the knowledge that, no matter how kindly Hannah was treating her and no matter how generous she was, she didn't consider Lissa to be anything more than an employee after all. She certainly wasn't like family.

And I never expected to be.

Still, it was a lesson worth remembering. It would be far too easy to forget her real place here, to believe that Hannah's kind treatment made Lissa something special, when in fact Hannah treated everyone that way.

"Sometimes," Hannah said softly, "it seems like it's just too much work to do this."

Here's your chance, Lissa told herself. "You don't have to do it all yourself, you know."

"Oh, my dear, I realize what a help you've been. I couldn't possibly have gotten so far in just a few days without you."

But we've barely scratched the surface, Lissa thought. "I don't mean me. There are auction companies—they'll come in and clear everything out, make arrangements—"

"And sell it all to the highest bidder."

There was no gentler way to put it. "Well, yes."

Hannah shook her head. "I hate the thought of an auction. All that sing-song talk, people yelling bids and pawing through things, hoping to get a bargain, dealers just wanting to make a profit…."

"You wouldn't have to be there to see it."

"I'd know it was going on."

Lissa considered, and then said carefully, "If it's the idea of an auction that bothers you, I've read about companies that offer tag sales instead. You could go ahead and move, and then they'd just take over the house and have a sort of gigantic garage sale of everything that's left."

She was so caught up in the idea that it took her a minute to realize that Hannah had gone even quieter than usual. "No," she said firmly. "Giving my belongings away is one thing, especially when they go to someone who needs them or who will appreciate them. But selling them—no. I couldn't stand to put a price tag on my china."

"I understand," Lissa said. "I have some precious things of my own. Like a quilt my grandmother had just finished when she died."

"Really? I'd like to see it."

Lissa wondered if that was true, or if Hannah was grasping at any way to change the subject. "I'll bring it down later, if you like."

"What about right now? I'm at a standstill here, and I'm ready for a glass of sherry."

In truth, Lissa was glad to escape for a minute. She needed a break from the weight of emotion in the room every bit as much as Hannah did.

Kurt was coming in the side door as Lissa started up the stairs. She leaned over the bannister and beckoned to him, and as he came closer she caught the fragrance of his aftershave. The scent—along with the memories it evoked of the way he'd kissed her yesterday—made her almost dizzy. She clung to the bannister. "Whatever you do, don't suggest she auction off the china," she said under her breath. "In fact, if you're smart, you'll tell her you're wild about her china, you always have been, and you can't wait to own it."

Kurt looked up at her as if she'd been speaking Swahili. "You mean those dishes with the pink cabbage leaves on them?"

"It's Havilland china, and they're roses."

"Never saw a rose that looked like that before. What's been going on?"

"Let's just say that my suggestion of an auctioneer didn't go over well. I'll tell you later. We don't want her thinking we're conspiring."

"Even though we are? Relax—she'll just think we're flirting in the dark corners."

Lissa remembered the almost-sharp way Hannah had looked at her, and the way she'd dodged Lissa's question about Kurt's parents. "I don't think that would be much better," she muttered and went on upstairs.

By the time she came back, with the quilt in her arms, Kurt had poured his grandmother a sherry and had one waiting for Lissa as well. "I don't like what all this work is doing to you, Gran," he was saying as Lissa came in. "You look worried... awfully stressed. I talked to a friend who's in real estate today."

Lissa stopped in mid-step. With her hands full, she couldn't exactly wave her arms to get his attention, and jumping up and down would be a bit obvious. At any rate, he wasn't watching her; he was too intent on his mission.

"He'd like to come and take a look at the house sometime," Kurt went on. "He could give you an idea of what it might bring on the market, and then you'd have a better idea of—"

"No, thank you, Kurt." Hannah set her sherry glass down with a thump that threatened to shatter the crystal stem. "I need to speak to Janet for a moment. Excuse me, please."

"Well, that was certainly a brilliant stroke of diplomacy," Lissa said. She dropped the quilt in a heap at the end of the couch and planted her hands on her hips.

Kurt's jaw had sagged. He stared after Hannah for a moment, then turned to Lissa. "What did I say that was so awful?"

"You told her that you think the easiest way to get rid of everything she owns is to sell it to the highest bidder."

"Well, it is," he said defensively.

"You know that, and I know that—but it's not just *stuff* we're talking about here. It's her memories. And since I just made the same mistake a few minutes ago...."

Kurt snapped his fingers and grinned. "I knew if I waited long enough, this would turn out to be your fault!"

"Thanks. I appreciate you giving me so much credit. Did you at least tell her you want her china?"

"What in the hell would I do with her china? Use it for target practice?"

"Are you *trying* to cause her a heart attack? Never mind." Lissa sank down beside the quilt, one fingertip absently tracing the wheel-like pattern.

"Is that my quilt?"

Lissa bristled. "Your quilt? I didn't sell it to you. In fact, you said you didn't want it."

"I'm coming to terms with the reality of the situation." He stretched out a hand. "I couldn't remember what it looked like."

"Too bad I didn't realize that—I could have substituted a less meaningful one and you'd never have known the difference. Anyway, I'll pay the loan back, Kurt—so don't get attached to my quilt. Did Mindy convince you to go climbing with her?"

"She didn't invite me."

"Really? Oh, I guess that makes sense. You could get a much better view of her figure from the ground than if you were up there with her, especially if she was wearing a skintight bodysuit. Was she?"

"Probably. I didn't go and watch, either. I figured dinner tonight was enough time to spend paying attention to Mindy."

"Dinner? She actually went for the bait?"

"It was *your* idea, Lissa."

"Kurt, she knew perfectly well it was a *let's-do-lunch* sort of invitation—you know, the kind of thing you say when you absolutely don't mean it. Oh, I suppose she arranged it to be just the two of you? Poor Ray. Have a good time."

"I said we'd pick them up at seven."

"*We?*"

"You're not getting out of this, Lissa. You're going to dinner, too."

Hannah had come back in. "A dinner date? Who's going?"

"Ray and Mindy, Lissa and me."

Lissa saw her chance and seized it. "Unless you object, Hannah?" she said smoothly. "It's awfully late notice to leave you on your own, and I wouldn't want to hurt Janet's feelings by walking out on the meal she's prepared."

She tried to ignore Kurt's sardonic smile.

"Don't worry about Janet," Hannah said. "She's making a casserole that always tastes better the second day, so we'll just have it tomorrow instead. And as for me—all this rich food might be why my ankles are swelling. I'll make up for it by just having a boiled egg on a tray in front of the television tonight.

I'll tell Janet you two won't be at home for dinner." She popped out of the room again, calling the housekeeper's name.

"That seems to settle it," Kurt said.

"Not necessarily. I can boil an egg for myself, Kurt."

"In Janet's kitchen? You must be joking. Besides…." He held out both hands, as if he were actually juggling the options. "Lobster Newburgh—boiled egg. Big decision."

"Not for somebody who doesn't happen to like lobster. Other seafood, yes—but not lobster."

"Steak, then. Or we could put it another way—staying home with Gran, Janet and the television, or going out for dinner."

"Getting dressed up and keeping company with you and Mindy…. I'd have to think about it." The trouble was, Lissa reflected, she *didn't* have to think about it. Kurt won that competition hands down.

But only because it would be fun to watch Mindy throwing out lures, she told herself. It certainly didn't have anything to do with spending the evening with Kurt.

"Don't forget that Ray's coming, too," Kurt reminded.

"Well, that fact certainly tips the scale in favor of going."

"Was that sarcasm I heard in your voice? I agree there's something freaky about that guy."

"Oh, you're just still holding it against him that he turned out not to be a woman."

"As if that would improve him. Go change your clothes— we need to get moving."

"Eager to see Mindy again?" Lissa said sweetly. She didn't wait for an answer.

Since there was only one good dress hanging in the guestroom closet, it didn't take her long to decide what to wear. When she came back into the living room Kurt was staring into the fire, glass in hand.

"Back already?" he said. "Maybe you're the one who's eager to see Ray."

She held her tongue until they were safely out of the house, but as she settled into the Jaguar Lissa said, "I want to make it clear that I only came because we need to brainstorm a new plan on approaching Hannah. She doesn't like the idea of an auction or a tag sale, or your friend in real estate. And arguing about it with her obviously isn't going to change anything—since you've already tried and she just walked out of the room."

"Then what do you recommend?"

"It's the idea of a sale that bothers her. She'll happily *give* things away, just not sell them."

"So maybe we just put a sign in front of the house that says *Free Stuff,* and let people in off the street to choose what they want?"

"And hire riot police to control the crowd? Do you want me to get in the backseat with Ray when we pick them up, so you can have Mindy up front with you?"

"I have an even better idea. You drive —"

"You're offering to let me get behind the wheel of your Jaguar? Pardon me a minute, I'm hyperventilating at the mere thought."

"Because then they'll take a cab home afterwards rather than risk another ride with you."

"You're funny," Lissa said. "Just for that I should take you up on it—and *you* can ride in back with Ray."

The address Mindy had given was two suburbs away, and rush hour was still going strong as they drove across the city. Kurt slid in and out of traffic with apparent ease, though Lissa closed her eyes every now and then, while he merged into a lane where she'd have sworn there wasn't room for a bicycle.

"What's the matter?" he asked finally. "Afraid I'm going to hit something?"

"Well, a nice little fender-bender would get us out of dinner," she pointed out.

"If this was my car, I'd consider it."

She frowned. "Whose is it?"

"A rental. I flew in from Boston."

"Boston? Do you have a store there?"

"Not yet. It's on the list for next year."

"You know, Kurt, I really don't understand why you don't want Hannah's house."

"For one thing, it's not in Seattle."

"But neither are you, most of the time—at least it doesn't sound as if you spend any time at home."

"Not a lot," he admitted.

"And that's my point—Minneapolis is much more centrally located, so you could have more time at home and still be able to get to all your stores in a hurry. The house is even reasonably close to the airport, and there must be a dozen airlines serving the Twin Cities. You could catch a flight to anywhere, anytime."

"Assuming I used airlines."

"You don't? I thought you said trying to fly off the garage roof with a couple of kites taught you a lesson."

"It did. I bought myself a corporate jet."

Of course he'd have a private plane. "Well, that's just one more thing we have in common," Lissa said dryly. "Neither of us collects frequent-flier miles."

He grinned at her. "You wouldn't know what to do with them, would you?"

She didn't bother to answer that. "Why do you live in Seattle, anyway? If your first store was in Denver, and you're such a fan of mountain-climbing—"

"I wanted to get out of Colorado. And Washington has mountains."

"Oh," she said. "Was it a girlfriend or a business deal that went bad?"

She thought for a second that he wasn't going to answer. "Neither," he said finally. "After four years of college I'd sort of forgotten how angry my parents were with each other. But as soon as I went home to Denver it all came back to me. I'd already started the first store, so I had to stick around for a while—but as soon as it was established enough that I could hire a manager I moved."

"They were getting a divorce?"

"No, they did that when I was three. The odd thing about those two is that they never moved on. Even after twenty years they were still so angry at each other that they couldn't talk about anything else."

"What were they fighting about? Custody of you?"

"Sort of. And money, of course. And new spouses—every one of them. And who'd broken whose favorite possession when they were still married. And where they should live."

"They argued about where to live *after* they were divorced?"

"Yeah. What was that address again?"

"I've got it here somewhere." Lissa dug into her coat pocket. Obviously the subject was closed, though her curiosity was far from satisfied. How did a couple *sort of* fight over custody of their son? And that bit about his parents' favorite possessions—did that explain why Kurt lived in a shoebox and didn't want to get attached to anything material?

She knew better than to pry; he'd told her as much as he was going to. He'd shared just a bit of what had made him the man he was.

And he'd left her wanting to know a whole lot more.

By the time they dropped off Mindy and Ray at Marian Meadows's house after dinner and dancing, it was threatening to snow again. The sky was low, the air felt heavy, and despite valiant efforts the streetlights seemed to make no dent in the gloom. Which made the weather pretty much a perfect metaphor for the entire evening, in Kurt's opinion.

He turned the Jaguar back into the street with a sigh of relief, and then wished he hadn't inhaled quite so deeply. The cloud of scent which had surrounded Mindy all evening seemed to have remained behind in the car. He'd no doubt have to air the vehicle out before he could return it to the rental agency.

Lissa, newly settled in the passenger seat beside him, stretched, dug her hands into the pockets of her overcoat, and started whistling under her breath.

Whistling. Kurt couldn't believe his ears.

She broke off after a block or two and said, "Well, that wasn't bad. As dates go, I mean."

"It wasn't a date."

She looked over at him, brows arched. "Well, don't bite my head off about it. I think I was pretty tolerant, considering you left me no choice at all about going."

"What's that you're whistling?"

"I'm not whistling anything."

"You are. Either that or you're having a low-grade asthma attack."

"So what's the matter with whistling?"

"Nothing. I'm glad one of us had a good time."

"I did, as a matter of fact—thank you for asking. The steak was very good, and once Ray had made a clean breast of the whole plot he was quite a pleasant companion. I really enjoyed watching Mindy perform. I see sorority girls all the time at the student union, but this was the first chance I'd had to observe closely and see why they're so different from other people. It all seems to lie in the expectations."

Kurt growled, and she shut up. But, as he'd expected, the

silence was too good to last. After a single minute of quiet, she started in again.

"You know, it was pretty funny, actually," she said. "I thought you were going to drop your fork when Ray finally spit out what he wanted. All that posturing and scheming they've been doing—everything you thought was intended to get Mindy and you together—and it turns out all Marian wanted was for you to give Ray a job."

"Are you really naive enough to think that was the whole plan, Lissa?"

"And are *you* really arrogant enough to think they're still after you? Or are you disappointed to find out how wrong you were?"

"I've been around this track before. No matter how many times you run the race, the scenery never varies."

"Well, that's poetic. Are you going to hire him?"

"Actually, I find it humorous that someone who wants to work in Human Resources has to pull strings to get a job."

"That's no answer."

"You're right, it wasn't. Why are you interested? Are you making sure he can afford to take you out in style before you encourage him?"

"No. Because if the tactic works, I might try it myself."

He swung the car into his grandmother's driveway. Most of the lights were off, but the bulb above the porte cochere was burning brightly. He parked the Jaguar directly under it.

"Hannah's left a night-light on for us," Lissa said. "Isn't that sweet? She probably thought it would be the wee hours before we got in."

"Instead, it only feels like we've been gone for three days. Are you going to get out of the car and come in, or just sit there getting high on Mindy's perfume the rest of the night?"

Lissa didn't move. "I'm waiting for you to come around and open my door," she said with dignity.

"I'm not the chauffeur—or the parking valet."

"You did it for Mindy," she reminded him. "It's that expectation thing, I suspect. She sat still, and you finally remembered your manners."

"I was anxious to get rid of her. You, on the other hand—"

"You're not anxious to get rid of me?" she asked brightly.

"The situation's completely reversed. If you sit out here I won't have to deal with you at all. Good night."

But, though his door was already open, he didn't get out of the car. Something—he couldn't put his finger on what it was—seemed to be pressing him back into his seat, keeping him there.

You're not anxious to get rid of me? Of course he was. And yet….

Because if the tactic works, I might try it myself….

The very idea of Lissa trying to seduce him into hiring her made his head swim. Which was a whole lot more than he could say for Mindy's methods. Maybe he'd just play along for a while and see what happened.

He leaned back against the headrest and half turned to face her. "You're sure you're waiting for me to open your door? You wouldn't—just possibly—be waiting for something else, would you?"

"Like what?" An instant later he saw comprehension dawn in her eyes, and he reached across her and intercepted her hand just as she touched the door handle. "Kurt, if you think I'm sitting here waiting to be kissed—"

"You kissed Ray good night."

"That was different." She blinked. "I mean…."

It was, Kurt thought, the funniest thing any of them had said all evening. "Different from how I'm going to kiss you? You can take that to the bank."

"It was just a peck on the cheek. It wasn't even intended to be a kiss. There was an audience, for heaven's sake, and—"

"And now there isn't," he murmured. "And you might think about how I'm doing you a favor at the moment by shutting you up so you can't dig yourself in any deeper." His fingers were still encircling her wrist, and he drew her slowly closer to him across the car.

She could protest all she wanted, he thought, but the truth was in her eyes. Even in the dim interior of the car he could see uncertainty mixed with desire in the deep brown pools. And the truth was in her body, in the way she went limp in his arms, as if she'd lost control of every muscle, every nerve. Everything but her mouth, which more than made up for the rest.

Just as it had that first time, so many years ago. The very first time he'd kissed her, when he'd realized that the most explosive substance on earth wasn't plutonium, but Lissa Morgan's innocence.

That was different, she'd said. Yes, it sure as hell was. If she'd made any move to kiss Ray like this….

Anxious to get rid of her? Not on her life. Not just yet, at any rate.

It was the wind whipping through his opened car door which finally brought him back to reality. "Let's go inside," he said. Obediently, as if half-asleep, Lissa reached for the passenger door handle again. But Kurt didn't let go—instead, he gently tugged until she slid across the seat and out his door.

He didn't have a plan, and he hadn't thought any further than getting inside where it was warm—or at least he hadn't given the matter any conscious thought. But the instant the door opened and he saw the pool of dim light in the living room he realized that what he really wanted to do was absolutely impossible. He could hardly hustle Lissa up the stairs and into his room—into his bed—when his grandmother was sitting up waiting for them.

Hotel, he thought vaguely. Why hadn't he insisted on staying in a hotel?

"You're home already?" Hannah called, and Kurt pushed the door shut and crossed the hall.

His grandmother was settled on the couch with a pot of hot chocolate on the table beside her, a magazine open on her lap, and Lissa's quilt spread over her knees.

"I hope you don't mind me using your quilt, dear," she said. "It was getting chilly, with the fire dying down."

"Of course I don't mind." Lissa's voice had a breathy catch and she looked dazed, Kurt thought. In fact, she looked as if she'd been thoroughly kissed.

He tried to stay between her and Hannah, hoping Gran wouldn't get a good enough view to figure out what had happened.

"It's actually sort of Kurt's quilt, though."

Gran looked intrigued. "Really?"

"Just a joke, Gran," he said hastily, before she jumped to the conclusion that he'd changed his mind about all the heirloom junk she wanted to give him.

"I'm going on up to bed," Lissa said. "It'll be a busy day again tomorrow." She managed a smile. "Since you've had a rest, Hannah, I imagine you'll be a slave driver in the morning." She stumbled a bit as she left the room.

"Isn't she a lovely girl?" Gran murmured.

Every warning buzzer Kurt had ever heard seemed to be chiming in unison in his head. What was his grandmother up to now? Maybe it *wasn't* Mindy she'd been aiming at him...?

He shrugged and made sure that not even a hopeful grandmother could read enthusiasm into his voice. "I suppose so."

"Oh, I'd say there's no doubt at all about it. And they make such a cute couple, don't they? Ray and Lissa, I mean."

"Yeah." *Wait a minute. What's she talking about?* "Gran, did you say *Ray and Lissa*?"

"Yes, dear. What's wrong? Surely you didn't think I was trying to pair her up with *you?* Heavens, Kurt—I *like* Lissa too much to see her be wasted." She picked up her mug and sipped. "I only stayed up to apologize, you know—I'm sorry I was a bit sharp with you earlier, about your friend in real estate. Would you like some hot chocolate? There's more here in the pot. Do sit down, Kurt, and let's have a heart-to-heart chat—about everything."

CHAPTER EIGHT

LISSA LAY AWAKE for a long time, thinking about what had happened in the car. Why must she be such a—such a *sponge* about being kissed? Add water to a sponge and you could mold it into any shape you liked. Add a simple kiss to Lissa Morgan and she, too, went all pliable and soppy….

Of course, she admitted, that analogy wasn't quite true, because it hadn't exactly been a simple kiss. If a simple kiss was like a jazz piece, then this embrace—with its multiple undertones and nuances—had been a full-fledged symphony.

And it wasn't just any kiss which could affect her that way, either. She'd been kissed her fair share of times, and never with anyone else had she reacted the way she did when Kurt Callahan touched her.

Of course, that didn't mean there was anything incredible going on here. No once-in-a-lifetime fireworks exploding. All it meant was that Kurt was far more experienced than the usual guys who'd kissed her goodnight at the door. And it wasn't exactly something to be proud of that she reacted like clockwork to a professional. Particularly when she knew from first-hand experience what an experienced charmer he was.

Maybe it was the unexpectedness that really got her, she speculated. Every time he'd kissed her, she'd had only an instant's warning, barely time to brace herself and certainly not enough to mentally prepare. So what if next time she didn't wait around for him to get the idea? What if she seized every opportunity to kiss *him,* rather than let him kiss her? Then she'd be the one in control. She'd be ready. And before long she'd be bored out of her skull and he wouldn't affect her at all anymore...

Dreamer, whispered a little voice in the back of her brain. *You just want an excuse to kiss him again.*

She punched her pillow into shape and thought about what little he'd said about his parents and Denver. No wonder the man was skittish about women, about commitment, about sentimental attachment to material goods.

And no wonder her resistance had been softened. Who wouldn't be sympathetic after a tale like that? Even though the details were few and the emotions were mostly ones she'd imagined for herself?

She wondered what Kurt and Hannah were talking about down in the living room, and why it seemed to be taking so long. She didn't even realize she was listening for footsteps on the stairs until she heard them come up. Hannah's steps were slow and careful, as if she were tired or discouraged. Then, quite a bit later, Lissa heard Kurt—though he was obviously trying to be quiet. Was it her imagination, or did he pause outside her door before going on upstairs to his own room?

Surely not. Kissing her was one thing, but coming to her room.... Unless there was something he needed to tell her, to warn her about. Perhaps something concerning his conversation with Hannah.

How much did Hannah know—or suspect?

Her comment about expecting Hannah to be a slave driver in the morning, after her evening's rest, had been nothing more than a casual phrase, but Lissa had barely left her room before she was starting to feel that she'd had a psychic moment.

A muffled thump drew her attention to the dressing room right next to Hannah's bedroom. Her "extra wardrobe," Hannah had called it, and Lissa had taken one look through the door at a couple of bulging closets and decided to postpone the job as long as she could.

Now, she opened the door and paused in horrified surprise at the sight of Hannah, standing on a chair, taking boxes off the top shelf of a closet. One of them had escaped her and bounced on the carpet.

She was eighty, and the woman was standing on a chair cleaning out shelves. It was a wonder she hadn't fallen off.

"Good heavens, Hannah," she said. "How did you get up there?"

"I climbed on the hassock and then onto the chair. I thought I'd get an early start, and I didn't want to bother you since you were out late last night."

Lissa, feeling guilty, stooped to pick up the hatbox Hannah had dropped, and eyed the row of similar boxes which marched across the top of the dresser. The woman had obviously been at work for quite a while. "What's got you so fired up today?"

"I had a chat with Kurt last night."

Lissa wondered if that was good news or bad. If Kurt had told his grandmother he wanted to use her china for target practice....

Hannah pulled another box from the closet shelf and opened it. "Oh, this was one of my favorites—back in the days when women wore hats everywhere. Maybe I should bring them back into style."

Lissa blinked at the bright-eyed bird—it looked real—perched atop the forest-green velvet. "Well, I wouldn't suggest starting with that one, or all the animal lovers will be on your case. Of course you could wear it with the mink and give them a two-for-one thrill." She took the box and added it to the row on the dresser.

Hannah didn't seem to share the joke. "There's a suit in here—the hat matches it. The same shade of green, but it's wool trimmed in velvet." She bent over, wobbling a little, so she could flip through the dress bags which hung under the shelf, peeking at each hanger.

Lissa's throat tightened. "Hannah," she said firmly. "You get down this minute and let me look for it."

"I wonder who might be able to use these things?" Hannah mused. Obediently, she took Lissa's hand and got down from the chair to the hassock, and then to the floor, groaning a little. Lissa felt the pressure in her chest ease a bit with Hannah safely back on firm ground.

"Why don't you go downstairs for a rest and a cup of coffee? I'll think about who would want them," Lissa suggested. "Oh, this must be the one you were looking for." She pulled out an organdy dress bag and opened it. "This is gorgeous."

The cut of the suit was severe and so old-fashioned that it was now back in style. Lissa could almost covet it herself. She laid the bag across the bed and set the matching hat on top of it. "I bet the drama department at the university would like having authentic period costumes."

"Oh, goodness." Hannah sighed. "Hearing my wardrobe referred to as *authentic period costumes* is a bit of a jolt."

"Sorry."

"It's all right, dear. It's true, after all. I'll bring you a cup of coffee—or would you like to have breakfast before you start sorting?"

"I'm not hungry. But I'd love coffee." Lissa climbed up on the chair and took out the next hatbox in the row.

She was admiring a confection of ivory silk and net, with iridescent beads scattered over it to catch the light, when she heard a footstep behind her. "What did you do with all these clothes, Hannah?"

It was Kurt who answered. "She wore them, I presume."

Lissa spun around, forgetting she was standing on a chair, and only kept her balance by dropping the hat and bracing both hands on the molding atop the closet door. She must look as if she were hanging by her fingernails, she thought irritably. Very carefully she shifted her grip and regained her balance. "I thought you'd already left."

"I slept in this morning." He retrieved the hat and handed it back to her.

"Thanks. Still recuperating from the talking-to you got from Hannah, perhaps?"

"That would take a while." His voice was dry.

The almost-devious answer was all the confirmation Lissa needed—it was obvious to her, if she'd needed confirmation, that the subject had been Lissa herself. "I'll accept your apology now, for causing all this trouble."

His eyebrows tilted upward. "If you're expecting me to say I'm sorry for kissing you last night, get over it. You were much too cooperative to deserve an apology."

Lissa bit her lip. She could hardly deny that. *You're nothing but a sponge,* she accused herself. "Then I'll accept with gratitude your offer to explain to your grandmother that there's nothing going on between us."

"With *gratitude,* yet? That's too bad. Because I'm going to do nothing of the sort."

"But there isn't, Kurt. A few kisses don't mean anything." She didn't look directly at him. She wasn't sure she wanted to see the expression on his face. Would it be relief to find that she agreed with him? Satisfaction, perhaps, that she hadn't misinterpreted his intentions?

He moved the forest-green suit and sat down on the corner of the bed. "What do you think our talk last night was about, anyway?"

"Well…." There was no easy way to put it. "Me. Or I should say, you and me? Right?"

He grinned. "Now who's being arrogant?"

"But what else could it be? She talked to you last night, and today she's suddenly gung-ho to get this room cleaned out. I thought it must be because she's suspicious of what's going on, and she wants to hurry things along and get me out of here."

"I thought," Kurt said meditatively, "you said there was nothing going on."

"But if she thinks there is…."

"She doesn't."

Lissa frowned. How could Hannah not be suspicious, considering the way Lissa had come staggering in last night after that assault on her senses had robbed her of all fine motor control? "I suppose as a cover story you told her I'd had too much to drink?"

"I didn't tell her a thing—because she didn't ask. In fact, I think you're just feeling guilty, Lissa—and considering that you say yourself there's nothing to feel guilty about, I find that very interesting."

She could feel herself turning slightly pink.

"Relax. Gran thinks you and Ray make a cute couple."

Lissa blinked in surprise. "Okay. Well, I suppose that makes things easier."

"One would think so. Of course that's not what she wanted to talk to me about either. But I don't suppose it'll come as any surprise to you that she's giving you the house."

Lissa's foot slid off the chair cushion, and this time she *was* literally hanging from the top of the closet door.

Kurt stepped forward, slid an arm around her waist, and lifted her down.

"Thanks." She was feeling shaky. "You know, maybe I should have something to eat. I'm so out of it that I'd have sworn you said—"

"I did say it. She's planning to give you the house. This house."

Blood was pounding in Lissa's ears. "That's impossible. She hasn't said a word to me about it."

"Since when did Gran consult anybody—unless it was convenient for her to blame somebody else for the idea?"

He had a point there. As her breathing finally steadied, Lissa's mind finally started to work right again. "Oh, now I understand. Of course she wouldn't tell me about it. She told you she was going to give me the house because she has no intention of actually doing it."

Kurt shook his head as if it hurt. "Run that one by me again."

"It was a shock tactic. She tells you that you're not getting the house, the shock makes you realize that you'd be heartbroken to lose it, so you argue with her about how she shouldn't give it to me, and *voilà!* She allows herself to be persuaded that it should stay in the family and then everybody's happy—including Lissa, who never knew what she missed out on."

"That's not what happened."

"You didn't have a sudden revelation that you want it?"

"Nope. I think it's an idiotic idea, but not because I had an attack of envy. The way is clear for you."

"But I don't want it! I don't know what on earth made her think I might."

"You haven't dropped any little hints about how wonderful the place is?"

"Well…only to make her think about whether she really wants to leave it."

"No chats about how if I would only stop to think I'd change my mind, because it's such a wonderful house and a family treasure? No discussions of how a central location would be better for my business?"

"Not to her. I swear, Kurt, I only told you that on the spur of the moment last night. What would I do with this house, anyway? It's way too big for her and Janet, so why she'd even consider giving it to me…. I could live in the linen closet and never touch the other rooms."

"Well, there you have it." Kurt's voice was dry. "You'd have plenty of room, now that the sheets and towels are all gone, and she could leave all her stuff here and come visit it whenever she liked."

"You think I conned her," Lissa said quietly. "Don't you?"

"No," Kurt said finally. "Not exactly." He pushed himself up off the bed and left the room.

A couple of minutes later Hannah came back, with two big mugs of coffee. "Here you go, Lissa. Maybe we should talk to the people in the drama department before we drag all this stuff out of the closets."

Lissa's jaw dropped. Now that she'd started the job, Hannah was suddenly ready to quit? What could have changed the woman's mind? Had Kurt run into her on the stairs and said something?

"We should look everything over and make a list anyway. I think they'd be more interested if there was some sort of inventory they could look at before deciding." Lissa took a long pull from her coffee and felt warmth creep through her veins.

She still couldn't believe what Kurt had told her. He must have been mistaken. She would have to think of a way to gently broach the subject with Hannah. She could hardly just say, *Is it true you want to give me your house?* Because if that wasn't what Hannah had said…well, the uproar would be incredible.

"I can take care of the inventory," Lissa went on, "as long as you'll pop in once in a while to identify things. I'm afraid I wouldn't know a cloche from a cloak without help."

"No, I'll just sit here and write it all down as you go. Are you sure you don't want a break, though?"

Lissa shook her head, finished clearing the shelf, and looked with interest at the set of cabinets which had been built in above the closet doors to take advantage of the enormous height of the ceilings. How was she supposed to get to those? The items in those cupboards—and she had no doubt the space was full—would probably be even older and more interesting than what was in the closet.

She decided to think about it later, and climbed down off the chair.

"Did you have fun on your date last night?" Hannah asked. She had dug a box of stationery out of a desk drawer and was trying pens, tossing one after another aside before finding one which worked. "Goodness, I didn't realize it had been so long since this room was used."

Kurt pushed the door wide and brought in a shiny new aluminum ladder. "Stop climbing on chairs. You can't come to the party at the store on Friday if you're in the hospital with a broken hip, Gran."

"A Christmas party?" Hannah asked brightly.

"As soon as the doors close on Christmas Eve."

"I love Christmas parties," Hannah said. "And I bet Lissa does, too. As long as you promise to get us home in time to be tucked in before Santa Claus comes."

Kurt left for the store before Lissa could catch him alone, and a couple of hours later the closet was empty. The bed was piled with dresses and suits, shoes and handbags, and Lissa was tugging the ladder into position for an assault on the top cabinets.

Hannah sighed. It was a long, heavy, tired sigh, and to Lissa it seemed to echo through the room.

"Kurt thinks the same thing you do." Hannah didn't look up

from her list. "That I should just walk away from all this and have a sale."

"He doesn't want to see you exhaust yourself."

Hannah didn't answer.

Lissa sat down on the bed, where she could watch Hannah's profile as she wrote. "Actually, that's where Kurt and I disagree," Lissa said. "I don't think you should hire an auctioneer."

Hannah raised her eyebrows. "Indeed?"

"Maybe the university would like to have the house. Perhaps they could turn it into a museum of costume and design."

Hannah turned the sheet of stationery over and began a new column. "I'm sure Kurt told you that I've decided what to do with the house, Lissa. I'm going to give it to you."

Until that moment Lissa had kept telling herself that Kurt had been mistaken, that he must have heard his grandmother wrong.

"But *why?*" Her voice sounded like a screech. "Hannah, what are you *thinking?*"

Hannah sounded perfectly calm. "I want you to have it because I like you, and because you like my house."

"But what on earth would I do with it?"

"Live in it, I hope."

"Hannah, I couldn't possibly afford…." Lissa's voice failed, and she had to start over. "The electric bill alone must be staggering. To say nothing of how I'd manage the upkeep, along with going to school. And how I'd even *get* to school—"

"Because the house is too far from campus for easy commuting?" Hannah asked calmly. "I know that. It's exactly why the university wouldn't possibly want to make it into a museum, either. It was a good try, though, Lissa. Was that Kurt's idea, or yours?"

"Mine," Lissa muttered. She eyed Hannah suspiciously. "You're not serious, of course. You only told me you want to give me the house so I'd have to admit the museum idea wasn't a very good one—right?"

"Oh, no. I'm quite serious. I figure you can rent the house out until you're finished with school, and that will help with your tuition and living expenses. Then, when you have a job and an adequate income, you'll be able to afford to live here yourself."

Lissa put her head in her hands. "That's the most—"

"Careful, my dear. I'm only an old lady, and everyone keeps insisting I'm in fragile health. I'm sure you don't want to upset me."

Upset her? At the moment the woman bore an uncanny resemblance to an Abrams tank; Lissa thought—capable of running straight over any opposition.

"And then you can remodel it however you like," Hannah went on comfortably.

Lissa grabbed for the straw. "You wouldn't mind if I changed things?"

"Oh, I'm not silly enough to think the house is perfect just as it is. It could be made much more comfortable."

"But *that's* the answer, then. You stay right here. Instead of investing in a retirement community, put the money into making the house easier to handle for you and Janet. And leave everything else alone. You don't need the room, so you can stop cleaning closets and dragging boxes out from under beds—"

"I'd still have all the headaches of owning a house. And someday when I'm gone, Kurt would still hire an auctioneer to come in and sell everything."

Lissa bit her lip. She didn't think it would be much comfort to remind the woman that after she was dead she wouldn't much care what happened to her hats, her china, her Christmas ornaments....

"He means well," Lissa said finally. "He just doesn't realize that things can be so important. But that doesn't mean he never will appreciate sentiment."

Hannah smiled then. "And if I live to be two hundred I might yet see it. Do you want to call the people at the drama department about all these clothes, or shall I?"

* * *

The caterers had set up the buffet tables even before the mall doors were locked, and within minutes of closing time on Christmas Eve the food was arranged and the staff had begun to gather in the large center atrium of the store. Kurt could hear the rumble of conversation as he made a last-minute check of total sales figures in all the stores.

"How's it look, boss?" the store manager asked. "How are we doing in comparison?"

"Pretty well. The bonus checks came in, didn't they?"

The manager patted his pocket. "I thought I'd start with that, as soon as everybody's here." He grinned. "Nothing like some unexpected money to loosen up a party. Do you want to do the honors?"

Kurt shook his head. "That's your job. I'm only here by accident." He signed off the network and left the computer to idle.

"Fine with me—I'm happy to be the bearer of good news. I saw your grandmother come in, by the way. She and a gorgeous girl are waiting for you down by the buffet. The girl asked where you were."

Gorgeous girl. Lissa, of course. There was no reason for the manager's comment to send his blood pressure up; any man with eyes could see that though Lissa might not be conventionally beautiful, she was stunning in all the ways that mattered.

He saw them from the top of the escalator. Hannah with her coat slung carelessly around her shoulders, Lissa wearing a dark green suit that hugged her figure and made her look even more like an undernourished waif.

He joined them near the buffet table. Lissa was holding a plate, he saw. It was decorated with a chunk of broccoli, a bit of cauliflower, a radish, and a celery stick. He took it away from her. "No dieting allowed on the premises tonight. Have a pile of shrimp instead."

"Maybe later." Her gaze followed his grandmother a few steps toward the table, and she lowered her voice. "I need to talk to you. Alone."

Kurt didn't miss a beat. "Your climbing gear came in. Want to come take a look?"

Lissa rolled her eyes, but she grabbed the cue. "Of course. We'll be back in a minute, Hannah."

His grandmother waved a casual hand, seemingly too intent on inspecting the ice sculpture centerpiece to notice whether they were present or not.

As they walked away, Lissa muttered, "You couldn't think of a better cover than suggesting I'm going to be climbing that stupid wall?"

"Hey, it worked. That's a nice suit, by the way. When did you and Gran fit in time to shop?"

"We didn't. This came straight out of Hannah's closet and it's older than I am. But we are making significant dents."

"Dents? And that would explain why I've been climbing over piles to get in and out of the house?"

"At least it's not the same pile," Lissa defended. "In the last two days I've been back to the homeless shelter, to the library with books to donate, to a support group for single moms to drop off yarn and knitting needles to make baby booties, and to a senior citizens' center where they sew stuffed animals from old fabric for the Red Cross to hand out at fires. Hannah's dressing room is still a wreck, but that's because the drama department at the university is closed down along with everything else this week, so we can't get rid of the vintage clothes." She flicked a hand across her skirt.

"So you're wearing the stuff instead? Have you decided to accept Gran's gift?"

"The house? Do I look like I'm nuts? I don't need an ulcer on top of everything else."

"Then you understand how I feel about it."

"But what are we going to do, Kurt?" She paused for a deep breath and said thoughtfully, "You know, sometimes I get the impression that she'd really like to stay. I've been talking to her about remodeling, to make the house easier to live in, and if it wasn't for the work and mess and confusion that's involved I think she'd love your ideas."

"Wait a minute. *My* ideas?"

"Yes—that's why I needed to talk to you. To fill you in so you don't blow it if she happens to mention remodeling."

"Thoughtful of you. What great ideas have I had?"

"The main one involves turning the linen closet into a master bath and laundry room combination."

"Why on earth would I want to do that?"

"Because most laundry originates in the bedrooms. It's handier not to have to carry it all the way downstairs and then back up again. And the extra bath will be very useful when there are children."

"Hold everything right there. *Kids?* What are you telling her?"

"Just that you're still a young man, and eventually you'll settle down and—"

"You told Hannah *I* want the house? After all the fuss and frustration I've had to convince her otherwise?"

Lissa looked so innocent that he was tempted to wring her skinny little neck before she could zing him with any other surprises. Though he supposed it would be more sensible to wait till she'd spilled all the current ones first—just in case.

"Not exactly," she said carefully. "I may—possibly—have hinted that you're actually more fond of the place than you're letting on."

Which meant, of course, that she'd actually come straight out and said it. "Why?"

"Why am I sure that down deep you want it? Because it offended you so much when she tried to give it to me. And don't pretend it didn't, because I won't believe you. You were seething when you told me. Maybe you're planning for it to be your summer retreat? It's not like that would be anything new. And then eventually—"

"You've been telling her I want her to remodel the place and live in it till I'm ready to take it over? And that would be when? When I retire in forty years, maybe?"

"Well, yes. Sort of. Only I don't think she's going for it," Lissa admitted. "All the dust and noise of remodeling puts her right off the idea. So I was thinking, Kurt—if you were to send her and Janet on a round-the-world cruise…"

"And rebuild her house while she's gone? What if she comes home and announces that she still wants to move into the retirement home?"

She sighed. "Then I guess you'd have a very updated Dutch colonial."

"Or *you* would. She sounds pretty determined that you're going to end up with it."

"Maybe if I tell her I plan to turn the porte cochere into a party room, with a hot tub to seat eight, she'll change her mind about me being the right person to take care of her house." She looked over his shoulder. "Oops."

"What? Gran's on her way to find us?"

"Not quite."

Kurt turned around to see Mindy, simpering her way down the aisle toward them, a wide fake smile plastered on her face.

"Hello," she said. "This is odd, finding you two here. Hannah told me you'd be in the climbing department."

"We're just on our way back," Kurt said smoothly. "What brings you to the party?"

"Oh, Ray invited me. He said all the employees were told they could bring a guest."

Lissa's eyebrows had climbed. "Ray? You didn't tell me you'd hired him, Kurt."

And when, he wondered irritably, would he have had the opportunity? Every time he'd seen her in the last few days she'd had her head in a cabinet or her hands full of boxes and bags. "Not all the new salespeople we hired when the store opened have worked out. That happens with any new store when there's an entirely new crew of workers."

"Nobody here is experienced?" She sounded disbelieving. *She's doing her accountant impression again.* "The manager has been with me for years, and a few of the assistants."

"So that's what you've been doing all week—working as an ordinary sales clerk?"

"Among other things. It keeps me in touch with the customers."

"I'd imagine it does."

Mindy, obviously annoyed at being left out of the exchange, said, "So you've decided to start climbing after all, Lissa. I wonder what could possibly have made you change your mind about that."

"Isn't it obvious?" Lissa said sweetly. "It's my utter fascination with everything about Kurt. I'm sure you understand the feeling…."

Kurt could have cheerfully knocked their heads together. "I'm going after some food," he announced. "The boxing ring's over that way, if you two want to suit up and go at it."

Boxing ring, Lissa thought. As if she'd fight over him—though she had no doubts that Mindy would. Much as she'd enjoyed jabbing Kurt about his ego, she had to admit that Mindy's intentions were pretty obvious.

Mindy laughed, a mincing little tinkle that—to Lissa, at least—didn't sound at all amused. "How very tacky it would be of us to squabble in public—as if you're a toy we both want." She slid a hand through the curve of Kurt's elbow, and the two of them moved off toward the rising noise from the party.

Lissa followed along in their wake, quite happy to be ignored for the moment. What on earth had inspired her to descend to Mindy's level, anyway?

The party was in full swing. The tables of food already looked ravaged, the store's music system had been turned up, and a few employees were dancing in the atrium. Kurt and Mindy were immediately swallowed up in the crowd, but Lissa dawdled behind.

She wasn't unnoticed, however, for as she paused on the edge of the party Ray came up beside her, his plate loaded with snacks. "Hi, Lissa."

"This is a surprise, Ray. Kurt tells me you're working here now." She took a closer look. She'd gotten the distinct impression from Kurt just a few minutes ago that Ray was just one more salesclerk. Yet, in a sea of Maximum Sports' standard blue employees' pullovers, here was Ray, dressed as neatly as any vice-president in a white shirt and a necktie any CEO would be proud of. "What are you doing?" The question was idle; Lissa was watching Mindy, who hadn't loosened her hold on Kurt's arm, playing hostess.

"Not the job I wanted, of course." Ray sounded defensive. "And not anywhere near what I'm qualified for. But he was short-handed, so I'm happy to help out."

Sales, Lissa thought. Well, if Kurt was working the floor

himself, it wasn't too much to ask Ray to do the same. "Lots of us don't get the jobs we want, Ray."

"You've got a pretty sweet deal right now," he said. "Hey, with all your connections, have you heard anything about Kurt moving the company headquarters here?"

That's a big oops, Lissa thought. *I just hope Kurt doesn't hear that one.*

It wasn't hard to figure out where the story had come from, of course. Lissa had hinted to Hannah that Kurt would like to keep the house in the family, and from there it would have been only a small step for Hannah to convince herself that he actually wanted to live in it. Which, of course, meant that he would want to work nearby. And if she'd breathed a word of that line of thought to her friend Marian….

"Where'd you hear that?" she asked casually.

"Around." Obviously he wasn't going to confide in her.

"From Marian?"

He looked genuinely surprised. "Does she know?"

Lissa could have sworn at herself for the slip-up. "I doubt there's anything to know. If there was something to it Hannah would probably have told Marian—that's all I meant."

"Yeah, I suppose." Ray didn't sound satisfied. "I hear he's been talking to real-estate people."

She was relieved to be able to quash part of the story. "Oh, that's because of Hannah's house. Nothing to do with the business. Put it out of your mind."

"Well, you see, I was hoping that if he *did* move the head-quarters there would be a spot in the personnel office for me."

Lissa smiled at him. "Good luck. But I don't have any in-fluence, I'm afraid."

The music died and the store manager stepped forward. "Is everybody having a good time? Don't worry, I'm not announc-ing work schedules for next week, and I'll let you get back to partying in a minute. In the meantime, though, Santa made an early stop—assisted by our boss—" he paused to let the applause die down "—and he asked me to distribute a few small gifts." He pulled a pile of envelopes from the inside pocket of his jacket. "I'm going to call names."

Ray was intent on listening, but because there was no reason for Lissa to pay attention she tuned out and wandered toward a display of windchimes. They were so perfectly balanced that even the movement of people in the atrium caused them to murmur. She closed her eyes and listened to the soft music of the chimes, to the voice droning names, and the happy chatter of those who had already opened their envelopes.

"Let's all thank Kurt," the manager suggested, and this time the applause seemed to take forever to die down. "Now, just one more thing. I'd like to introduce someone else who has a few words to say—someone who just this week received a donation from our boss: a full gym setup for the men of the Mission Shelter downtown."

That got Lissa's attention. The Mission Shelter was where he'd gone with her just last Sunday, to deliver a load of sheets, towels and soap.

It was very interesting, she thought, that when she'd told him just a few minutes ago about going back to the shelter with another donation he hadn't mentioned his own gift. Interesting—and also very much like Kurt, she thought, to try to avoid getting the credit. He hadn't bragged about hiring Ray, either. And Hannah had told her he'd even tried to duck out of that banquet in his honor at the university.

Well, she was glad he hadn't managed to avoid that evening's festivities, or she would never have met him again. She would never have come to love him....

The realization was so smooth, so natural, that for a moment Lissa didn't even realize what she was thinking. Then the fact hit her as hard as if the climbing wall had suddenly crumbled on top of her.

For the last six years he'd always been at the back of her mind. He'd been her first lover, and there was *no* forgetting that. But all this time, while she'd thought she'd been nursing her irritation at him, and the hurt and humiliation of the past, she'd been fooling herself. She'd been getting more deeply involved with each conversation, each smile—each kiss. And as she had gotten to know the real man, she had fallen in love with him.

There's nothing going on between us, she'd said. Which was true enough.

The problem was, she didn't want it to be true—because she wanted Kurt to care as much about her as she cared about him.

CHAPTER NINE

LISSA WAS HORRIFIED by the sudden realization. How was it possible that she'd fallen in love with a guy who had actually made a bet on whether he could turn a tutoring session into making love? A guy who had not only made the bet but carried it through, won it, and bragged about it?

I didn't tell them, he'd said a few days ago, and he'd sounded perfectly sincere. Was it possible she'd been mistaken? Had he really been the arrogant and self-centered jerk she'd convinced herself he was back then?

Or was he the young man whose bitter, angry parents had fought over him and left him scarred?

In any case, he wasn't like that now. He'd proved it, because she had given him plenty of opportunities to take advantage of her again in the last few days and he hadn't done it.

Lissa didn't think that his failure to act was entirely due to respect for his grandmother, or even the fact that for the moment he was living under Hannah's roof—some of those occasions hadn't involved Hannah at all. In Lissa's room at the boarding house, where he'd kissed her and she'd melted into him, it hadn't been respect for his grandmother's feelings which had stopped him—any more than it had stopped Lissa herself. In his car, after that ill-conceived dinner date, the idea that Hannah might be waiting up for them had barely entered the equation. Then there was the apartment he'd offered to rent for Lissa—and the fact that he hadn't suggested it be a love nest for the two of them…

No, he hadn't take advantage of her—despite the many opportunities he'd had.

The many opportunities you created, Lissa admitted. Though just an hour ago she'd have let her toenails be pulled out rather than confess it even to herself, now she couldn't dodge the knowledge any longer. She hadn't exactly tried to avoid his kiss at the boarding house that day. And, no matter how she explained it, the fact was that Lissa herself had managed to arrange that dinner date and opened up the opportunity for a good night kiss.

But in every case Kurt had acted like an almost-perfect gentleman. Which, she had to admit, was a very lowering thought—for if it wasn't simple respect for his grandmother which had kept him from acting on the invitations Lissa had offered him, then what had stopped him?

Was he afraid that Lissa would misinterpret his intentions? Or was she fooling herself to think that the craving he'd felt on those occasions was as overwhelming as what she had experienced?

She didn't believe she could be mistaken altogether—there was no question in her mind that he had felt desire, for if he hadn't why would he have kissed her a second time, and a third? But maybe for him it hadn't been the same mind-blowing sort of hunger that had threatened to knock all common sense out of her head. Perhaps for Kurt it had just been ordinary lust—and not important enough to throw him off balance or make him forget simple caution.

Lissa had fallen in love—but it seemed that to Kurt she'd been nothing more than an interesting novelty, something to entertain himself with for a few days, but certainly nothing important enough to make him risk offending his grandmother.

She'd fallen straight into the same trap she had as an inexperienced coed—letting herself believe that the popular guy, the most handsome in the class, could be seriously interested in her. Only this time there hadn't been a bunch of his friends in the wings to make it clear how she'd been duped, so instead of quickly realizing her mistake—and running while there was still time—she'd fallen farther and faster than before. Because he was so different now she'd fallen even harder. And now there was no turning back.

She remembered how sure she'd been, after the foursome's dinner date, that Kurt had paused beside her bedroom door before he went on upstairs to his own. She remembered feeling left out and lonely that night, wanting him and hoping he wanted her—though at the time she hadn't begun to recognize what she was experiencing.

Had his feelings been entirely created in her imagination? Had she taken a few sparse, careless kisses and dreamed them into a passionate affair?

Or perhaps the entire situation was even worse than that. It would be bad enough if she had imagined that Kurt felt the same desire, the same longing that she did. But if he'd caught a hint of what she was thinking…that would certainly account for why he'd kept himself so busy all week.

Lissa had told herself for days that she was glad he was staying away from the house so much, that his absence made her life a great deal easier. Only now, after facing the greater truth, could she admit the reality—she had missed him almost beyond bearing.

She'd awakened every morning eager to see him, and she'd been disappointed to find that he was already gone for the day. Every precious minute that she had actually spent in his company—always, it seemed, with Hannah there, or Janet—she'd been jealous, because she'd wanted to have him all to herself.

No wonder just half an hour ago, when Mindy had chased them down, interrupted their conversation, and started to flirt with Kurt, Lissa had reacted like a cat whose tail had been stepped on.

It's my utter fascination with everything about Kurt, she'd told Mindy. She'd intended the comment as sarcasm, but it was far from that. It was simple truth. She *was* utterly fascinated with everything about the man.

It was too late to erase the fact, to back out of loving him. And there was not a thing she could do to make him return her feelings. She'd done this to herself—and now she was stuck with the results.

Though it felt to Lissa as if a month or two had passed while she was standing at the fringes of the party and sorting out what had happened to her, in fact only a few minutes had gone by. When she pulled herself back to the atrium at the center of Maximum Sports, the windchimes were still murmuring softly and the director of the Mission Shelter was still giving thanks for the generous gift.

Kurt, she noticed, was looking around as if he wished he were anywhere else.

Lissa couldn't quite keep herself from smiling at the way he was shifting from one foot to the other, looking in turn at the marble floor and the glass dome of the atrium. Definitely he wasn't the same guy he'd been in calculus class, she thought. Then he'd been nothing short of arrogant, while now he exuded a self-confidence that was based in fact rather than attitude. He'd gone out into the world and made it his.

The rush of warmth which surged through her at the thought took her by surprise, almost rocking her off her feet. Was this what love felt like? Not a flood of passion—though she didn't doubt that it lurked not far under the surface—but an incredible wave of tenderness. Fondness. Affection. Sheer liking.

It wasn't at all what she would have expected.

The shelter director stopped talking, and there was a burst of applause. Then Lissa heard Kurt's voice. It seemed to her to ring out above the noise of the crowd, even though his tone was actually low and almost intimate. How was it she could hear him so clearly? Had she simply tuned her hearing so that she wouldn't miss anything he said?

He was talking to Mindy, and it was very clear to Lissa what the woman had been saying. Something about the incredible generosity of his gift, what a wonderful guy he was, how his openhandedness should get the widespread publicity it deserved. Lissa thought she caught something about a Man of the Year award, as well.

Kurt said, sounding short-tempered, "The gift was from this store and Maximum Sports as a whole. Not from me."

Mindy gave a little trill of laughter. "But that's exactly what I mean, Kurt. Just pretending that it wasn't all your idea is another very big-hearted gesture."

She hasn't got any idea what makes him tick, Lissa thought with a tinge of amusement. Then she pulled herself up short. *And you think you do, Lissa?*

Even if she did understand him far better than Mindy ever could, she warned herself, the talent wasn't likely to get her anywhere. Just because she claimed to have some great insight into his character it didn't mean Kurt would appreciate being analyzed. Probably far from it.

As if he had felt her gaze on him, Kurt ran a hand over the back of his neck and looked over his shoulder toward her. Lissa ducked behind the windchime display.

Hannah came up beside her. "What are you doing hiding back here?"

Lissa wondered what Hannah would say if she told the truth. *I'm contemplating how I happened to fall in love with your grandson.* No—that wouldn't be smart at all. Lissa fumbled for an acceptable excuse. "I thought I recognized one of the employees," she said. "He's a basketball player at the university, and he asked me for my phone number once." It was true enough, as far as it went. She'd noticed almost as soon as they arrived that one of the employees looked very much like one of the athletes who had been hanging around the cloakroom the night of Kurt's banquet.

Kurt's banquet. The night her life had changed—though she'd had no idea of it at the time.

"I don't mind if you get calls," Hannah said absently.

Lissa figured there was no point in explaining about the time and temperature in Winnipeg, or why the athlete just might be nursing a grudge.

"I'm very tired," Hannah went on. "I'm going home now, but there's no need for you to leave the party yet."

"I don't mind at all, Hannah. Just let me grab your coat— did you leave it over in that pile on the billiard tables?"

"Don't forget to say good night to Kurt."

Lissa darted a glance in his direction. "It appears Mindy's taking good care of him," she said dryly. "I'd hate to interrupt when she's on such a roll."

Hannah didn't protest, but followed meekly along to the door. Her unusual mildness drew Lissa's attention away from her own preoccupation.

"Are you really just tired tonight?" she asked suspiciously. "Or are you not feeling well? You still haven't called a doctor, have you?"

"I'll get around to it," Hannah said vaguely.

Lissa ran out into the frost-coated parking lot to warm up the SUV and bring it to the door, so the winter air wouldn't hurt Hannah's lungs. Then she spent the drive home quietly plotting. Maybe if she waited up tonight to share her concerns with Kurt he would put his foot down....

Are you certain you aren't just looking for an excuse to talk to him? To have any sort of meaningful contact with him at all?

By the time they reached the house Hannah seemed to have regained all her spirit, if not her energy. "I can't have you stuffing your own Christmas stocking, you know," she said. "But if you'll do Kurt's and Janet's for me I'd appreciate it." Hannah sat down by the now-dead fireplace to supervise. "I left the goodies on the table in the library."

Lissa retrieved two huge bags, studied the stockings, and wondered how she was to make everything fit. "Just in case you're putting a shoehorn in my stocking, Hannah, may I have it early? It would make this job a little easier."

"No shoehorn, I'm afraid. I didn't realize you wanted one." Hannah's tongue was obviously just as firmly in her cheek as Lissa's.

By the time Lissa had finished, the two stockings were fat and heavy enough to almost drag down the bright red bricks which anchored them to the mantelshelf. Even Hannah's stocking, though Lissa hadn't added anything to it, had a suspicious bulge in the toe and a very swollen calf—Janet must have been busy while they were gone.

But Lissa's, the only one without a name needlepointed on it, was still just as limp and empty as when she had hung it last weekend.

She didn't feel sorry for herself, or even left out. She'd been on her own too long for that sort of indulgence. She'd long ago learned to face the painful realities straightforwardly and without excuses.

This was just one more good lesson to remember. When Christmas was over and the holiday break came to an end everything would go back to normal. The generic stocking assigned to Lissa this Christmas would be returned to Hannah's stash of seasonal decorations to be used again some other time, for someone else—or given away, if Hannah found someone who would appreciate all her Christmas treasures. Lissa would return to her classes, her work at the student union, and her boarding house room—or one very much like it—all alone.

The only things she would be able to keep from this precious time would be her memories, and her dreams of what might have been.

Christmas morning was unusually bright and beautiful, and despite the party running late the night before Kurt was up almost as early as the sun. Still yawning, he threw on jeans and a sweater and went downstairs.

His grandmother was already in the living room, tucked up on the couch under a knitted blanket, wearing a fuzzy pink dressing gown and matching slippers. "Are you eager to tear into your presents, Kurt?"

"I'm not six years old anymore, Gran." He poked at the fire and added a log. "Besides, at least I took the time to get dressed. What's your excuse for eagerness? You can't wait to see what Santa brought you?"

"I'm eager to watch Lissa's face. What a good child she's been, waiting patiently for the days to go by."

Kurt wasn't about to admit it, but he was feeling just about the same—impatient to see the glow in Lissa's eyes at what must be her first real Christmas in a long time. He eyed the weighted-down stockings and the pile of brightly wrapped gifts under the tree. "And what a big heart you have, Gran," he said softly.

Janet came in with coffee mugs on a tray. Three of them, Kurt noted. "You're actually going to sit down and join us, Janet?"

The housekeeper sniffed. "No. I brought three because I thought the young lady would be hurrying down so she wouldn't miss out on anything. I have pecan rolls in the oven for breakfast, so I can't dawdle." She set the tray on the table in front of Hannah with a thump, and went back to the kitchen.

"Speaking of missing out on things, you and Lissa left last night before the goodbye gifts were handed out." He went out to the hallway and retrieved two small silvery boxes from the pocket of his overcoat. He tossed one to Hannah and perched the other in the overloaded cuff of Lissa's stocking.

Hannah sat up straight, her excitement palpable as she tested the weight of the box.

"Don't get your hopes up," Kurt said dryly. "It's not a diamond necklace—everybody who was at the store last night got one of these."

Hannah ripped the box open. She was exclaiming over the sterling silver Christmas ornament—the Maximum Sports penguin mascot, wielding a finely crafted tennis racquet and ball, engraved with the store name and date—when Lissa came in.

"You haven't turned on the Christmas carols?" she asked.

She, too, was dressed in jeans and a pullover. With her auburn hair and bright green sweater, Kurt thought she looked a bit like a Christmas package herself—just as intriguing, just as full of secrets, just as much fun to investigate and unwrap....

He especially liked the idea of unwrapping her. He spent a moment enjoying the view as Lissa bent over the stereo set to choose the morning's music. She was still too thin, but how could he ever have thought her to be shapeless?

Finally, Kurt tore his gaze away from her nicely rounded little rear. "We were waiting for you. If you'd been another five minutes I'd have blasted you out with 'Jingle Bells.'"

Or maybe I'd have done something which would have been equally sure to wake you up—even if it didn't involve getting you out of bed.

"The youngest person in the room has to sort out the gifts," Hannah ordered. "It's tradition in the family."

Lissa bit her lip, and Kurt saw a shadow flicker in her eyes. *It's tradition in the family....* But Lissa was obviously remembering she *wasn't* family. He was annoyed with his grandmother for tripping over her tongue like that, saying something which was so carelessly hurtful.

"You sort out the boxes, Lissa," he said. "I'll get the stockings down."

The soft strains of an *a capella* choir mingled with the crackle of the flames as he took down the stockings. He set Janet's on the loveseat, a bit away from the fire, because Janet's stocking was always loaded with chocolate and other goodies which didn't react well to heat. Hannah instantly dumped hers in her lap, and tiny packages spilled out over her blanket. Then Kurt paused to watch Lissa dragging packages out from under the tree. It was a sight well worth considering.

With all the boxes distributed, Lissa dropped cross-legged to the floor in front of the fire, so he set her stocking on the hearthrug in front of her before he took his own back to his chair. He sat down at an angle, where he could see Lissa's face.

Nobody moved.

"Go ahead," Hannah urged. "Dump the stocking and dig in. Unless you want to start with your packages instead?"

"Aren't we waiting for Janet?" Lissa asked.

"She'll be along when she's ready."

Finally Lissa reached out and touched the top bulge in her stocking with a tentative finger, picking up the silvery box Kurt had tucked in just a few minutes before she came downstairs. Her ornament showed the Maximum Sports penguin mascot decked out as a skier with poles braced, crouched for a jump.

"Darn," Kurt said. "I was hoping you'd get the rock climber."

Lissa stroked the sterling silver ski mask with a gentle fingertip. "There's a set?" Her voice was wistful.

"We do four ornaments each year, just for employees."

"I never did ask you why your mascot is a penguin."

Kurt grinned. "His name's Tux. I chose him because he's awkward and unwieldy except in the water."

Lissa frowned. "I don't get it."

"People don't have to be graceful or elegant or professional to enjoy sports, any more than Tux is. On land, he waddles and falls over—but he's a heck of a swimmer. The point is that everybody can find a sport they're good at—even if they're awkward, it's all right."

"Enough with the fairy tales," Hannah interrupted. "Get on with those packages, girl!"

Lissa reluctantly set the silver penguin aside and dug into her stocking. The next item wasn't even wrapped—in fact it was just a simple chocolate orange in a decorative box—but she studied it, sniffed it, and smiled.

Hannah was fidgeting. Kurt didn't know which he was enjoying more—watching Lissa make the most of the holiday, or watching Hannah being driven wild by such care and patience. The longer Lissa took to slit the tape and unfold the paper from each box, the more Hannah bounced on the couch. He found the show quite entertaining to watch.

The stack of discarded paper and empty boxes grew. Kurt unwrapped a package which had no giver's name on the tag—not that it needed one, since it was clear as soon as he saw the title of the book whose idea this gift had been.

"You must have ransacked the bookstores to find this," he said dryly as he held up *The Calculus Cheat Sheet.*

So that was how she'd spent part of the money she'd borrowed from him. Now he was glad he'd indulged his own whimsical side.

He set the book aside and rummaged through Lissa's pile of gifts. "Here, open this one next."

It was small and flat, wrapped in paper emblazoned with

Maximum Sports' logo. As she lifted a gold-embossed certificate out of the box, she eyed it warily. "You gave me a ticket for the climbing wall?"

"Not just one ticket. It's a free pass, so you can climb whenever you want."

"Gee, thanks," Lissa said. "It's so thoughtful of you."

He grinned, enjoying her discomfort. "You've been on a ladder so much this week that the climbing wall probably won't even be a challenge. You must be over your fear of heights by now. When would you like to make your first climb?"

"Oh, I think I'll savor the idea for a while first," she said dryly. "Or maybe I'll just wait till you visit again. I'm sure you'll be back sometime in the next decade."

His grandmother was ecstatic over the seed-pearl choker that Kurt had slipped into her stocking. "You've still got the prettiest neck around," he said, kissing her cheek when she thanked him.

But she seemed just as pleased, he noticed, by the pair of Austrian crystal earrings Lissa had given her. She put them on instantly, and leaned forward to point out a package in Lissa's pile. "Open that one next," she said. "I can't wait to see your face."

Lissa's eyes widened and she looked at Kurt, as if begging him to rescue her. With obvious reluctance she picked up the package. Small, flat, and apparently almost weightless, it looked as if it might be a box of stationery. Or...

"What is it, Gran?" he asked lazily. "The deed to the house?"

"No, dear. You should know better than that."

Lissa relaxed visibly and started to pull tape loose from the red foil paper.

"Some things just aren't appropriate Christmas gifts," Hannah went on. "And in any case, I've reconsidered."

Lissa paused. "You have?"

Kurt leaned back and folded his hands behind his head.

"Why? You didn't like the idea of a hot tub for eight right out by the neighbors' side door?"

Hannah laughed merrily. "Only if I get to come and use it—and enjoy seeing the shock on their faces. But Lissa's right—if you don't want the house, then I shouldn't saddle you with it."

"So you're staying here?" Kurt asked casually.

"Oh, no, dear. I still want something much smaller, much simpler, with much less responsibility. This solution was Lissa's idea, really. Well, not directly—but when we were choosing charities to donate things to it seemed such a pity that the only thing I could give to the group of unwed mothers she's so attached to was a few skeins of yarn and some knitting needles. Since there haven't been any babies in this family for twenty-five years, I don't have high chairs or cribs to give away."

They must be the only things she doesn't have stuck back in a closet somewhere, just in case she might need them someday.

Lissa shifted, as if the hearthrug had suddenly grown hot under her. "Hannah—"

Lissa had gone pale, Kurt noted. *Because she isn't going to get the house after all?* But he'd swear she'd been sincere all the times she'd said she didn't want it. Besides, Lissa was the most pragmatic female he'd ever run across, and she certainly knew how impractical it would be for a young woman with no job to take on a house the size of Hannah's.

So why was she turning white now, instead of looking relieved?

"Young women in difficult situations need options," Hannah said, "not booties. The more we talked about it, the more I realized Lissa knew what she was talking about when she said if those girls had real choices, they'd make better decisions. Decisions they wouldn't regret later. So, when neither of you seemed to want this big old house, I got to thinking about how it might do as a group home—a place where single mothers could come for a while, rent-free, till they get on their feet. There could be classes in how to be good parents, help to get jobs, a cooperative nursery to take care of the babies while the mothers went out to work so they didn't have to pay for daycare."

"Good idea, Gran," Kurt said. He hardly heard what he was saying. "Of course there may be a bit of a hitch in how to pay for it all, but—"

Hannah didn't pause. "So as soon as the holiday's over, Lissa, I want you to invite your friend who runs the women's shelter out here, and we'll sit down and talk about it—about how we could make it all work."

Lissa swallowed hard. "Whenever you like, Hannah. But let's talk about it some other time. Aren't you going to open the rest of your gifts?" She reached for another package herself and started to tear off the paper.

Kurt's stomach felt as if he'd just topped the first peak of a rollercoaster and dropped into freefall, without the slightest idea of how he'd gotten on the ride. All his suspicions came rushing back like a tidal wave. *There haven't been any babies in the family for twenty-five years*—as far as his grandmother knew. But was that the truth?

I realized Lissa knew what she was talking about, Hannah had said. *If these girls had real choices, they'd make better decisions. Decisions they wouldn't regret later.*

Lissa knew what she was talking about…*how?*

From firsthand experience?

In some situations there aren't any good choices, she had told him once. *You just deal with it and go on, that's all.* It had been the voice of experience speaking then—matter-of-fact, almost toneless, with no pain. Not because there hadn't been any pain involved, but because she was long past feeling it. It had been the voice of a woman who had looked a bad break in the eye, dealt with it, and survived.

That had been the moment when he'd first started to wonder if she was talking about something other than her father's terminal cancer and her own bout of illness. But when he'd confronted her about the possibility of a pregnancy she'd almost ridiculed the idea.

What do you think I did with this supposed infant?
I hope you're satisfied that it never happened....

She had assured him there had never been a baby.

Or...had she?

He was struggling to recall exactly what she had and hadn't said when a crash reverberated from the kitchen. It was a full three seconds before Kurt, his reflexes paralyzed by the sudden shocking questions whirling through his mind, realized that the echo of metal clanging, glass shattering, and something heavy thudding to the floor was real.

Janet had taken a fall.

Maybe, he thought, his grandmother had waited just a little too long to make her move into retirement.

Hannah jumped up, untangled herself from her blanket, and rushed toward the kitchen. Lissa was only a couple of steps behind her, but as Hannah vanished around the corner and into the hall Kurt reached out and grabbed Lissa's arm, holding her back.

She skidded to a halt and glared at him. "What are you doing? We should go see what's happened out there!"

"In a minute. I can hear Janet swearing a blue streak—she sounds a whole lot more angry than hurt. Lissa...." He took a deep breath. "About this woman who runs the shelter..."

She couldn't believe her ears. "Can we do this later, Kurt? *After* the crisis is past?"

"No, we can't. How long have you known her?"

"Several years. If you're asking whether she's the sort of

person who would take advantage of a kind-hearted old lady who only wants to help girls who are in trouble—"

"No." His eyes were dark, the lines around them deeper than usual, as if he had a sudden, splitting headache. "I just wondered how you'd happened to meet her. And how you know all that stuff you told Gran—about young women and choices, and decisions, and regret."

Lissa bit her lip. The moment Hannah had started talking she'd been afraid of how Kurt might react, what he might say. If he let any of this slip to Hannah it would only cause pain, without doing anyone any good. She had to try to stop it, to convince him. "Are we back to that again? I told you, Kurt—I did not have your baby. I did not give your child up for adoption."

He was silent for a long moment. But not, she thought warily, because he was convinced.

When he finally spoke, his voice was very low. "Those aren't the only possibilities. You never said you weren't pregnant, Lissa. Just that you didn't have a baby."

They say men don't have intuition, she thought. *Well, this one must.* "And that's the truth," she said, as firmly as she could. "I didn't."

"But it's not the whole truth, is it?" He paused, took a deep breath. "Why didn't you tell me you were pregnant?"

In the face of his certainty, Lissa couldn't keep silent any longer. "Because there was nothing to say, Kurt."

All right, you're going to have to tell him. The man's a bulldog; he's not going to back off till he gets an answer.

She took a deep breath and tried to think. *I didn't tell you I was pregnant because I didn't know myself...not for sure.* It was the absolute truth; it would have to do.

"You'd already made up your mind what you were going to

do, hadn't you?" His voice held a hard edge. "So what I might have thought about it didn't matter a damn."

"Made up my mind about *what?*" Then it hit her—the unthinkable thing he was accusing her of—and Lissa reeled from the impact. "If you're saying I had an abortion, Kurt—"

"What else am I supposed to think? *Sometimes there aren't any good choices.* You said that yourself. If there was no baby, no adoption, what else is left? And you didn't even bother to tell me—"

Fury roiled in her stomach. "If I *had* told you I was pregnant, Kurt, what would you have done about it?"

"I sure as hell wouldn't have let you kill my baby."

My baby.

He had made a bet with his buddies that he could get her to sleep with him, and no doubt he had celebrated with them and collected his winnings. He had given her not a single additional thought. Not then. Not when his buddies had tormented her. Not when she'd vanished from the class.

But if that night of carelessness had resulted in a child…*that* he would have cared about. Not Lissa—she didn't matter. She had never mattered to him. But a baby…

You've always known where you stand with him, Lissa told herself. *Nothing's changed.*

But it *had* changed. Everything had changed. For him to coldly look at her and assume that she was capable of ending a child's life simply because she'd found it inconvenient to be pregnant….

Rage rose in her. She was damned if she'd beg him to believe her. He had appointed himself judge and jury and issued a verdict. The overwhelming urge to hurt him just as deeply as he'd hurt her swept over her.

Her conscience whispered, *A lie is still a lie. No matter how much he deserves to be wounded, you shouldn't sink to lying to him.*

But the words were out before she could think it through. "Sure—that's what happened," she said coolly. "You're always right, aren't you, Kurt? But then it wasn't a baby. Not really. It was a nuisance, that's all."

The instant the words were out she hated herself for saying them—though not because they had hurt him. She still felt he deserved all the pain she could inflict because he'd assumed she could do such a heinous thing.

What she regretted was that in her fury she'd soiled the memory of her child—the baby she was morally certain she had carried for just a few brief weeks. So short a time, in fact, that a pregnancy test hadn't yet shown up positive when the bleeding had started and wouldn't stop....

"Kurt," she said desperately. "I'm sorry. Let me explain—"

His face was like stone. "Sorry you did it? Or sorry I found out?"

Hopelessness swept over her, but she was taking a breath to try again when Hannah came back into the room.

"It's a pity," she said cheerfully, "but there won't be pecan rolls for breakfast. Janet's wrist gave out as she was transferring them to a plate and she dropped the whole lot on the floor. Kurt, you'll have to run down to the grocery and get some donuts." She looked from one of them to the other and frowned. "Are you two all right?"

"Sure," Lissa said. "Fine. I'll go help clean up."

"That's a great idea." Kurt's voice was hard. "You're so experienced at getting rid of messes, Lissa. Aren't you?"

CHAPTER TEN

KURT SEIZED HIS coat from the closet and stormed out of the house. The silence he left behind was thick, the atmosphere so heavy that it was like trying to breathe underwater.

"Do you want to talk about it?" Hannah asked.

As if, Lissa thought, this was a simple lovers' spat. *Kiss and make up....*

"No." She shuddered uncontrollably; chills were coursing up and down her spine. She wanted to follow Kurt, explain, but how could she? "No, I don't want to talk about it. If you'd like me to go away, Hannah—"

"Where would you go?" Hannah asked practically. "It's Christmas Day."

The reminder would have brought tears to Lissa's eyes if she hadn't been in too much pain to cry. How could she and Kurt have forgotten the holiday, and how much it meant to Hannah? "I'm sorry to ruin your Christmas."

"It wouldn't be the first time." Hannah's voice was matter-of-fact. "When Kurt's parents were still together—" She seemed to think better of saying it. "If you'd give Janet a hand in the kitchen, I'd appreciate it."

Lissa nodded, and looked over her shoulder as she left the living room. Hannah was already standing by the sideboard, sherry bottle in hand. Lissa might have joined her—only for her the sherry wouldn't have been nearly strong enough.

Still-steaming pecan rolls lay scattered on the kitchen floor in a puddle of caramel sauce, absurdly crowned with shards of the milk-glass cakestand that Janet had been transferring them to.

By the time the mess was gathered up and the floor scrubbed, Lissa was starting to wonder if Kurt was going to come back at all. But just as she was wringing the last of the sticky sauce from the mop the side door banged open and he came into the kitchen, two big white bakery bags clutched in one hand.

I'm sorry I let my temper get the best of me, she wanted to say. *I shouldn't have lied to you. I should have told you that I think I had a miscarriage so early that there's nothing to prove I was ever pregnant at all.* But it was too late for that; he'd never believe her now.

He came straight toward her, and the iciness in his eyes chilled her blood. "We aren't going to ruin Gran's Christmas." There was a thread of steel in his voice.

"Now's a fine time for you to consider that." Deliberately she let a hint of sarcasm creep into her tone. It was better than breaking down in tears. "But I suppose an afterthought is better than nothing. What's your plan?"

"I pretend you don't exist, you pretend I don't exist, and we get through the day the best we can."

She felt compelled to say, "I've already offered to leave."

"Don't bother. I've bought a ticket. I'll be flying out late this afternoon."

He was so anxious to get away that he didn't even want to wait for his private jet to pick him up. It was no surprise that he wanted to avoid her. Still, for her own sake there was something she had to say.

"Just for the record," she said, trying to hold back the emotion. "I didn't have an abortion." She shoved the mop into the tall cupboard beside the sink and left the room without a backward look.

Just get through the day, Lissa told herself. *Just get through this day and you'll never have to see him again.*

The winter felt endless, and spring was late, wet, and cold. Some days it seemed to Lissa that the sun would never shine again. But the months went by, and she plodded through the last of her classes and the last of her shifts at the student union, and eventually she reached a level of acceptance and almost peace. Whatever Kurt thought of her, it no longer mattered.

Her graduation day, late in May, was perfect—sunny, but not too warm. The scent of lilacs drifted across the campus from the rows of groomed bushes near the quadrangle where the ceremony was being held, and the long tassel on her mortarboard stirred in the breeze and tickled her ear as she half listened to the speaker.

Perhaps, she thought, it had been silly to dress up in cap and gown and go through the motions of the formal ceremony. She'd be a graduate just the same, whether she walked across the stage or not, and she could have spent the day polishing up her job applications. Between working, studying, and writing her senior project, the not-so-small problem of what she was going to do next had not gotten the attention it deserved.

And it wasn't as if there was a proud family waiting in the stands to cheer her accomplishment.

She hadn't invited Hannah to the ceremony. In fact, Lissa hadn't seen her for several weeks—and even then they'd been meeting with the director of the women's shelter, so the only subject had been the transformation of Hannah's house to make it accommodate more than half a dozen young women and their babies. But, even if the agenda had been less crucial, Lissa was reasonably certain Hannah wouldn't have mentioned

Kurt. In fact, since he'd left the house late on Christmas afternoon, Hannah had not once brought up his name—even during the following week, when his presence had still been palpable and the scent of his aftershave still hiding in unexpected corners of his grandmother's house, lurking as if to ambush Lissa.

Lissa didn't know what Kurt had told his grandmother—if anything—about that last fight. She was fairly sure he hadn't breathed a word, and that Hannah was still as much in the dark as she'd been on Christmas Day, when they'd been frigidly polite to each other over the dinner table. For if he'd told his grandmother about Lissa and his suspicions that she'd deliberately ended a pregnancy then he'd have had to admit that he was the man who'd caused it.

Not long after the pumpkin pie was cut Kurt had left for the airport, and Lissa hadn't heard from him since. Not that she'd expected to, though for a while she'd felt the clench of fear in her gut whenever she went to work and found a message waiting for her at the union—because, she thought, that was the only place he'd have known to reach her.

But as the weeks had gone by she'd gradually come to accept that it was really over. She was still angry at him for judging her, hurt that he could have thought her capable of such a thing. And she still regretted that she'd lied to him—even though she knew he wouldn't have believed her if she'd told the truth right then.

She wished the end could have been less painful and less public, and that Hannah hadn't walked into the crossfire and been hurt. She wished that she could still consider the old woman a friend, not just an acquaintance.

And, in a few dark, middle-of-the-night contemplations, she'd found herself wishing all over again that things had turned out differently. Not because having his baby would have kept Kurt in her life—she wouldn't have wanted him there if he'd had to be forced, and he'd made it clear enough that nothing

short of a child would have drawn him to her. But, as complicated as her life would have been under those circumstances,
she would have had her reward in watching her child grow.

Instead, she'd barely begun to suspect the existence of a
pregnancy, much less come to terms with how she would
manage life with a baby, before it had all been over.

But the time was past for all those sorts of thoughts. This
was the end of a long and difficult chunk of her life, and it was
time for a fresh start.

The university president called her name. Lissa held her
head high as she climbed the steps to the temporary stage set
up in the center of the quadrangle and walked across to receive
her diploma. There were a few cheers; she saw her fellow
workers at the student union in a clump right down front,
yelling, and her heart warmed. The dean of the business college
presented her diploma, shook her hand, and whispered, "Congratulations, Lissa. You have a bright future, I know."

The parade of names was the very end of the ceremony, and
as the black-gowned graduates came down the steps at the far
end of the stage, diploma in hand, they moved off to the side,
out onto the quadrangle where they could mingle and celebrate.

The stairs were makeshift, and she had to watch that the heel
of her shoe didn't slide down into the metal grid, or that her toe
didn't catch in the hem of the long black gown. Going down was
harder than ascending had been, and she was grateful for the arm
which was offered in support as she climbed off the stage.

Until she drew her next breath and caught the scent of an
aftershave she'd thought she would never smell again.

Her hand stilled on Kurt's arm.

"Congratulations," he said.

She nodded. It was the only thanks she could manage; for
her life, she couldn't have forced a word out.

Though she was off the stairs, once more on solid ground,

the grass seemed to sway under her, and Lissa was afraid to trust her feet. As if he'd read her mind, Kurt pulled his arm closer to his body, trapping her hand, and drew her away from the stage.

She looked around. "Is Hannah here?" Her voice was little more than a breath.

Kurt shook his head. "Since you didn't officially invite her, she couldn't get a seat—and she didn't think she could stand through the whole ceremony."

"It was nice of you to come as her delegate." *Let's make it clear right up front—you're not here because of me, and I know it.*

"Would you like punch and cookies?" Kurt asked.

"No—I'm not staying for the reception."

"Because you have too much to do?" His tone was light, conversational.

As if he cares. "Yes, I thought I'd take the rest of the day off to do some serious relaxing before I get down to the task of finding a job."

"Then my timing was perfect." Suddenly he sounded serious. "Lissa, I want…I *need* to talk to you."

"Oh, I think you said everything that was on your mind at Christmas, Kurt. Pardon me if I'd rather not sit through a repetition. So, thanks again for coming. Tell Hannah I'll talk to her sometime, and…" She pulled the mortarboard off her head and ran her fingers through her hair. *And don't send me a Christmas card; if I want to know what's going on with you I'll just read the business magazines.*

"Lissa." His voice was quiet. "I'm going to say what I came here to tell you. You can stand here and listen to me, or you can walk away and I'll follow you and shout as loud as I have to, to make sure you hear. So it's up to you, really. Do you want to keep this between us, or not?"

That would make a nice scene for the crowd—on the stage, the university president still reading off the last half of the

graduates' names, while mere feet away Kurt boomed out—
what? More accusations?

A crowd had gathered around the refreshment table, and
newcomers from the stage sidestepped Kurt and Lissa to head
in that direction. Off to one side of the quadrangle lay an almost
deserted path, and Lissa moved toward it. "Why right now?"
she said wearily. "It's been months, Kurt. Why did you have to
ruin my graduation day?"

"I didn't intend to ruin it. I came to tell you I'm sorry."

She turned to face him. "Sorry for what? There are so many
possibilities I don't have any idea where you might begin."

He winced. "Let's start with the biggest one, then. I'm sorry
that I accused you of having an abortion."

She thought about it for a moment, not quite sure what he
was saying. Was he sorry he'd believed it, or only sorry that he'd
voiced the thought?

"I suppose I'd have to call it temporary insanity," he said.
"What happened to me on Christmas, I mean. Everything seemed
to fit—what you'd said to Gran, the whole idea about the home,
the fact that you'd been very careful what you'd said to me. You
never exactly told me that you *hadn't* been pregnant, you know."

"I couldn't assure you of something I didn't know myself,
Kurt."

But he didn't seem to have heard her. "You only said that you
hadn't given up a baby for adoption. Suddenly all of that seemed
to fall into place in my head, and the pieces formed a picture—
one I didn't like. One I didn't want to believe. But when I confronted you, you didn't deny it. And the look on your face—"

To his already suspicious eyes, she realized, she must have
looked and sounded guilty. No surprise there, because she'd *felt*
guilty—even though she had done nothing wrong—simply
because she'd kept her own suspicions to herself for six long
years.

"Not that it excuses what I said to you. Lissa, I'm sorry the idea ever crossed my mind. It didn't occur to me then that there was yet another possibility—that you'd miscarried. That's what happened, isn't it?"

She hesitated. "I think so."

Kurt frowned. "What do you mean, you *think?*"

"It all happened so quickly. As soon as I began to suspect I might be pregnant, I got a test kit. The results said I wasn't, but the instructions made it clear that if it was too early the test wouldn't show up as positive. So I was going to take it again in a few days, but before I could I started bleeding, and…well, it was all over. So I've never really known…even though in my heart I was pretty sure."

"You looked so guilty. And—I wasn't thinking clearly, that's all."

"I'd noticed that," she said dryly.

"But when I finally stopped letting myself be blinded by anger and thought it through, I knew that had to be the answer. If you had been pregnant, you might not have told me—"

"As if you'd have been eager to hear that sort of news."

"But you wouldn't have acted in your own selfish interests. Not if it would hurt someone else."

She supposed she should be pleased that he'd finally worked it out. "I'm glad you at least got that much straight. How long did it take you, did you say?"

"A while. A month or so. I was pretty angry." He paused. "So were you, or you wouldn't have told me that raft of lies."

"Don't try to shift the blame, Kurt."

"I'm not. I take full responsibility for that, too. If I hadn't been such a—"

She could think of several words which fit the situation, but Kurt seemed to conclude that none of them was quite severe enough as a description.

"I attacked you," he said quietly. "I hurt you in the worst possible way. It just took me a while to realize why you would admit to something like that when it wasn't true. But of course you fought back—you wanted to hurt me."

"I'm not proud of what I said," she admitted. "I didn't help things, did I? But even if it took you a full month to figure all this out, why wait till now to talk to me?"

He looked down at the toe of his wingtip and drew an invisible line on the sidewalk. "I know it sounds like I was too scared to face you. And perhaps I was, for a while—because I knew what a horrible thing I'd done to you, and I couldn't imagine you being willing to talk to me no matter what I did. Last time, you wouldn't listen at all."

"By *last time,* you mean when you caught up with me that day after calculus class? The day after we… You didn't try very hard to talk to me then, Kurt."

"Maybe we've both learned something in the last six years."

Maybe, she thought doubtfully. Though if he'd called her up anytime this spring she might have slammed the phone down. She'd been plenty angry, too. Even this afternoon she hadn't wanted to hear him out.

"But I couldn't just let it ride," Kurt went on. "Whether you listened to me or not, I had to at least tell you I was sorry—for everything. At the same time, I knew everything you'd been through the last few years in trying to finish school, and I didn't want to risk that. As long as you were doing all right, I didn't want to upset you all over again. So I waited till the semester was done—till today. And I thought if I approached you in public…"

Shanghaiing her was more like it. "I see."

"If I've done the wrong thing by coming to talk to you, I'm sorry—but at least by waiting I didn't throw you off course again and keep you from graduating."

"Very thoughtful of you. You said you knew I was doing all right? How? Oh, from Hannah, I suppose."

"No. Gran wouldn't so much as breathe your name. I called up the dean of the business school."

The dean—the man who had just shaken her hand up on stage and murmured, *You have a bright future.* Much he knew about it, Lissa thought. "I suppose he read you my report card in return for a nice contribution?"

"Not exactly. But he did agree to keep an eye on you—and he seemed to be impressed by what he saw."

Lissa said dryly, "He was probably only impressed because you were the one who was asking about me. He loves to use Maximum Sports as a good example—of everything."

"What are you going to do next, Lissa?"

He was finished, she realized. The apology was over, the discussion complete, and now he was moving on to civil chit-chat for a few moments before saying goodbye. "Look for a job. So far I haven't had anything but nibbles."

"If you're interested, there's a position with Maximum Sports."

"That wasn't a hint for you to hire me, Kurt. Besides, I'm terrible at sales, and I'd scare people away from the climbing wall—so, thanks, but no."

"It's corporate," he said. "I'd like you to set up that new simplified tracking system you told me you could create."

It would be her dream job, and for a moment Lissa let herself wallow in the thought of how perfect it all could be.

"I feel bad about the internship," Kurt went on. "You kept your part of the bargain—Gran's finally moved out of the house, and everything's settled—but I didn't keep mine. I wanted to, but I thought if I offered you a job—or suggested I pay your rent —you'd throw it in my face after what I'd said to you."

"I might have," she admitted. "And I didn't exactly accomplish what you wanted, anyway. It took Hannah all spring to get the house mostly cleared out, and even though they're re-modeling now, she's still got the china stacked in an upstairs closet because she swears you're going to want it someday—so I didn't figure you owed me anything."

"Well, that's past. Now that we've got things straightened out...."

Oh, yes. Everything's just peachy, now.

"What about the job, Lissa? A real job, I mean—not an internship."

She eyed him narrowly. "I thought you said the dean didn't read you my report card."

His eyebrows furrowed. "What are you talking about?"

"Never mind. It's nothing. Thanks for the offer—but I don't think so, Kurt."

It was the only thing she could say. Working near him, working for him, but not being with him, would be more than she could bear.

He nodded, obviously not surprised that she'd turned him down. She wondered if there was a flicker of relief deep inside him. If so, at least he'd had the decency and self-control not to show it.

They'd reached the far edge of the quadrangle, where the shade of a row of pine trees kept the sidewalk even cooler than the grassy expanse they'd crossed. The campus boundary was just ahead, and beyond that was only a neighborhood of student housing. There was no further excuse to linger, so she tipped her head back and looked directly up at him. "Anything else you want to get off your chest before I go, Kurt?"

He took his time answering. "I've really ruined things, haven't I?"

She wanted to say, *Yes. You ruined everything.* But she had ached so long and so deeply that she was too guarded to admit that there had been anything between them at all, anything which could be ruined. So she only shrugged and turned away, hoping that she could get out of sight before she broke down and cried.

"At least let me walk you home, Lissa."

She clenched her fists on the hard leather binder that held her diploma until her knuckles ached. But there really was no reason she could give for not allowing him to share a public sidewalk with her on a beautiful spring day, so she shrugged and started off, setting a brisk pace.

"You haven't asked why it was so easy for me to convince myself that there had been a baby," he mused.

"Oh? Your being a bit paranoid wasn't enough of a reason?"

"I don't think so. And neither was remembering that you'd supposedly been sick that spring. You see…what I finally realized was that part of me *wanted* there to have been a baby."

The admission was so startling that she tripped over thin air. Kurt grabbed her arm to steady her and didn't let go. "My parents…." he said slowly. "They didn't fight all the time because they both wanted me, they fought because they didn't."

There was no pain in his voice, only acknowledgment of the truth. But she felt his hurt nevertheless. "I'm sorry, Kurt."

He shrugged. "They only got married because I was on the way. I've always thought it would have been better if they hadn't bothered."

She listened to the rhythm of their footsteps, almost in tune against the concrete. "I don't understand. If it was so bad for you, why would you want another child to feel like a burden?"

"Because it would have been different. I'm not my parents."

She nodded. "But…"

"I would have wanted my baby. And when for that instant of time I thought that there had been a child and I'd lost him—or her —"

It wasn't a baby, she'd said to him. *It was a nuisance.* It had been a blow struck in anger, a lie told in a moment when she'd have done anything in her power to wound him. Now she wondered how many times he'd heard *himself* called a nuisance by the people who should have loved him most.

No wonder he'd turned to stone when she'd said it. She couldn't have found a way to hurt him more.

He looked down at her, almost as if he were seeing her for the first time. "I went crazy—I'm not making an excuse, because there isn't any. If I'd only stopped to consider I'd have known you couldn't do that—but I didn't take the time to think it through. Lissa, I'd give my right arm if I could go back and relive that fifteen minutes."

Something deep inside her relaxed—something which had been so tense since Christmas that she had grown used to it, even begun to think it was normal. "Oh, not the right arm, Kurt," she murmured. "It would make climbing that wall much too difficult."

He frowned at her as if he didn't appreciate the feeble effort at humor. "It's taken me six years to figure out what's wrong with me. Six long years to figure out that what happened between us that night was no accident."

She wanted to snort. "Of course it wasn't an accident. You planned it."

He shook his head.

"Come on. You can't deny there was a bet."

"It wasn't what you thought. I didn't set out to go to bed with you. I told one of the guys that you were going to tutor me, and he started making jokes about how I must want something more than a calculus lesson, and I said, yeah, sure, I had all kinds of plans. It was the sort of thing all stupid young guys say when they're trying to sound macho in front of their buddies. Before I saw what was happening everybody knew about it. I tried to squelch the talk, but then after that incredible night…."

He had thought it was incredible, too?

Calling it incredible doesn't necessarily mean he thought it was wonderful, Lissa reminded herself.

"At first I was too stunned to think. Nothing like that had ever happened to me before. But you were like a startled rabbit —jumpy and anxious, in such a hurry to get out of my room that of course I said all the wrong things. Did all the wrong things." He sighed. "And by the next day, we both must have been giving off vibes—because it was obvious to everyone what had happened. Then there was no stopping the gossip."

And as soon as she'd heard about the bet she'd refused to speak to him at all....

Kurt had been a fool, there was no argument about that. But so had she. They had let their passion carry them away, long before their tentative friendship had been strong enough to stand the pressure. Then, in their proud refusal to be the first one to confess—in their fear of being embarrassed if feelings turned out not to be mutual—they'd squashed any possibility of finding out if their attraction could turn into something more lasting.

At least now there's no more need to wonder what happened. We did it to ourselves, in equal measures.

"Then you wouldn't even give me the time of day," Kurt went on. "So I assumed that it hadn't been so wonderful for you after all, and I stopped trying. But even while I was telling myself that women couldn't be trusted, that you'd slept with me and then turned your back—"

"Wait a minute. *I* turned my back?"

"I didn't say I was right, Lissa, just that it's what I thought back then. It hurt me, that you had walked away without seeming to care. And I was still hurting when I saw you again at the cloakroom that night, when you told me to get lost. By then, I'd buried it so deeply that I didn't recognize what was happening—but that's why I was so nasty and suspicious at first. And when I began to suspect that you'd been pregnant—and hadn't even told me…."

She sighed. "I would have told you, Kurt—if I'd been sure. But there was never anything definite to tell you. I certainly wasn't going to walk up to you and say, *I just wanted you to know I thought I might be pregnant but I'm not.*"

He smiled a little. "Yeah, I can see that. Lissa, I know it must have been a relief to you when it was all over…but I almost wish it had been different."

She stopped at the foot of the steps outside her boarding house. "It wasn't a relief," she said, almost under her breath. "Well, this is the end of the road."

He didn't look at her but at the façade of the house, and for an instant she saw it through his eyes. The porch was even more rickety than it had been at Christmas. The stairs sagged. The paint was peeling off the front door, and a panel of glass that had been loose then was gone now, replaced by a board.

Kurt's jaw tightened. "I wanted so much to take you out of here. But I messed that up, too."

She was so glad that he hadn't picked up on her admission—or at least she told herself she was glad—that she was almost giddy. "Oh, really? Then why did you raise such a fuss when Hannah tried to give me her house?"

"Because I didn't want you to have it," he admitted.

"Seems a little contradictory, Kurt."

"I didn't want the house to get in the way. I didn't want it to be a possession to come between us, something to fight over the way my parents fought over everything." He turned her to face him, his hands tight on the shoulders of her black gown. "I didn't want you to get attached to the house—because I wanted to take you with me."

Her heart was suddenly beating in a staccato rhythm she'd never felt before. "And I suppose that's why you offered to rent an apartment for me here, right? You aren't making sense, Kurt."

"I know I'm not. Give me a chance, Lissa. This is hard for me."

She looked up at him for a long moment. There was something about his expression, a turbulence in his eyes... "I'm going inside."

His grip tightened almost painfully for an instant, and then he let her go. "All right. Thanks for listening. I—Can I call you sometime?"

"I just meant you can come in—if you want." She climbed the steps, trying not to care whether he would follow—and knowing by the way her body reacted that he was right behind her.

She unlocked the new deadbolt on her door. "I've got a microwave now, so I can heat water for coffee or tea." She laid her diploma and mortarboard aside and unzipped the black gown, laying it carefully over the back of the futon sofa.

He shrugged. "Coffee, I guess. If you don't mind the bother."

At least it was something to do with her hands. She poured water from a carafe into two mugs and set them into the tiny microwave, watching from the corner of her eye as he walked across the room to the mantel.

Her little Christmas tree was long packed away, but in the center of the mantel sat Tux—the penguin mascot in skiing gear that he'd given her at Christmas.

She knew the instant Kurt saw the silver ornament, for he released a long, startled breath. "You kept him." He turned to face her and his eyes held a new light. "You didn't throw him away. Why, Lissa?"

"Because he's silver."

"Only plated. Not enough to be valuable. You should have jumped up and down on him, to get even with me."

She took the mugs out and stirred instant coffee powder into the hot water. "It wasn't Tux's fault."

"No," he said softly. "It was mine. Every bit of it. You said a minute ago that it wasn't a relief to find out you weren't pregnant. Why, Lissa? Because you wanted a baby?"

Your baby. But something prevented her from saying it. If she admitted how much she cared about him and he didn't return the feeling…. It *seemed* that he was telling her he cared, and yet….

Have you learned nothing at all? she asked herself. Wasn't this exactly what they'd done six years ago? Then they'd both been afraid to be the first to speak, and so neither of them had said anything. Now—it might not make a difference, but at least she would know that she had done her best, that she had told the truth even if it caused her pain.

"I should have been relieved," she said. "It would have been…very difficult. And yet…. I've tried to convince myself over the years that I couldn't have been pregnant at all, that it was only my imagination, that there was nothing to mourn. But…I couldn't forget."

"The baby?"

She bit her lip. "No, Kurt. I couldn't forget you."

He didn't move. Had she torn herself in two for nothing?

His voice was very soft. "You asked me once why, if so many women were after me, one of them hadn't tripped me up yet. You're the reason, Lissa. None of those women was you."

Her nerves were jangling. "If you're expecting me to believe that you've nursed some sort of crush on me for the last six years—"

"It's true. That night in the cloakroom, even before I knew who you were, I was ready to punch out the jocks who were hanging around drooling over you. You were already mine, and somewhere deep in my gut I knew it."

"Then I told you to get lost."

"And even that didn't stop me from wanting you. It wasn't until you said you didn't want to date me—"

She wiped up a few drops of coffee and dropped the paper napkin into the wastebasket. "What I was really saying was that I didn't want to pretend."

His eyes narrowed. Very slowly, he set his mug down, and then reached for hers and put it safely out of the way. "What about if it's for real, Lissa? All of it?"

For real. Was he truly telling her what she had so longed to hear?

"Being raised by parents like mine doesn't spawn much confidence in catchphrases like *happily ever after* and *till death do us part*," he mused.

"I understand, Kurt—"

"But when I look at you, Lissa, I believe in those things. I love you."

She wanted to cry, to laugh, to yell at him for keeping her in suspense so long.

"I know I haven't done a very good job of showing it. I'll make up for it, I swear—"

"Yes," she said. "You certainly will. Starting now."

He pulled her against him, and his mouth came down on hers with a hunger which told her more than words could say.

Eventually he let her go, still cupping his hands around her face, and just looked at her for a while. Then he draped an arm around her shoulders and said, "We've got a lot to talk about. But let's not do it here. Would you like some real coffee? This stuff is cold."

"That's not my fault," she pointed out. "Where are we going? Hannah's place?"

"You're kidding, right? Have you seen her new apartment? There's no place for a guest, so I checked into a hotel."

"That's convenient," she murmured.

"Very. They have excellent room service…. Then in a few days…" He sounded anxious. "You'll come with me, Lissa?

You'll work with me? And you'll marry me and take over all Gran's china?"

A last doubt flared deep inside her. "I don't know, Kurt. I love you, honestly I do—but I'm scared."

His eyes were full of pain. "Because I wouldn't listen to you. Because I wouldn't believe you, or trust that you couldn't do something so dreadful. It won't happen again, I swear it. I know saying it doesn't prove anything—so take as much time as you need to be sure. Just give me the right to convince you, Lissa. That's all I'm asking for right now."

Slowly, she nodded. He lifted her hand and kissed each fingertip as gently as the touch of a butterfly's wing, and she relaxed, feeling safe in his arms. "Then—all right."

"You mean all right you'll marry me? Or all right I can start convincing you?" He didn't wait for an answer. But a bit later he broke off the kiss and held her just a little distance from him. "And you'll set up that tracking system for me?" He was suddenly all business.

Lissa had to laugh—for the abrupt shift from lover to businessman was somehow more convincing than any number of sweet words could have been. "You're impossible, Kurt."

"I'll make you vice-president of marketing."

"What is this? Nepotism?" It felt so good to be able to tease him.

"Of course not. I really do need that tracking system, you know—the sooner the better."

"Is this afternoon quick enough?"

He frowned. "It can't be that simple."

"Of course it's not. I've spent all semester writing it—it was my senior project."

He rubbed his temple as if it hurt. "After all the pain I've caused you, you spent the whole semester trying to improve my business?"

"Sort of." She didn't look straight at him. "Though I never intended to give it to you. And I have to admit I started out to prove your business plan was badly thought out and you were going about it all wrong—"

He laughed and pulled her closer. "So that's what you meant about your report card. You thought the dean told me about your senior project."

"He was my adviser. I told you that he thinks Maximum Sports is the greatest. Besides, I know firsthand that you can be very persuasive when you're determined to get what you want."

"Well, yes," he admitted. "But take all the time you need— tomorrow will be fine."

Then he was kissing her again, and she quickly forgot about inventory tracking. "Kurt, about that incredible night we spent together...." Her voice was very small. "What if it isn't so incredible now?"

He tucked her head under his chin and let his hand drift over her hair. Then he smiled down at her with mischief dancing in his eyes and said, "It will be. But I've got a surefire idea—let's make it a bet. Then we can't possibly go wrong."

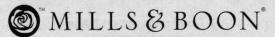